"Stories tend to run in cycles. Last year, I received many stories of what could be classified as 'rape and revenge,' a story which is written and rewritten in new ways because it resonates in the minds of the readers as an archetype. This year, for some unknown reason, many stories came in on the theme of the 'Chosen Maiden.' Perhaps the popularity of the film *Dragonslayer* had something to do with it, because one of the themes of that film was a lottery where one maiden in the village was chosen yearly as scapegoat to appease the dragon and save the others. I ask myself: is this feminist Christ-symbolism? 'It is fitting that one shall lay down his life for all mankind.' I think not. In Greek mythology Andromeda was chained for a dragon until the hero Perseus came along with the Gorgon's head to turn the evil dragon to stone . . . The Chosen Maidens in these stories, however, do not await a Hero to rescue them from their allotted fates. Each of the Chosen Maidens I have chosen to bring you has a different approach . . . and each is a heroine in her own right."

—MARION ZIMMER BRADLEY

SWORD AND SORCERESS II

An Anthology of Heroic Fantasy

Edited by

MARION ZIMMER BRADLEY

DAW BOOKS, INC.

DONALD A. WOLLHEIM, PUBLISHER

1633 Broadway, New York, NY 10019

First Printing, May 1985.

4   5   6   7   8   9

Printed in Canada

CONTENTS

Introduction

Here we are again—a second volume of *Sword and Sorceress*. And already during the reading for this volume, I was being asked about every third letter if there would be a *Sword and Sorceress*, Volume III.

The answer to that is—it depends on you, the readers. If this volume sells like hot dogs in the ball park, or Popsicles at a fifth-grade picnic, if DAW Books is deluged with letters about how great this series is, probably yes. If it has a mediocre sale, probably not. So if you like these volumes and want more, you know what to do. Write the publishers (not me—letters to me are great for my ego, but won't convince DAW Books to buy another *S&S*) and tell them how much you like the anthologies. Also, it wouldn't hurt to buy extra copies as presents for your sisters and your cousins and your aunts.

One of the few critical comments made by a reviewer was that *Sword and Sorceress* tended to lean heavily in favor of swordswomen, and stories of adventure. While we do not cater to women in the martial arts, it's true—this editor *does* have a strong bias in favor of the adventure story in preference to the story which has mostly interior action—the "come-to-realize" story. Women's fiction in general, from the *Ladies'*

Home Journal to *Sue Barton, Student Nurse* and the maunderings of Barbara Cartland, has been heavily skewed toward the domestic, the story where the heroine spends much of her time romantically mooning about the hero and her own inner passions; her life will begin when she finds love. One of the things I determined when I began this anthology is that it would concentrate on women *doing* things; having adventures of their own rather than being secondary to the men's adventures. This because, like many women who read science fiction and fantasy when the readership was still 98 percent male, I ran to it because "women's fiction" bored me to tears—and still does. I have no interest in the modern kind of "women's science fiction" which is right out of *Good Housekeeping* with a few robots and computers thrown in. I believe women deserve more than domestic or romantic fiction centering upon their roles as housewives, consumers and love objects, even when made more "palatable" with a few futuristic trimmings.

And too many of the "sorceress" stories submitted to me for this anthology were either too domestic (love potions on campus) or too cutesy-pie: the "Hearthwitch" school, all ready to be made into Disney cartoons, or retelling of fairy tales, also Disneyfied and saccharine enough to tip an incipient diabetic over the edge. The stories about swordswomen, at least, were more resistent to cutesification.

Stories tend to run in cycles. Last year I received many stories of what could be classified as "rape and revenge," a story which is written and rewritten in new ways because it resonates in the minds of the readers as an archetype. This year, for some unknown reason [perhaps the same phenomenon which meant that two different concepts for transmitting pictures over wireless broadcast—essentially television—were patented within a few weeks of one another] many stories came in on the theme of the "Chosen Maiden." Perhaps the popularity of the film *Dragonslayer* had something to do with it, because one of the themes of that film was a lottery where one maiden in the village was chosen yearly as scapegoat to appease the dragon and save the others. I ask myself: is this feminist Christ-symbolism . . .? "It is fitting that one shall lay down his life for all mankind." I think not. In Greek mythology Andromeda was chained before a dragon until the hero Perseus came along with the Gorgon's head to turn the evil dragon to stone. In the original ballet version of Stravinsky's *The Rite of Spring* (better known to most of us, perhaps, through Disney's *Fantasia* and the dinosaurs) there is a Dance of the Chosen Maiden in which the Chosen sacrifice dances herself to ritual death.

The Chosen Maidens in these stories, however, do not await a Hero to rescue them from their allotted fates. Each of the Chosen Maidens I have chosen to bring you has a different approach . . . and each is a heroine in her own right.

Every anthology must achieve a balance between short stories and long; known writers and unknown—and in the case of "series" anthologies, another balance must be kept; between "repeat" stories and new ones. I am pleased to bring back some of the heroines and series characters from Volume I; another Dossouye story in an African setting by Charles Saunders, and another adventure of the well-loved Frostflower and Thorn by Phyllis Ann Karr were definite pluses, and repeat adventures of Diana Paxson's Shanna, and the rogue-thief Cleo of Stephen Burns were sure, we felt, to please our readers.

When I was reading for this year's anthology, I sent out a lot of guidelines, attempting to "head off at the pass" the overdone cliché stories I never wanted to see again. Reaction to this list was mixed, to say the least—one writer suggested it should be required reading for all writers. While I would hardly go so far, at least it meant I didn't have to read three dozen stories this year about how a strong, independent woman found true happiness in giving herself up to an even stronger male, nor did I get more than one or two stories of gratuitous rape.

(For further information about stories I never want to see again, see Elizabeth Thompson's "On First Looking Into Bradley's Guidelines.")

In general, though, the stories submitted were better than last year's. Or so I feel. Now it's your chance to decide what you think.

MARION ZIMMER BRADLEY

A NIGHT AT TWO INNS

Phyllis Ann Karr

Phyllis Ann Karr's stories about the ill-matched (or are they?) pair, sorceress Frostflower and swordswoman Thorn, have been delighting readers ever since the first novel about the pair *(Frostflower and Thorn)* was published in 1980. A second novel, and a slender handful of short stories, have kept the sorceress and her swordswoman friend before the public eye, and last year a Frostflower and Thorn story led off the first volume of this anthology so successfully that as soon as I knew there was going to be a Volume Two I wrote to Phyllis and asked specially for a story about her odd couple, because, for me, the matching of swordswoman and sorceress plying their trades is what *S&S* is all about.

Many writers have used the device of bringing their characters to an inn between worlds where they encounter characters from other fantasy universes. But *two* inns? When one professes to be heaven and the other hell? And which is which? This story is less predictable than that bare summary sounds.

—MZB

Frostflower finally teased the Circle into showing a familiar bank of the sluggish old Glant River by sunrise.

But when she brought them through and the mist cleared, they stood ankle deep in snow beneath a night sky where three small green moons fought a losing battle against stars clustered thick as mosaic tiles.

East to west—assuming directions were the same as in the Oldhills—the snowline was only about a hundred paces wide. To north and south it stretched away farther than eyesight would follow, broken only by a big ice sculpture, looking something like a grotesque, double-headed bird with scrawny wings, about forty paces to the north. Roughly opposite the statue were two large buildings, one on each side of the snowline. The one to the west had most if not all of its windows lighted up and was sending noise out over the snow. At this distance, the one to the east seemed completely dark and quiet.

Frostflower's dog Dowl whined and huddled up closer between the two women.

"All right," said Thorn, "what happened to the Glant?"

The sorceress spread her arms in a gesture of confusion. She did not hold her left arm out too far or too long, burdened as it was with the bag containing Dathru's bulky book, the only nonedible item besides his white-gold Circle and his pendant of inlaid wood that they had carried along from the Oldhills.

Four days ago, this demon's turd Dathru had sorcered them out of their own Tanglelands into his Oldhills world. (Frostflower seemed to understand this "worlds" business better than Thorn did.) Dathru had intended their destruction or the next thing to it, but thanks to Frostflower's strategy, Thorn's recent hours of practice in throwing weapons, and a lucky fluke, he was the dead one.

Being dead, he could not explain how he had brought them through. So Frostflower studied his book and tools until she could take the Circle, which was not much taller than Thorn's knife, make it show a Glant riverbank, bring a mist down around it and them, and then somehow enlarge the little hoop until they could step through it like a doorway, catching it back down to its former size in her hand right afterwards. Three days of puzzling over a new system of sorcery with no teacher but herself, and she had already figured out that much! Probably the best little sorceress who ever came out of a Tanglelands retreat, so why grumble about her failure to hit the target dead center on her first try?

"Forget it, Frost," said the swordswoman. "You know my demon-twisted tongue. You brought us all through safe, and that's good enough for the first throw. Now try it again before we freeze."

The sorceress shook her head. "Not yet. It has left me very tired. And I must try to learn why I failed this time."

Thorn swallowed a curse and started stamping around to keep her blood moving. They were dressed for Tanglelands summer, Frostflower in black robes that were thinner than they looked, Thorn in lightweave wool trousers and linen tunic, fortunately long-sleeved. "Good strategy," she remarked. "Let's find someplace warm where you can sit and study it out." She waved at the buildings ahead. "Lights and noise or dark and quiet—which?"

Frostflower looked from the lighted building to the dark one and then started walking straight up the center of the snowline to the ice sculpture. Thorn shrugged and walked along, Dowl tagging between them.

As they neared the statue, Thorn saw it was shaped like a pair of giant hands held back to back, thumbs stretched out in opposite directions and fingers cupped forward from the middle knuckle. The thumbs were on a level with Thorn's shoulders.

Frostflower brushed snow from a line of symbols along the length of the west thumb. They were deeply indented, as if burned in with hot metal.

"Unh, writing?" Thorn guessed.

Frostflower sighed. "I have also failed to touch your mind with Dathru's spell for understanding new languages."

"Hellstink, Frost, I'm not that quick even at reading Tanglelands writing! What does it say?"

"It seems to be a pointer guide." Sighting along the west thumb, Frostflower nodded at the bright, noisy building. "That will be the Inn of Good Fellowship. And the other," she went on, walking around to the east thumb and brushing off the snow, "is the Inn of Ultimate . . ." She frowned. ". . . Something. There's one more word, but the letters seem to have melted together, or . . . oh. I think that someone has burned in a vile word over the true name."

"What word? Never mind," Thorn corrected her curiosity. "Sounds like a fair warning, so let's go peek into the Good Fellowship before someone sees us and thinks we look suspicious."

"Wait." Frostflower gazed again at both sides of the snowstrip, each in turn.

"Yes. I see what you mean, sorceress! Looks like patches of snow on black mud all around the Good Fellowship."

"And on the other side," said Frostflower, "orchards in bloom and fields in grass?"

Thorn took a few more squints in each direction, shrugged, and blew on her hands. After the first six or seven marvels, an ordinary, hard-working warrior started to value action more than wonderment. "Could be this blasted green moonlight on a fresh snowfall that came down on that side only. Cloudleaks have to have borderlines somewhere. Anyway, the Good Fellowship looks a lot warmer inside than the Ultimate Whatever, and sounds as if it has a lot more people to answer questions for us."

"Yes . . . perhaps." Frostflower continued gazing toward the quiet inn. "Or they might have some sorcery on that side. And would we not be safer to go first where there are fewer people?"

"Not if they're like that demon's pimple Dathru."

"Surely it must be gentle sorcery, Thorn, if they have used it for grass and orchards. Dathru had blighted the land around his dwelling."

Thorn guessed what her friend was thinking: sorceri on one side, everybody else on the other side, the same kind of fear and distrust that existed in the Tanglelands, and that would explain the vile word on the eastward-pointing thumb. All the same . . .

"Look, Frost," said the warrior, "getting us from one of these worlds to another is your worry. Looking out for us once we're here—wherever—that'll be my worry."

"But . . . Very well, Thorn. Your choice." After one more glance at the Ultimate, Frostflower wearily gathered her skirts and turned toward the Fellowship.

At that moment its door burst open and a pair of fighters tumbled over the step, regained their footing, and went at it again with swords clashing. Instinctively, Thorn pushed her friend into hiding behind the ice sculpture, squatted down beside her, and told her to clamp a hand round the dog's muzzle.

One of the fighters was female, all right, and must have been sneak-attacked while dressing or undressing, since all she had on were an inadequate halter across the chest, some kind of triangular loinpiece with barely visible hip straps, and knee-high boots. But by the way they glinted, her breast- and loin-coverings were metal. Who the hell wore metal underclothes? A connecting whack from her opponent could drive some of that metal deep into her flesh and wound her that much worse! Even at best, she'd be lucky to escape frostbite or metalfreeze. To add to the stupidity, she wore her red hair elbow-length and loose, so that it went flopping and flying around her head and upper arms. And—Warriors' God tighten our grip!—the soles of her boots! Had some bogbait driven spikes through the heels to make her overbalance? She'd be better off fighting stark naked, bald, and barefoot!

Her opponent was a male, bare-legged and bare-chested,

but wearing an animal pelt over his shoulders and a wide
band of fur round his waist and loins. Thorn was starting to
lose a little of her shock on seeing male warriors. His hair
was tied sensibly in back. He looked big enough to wrestle an
ox.

"You red-haired she-devil!" he shouted. "You want it as
much as I do!"

"Come on then, you big barbarian!" she shouted back
with a husky laugh. "I'll let no man bed me unless he can
best me first in fair battle!"

Thorn muttered, "She's got caterpillars in her skull!"

Frostflower twitched her sleeve and whispered, "Thorn?
You understood their words?"

"Never mind, Frost, they're addlebrained as . . ." Suddenly Thorn grinned. "Yes! So you did spellcast the bloody
languages into me. That'll help—"

"By Crom's teeth, you arrogant wench!" bawled the
barbarian.

"You semi-civilized savage," responded the she-devil.

They stanced back and forth, banging their swords together,
shouting, laughing, and kicking up snow at each other.

"If we can find anybody sane enough to talk to," Thorn
added.

A third person appeared in the open doorway, a man in
bright green tunic and furry trousers. Two little points stuck
up from his forehead. Hairlocks combed up and stiffened
with wax, Thorn guessed. "Reverence and lady!" he called.
"Would it please you to come back inside and finish your
fight in a warm, well-lit chamber? We have several other
patrons laying wagers on the outcome."

"Well, flame-haired she-devil, what say you?"

"It suits me, barbarian, provided we take a share of the
purse afterwards."

They lowered their swords and swaggered back inside, arm
in arm, singing a bawdy song. The inn servant closed the
door behind them. Thorn sighed and got to her feet. At least

people were civilized enough in the Fellowship to gamble. But to gamble on which one of a pair of slopbrains would win a fight that was as much shouting as swordwork? "Come on, Frost. We'll look into the quiet place first."

The Ultimate looked as black inside as outside. The door opened directly into the deserted mealroom, where one miserly lamp guttered on a table near the back wall. Less by its light than by the nightglow coming in through the windows, they could make out a trough, about a pace wide, that ran half the length of the floor. It was full of dead ash and charred wood. When Thorn stepped across it she felt no lingering warmth whatever.

Frostflower took the long way around the trough to the lamp table, where she sat, put down her bundle, and warmed her fingers over the tiny flame. The dog padded after and lay down at her feet. For once Thorn did not blame Dowl for whining. The floorstones felt colder than the snow outside. They were also uneven. Frostflower put her elbows on the table, and it wobbled with a click that echoed throughout the room.

Thorn found a doorway to the back part of the building. The shadows were dark as an unlit escape tunnel, so she stood in the arch and called, "Hey! Is this an inn or a bloody deserted cowhouse?"

"That is not entirely fair, Thorn," the sorceress murmured. "At least the air is sweet."

Surprisingly, it was. Instead of smelling like a stale chickenyard, it smelled like a spring garden. But that did not make it feel any warmer, and Thorn would have preferred the fragrance of roasting meat. "Hey, you! Innkeeper! Anybody!" she shouted again.

"All right, all right, rot you," a voice rasped from the darkness. Frostflower gave a start, Dowl sat up, and Thorn stepped back from the opening as the keeper came into sight.

He had a pale face, balding skull, and bony hands. The rest

of him was shrouded in cloth so nearly the shade of the surrounding gloom that it took a few moments to determine its outlines. "No need to come caterwauling in honest people's ears," he grumbled.

The warrior demanded, "Is this an inn, or isn't it?"

"Unh," he replied. "The Inn of Ultimate Happiness."

Hearing a short gurgle, Thorn glanced round and saw her friend hunched over to stifle a laugh. She turned back. "And are you the innkeeper or his great grandfather?"

"I'm the keeper. Why didn't you go to that den across the border, like all the rest of them?"

"Maybe we'll just do that!" said Thorn.

But Frostflower stood and faced the innkeeper, speaking gently. "When travelers need rest, they seek the place that is quiet and softly lit."

"Well, if you want to stay here, you'd better keep the peace and quiet. Let's see your trading stock."

"We're not merchants," said Thorn.

"I didn't ask what you do for a living, and I don't care. I asked to see your stock—wampum, money, spicecubes, jewels, moola, icing, crumbles, credits, pikunes, whatever you use and whatever you call it."

Thorn reached into her moneypouch, brought out several coins, displayed them on her open palm long enough for him to blink at them, then curled her fingers around them again and returned them to safety.

He grunted. "It's a new mintage to me. They probably know all about it across the way. Well, I'll accept it, but likely you'd get more for it over there."

"Fine!" said Thorn. "There's a fight on over there, and maybe I've still got time to triple this on the betting."

"Wait," said Frostflower. "Keeper, where are we?"

"The border. One side is Slagland, the other's Limmervale. Slagland's a bloody wilderness and Limmervale's a land of heart's desire."

"A what?" said Thorn.

"A paradise, a utopia, a glorious harvest before death, a heaven on earth," he replied impatiently. "And Slagland's a hellbog, an inferno, a hades on earth. Some like one and some prefer the other. Now take your choice and leave me in peace."

"Right! Come on, Frostflower."

"Thorn—" the sorceress began, but the swordswoman was halfway to the door and did not break stride.

Dowl caught up with Thorn at the doorstep, Frostflower a few paces later. The people on the other side of the snowstrip had gone back into the Good Fellowship, leaving the door closed and the border deserted.

Frostflower pointed out, "He did not tell us which side was which."

"Obvious, isn't it?"

"Is it?" said the sorceress. But she followed her friend across the snow. It should have been churned up pretty thoroughly where the two slushbrains had fought. Some brisk puffs of wind were blowing, however, and they had already drifted much of the battleground smooth again, as well as filling in Thorn's and Frostflower's own footprints.

They entered the Fellowship to find light, warmth, song, laughter, and the aroma of roasting meats. The firetrough down the middle of this floor was cheery with glowing coals over which handsome, smiling young inn servants turned spitted fowls and cuts of beef. All around the trough cheerful-looking men and women sat elbow to elbow at gleaming wooden tables with steady legs. More servants bustled around politely, bringing food, pouring drink, wiping the tabletops, and winking at pinches. Colored lanterns and flowery festoons hung from the artfully carved rafters. On a platform at the mealroom's far end two ballad mongers were singing a lively tale, accompanied by three musicians, one with a fancy harp, one with bells and drum, and one with a horn shaped like a deer's head.

The man with furry trousers hurried up to the newcomers,

bringing two silver cups. "Lady!" he exclaimed, looking at Frostflower, who was holding a fold of her hood over her nose. "What's wrong?"

She shook her head. "Nothing. A small weakness."

Thorn explained, "She can't stand the smell of cooking meat."

"Ah! We understand, we understand. Come: we have specially ventilated alcoves for abstainers." Nodding eagerly, he presented them with the cups.

Thorn sniffed hers and handed it back. Wine. "I never drink this stuff. Bring me something that doesn't fume up a person's brain."

"Of course, of course! Goat's milk, cow's milk, siren's milk, kawfy, tea, apple juice, peach juice . . ." Trailing out the list, he led them to a row of raised, semienclosed alcoves against the inner wall.

As he settled them at a private table in one of these little alcoves, he pointed to the overhead decorations. "The vents are in the birds' beaks. Windwheels between this ceiling and the floorboards above draw in fresh air from outdoors. The distance warms it and flower-petal filters sweeten it. We hope you find it satisfactory?"

"Very satisfactory, many thanks." Sinking into her chair, Frostflower sighed and sipped her wine. Dowl lay down beside her and thumped his tail.

"Seems all right," said Thorn. "Understand now, *I* eat meat."

He blinked, then nodded. "We can manage. If you'll just allow me to move your chair a little toward the edge of the alcove . . . There! Now: goat's milk, cow's milk, siren's—"

"Water! Just good, plain water, charcoal filtered if you have it, and a nice, big pitcherful."

"Plain, pure water. Melted hourly from the cleanest and newest wind-driven snow. Will that be satisfactory, lady?"

Thorn grunted and nodded.

"And you, lady?" He turned to the sorceress. "Do you consume fish? Milk? Cheese?"

As he spewed out a long selection of meatless edibles for Frostflower's choice, Thorn studied him. His body seemed comfortably shaped, and his face was handsome, but those were not spikes of waxed hair on his forehead. They were little horns like a nanny goat's, to all appearances sprouting up from his own scalp. And she finally decided that his fur "trousers" were the natural hair of his legs, long, thick as a bear's coat, silky, neatly combed and curled.

Gazing down at the happy crowd, she noticed a lot of garments that might be growing directly from the wearers' hides. And they included green, crimson, and blue coverings as well as brown, orange, black, white, and yellow.

"Barley bread, one small loaf," the sorceress said at last. "And perhaps a few radishes?"

"You will have them before that song is finished, lady." Nodding again, he turned, but before he could step down from the alcove, Thorn caught his arm.

"Just a moment," she said pleasantly. "Can you tell us where we are?"

He flashed her an amiable smile, full of even white teeth. "You're at the border between Limmervale and Slagland, ladies."

"Slagland's a hellbog and Limmervale's a glorious harvest, hey?"

"Limmervale's a utopia, lady, but Slagland is less a hell than a valhalla."

"A what?"

"All this area," said Frostflower, bending forward. "It is a place where many different worlds somehow touch. Where travelers between the worlds may find themselves drawn as to a magnet?"

He nodded eagerly. "Yes, lady. You have seen it exactly. And a valhalla, you understand, is a gathering place for mighty warriors and great sorceri, where they are chosen to fight heroic battles.''

Thorn asked, "Who chooses them?"

"The High Controllers. They come at intervals to sweep the assembled heroes up into their garrisons."

"That explains why the Ultimate over there is empty," Thorn reasoned. "These High Controllers must've just made a sweep."

"Oh, yes, lady, that would explain it! Now, if I may go—"

"Just one more thing." The warrior shook a few coins from her purse onto the table. "Will this pay for our meal?"

He studied the Tanglelands money and picked out a single kip. "This will buy both your suppers, two fine beds with linen sheets and feather-stuffed blankets, and your entertainment." He winked at Thorn. "And for the mealservice, no tipping."

He left. Thorn tilted back with a contented sigh, bracing her chair against the alcove post, and loosened her belt slightly.

"Why would anyone prefer a valhalla to a heaven?" said Frostflower.

Thorn shrugged. "Didn't see anyone over there on the Slagland side, did you?"

"But that denies the explanation that it is empty because the High Controllers swept them up a few hours ago. Does it not?"

"So it had a couple of bogbrains inside bickering with that bloody innkeeper, the Controllers came and swept them up, the keeper got thin pay because the sweepings were poor, and that's why he's sour enough now to pickle beans with his spit."

Frostflower gagged and took another sip of wine. "The innservant here spoke as if some warriors and sorceri might desire to fight these Controllers' heroic battles."

"So they're bloody idiots."

"Thorn, we sorceri of the Tanglelands believe that after death we continue to practice our skills. It is one of the three chief happinesses of our heaven. But I would hate to practice any sorcerous skill as a battle weapon!"

"Then relax and enjoy being safe."

"But your training is for battle. Do your farmer-priests continue raiding one another in their Glorious Harvest, and do you warriors look forward to it as part of your afterdeath happiness?"

"Not that I've ever heard of. Bloodrastor! Would a muck carrier want to go on carting muck forever?"

The servant reappeared, bringing bread, radishes, a crystal cup, and a pitcher of clear water, all on a silver tray. He put it down in the middle of the table, filled the cup from the pitcher, and set them before Thorn with a flourish and a broad smile. She grinned back. He smelled clean, and a woman might even get to like those dinky little horns on his forehead. Did he take tips for other services than bringing meals?

"Those two who were fighting outside a little while before we came in," she said. "Wasn't there some betting on that? How did it come out?"

"They are sitting down there at the third table, lady, resting and drinking together. They have kindly agreed to finish their fight on our stage after this round of ballads is sung. If you'd like, you can place a bet through me. The Inn of Good Fellowship promises honest holding of stakes and prompt payment at a guaranteed minimum of seven to five."

Thorn looked until she located the she-devil and barbarian. They were both drinking heavily. "I'll hold off and make my choice at the last minute."

"As you wish, lady. The inn accepts bets up until the third blow is dealt." With another wink, he departed.

"Thorn," said the sorceress, "that is a very unpleasant ballad."

"What?" Thorn started listening to it. Someone called

Gworkin the Great was getting killed by bits and pieces hewn off in the heat of battle, on a field already ankle-deep in other heroes' mangled remains. Having missed the earlier part of the story, Thorn could not tell who was raiding whom, but the refrain was a list of the dead heroes, chanted off so fast that their names melted into one another, with Gworkin's name recognizable at the end. Those of the assembly who were listening to the ballad laughed and applauded. The singers took a breath and started the next stanza, describing a new hero getting chopped bravely apart in glorious combat.

"Damn stupid way to fight," Thorn commented. "Wasteful, too." The object of Tanglelands raidfare was to defeat with a minimum of killing and maiming, since tonight's enemy might be next year's companion. "Must be singing about the bogbrains who go over to the Ultimate Foolishness for the High Controllers to sweep up."

"Perhaps." Frostflower took out Dathru's book. It was almost as long as her forearm and had been cased in crumbling leather, but the sorceress cringed from the feel of that, so Thorn had cut it off and bartered with the peaceable Oldhillers for a woollen bag to use instead.

While Thorn rolled mouthfuls of snow-water around her tongue and mused on the stupidity of the overlong ballad, Frostflower frowned over the book, chewing an occasional bite of bread and radish, and shaking her head from time to time as if to ward off gnats.

At last the sorceress sighed, slipped the book back into its bag, and stood up. "Thorn, I . . ." She smiled. "Thorn, if this is a glorious harvest, then the farmer-priests may be right when they say that sorceri belong in hellbog."

"What?"

"I would rather return to the Ultimate Foolishness. There at least it will be quiet."

"Oh. All right, we'll settle for a bedroom and you can go upstairs right now."

Frostflower shook her head. "All this noise and merriment must permeate the entire building."

"The Ultimate may be quieter, but it's about as safe as the palm of Azkor's left claw."

"Having been so recently swept, it ought to be safe tonight."

"Yes, maybe. But I don't think we should separate in strange territory."

"We would have separate bedchambers here, would we not?" Frostflower's smile was as close to a smirk as it ever got. "He is very handsome, Thorn, antler-buds and all. Will a hundred paces of snow put us so much farther apart for a single night?"

Thorn shrugged and grinned. "All right. Just don't fall asleep studying. They may sweep the place oftener than we think. And don't try going through the Circle again and get stuck somewhere without me. This place should quiet down before dawn. Why don't you come back when it does? Or else I'll go over and meet you. Have enough money?"

"A silver and four kips."

"That old brinesqueeze may set his prices pretty steep, especially when you come waking him again."

"I will only sit at that table with the lamp, and not wake him again. Happy gaming and sport, Thorn."

"Happy studying and quiet, sorceress."

Frostflower tucked her bread and radishes into the pockets of her robe, took a last swallow of wine, left the cup on the table, and went. Dowl got up and stood looking back and forth. "Well, go on," Thorn told him with a mock kick in his direction. He looked at her again, turned, and jumped down from the alcove to follow Frostflower.

Thorn watched them edge their unobtrusive way out the door. Feeling unaccountably empty, she gave another shrug, refilled her cup with snow-water, and sat back to make up her mind how much money to gamble, and on which of the sleazy pair drinking themselves silly.

Furry Legs brought her a platter of roast beef, still steaming, garnished with green and purple lumps that she guessed were boiled vegetables. Disappointment seemed to flicker across his face as he looked toward Frostflower's deserted place. "Where has your companion gone?"

"Over to the bloody Ultimate."

"Why?" he asked anxiously. "Have we failed to please?"

"You haven't failed to please me, hornhead. Not yet, anyway. But my friend wanted a little more quiet to study by."

"Is she a great sorceress?"

"One of the greatest. And one of the most gentle. She couldn't take that bloody longwinded ballad about warriors getting hacked apart, let alone the battle to come."

"The battle to come?"

"Epic combat between She-devil and Barbarian."

"Ah, that!" His expression calmed into the old, smooth smile. "They will begin in a few moments. Have you decided on whom to bet?"

Shrugging, she tossed him two kips. It wasn't worth any more. "On the barbarian."

The servant bowed, smiled, and slipped her money into a yellow pouch at his belt. "If you should wish to change your bet, lady, just tell me before the third blow."

"One more thing, sweetfur. These High Controllers. Why do they mess around with the Slagland side when they could sweep up a real harvest from Limmervale here?"

"Limmervale is protected by ancient spellcasting."

"And the Controllers aren't smart enough to break it, hey?"

"If they ever did, it would be for the sake of a very fine catch indeed, because customers would be shy of Limmervale ever afterwards."

"But they're not likely to make another sweep on the Ultimate tonight?"

"Oh, no, lady! They're very far from likely to sweep the

Ultimate tonight." He grinned and patted his yellow pouch. "Now, if you'll let me carry your bet to our good keeper?"

"Fine." She waved her right hand, hooking one finger in a gesture that should carry the same hint anywhere. "See you after the fight, sweetfella."

He winked, bowed again, and left.

Thorn had a finger-length meatknife these days, but she did not need it tonight. The Good Fellowship provided brass meatknife and small skewer, wrapped up in a silk napkin tucked through a little hoop on the side of the platter. She carved in.

A lot of bogbrains down at the lower tables were slicing their dinner with their fighting knives, or picking big hunks of meat up whole and biting in as if they were out in a wilderness, and using the inn's meatknives and skewers for throwing at one another or playing nick-up on the tabletops. Drunken idiots. For once, Thorn would not have blamed an innkeeper for clearing out the rabble. The keeper of the Fellowship was maybe a little too polite. But the beef was excellent.

She heard a new roar of laughter and looked over to see the balladeers climbing down and the she-devil and barbarian jumping up on the stage, still holding their winecups. They took their stance three strides apart, lifted their cups and drank a salute, then tossed the cups at each other. Done deftly, it could have been a nice juggle, but since they were too tipsy to catch each other's cup and drink again, the cups just grazed their fingers and clattered to the stage floor, sluicing wine over everything in reach. Thorn returned her attention to her meal.

The rest of the assembly sent up a new cheer every few heartbeats. The first several times Thorn glanced back at the fight, but it was always some stupidity or clumsy braggery that roused the enthusiasm, so she lost all interest. She should have saved her kips for dicing.

She wished one or the other would win so the balladeers

could take the stage again. This crowd was getting too rau-
cous even for her. When a crooked chair by a cold firetrough
in an empty mealroom with only the service of a surly old
leatherface started not to look like such a silly choice after
all . . .

Suddenly she realized that not all the noise was coming
from inside the Fellowship. A deep rumble had begun somewhere outside the building.

At first she thought it was thunder. On a starry night in
winter? Well, possible. But it went on too long and too
steadily, swelling in volume with no waver in the rolling
rhythm. It sounded like a cart with wheels a spear-length
wide.

No one else seemed to have heard it yet. Everyone else had
been guzzling heavily, except the inn servants, and they were
all looking the other way. Nobody else had a friend on the
Slagland side, either. Thorn tried to catch the attention of her
lad with the furry legs and horny forehead.

He was busy refilling winecups and letting customers pinch
him, but since male warriors outnumbered female by about
five to one, he was not quite so busy as the two women
servants. When Thorn whistled, he glanced up, grinned at
her, and went back to pouring wine. By now the rumble had
started to make the walls vibrate a little, and still the soggybrains
weren't paying any attention to it.

Thorn jumped down from her alcove, waded between the
tables (ignoring shouts and dodging missiles aimed at her
because she blocked somebody's view or kicked somebody's
ankle), reached Furry Legs and took a grip on his shoulder.

"I am very sorry, lady," he said with the same old smile,
"but no bets or changes allowed after the third blow."

"Never mind that, what about—"

"For the other, when the fight's done and the lights turned
down." His grin broadened and he winked again.

Tightening her grip, she gave him a shake. "Damn it,
what's that rumble?"

"Rumble, lady?"

She shook him again, short and hard. "*That* rumble! Azkor's breath, you can feel it if you keep your damn feet on the floor. It's your bloody Controllers coming, isn't it?"

Looking down, he mumbled a confession that it was. "But they will not sweep the Limmervale inn, lady."

"Stone you, I've got a friend over there in the stinking Ultimate!"

He sucked in his breath and glanced up at her, eyes wide. "Gods, yes! Lady, you'd better fetch her back here at once."

She let go of him and started for the door. A bugger with green skin and white tusks stood up and blocked her way, towering high above her. His tongue was slurry with wine, but she thought he was telling her that without her clothes, she might look almost civilized. He threw off his own cloak—the freak had four arms, and three of them came groping for her while the fourth twiddled some strange, ugly weapon.

She didn't have the time to waste. She punched him in the gut with one fist, in the groin with the other, and hooked a kick to the back of his legs. Between the wine in his belly and the silly metal ornaments that sank into his flesh instead of protecting it, he crumpled almost before she could dodge out of the way.

Most of his fellow drinkers jumped up laughing and cheering and yelling that here was a new she-devil, good as the one on the stage. Four or five big ones lurched toward her while an old croaker in a long purple robe covered with gold symbols started bawling odds.

Thorn tried tact. Drawing Slicer and Stabber, she brandished them at the nearest noses and shouted, "Out of my way, turdbrains!"

"Four to one on Mighty Murdick!" babbled the oddsmaker. "But if she beats him, three to two on her against Grok the Savage."

Thorn added, "Azkor gut you all."

The one closest to her—Mighty Murdick, she assumed—

wore a metal hat topped with a tall, thin statue like a leering bird. Guessing that it couldn't be solid metal or it would've weighed his chin into his rib cage, she swopped Slicer at it. Her sword cut right through the bird's middle, which crumbled into feathery stuff, as the bird's upper half fell to the floor. Murdick howled as if he'd got a death wound and lost interest in everything except his broken bird.

"Three to two on her against Grok!" shouted the oddsmaker.

"Eat stones, you motherstickers!" Gambling that they would show at least enough comrade-sense not to jab her in the back, Thorn turned and dashed for the door. They left her back alone, but they hooted, "Coward!" and tried to trip her with legs, weapons, and dishes thrown into her path. She was within three strides of the door when a brown pricker roughly the breadth of two ordinary men lumbered out to block her.

His upper arms looked about as big as hams, his chest, shoulders, body and legs were in proportion, and all he wore above the waist was a sheep's-weight or so of gold jewelry. He presented no weapons: he just stepped in too close for her sword and started clamping his arms around her. She supposed the idea was to crush her against his jewelry.

Holding her knife four-fingered, she hooked her thumb into his dangling earring and gave one hard tug, yanking it loose through the lobe. He screamed and doubled over, clutching his ear. She jumped around him and reached the door.

It was rattling on its hinges, and the latch was stuck. "You bogbait idiots!" Thorn shouted, glancing back. "That rumble means—"

"We know!" the red-haired she-devil called back from the stage. She and her barbarian had suspended their own fight to watch the action below. "So why not wait here with us, swordsister?"

Furry Legs sprang forth from the sidelines, jiggled the latch free and threw the door open. "Hurry back!" he told Thorn, winking as she ran past. The door banged shut behind her.

Glancing toward the rumble, she saw a demon face bearing down on her, tall as an oak tree and broad as a scaffold, all fiery eyes and flaming teeth.

"Thorn! Thorn! *Rosethorn!*" That was Frostflower calling her, at last by her childhood name. The dog was barking, too.

The swordswoman jerked her stare from the demon and located the sorceress, who stood at the ice statue waving and beckoning, Dowl jumping up and down beside her.

Thorn risked another look at the demon. This time she made out that its face was lights on the front of a huge wagon trundling along somehow with no cart animals to pull it but with wheels high as an ox and almost as broad. Their rims were white, and snow avalanched leisurely away from them without clogging the thing's advance down the middle of the snowstrip.

It was within two spearthrows of the ice hand. Any moment it would slew off to the Slagland side. Thorn waved her knife. "Frost! Over here!"

"Behind you!" Frostflower screamed back.

Thorn became aware that the door was shuddering. She whirled just in time to see it swing open again. She sprang backwards.

There they all stood, crammed in the doorway—four-armed green man, gold-crusted, with his bloody earlobe, Murdick wearing half a gilded bird, laughing she-devil and scowling barbarian, not to mention the crowd at their back. Warriors' God! Thorn thought. The only place safe from the Controllers, and everyone in it greedy for my guts.

They brandished their weapons and started forward with a shout. Thorn sprinted for the ice statue.

Reaching the snowstrip, she found herself enfolded in a sudden blizzard. Frostflower! The sorceress had found enough wind to stir up a nice, sheltering little storm around them.

They found each other about midway between the statue and the Fellowship side. "Good work, Frost!" Thorn shouted above the sounds of wind, wagon, and warriors floundering in the edge of the snowstrip, where the sorceress had her blizzard raging three times fiercer. "Now if we can sneak around behind the Good Fellowship—"

"Thorn, no!" The sorceress was trying to tug her back toward the Ultimate.

And all at once Thorn understood. "Azkor's talons! Gods, come on!"

Ploughing forward regardless of the blizzard, the wagon was hardly a spearthrow away. They made it back to the statue and there, because even now Thorn couldn't quite believe she had been so wrong, she pulled her friend down into a huddle. The giant hand and the sheath of whirling snow would hide them, she hoped, from the High Controllers, wherever they were heading.

The wagon came on until its lights cast blotches on them, some shining through and some towering above the fingers of ice. Snowflake shadows flew thick and frantic through the spots of red and yellow glare, and the rumble drowned even Dowl's howling, close as it was to Thorn's ears. Thinking the wagon might roll right over the sculpture, she flexed her legs and retightened her grip on Frostflower's arm.

Then, with five paces to spare, it swerved aside—toward the Inn of Good Fellowship.

"The Ultimate Happiness was on the Limmervale side all along," Thorn mused, adding more chips to the fire that the surly innkeeper had let them build for themselves. "I should've guessed earlier. It's the Good Fellowship that stands to make a nice profit by having warriors and sorceri for the High Controllers to collect. That's why they're so bloody polite over there. The old pricker here doesn't care whether we go or stay because all he can get out of us is our own money."

"And our coins are strange to him," said Frostflower, "though I think he will be able to exchange them at the Fellowship. But also, the people of this utopia, this glorious harvest—I believe they fear crowding their land with too many inhabitants. They provide a refuge, here at their border, but only grudgingly, only for those who can solve the riddle.''

"Hospitable buggers! I don't think I'd be much happier settling down in Limmervale than fighting the Controllers' silly battles in Slagland. . . . Would you, Frost?"

The sorceress shook her head. "No. Tomorrow we will try again for home. But . . . all those others, Thorn! If only we could have guessed earlier."

"All what others? The wine fools in the Fellowship tonight?" Thorn shook her head. "They'll probably love it. I wouldn't be surprised if half of them knew exactly where they were and the other half would've stayed anyway. Bogbrains! That'll be another reason the Ultimate discourages customers. Get a bunch like that over here and they'd make a hellbog out of the glorious harvest."

"And the servant with horns and furry legs and the pleasant smile, Thorn? Do you regret . . .?"

"A little. Yes. He did open the door for me, there at the last . . ." Thorn caught back her thoughts with a shake of her head. "Hell, yes—he opened the door because he wanted me to get you back in time for the Controllers. Well, he'll have landed on his feet, all right. Too valuable a servant for the Good Fellowship not to protect. As for me. . . . Better luck next world."

She pushed the Ultimate's battered metal tub close to the fire. This time, she was melting her own snow water.

THE RED GUILD

Rachel Pollack

Early in the choosing of stories for each anthology, I choose two, or three, or four stories which color my choice of all the others; I call them "cornerstone" stories, since everything I choose afterwards must fit with these. The first "cornerstone" chosen for *S&S#2* was Rachel Pollack's *The Red Guild.* The "assassin's guild" story is an old chiché about this notion. Early in the story a client says to the assassin Cori:

"I didn't know the Guild took—"

"Women?"

"Girls."

"The Guild takes what belongs to it."

So that this is, in a sense, less a story of adventure than a riddle; *why* has the red guild chosen Cori—and why does she belong to it? I have seldom been so touched by a story.

Rachel Pollack lives in Amsterdam, a willing expatriate in a long tradition of writer-expatriates. A brief visit in Holland showed me that it must be a good place to live and work—if you can get used to climbing the ladder-like staircases which lead to upper floors in Amsterdam.

Rachel has written one novel, *The Golden Vanity,* in the science-fiction field, and two books on the Tarot, collectively entitled *78 Keys to Power.* She has also appeared in a number of anthologies.

—MZB

1

"I would like to see your master, please." The merchant stood in the doorway, nervously shifting his weight. Except for a first glance at Cori, his eyes slid right past her.

"There is no master here," she said. "I serve only myself."

"What? Oh. I mean, I'm sorry." She could see him shrink back as he looked over his shoulder at the single dirt road from town, empty of any other houses (must they *all* do that?). Then he looked her up and down, seeing the long deep red dress, the green scarf that covered her hair and then crossed around the back of her neck to tie at the throat, the long delicate hands slightly reddened from the scrubbing she'd given the house that morning, the small breasts and long slender waist, the delicate face with its thin lips, high cheeks, and wide eyes. "I'm sorry," the merchant repeated. "I must have made a mistake."

"If you must, you must," Cori said, and almost slammed the heavy wood door. Instead she reminded herself how much she needed a client. "Why don't you tell me what you want?" she said.

"Well—" The man swallowed. "The people, I mean in the town, they said, that is, the innkeeper, a bald man—"

"Jonni."

"Yes, that's right. Jonni. He told me—" He stopped. "That an—"

"That an Assassin lived here."

He caught his breath at the word. "Yes. A member . . . a member of the Red Guild. Yes."

"I am an Assassin," Cori said.

He stared at her. He was a tall thick man, this merchant in his yellow satin robes streaked with pink and purple velvet. He stood more than a head above the skinny girl, and probably weighed a good third more than she did. He could have knocked her down with a single shove; or so it looked. "I didn't know the Guild took, uh . . ." Again his voice trailed off.

"Took women?"

A smile played upon his fleshy lips. "Took girls."

Cori smiled back at him. "The Guild takes what belongs to it. Please come inside." She led him down the narrow center hall of her house, her black slippers silent on the tile floor, his embroidered leather boots clunking awkwardly behind her, to a wide, high-ceilinged room filled with sunlight and a cool breeze from the large curtainless double windows facing the open fields. Against one wall stood several paintings, dark and abstract. Cori had been trying to decide whether she liked any of them well enough to hang when the knock came at the door. Besides the paintings the room contained only two flat red cushions set on either side of a brass disc engraved with Earth Markings in the center of the stone floor. Cori sank down crosslegged, her back absurdly straight even for her; she restrained a grin as the heavy man grunted his way to the floor.

"My name is Morin," he said. "Morin Jay. Do you know the city Sorai? By the sea?" Cori nodded. "I've lived there for ten years now. It's a good place for a merchant. Opportunities from the sea trade, you know. But it's not overcrowded. That's important for a merchant."

"Mr. Morin, why do you want an Assassin?"

"Yes, yes, but you should know the background." The sunlight on his face brought out his paleness. Cori imagined him sitting before his ledgers all day, harassing even paler clerks. "I came to Sorai with enough money—from my family, I was the third son."

"Mr. Morin, please."

"Oh. Yes. Well, I sent out a caravan—I couldn't afford any ships at first, so I bought a cargo and anyway, the Yellow God stroked my camels as they say, and then my ships, when I could afford them, and now I find myself, well, not in a safe, but a comfortable position, one I can build on. But not safe. Not safe. That's the point. I need to expand, I need to keep my investments constantly turning over." Cori imagined a row of little money bags somersaulting. "The Yellow God doesn't like money sitting in cellars, you know."

Cori sighed. It was beginning to sound like the kind of offer every Assassin hated, when you knew you should say no, but found yourself hoping something would justify it. "Let me see if I can help you. A rival merchant has attacked your operations and you find no choice except to remove him."

"Rival?" he said. "My father's god, do you think I would hire—" He swallowed. "No, it's very different. Not a rival. A dragon."

Cori's eyes widened despite herself. Dragons may once have blotted out the sky, but that was long ago, before the Blank God had taken most of his servants with him into the World of Smoke. The last dragon kill, the only one Cori knew of really, had taken place a good twenty years before she had joined the Guild. She imagined a scaly monster laid out before her, imagined her Mark burned into its belly, imagined the line of Guild members shouting her name as she walked coolly into the great Hall in the Crystal City to formally announce her kill.

Morin Jay's sigh brought her back to reality. "I'm sorry. I should have realized it was too—too ambitious for a girl." He pushed himself up.

Cori's grip held him like a paper doll. "Please continue, Mr. Morin," she said, and lowered him to his seat.

"Is there any point? Look, Miss—"

"Coriia. No Miss. Assassins are forbidden all titles."

"Coriia, then. I don't mean to insult you, really. God knows I wouldn't anger a Guild member, even—"

"Even a girl, yes. Don't worry, Mr. Morin, assassins never get angry."

"But really, a thing like this—" He gestured. "A dragon."

"Do you think the Guild would credit me if I couldn't handle whatever jobs I took?"

Sweat dripped over his cheeks. "I don't really know the Guild has credited you. Maybe that innkeeper was playing a joke on me."

A flick of a thumb and forefinger yanked away the scarf that covered Coriia's head and neck. Morin Jay's eyes saw first the red hair, cropped closer than any normal girl would even contemplate; and then they moved down to the hollow of the throat, where the mark gleamed, as red and liquid as a fresh wound. A spiral cross, the arms curled clockwise. As the merchant stared at it, the mark appeared to spin, like the sun wheel of a meditator.

"Mr. Morin," Cori said, with just a hint of the Voice, enough to command obedience, "the knife hidden in your pouch. Throw it at me."

Morin didn't ask how she had known the jeweled blade was there. His eyes stayed on her mark as he fumbled in his pouch, found the blade, and with greater speed and accuracy than Cori expected, launched it at her throat. Her right wrist snapped; the scarf, with its pencil line of "diamond metal" sewn into the outer fabric, flashed out; the two halves of the knife clattered against the wall. "Am I an Assassin?" she asked.

Again he surprised her. Sweating, he whispered, "It takes more than a quick hand and a blade scarf to kill a dragon."

"Yes," she said. "Yes, it does." Again the mark spun,

slowly this time, and as the merchant stared, his face slackened and he began to moan. Cori knew what he was seeing. The image would grow, filling the room. He himself would shrink to a dot, the tiniest pin prick against a cloud. Darkness would surge through him, an invasion of utter cold, slowing the blood rushing through his body. Cori knew this feeling. Her teacher had used it to bring her back the time she'd run from the Guild. For Morin Jay it would seem as if the slightest noise, just a breath, a scratch of a fingernail against a thigh, and he'd shatter like a frozen bubble.

Abruptly it ended. He sat again on a thin cushion across from a young girl, her face as innocent as spring, her head and throat covered with a thin green scarf. She nodded, fighting a smile that attacked the edges of her mouth. "Tell me about your dragon," she said.

They traveled to Sorai separately, Morin Jay by coach along the sea road, Cori on foot, running with the "unwilled stride." Someone, not a Guild member, had once described the stride as drawing power from the Earth. It was nothing of the kind. Instead, she let the Earth enter and propel her, a hand moving a puppet. It felt good, the pull of the muscles, the slap of her slippers against the dirt and rock of the low hills leading to the sea, the changes in light and temperature as gray sea clouds rolled across the sun, the thick smell of late spring.

When Cori first learned it the stride had demanded an empty mind. Now she knew the further trick of experiencing thought without creating will. Undirected, her mind filled with memories. The sea and the time after her first kill, when she'd swum out in a storm, hoping to drown, only to find her desire to live stronger than shame, or horror at what she was. The Guild hall in the capital, with its stark brown chairs and wonderful wine. And Sorai, with its up and down streets and bleached white houses.

She thought also of Morin Jay's strange enemy. The house

Morin had bought for himself outside Sorai sat on a piece of land that also hosted, a little farther inland, the remains of an old castle or fortified town. No one really knew the name or purpose of the place except that the strange architecture, the oddly shaped and colored stones, suggested some old wizard centef. Very ancient. Harmless. Empty as long as anyone could remember. So they said.

Morin had lived there three years, building up his business, when one night, while he stood in his office watching a small fleet of his ships sail past his house on their way to the Sorai docks, he heard a wild rushing noise. A moment later, to his amazement as much as terror, a dragon, a genuine winged worm longer than any of his boats (Cori allowed for considerable enlargement through fear), fell upon the fleet, smashing the flagship and breaking the other ships' masts, so that one of them foundered and the other two barely made it to port. Miraculously, no one was killed, but half the cargo sank into the sea.

Over the next two years the dragon attacked three more times; the last two, however, had come only two weeks apart. Always the same pattern prevailed, ships, caravans, storehouses destroyed, but never the men and women who tended them. Morin Jay himself was the target, though the beast never went for him or his house.

From an overpriced wizard the merchant had learned that the creature apparently lived in the old ruined town, perhaps as a guardian for the long dead. Somehow Morin had angered it, maybe just by being there, and only its death could release him. Moving would accomplish nothing, the wizard said. Angry dragons never changed their minds. After two ineffectual tries at killing the creature the wizard admitted that the spells guarding the ruins lay beyond his comprehension. An obsolete style. When he'd collected his fee—Morin Jay had tried to haggle but a vengeful demon is trouble enough—the wizard had given Morin one last suggestion. If you want something dead—hire a specialist.

Cori slept one night in the wild, stretched out on a rock. There was no need for shelter. She knew it wouldn't rain— the Earth had "told" her—and even asleep an Assassin's reflexes were more than equal to any beast or bandit. She arrived in Sorai the following evening, only five hours after Morin Jay's coach had rolled into the center of the city.

Cori had visited Sorai twice before, and both times found it charming with its streets stepped like stairways, its open air jewel markets bringing traders and thieves from hundreds of miles, its wandering bands of child singers (half of them pickpockets), its thick black ale. But those times she'd gone disguised, first as a Free Messenger, and then as an aristocrat observing the common people. This time, when Cori stood in the center square, with its empty stalls from the closed markets and its rows of grotesque statues decorating the doorways of the guild halls, this time she wore the "uniform" of her calling: black leggings, soft leather slippers (rimmed, like the scarf, with a strip of diamond blade), dark green tunic with a small red leather bag tied to her waist, and the scarf covering her Mark. A simple enough costume; but one immediately recognized.

On all sides the traffic stopped. Some people stared, others darted into the guild halls (what would they say, she wondered, if *her* guild had asked to open a hall here?). Two teenage boys edged forward, their eyes partially on each other as if each hoped the other would stop first. Crossing her arms Cori looked them up and down, and the two ran back to the line of adults pressed against the buildings.

Somewhere in the crowd a child said, "Momma, why is everybody looking? I want to see." The mother slapped a hand on the child's mouth, then nearly smothered it when it started to cry. Cori could see the woman staring at an alley leading away from the square.

"Oh, let her alone," Cori called. "I'm not going to swallow her."

With a sob the woman grabbed up the yowling child and ran for the alleyway.

A man shouted, "Go back where you belong." Cori shrugged. *Where the blood would that be?*

She looked around the square. On one side the setting sun lit the gold plates of the different guilds. Everything else lay in shadows. Near her stood the tables and chairs of an outdoor café. Usually, she knew, people crowded it after the market closed, laughing, drinking, the merchants bragging of their sales, the artists drawing the statues or the crowd, the pickpockets with one eye on their "customers" and the other on the waiters who doubled as market police. Now the chairs stood empty, the tables bare except for a few abandoned drinks. Cori walked over and sat down.

She raised an eyebrow at the burly waiters lined up by the doorway of the café. "You've got a customer," she told them. "Why don't you see what she wants?"

"We don't serve murderers," one of them said.

Cori smiled at him. "You served me with enough eagerness last winter, when I came in different clothes. If I remember—yes, weren't you the one who suggested *I* could serve *you* below the Sea Wall?" A few people laughed; a few more joined in when the waiter blurted out, "That's a lie. I've never seen her before in my life."

An older waiter slapped him on the back. "Forget it, Jom," he said. "You've tried with so many, you might as well count an Assassin in with the rest of them." He stepped up to Cori. "What can I bring you?" he asked.

"Ale. A double tankard. And free drinks for anyone who wishes to join me." A safe offer; no one sat down. Cori sipped her drink as the crowd began to calm itself. She watched them slide away and she thought how it never changed. In the larger towns the people might show a little more sophistication, but behind each pair of casual eyes lay the same thought displayed so openly on all these frightened faces; *she's come for me,* someone's hired her to kill *me.*

They were mostly gone when a boy threw a rock at her. Cori caught it with one hand, slapping down the ale with the other. She'd half risen and had her arm cocked when the anger exploded out of her. She sat down heavily. *Idiot*, she scolded herself, *you've come for a dragon, you'll spill the hunger on some brat?* Shaking slightly she threw some money down and left the square.

Though Cori wasn't due to see Morin Jay until the following morning, she didn't much feel like imposing herself on some trembling tavern owner. She headed for the Sea Wall, still upset by the fury that had swept her. Anger—the worst thing that could happen to an Assassin. It threatened all the years she'd spent training, practicing, learning to control the hunger and not release it until she'd found the right target. If she let it burst out of her at the slightest insult then she deserved everything those pompous fools thought about her.

Maybe I deserve it anyway, she thought. *Maybe we all do.* "Choose a proper target." What gave her the right? She sighed. Necessity. And wasn't a dragon a better choice than a boy?

She climbed the stone stairs of the Wall, stopping for a moment to look through the bars of a cell. The Wall, which ran for several hundred miles along the coast, protecting the various towns and provinces from storms and pirates, contained catacombs of cells. In the small room the single prisoner looked up curiously at the face peering in at her. Either she couldn't tell what Cori was, or she didn't care, for a moment later she sank back on her cot, her elbows on her knees.

At the top of the stairs Cori stepped onto the wide grassy surface. To the right a solitary guard post shined its yellow wizardlight on the sea. Cori walked some few hundred feet to the left and sat down.

The sea leapt nervously at the sloping wall. Like someone trying to break in, she thought. In minutes the cold spray had coated her, soaking right through her clothes. She didn't mind; through narrow eyes she watched the waves, her hands around her knees as she remembered the time she'd swum a mile underwater to rip open the bottom of a ghost ship. What a beautiful kill that was. The hunger had exploded out of her with enough force to boil away the chunks of ice banging into her. She remembered how she'd half swum, half floated back to shore. So empty. So light. And she remembered the cheers of the villagers who'd lifted her from the water and wrapped her in fur blankets.

What a difference from Sorai. Or was it? She'd done a job for them. How would they greet her now if she ever came back for a visit?

She thought about Laani, speaking to Cori that first night in the Guild Hall. She'd just arrived, filthy and hysterical, screaming any time someone approached her. Only much later did she find out how much her anger and fear had threatened everyone sitting there. Then, all she knew was that she wanted her mother. Laani, not much older than Cori herself, had managed to grab the flailing arms and pin the kicking legs with her knees. "Forget your parents," she'd told Cori over and over. "We're your family now. No one else but us. No one."

Without thinking, Cori began to breathe along with the waves, following the Moon rhythm that lay underneath the wind-driven frenzy. Her body swayed as she closed her eyes and breathed in the dark water, breathed out all her memories, the kills, the loneliness. In and out, rising and falling. She could let herself open like the paper flowers in the Crystal City, let the sea enter her and carry her away until nothing was left but the waves, rising and dying forever.

With a sharp cry Cori shook herself loose. She stood up and rubbed her arms. What was happening to her? First she almost spills herself on some nameless brat, now she comes close to emptying the hunger into the sea. Was she scared? Of the dragon? Maybe she was just tired. Sick of it all.

She began to walk along the muddy road that formed the

top of the Wall. What would have happened if she'd let herself drift off like that? With the hunger so high. Burn the whole town probably. What they deserve, she thought sourly.

Memory again. Huddling in the corner of her parents' stone floor kitchen—her dress torn, blood spattered—her ears battered by her mother's gulping sobs, her father's groans and whimpers, the shouts from Rann's father and brothers, and from the mob throwing rocks at the walls and the closed wooden shutters. And then the stillness. It started outside the house and spread inside, even silencing her mother, as *they* appeared in the doorway, three of them, neither men nor women it seemed, despite their close-fitting tunics. Weaponless, silent, they walked her through the enraged crowd, and even Rann's father didn't dare throw the stone he held so tightly in his hand. "We're your family now. No one but us."

"Rann," Cori said softly and squinted at the wet night as if the sea would fling his burned body at her. She started walking again, then stopped when she saw another guard outpost. Don't want to give the poor boy a shock, she thought. She lay down on the road, so soaked it didn't make a difference. *Mother Earth*, she thought, *when are you going to let go of me?*

2

Morin Jay lived in a turreted house with too many rooms. A servant met her at the door. Despite his blousy shirt and balloon trousers, the costume of a middle-rank Hrelltan, the man's accent betrayed his local origins. He led her through a long hallway to a large room overlooking the sea. Cori glanced at the paintings in their gold-edged frames (expensive but she would never have hung them), the long desk covered with symbols of the Yellow God, the graceful gold and red rug before the desk, and she thought how the god had favored Morin Jay more than he cared to admit.

The merchant stood up, his hands politely extended, then

dropped them as Cori stood motionless. He offered her a room in his house; she said she preferred to camp on the grounds. He vaguely suggested lunch; she suggested they go look at the ruins. Obviously relieved he wouldn't have to entertain her, Morin dismissed his servant (even more relieved) and led her from the house.

The dragon's former town (or castle, or spell-casting ground) covered the flat top of a hill somewhat higher than that of Morin's house. Though the winding road upward appeared gentle, Cori soon found herself struggling, almost as out of breath as Morin Jay, who gulped air at every step. Entry barrier, she thought, probably very strong at one time. But when she tried to reach past it to ground her nerve ends in the Earth she discovered a very different barrier. For the first time in years she couldn't sink her mind through the pathways in the rock to that endless source of power. She could sense a kind of fever, a sickness in the Earth itself.

"What's wrong?" Morin whispered. "Should we turn back?"

"Shut up." Panic shook her like an infant who can't find her mother. Panic, and a wild urge to smash her elbow into Morin Jay's face, to cut his belly with her sharp, hardened fingernails. Calm, she ordered herself. The memory of what the Guild had done to Jabob, the "client killer," helped her to throw off the tension from her eyes and mouth, then move the calm down her body to the toes and fingers. "Come on," she said, and strode up the hill. Morin puffed behind her.

Cori had never seen ruins like these. The building or buildings must have been built of some artificial rock, if such a thing could exist, for she knew of no way to carve stone in such graceful spirals, or in such fine and regular points. Nor could anyone dye stone in such vivid delicate colors. There was rubble everywhere, from pebbles and formless chunks of jagged "rock," some as big and lumpy as a sleeping horse. Cori picked up some small pieces, found them cold, more smooth than the grainy look suggested, and amazingly heavy.

She stared at a flattish piece smaller than the palm of her hand—and found herself thinking how she could crack Morin Jay's skull with it. Shaking, she threw it behind her.

Though no complete buildings remained, several half structures rose from the ground like plants. One, a kind of vertical maze, began as a narrow tower, then impossibly curled around and back on itself, until Cori grew dizzy trying to follow all the twists of "stone." In the center of the ruins Cori found some sort of well, a tube of glistening dark blue stone about four feet in diameter and broken off a short distance above Cori's head. She found a smooth edge and hoisted herself up to look inside. Dizziness seized her; she got a glimpse of a deep tunnel, murky dark with a pinpoint of light far below the hill. Her fingers came loose and she fell heavily to the pebbly dirt. Morin hovered over her. "What was it? Did you see something?"

She ignored him, trying to ignore as well the urge to run down the hill. What was this place? What was it for? Cori sighed. To her client she said, "Where exactly does this dragon of yours keep himself when he's not smashing things?" She'd expected some cave, a building large enough to act as one.

"I don't know," Morin whispered, and added stupidly, "I'm sorry."

"What do you mean? You told me it came from this—this place. Well, where?"

"But that's all I know. The wizard—"

"The expensive master of wisdom."

"He told me it lived here—somewhere—but that's all he said."

Cori made a face. She'd have to search the whole area. Later, without this overdressed fool. She walked back to the road, her client scurrying after her.

They were just beyond the ruins when Cori sensed the ground trembling, and then the Earth itself seemed to come to pieces, torn open like a cloth screen. "Run," she shouted, and took off down the hill. Pain entered her through her feet, and a noise like grinding rocks. She fell, half got up and fell again, before she could break loose from the Earth's agony.

The ground was heaving now, and even Morin Jay could sense the terror. "I can't move," he cried. "Help me." Cori braked, swore against all clients, and ran back to hoist him from all fours onto her shoulder. "Stop squirming, you stupid ape," she shouted.

Noise. A boom, suddenly rising to a shriek, then sinking again to a shaky roar. Cori looked over her free shoulder—and sat down with a thud, dropping Morin beside her. On top of the hill the ruins shimmered like sculptured smoke, then suddenly vanished. A beast stood there, green scales heavier than ship armor, yellow tongue longer and thicker than a cobra and snaking out from a gateway of fanged teeth, hooded eyes bulging in a head all lumps of stone. Four wings unfolded across the entire sky, and then the largest creature Cori had ever seen took off into the air with the gracefulness of a gull.

Three times it circled over their heads, while Morin shrieked and Cori stood over him, staring at the granite hard underbelly and a dark red penis as thick as the battering ram the underdemons used against heaven. At last it flew off toward the sea. When Cori could breathe again and Morin's screams had settled into whimpers the Assassin looked up at the hilltop. The ruins had returned, still and silent. Gingerly her senses reached into the Earth. No barrier stopped her, no noise or agony; only a rawness.

Later that day, the news came, via runner, that the dragon had attacked a grain storehouse on the edge of the town, leveling the building and scattering the already sold grain with his wings. To Morin's loss was added the cost of placating his hysterical workers and the town at large with extravagant gifts and promises of action. "You've got to do something," he fumed at Cori, who sat cross-legged in a corner of his office.

"I already have," she said. "I saved your life." She wasn't sure that was true, but it sounded good.

"That's not enough. I mean—oh, you know what I mean."

"He's very selective, this dragon of yours."

Morin squinted at her. "What are you trying to say?"

"He's attacked six times without taking a single life."

"What's the difference? He's destroyed enough property."

She stood up. "It's a pleasure to work for you, Mr. Morin."

"You're awful uppity," he called after her. "I never knew a killer to care so much about life." He ran into the hall to shout at her back, "You better do something about that beast, do you hear me? Or else I'll notify your guild. Killer! Murderer!"

Cori made herself a small camp among a group of trees a mile or so from the dragon hill. There she sat down to work. *At least,* she thought, *I won't have to waste my afternoons finding mushrooms and berries, or whatever vile food grows around here.* For the kind of job she had to do, the first step was a fast.

Some prey you kill with your body, that exactly trained weapon. Some you kill with the mind, reaching in to unravel the core of energy animating the lump of flesh. Either way you release the hunger at the moment of the kill, losing yourself in that dreadful ecstasy. But there are some creatures that only the hunger itself will kill. For those that force must be nurtured, built up until you can direct it, like a needle-thin spear of fire with the force of a volcano.

First she fasted, not even water touching her lips for days; in some way, the hunger grew as you denied the body's more normal appetite. Fast and concentration. She needed to reach that storm gathering in her womb, somehow join it and gain control over it. Revulsion seized her, made her want first to run, as if she could get away from this thing inside herself, and then to cut herself open and spill the filth into the open air. She gained control over this horror, using the energy coiled around revulsion to increase her concentration.

Linnon, the first person to conquer the hunger, described seven steps to mastery. The last two, denial and emptiness, involved the actual dissolution of the curse, like picking apart a knot where each strand is a fire. Cori didn't know if she would ever master those last steps to freedom—to try was extremely dangerous, not only for herself but for the land around her—but she knew from her training she could reach the fifth level, direction.

From the first level, attention, she passed, three days later, to empathy, reliving the deaths of all her prey. From the ghost ship, and the mad farmer who went around mutilating any girl who looked like his runaway daughter, she worked all the way back to the first "safe" kill chosen for her by the Guild, an old sick woman whose healer son wouldn't let her die, but kept forcing useless medicine into her. The woman had wanted to die, the woman had hired her—but even so, the disgust had stayed in Cori for weeks. And now it rose in her again, only to float away as the recall slipped still further back, to Rann. Fear tried to shake her loose from her concentration. She sat immobile, eyes half closed, hands against the hard ground, and let it drain away into the Earth.

Next came fever, the body turned to oily mud, the mind lashed by hallucinations. She saw the Guild surrounding her, led by Morin Jay, who stood and laughed while her friends and teachers spit at her, kicked her. And then they changed into demons, clawing the skin from her face and belly—all except Morin Jay, who grinned, his face a mask. (Mask? The thought whisked away in a wave of fright.) Cori made herself a rock whose top alone jutted into the air while the mass remained invulnerable, rooted deep in the Earth. Against that rock the fever fell to pieces. And the hunger grew.

Finally the most dangerous stage came, forgetfulness. Her

knowledge of herself, her purpose, dissolved, blown away like a fluff in a breeze, and every time she caught it there was less of her. Worst of all, the need to remember became less and less real, more and more an illusion that at last was slipping away. Peace, it offered her. Let go. You've reached the emptiness. Let go. It's only the fore-mind, after all, just a mask. Release it.

Soundlessly, over and over, Cori repeated her true name, and when the syllables threatened to become a meaningless chant she carved her face into the world, on the rocks, the trees, across the moon and under the sea. When her face became meaningless lines and blotches, Coriia imagined herself naked, stripped down to her true self, that which can never be dissolved or blown away. Motionless, more real than the universe.

And when she'd overcome forgetfulness Cori dove into the hunger. She took hold of it, pressed it into a tight ball then pulled and shaped it to a whip, a wire. On the eighth day of her fast Cori stood, feeling her mass greater than the Earth itself, lighter than the wind. She turned to the hill, and from her eyes the hunger snaked out. The rock appeared as a sponge with a thousand holes for the hunger to enter. And probe; and push.

There, in the center, that thick green mass. She pushed it, and the hunger whipped back at her. Again, and suddenly a roar of pain and fury battered her. She pushed again. Another roar, a shriek. All at once, like a creature buried in mud and suddenly awake, the dragon lifted into the air, biting its wings and shrieking.

Cori bounded it, using part of the hunger to make a fence. The creature crashed and kicked and beat its head against the ground.

For a moment Cori wavered. The noise—as blindly beautiful as a hurricane. Her hands clenched and opened, the sweat poured off her, the mark in her throat grew cold as ancient death. Before her the dragon's eyes hovered, begging for release. With a shout Cori tightened the fence.

The Mark appeared, the curled arms spinning before the dragon's face wherever it turned. Through the still center Cori drove the hunger down between the dragon's eyes, probing through the complex streams of being for the image that formed the dragon's true self. When she found it she would kill.

Layer after layer burned away, until she saw, like a carved jewel, the tiny image. The hunger lashed out—

No! Desperately Cori tried to pull back, send it somewhere else, anywhere. For what she saw was not a beast but a man, naked and in chains. And at that moment she heard the laughter of the thing that had called itself Morin Jay.

Wildly Cori turned the hunger around—she had only an instant before it would escape her to rage across the land, picking up energy from anything alive in its path. She threw the hunger at Morin Jay—only to have it thrown back by a mind shield stronger than Cori would have thought possible.

No time. As best as she could she barricaded herself. Then she called the hunger home.

Light. Blinding, a thousand colors, all the cells of her body burning into light. Her mind burst apart into screams, rage, agonies of hate. A thousand years of pain passed in a moment, wave after wave of blinding fire—until the Earth took pity on her, and darkness, blessed empty darkness, swept it all away.

3

Sky—hazy, grayish blue, a summer morning trying to decide whether to be clear or overcast. Whispers—leaves? people?—maybe the rocks and pebbles were talking to her. When she strained to hear it the sound receded.

She was lying naked on her back, she realized. On what? She patted a hand to the side. Something resisted, something as hard as packed dirt or stone; so why couldn't she feel it?

She touched her naked thighs, belly—solid, too smooth, too hard and cold. She made a frightened little noise.

"You're awake. Hello," said—what? Cori turned her head, saw for a moment a vast scaly— No, it was a man, wide shoulders and terribly white arms crossed on his chest, a smiling somewhat pointed face, with a smooth chin, a narrow nose, and very round lovely eyes. Curled blond hair fell loosely almost to his shoulders. Naked, he was squatting on his heels, his knees up covering his genitals (a red battering ram?).

"What happened to your chains?" Cori asked, her voice sounding flat.

He made a sound between a laugh and a grunt. "They're all around." Stupidly, she looked about, then tried to get up. Incredibly weak, she sank down again. "Relax," he said. "You've been away, asleep, a long time."

Angry at her weakness and dependence (an Assassin doesn't need anything from anyone), she asked, "Where the blood am I?"

"Nowhere."

"It sounds like a title."

"Why not? It's as good a name as any."

"But *where* is it?"

He frowned and sat back, crossing his legs under him. Cori was relieved to see his genitals were the normal size and color. He said, "I used to think it was a special place created just for me. My prison. But now that you've shown up, well, I don't know. Maybe it's where you end up when you don't fit into any category. Not alive or dead."

An old joke came to Cori's mind. She grinned. "Everybody's got to be someplace." She thought of the shield she'd put up the moment before the hunger turned on her. If her body couldn't survive and couldn't die either, something had to happen. "Am I really here?" she said. "I mean, is this my body? Damn, you know what I mean."

He shrugged. "Is this *my* body? It doesn't need any food or sleep. I really don't know."

"But if my body is lying out there—"

"Wherever your real body is, it's not—not out there." He tilted his head upward, as if the real world lay above them.

"How do you know?"

"I checked." When she just stared at him, he added, "My representative."

"I don't know what you're talking about."

"An ugly green dragon. Remember?"

"Oh. Oh, of course. Look, I'm sorry."

"But you didn't do anything. Except to yourself. Believe me, being *here* is punishment enough for any mistakes you've ever made in your whole life."

Cori studied his face, the smile that stayed just this side of bitterness. "Who are you?" she asked.

The smile broadened. "Haven't you guessed? I'm Morin Jay."

Between them they pieced the story together. Morin Jay was indeed a merchant, or at least had planned to be, having been a student until his father's death. And yes, he had bought the house overlooking the sea, acting through his father's agents so that no one in Sorai had actually met him. Eager to see his new home he had ridden out alone, before the servants had actually come from Sorai to open the house. The ruins had captivated him immediately, so that he used the house only for sleeping, and after a couple of nights did even that among the stones. Whether the demon or simple curiosity had gripped him he couldn't say, but slowly he became more and more drawn to the black well and its pinpoint of light. Like Cori he'd grown faint just looking over the blue stone; unlike her he couldn't stop himself looking again and again, even when the light glowed, then rushed up at him. He made one great effort of will to break loose; and failed. There was a roar that might have been laughter if it had been human. For an instant he sensed himself alive but changed, vast, and tenuous as smoke. Then that too vanished, and he was "Nowhere."

But if the demon had hoped to take Morin Jay's place and be done with him, he was disappointed. Though hardly a wizard Morin had learned in his studies to direct his will, and after an endless time he found he could glimpse or sense the "outside." Just for a moment, and then his will collapsed, but it was enough to see the demon enjoying its freedom. Again Morin focused his will, powered by a hate he never would have thought possible for him.

Then suddenly, one day he was free, he could taste the air and touch the living Earth. It took only a moment before exhilaration gave way to horror as he discovered the monstrous form his rage had taken.

"Do you suppose that was Morin—the demon's original form?" Cori asked.

"And we changed places? I don't know. I'm not sure that thing ever owned a physical form at all, at least one that wasn't an illusion. It might just be wild energy. Do you know what wizards mean by a pattern breaker?" She nodded. "Maybe someone, with a lot of effort, managed to imprison this particular breaker in that black well. Hoping no useless fool would set him free."

Cori ignored his bitterness; she needed information. "Well, where did the dragon come from?"

Morin looked away. "I'm afraid that monster was me, what I'd become, made myself through hate and fear. A very graphic demonstration."

"But you don't know that." She took his hands, disoriented by the dreamlike sense of feeling and not feeling at the same time. "The demon might have made that form, had it waiting for you, you could say, in case you ever broke loose. To make you give up."

A weak smile broke his despair. "If he did, it backfired on him." That first time Morin had stayed outside only a few moments, hurled back by shock. But success, strange as it was, had strengthened him. He tried again and again. Why the demon didn't (or more likely couldn't) kill him he didn't know, but he used his small powers to devastate the "merchant's" wealth.

And so the demon had hired an assassin, hoping to blast Morin Jay once and for all. But not just any assassin. Someone too experienced might have sensed the malignant force hidden in the plump merchant. No, he must have looked around carefully until he found just the Guild member he wanted; a stupid, arrogant girl.

When she'd finished telling her part of the story Cori stared off at the endless dull brown emptiness, where the flat "ground" merged with the blank sky. Morin asked, "What are you thinking?"

She said, "I'm wondering what ugly toad shape I'll become if I break loose from here."

Morin Jay laughed.

Their non-world never changed, always the same dull light without a sun or moon, the same brown flat ground you couldn't really feel, even though it met your foot when you stamped. They walked, sometimes for hours, their minds insisted, though these bodies of theirs never tired, and it always stayed the same. Once, Cori tried to teach him the unwilled stride. But when she emptied herself of will to let the Earth move her feet, nothing came, a true emptiness that so appalled her she could only stand, paralyzed, and whimper, until Morin Jay came to hold her, lightly stroking the cold smooth body.

They fought at first. Cori wanted to get out, through will or hate or whatever means she could find. Morin Jay wanted company. He reasoned with her; her body was safe—probably— and when it woke up she would snap back to it— probably. He shouted, called her a "selfish bitch murderess"; he cried, trying in broken sentences to tell her of his loneliness.

Cori stamped off, thinking how she had always been alone, how only an assassin really understood loneliness, thinking, "I can't stay here. I can't stand this place." And thinking finally that Morin Jay had stood it, by himself, for years. She walked back to him, and never mentioned leaving again.

It was the cold that moved them closer. Not the air—that always stayed insipidly warm—but the cold deep in their "bodies." They began to huddle together, fighting for warmth. They pressed and stroked each other and suddenly Cori was thrown back a dozen years to Rann kissing her breasts, her belly. "No," she said, "I can't." She tried to pull away, but not very hard, for Morin was able to hold on, whispering, "It's all right. Believe me."

"It's not all right," she wept. "You damn idiot. You don't understand. I'm an assassin."

"Not here."

"Here, anywhere. You don't know what that means."

"Not here. It doesn't count here."

She stared at him as warmth moved in her for the first time since she'd arrived, no, for the first time in years. The warmth opened up inside her and Cori sobbed, in fear, in joy, in memory at the infinite loneliness that ended as Morin Jay entered her.

Years later, Cori would try obsessively, like a bleary alchemist mixing formula after formula, to work out how long she and Jay had spent in that place without time, how many days in a world without night. However long was too short.

Their lovemaking was curious, wondrous and unsatisfying at the same time. Their bodies nearly melted into each other, yet neither would ever climax in the usual sense. Often they simply lay in each other's arms, talking of their lives outside, while their hands moved of their own accord across each other's body. Jay told her of his studies, of his childhood in a house so big he grew scared he'd get lost and no one would ever find him. Cori also talked about her childhood, and sometimes about her life now, and the way people looked at her or left the room if she entered in her uniform. She never told him, however, about the moment those two lives merged, that day with Rann on a grassy hill.

They talked and made love, and played silly games and made love, and when Jay started to speak of all the things he missed outside, Cori kissed him or joked or picked a fight. One "day," in the midst of their peculiar passion, Cori lost, for just an instant, even that dreamlike sense of her body pressed against his. For a moment she was alone and lying on her back, with a cloudy sky and a warm breeze washing her face. Then it flickered away again, leaving her rigid and scared, with Jay holding her, asking what had happened. She tried not to tell him, to make something up. When he insisted and she gave in, he said nothing, only sighed and walked away. "Are you angry?" she asked. From the beginning she always expected him to in some way dismiss her, from boredom, or from disgust.

"Angry?" he said, and turned his stricken face to her. "Oh, Cori." They held each other, trying to form one creature stronger than the emptiness surrounding them.

"You ran away from me," she said.

He shook his head. "Darling Cori, don't you understand? *You're* leaving *me*. And I'm so damned jealous."

"No," she said, "it's not true. I'll never leave you." As he held her she heard a sound, like whispers, like the movement of grass, or faraway waves.

The next time they made love it happened again, this time long enough for Cori to glimpse rubble around her. Without a word she and Jay stopped making love, stopped even holding each other except when the nearness became unbearable.

What amused them before—Jay's stories, Cori's acrobatics or self-deprecating jokes—now became embarrassments, as if they could hear a voice saying, "Is this all you can think of to spend your last moments together?"

When it came it happened in such a simple way. Jay was

telling her something about his father; long afterwards Cori tried to bring back what he'd been saying and could never remember a single word. As she watched him his voice vanished, just as if he were playing a child's game to make her think she was deaf. In its place she heard birds, and the vague sound of summer wind. He must have seen the look on her face (what had happened to her assassin impassivity?) for his mouth hung open a moment, then simply closed. She shouted his name, not knowing if he could hear her, and reached for him.

Too late. The birds grew louder, filling her head. Light burned her eyes.

Suddenly she was lying, no, tossing like a woman in a fit, on a rock-strewn hilltop, her body impossibly heavy and hot, soaked in sweat. She stopped shaking. The Assassin muscle control was returning automatically, and she hated it. Slowly she got to her knees under a blinding sun.

"Jay," she called, and turned, hoping at least to see the monster that stood for him. She knew she wouldn't. She could sense the block in the Earth again, but that was all.

And she could sense something else as well: a force as brutal as a forest fire, yet somehow unsure of itself, or maybe limited by some ancient laws Cori didn't understand. Whatever held her enemy back, the assassin was grateful. She needed time, to gather her strength, to make a plan. Because now that she'd returned, Coriia wanted only one thing. Revenge. For Jay, for herself; and for the Guild. Years now they had been her family, her people, and no demon was going to play them for fools.

She didn't dare go for the thing on her own, not without real knowledge of its powers, and herself still fragile. So she ran, as far from the hill and the sea as the Stride would carry her. The warm wind blew away her tears.

Back in her house, protected (she hoped) by the markings on the door and windows and along the foundation lines, Cori sat in perfect stillness in the room where she'd first promised her services to the thing that had stolen Morin Jay's name. The paintings and the cushions were gone, the windows draped in black cloth. Eyes half closed, Cori sat before the engraved disc, emblem of her guild. Furiously, she drove away all thoughts, until she remembered that she needed calm as well as emptiness. She allowed the thoughts to approach her, then drift away, the whole time fighting the feeling that she was betraying Jay by releasing her memories of him. The thoughts became birds seen far away and then gone.

A deeper darkness rose in the dim room. It covered her, like smoke, and then like a thick jelly. Terror nearly came in with it, but Cori knew they were not the same, and released the fear even as she embraced the Dark. At last there was nothing left, no thoughts, no room, no memories, not even her body, just the Dark filling her existence.

In that blackness a light began, a point of dull red quickly growing in size and brightness, gaining form as it grew until it became Cori's mark, sprung from her neck and burning like a newborn star.

All across the land her sisters and brothers saw it, in Guild halls, in homes and forests, in taverns and markets. It woke them up and stopped their meals; it even turned them away from their contracted kills. Wherever they were they found some place where they could open their necks to the air. The hunger rose in them. At the moment that it flared they propelled it, like lovers thrusting toward orgasm, through the image of Cori's whirling mark.

She reeled, pressed down by the weight of all that power. Somehow, she stepped back from the onslaught, seized control of it, and then, with a shout of hate and joy, sent it hurtling at a house on a hilltop outside the town of Sorai.

Cori never knew what defense the demon mounted. She felt a moment's resistance, and then the uncontrollable hunger of the entire Guild swept over the house and its owner like a hurricane striking a nest of bees.

In the very moment that the storm blasted the ancient center of the monster's being something struck Coriia as well. Ecstasy. Floods of joy roared over her body, wave and wave of release, from her own hungry body, and from the joy of all those other men and women linked together in a way no one who was not an assassin could ever understand. No one.

Cori tried to hang on to her memories of Jay, of the time they'd spent together. Shame filled her as she realized the pettiness of what she'd given and taken from him. Then all memories and thought gave way to that ecstatic sea.

4

Cori knew it was him as soon as she heard the knock. Slowly, she set down her brush and paint and walked through her bare house to the door. "Cori!" he cried, arms out, only to drop them clumsily when she stood there, impassively looking at him.

"I thought you'd find me," she said, not inviting him.

"It was quite a search." He laughed, trying to make it a joke. "Are all your Guild halls pledged to secrecy or something?" He wore a yellow silk robe, unembroidered. The bright clothes set off the color that was coming back to his skin, and Cori had to clench her fists to keep from touching his face, from feeling just once, the full weight of him pressed against her. "Aren't you going to let me in?" he asked. "I've never seen an assassin's home."

"There's nothing to see. Jay, I'm sorry you came all this way, but please, there's nothing for you here. Believe me."

"Nothing? All this way? Cori, darling, what are you talking about? You know how far I've come to be with you. No one in the world can know that but you."

"I'm sorry."

"You're sorry? Oh my gods, Cori, what's happening? When I came back I looked around for you. I thought you'd be there on the hill waiting for me. But I told myself, she thinks I'm dead, she thinks I didn't make it. All I've got to do, I told myself, is find you. Then we'll be together again. Really together.'' He stepped towards her. She pushed him back. ''Cori, you're my lover. Have you forgotten or something? Is that it? Let me touch you and the memories'll come back. Believe me, they'll come flying back.'' He reached out.

Cori stepped away. ''I'm an assassin, Jay. A killer. Don't you understand that? That's my only pleasure, my only love. Murdering helpless people.''

''I know what you are,'' he said. ''What you've been. I've thought and thought about it. Cori, darling, I don't care. We'll—in some way we'll handle it.''

She half shouted, ''Won't you please just *go away*?'' Tears threatened to ruin the whole thing, so many times rehearsed.

''No. I won't let you chase me. What we had, it wasn't just to pass the time. I know it wasn't.''

''What happens in Nowhere doesn't count. We were just keeping each other from losing our minds. That's all it was.''

''We were lovers, Cori.''

''We were nothing.''

He shook his head, started to say something, and found his throat too full of tears. Abruptly he turned and walked down the road back to the little market town, his back straight, his steps jerky.

Cori closed the door, shaking. Would he come back? Probably. Jay wasn't the type to just give up. She hoped it would go easier the next time, but she didn't think so. If only she could do it without hurting him. ''Jay,'' she whispered, feeling his name inside her.

But when she sat down in an old green leather chair and closed her eyes it wasn't Morin Jay she saw but Rann, the skinny red-faced boy who'd led her, a girl of twelve, with promises and fantasies and caresses to a gentle hill on his father's farm. For the thousandth time Cori remembered every touch, his grin as he broke her hymen, the sudden fury of her own desire. And then the flames, the shrieks of pain and terror, Rann's stunned look as he pulled back from her, his mouth and eyes open until the flames roared over them, and the way he rolled on the ground, then slowly came to a stop, lying there all charred and stiff, the last flames dying out, with nothing left but smoking flesh and bone.

She remembered running back to town, remembered the mob and her mother's shrieks, remembered the assassins walking her through the crowd, whose fear had suddenly overcome their rage. From now on, they told her, forget any life but us. Any lover but us. What happened to Rann will happen again and again, to anyone you touch with desire. And once it gets stronger it will happen without sexual contact, once, twice a year, destroying people, land, anything near you. Unless we train you. Unless you release it before it builds up. Release it the only way possible.

"No!" she'd shouted back. "I won't kill. You can't make me."

You must, they told her. When the hunger rises you cannot fight it. You can only choose your target.

"How can I make a choice like that? How can anyone?"

Because you must. There is no other answer. We will help you. Remember, Coriia. You belong to us now. To the Red Guild.

SHADOW WOOD

Diana L. Paxson

One of the best-liked stories in *Sword and Sorceress I*, judging by letters I received, was Diana Paxson's "Sword of Yraine." Her main character, Shanna, made her first appearance in Andy Offutt's *Swords Against Darkness IV* and after half a dozen short stories Diana felt it necessary to begin writing Shanna's adventures in chronological order. When I asked for another story this time, after "Sword of Yraine," she told me that she should be writing Shanna's story in chronological order, perhaps as a novel.

I persuaded her to change her plan and give us at least one more Shanna short story before she began work on the novel. "Shadow Wood" is the result.

In addition to stories in several anthologies—including all five of the ones I have edited—Diana Paxson has written two novels for Timescape, *Lady of Light* and *Lady of Darkness*, and a third, *Brisingamen* (Freya's Necklace), will be published this October or thereabout.

—MZB

hadow Wood . . . Shanna tested the name against the reality of the forest before her. On maps the sea of trees that flowed across the rising land between Sharteyn's fertile farmlands and the mountains had some ancient name, but Shanna preferred the title the countryfolk used. The sky looked very dark beneath the massed trees, and after the heat and dust of the road, very cool.

She straightened in the saddle and snapped open the clasps of the quilted jerkin of red leather she wore. Her new breeches were sticking damply to the saddle, and sweat trickled down her backbone. She wondered how the men in her escort stood the additional weight of breast and back plates of leather sewn with little plates of iron. They had become accustomed, she supposed.

After the half-hour it had taken to argue her old nurse, Nellis, into allowing her to wear her warrior gear instead of the draperies of a Royal Daughter of Sharteyn, Shanna did not dare complain. She had won only on the grounds that they were nearly past Sharteyn's borders. But many leagues stretched between the forest and the Imperial City of Bindir, where they would meet her brother Janos and bring him home again—this was the Old Road, easier on the wagon, but longer and less-traveled than the one the Emperor's couriers used. Shanna shifted her shoulders beneath the thick leather and grinned. *I will become accustomed, I suppose.* . . .

Her bay mare danced forward, responding to an involuntary, excited squeeze of Shanna's long legs, almost colliding with Big Hwilos' gray.

"Peace, Calur!" Shanna shortened her reins, avoiding the old soldier's eye. The road unreeled before her like a white banner, she had a good horse beneath her and the sword she had risked her life to win hung at her side. She was finally free!

Or if not free—she considered her escort—then at least she had escaped the intrigues and etiquette of the Court of Sharteyn.

And perhaps somehow, somewhere, along her way, she would find the liberty her soul craved as a hawk craves the skies.

The trees loomed larger as they plodded on. Shanna identified oak and hazelwood, the narrow-leaved ash and stately elm. Crows flapped toward the forest from a day spent gleaning the rich harvest of Sharteyn, black against a golden sky. The road ahead was dim beneath its canopy of gilded leaves.

And then abruptly they were inside. Shanna blinked, trying to adjust her sight to the shadows, then jerked on the reins as her cheek felt the swift flight of something she could not see. A soldier ahead of her cried out; to her returning vision the arrow-shaft seemed to sprout from his throat as he fell. Men shouted, a horse screamed. There was a crash and Shanna saw the gaudily painted wagon in which Nellis had been riding tipped over on its side, wheels still spinning helplessly.

"Stand! Put up your weapons or you die!" came a deep shout, but it was too late.

Three more arrows flicked accurately past. Two of her father's men screamed as feathered serpents found gaps in their armor. The other arrow glanced off a helm and rattled past a tree. Shanna crouched over her mare's mane, twitching when a bowstring twanged, for the fine-linked vest of gilded mail she wore under her jerkin would not protect against a bolt from a powerful hunting bow.

Trees shuddered at the movements of invisible enemies. A superstitious shiver tightened Shanna's grip on Calur's black mane, but she forced the fear away—*Wood spirits don't need mortal weapons to kill.* . . .

"Dismount and scatter!" shouted Hwilos, and Shanna realized without time for emotion that the leader of her escort must have been killed. "We're only targets here!" He turned to her— "Quick, my lady! I'll cover you!"

Her feet already free of her stirrups, Shanna kicked the mare forward, rolled from the saddle and, still rolling, hit the road and scrambled toward the trees. Tufted grasses were crushed beneath her clutching fingers, a berry bush scratched her face; she saw a tree trunk—no, a man's leg, before her, and uncoiled upward. The little dagger in her hand scarcely gleamed in the dim light.

She felt the knife go in, pulled free to strike again as his bow and arrows clattered to the ground, then hard hands closed on her arms; she was jerked backward and felt the chill sting of a blade at her throat.

"Hold still, lad, if you want to live—" came a growl at her ear.

Shanna remembered the sour breath of the man from whom she had won her sword. Better death than to live in such a man's power! She knocked her head back against her captor's unprotected face and jabbed her elbows into his ribs as his fingers relaxed in the first moment of shocked pain.

Then a long arm jerked her around, she struck out and his return blow thunked dizzyingly against her steel cap. As it fell, her black braids uncoiled from around her head and swung free. Half-stunned, Shanna could only struggle weakly as her captor bore her down and bound her wrists and ankles.

She stared upward, her clearing vision showing her a big man—from that angle he seemed like a tree—grinning and attempting to stanch a bloody nose. There was an infuriating twinkle in his gray eyes.

"Well, by all the gods." The man's voice came muffled from behind his hand. "Perhaps fortune is blessing us at last. It's a maid!"

The brush crashed behind him and more men appeared, none his height, but all dressed in the same rough tunics and leggings of brown and green. Some, Shanna noticed with satisfaction, were bleeding.

One of the newcomers stopped before her captor and brought up his fist in a salute. "Lord, all's secure. Andros is dead and Tam's got a thrust through the lung—"

The big man nodded, the lines of authority in his face deepening as he frowned. "And this vixen knifed Vand. Did we lose any others?"

"Just wounds, my lord—nothing that won't heal."

Shanna struggled to sit upright, croaked, found her voice and gasped, "You bastards, what have you done with my father's men?"

A dozen pairs of eyes fixed on her, then turned to their leader with dawning comprehension. "I knew that old bitch in the wagon couldn't be all they were guarding!" exclaimed the man who had been reporting, then met his commander's eye and continued more formally, "We killed five. Two are wounded, I don't know how badly. Arni and Farel are guarding them and the three we overpowered."

Shanna closed her eyes and swallowed, sick with grief for men she had become fond of during the month's journey from the city of Sharn, and sick with outrage. They had been attacked when they were still on Sharteyn land! When her father heard—

"I see you had good hunting too," the hateful voice of the lieutenant continued. "What have you got there?"

"I do believe—" the big man bent and forced up Shanna's chin. "I do believe I have the honor to present to you the Royal Daughter of Sharteyn!" He straightened, sketched a bow. "Lady, permit me to introduce myself and my men. You are now the prisoner of Roalt Larsenyi, lately Prince Governor of Norsith. If all goes well, you will also be the key to recovery of my throne!"

Shanna shook her head, forcing her mind to function again. "You want my father to help you?" Now she was remembering—the Lord of Norsith had been dispossessed by his cousin some two years past. As long as the taxes were paid regularly, the Emperor did not appear to mind. Roalt had sent to her father, seeking alliance, and had been denied. Busy with the depredations of the outlaw Kintashe, Prince Artinor had neither time nor resources to deal with injustices on somebody else's lands.

"By Yraine's holy fire," spat Shanna, "my father will nail

your foul hide to the walls of Sharn! Why did you have to kill my men? Couldn't you simply ask me to plead for you?''

Roalt sighed. "We guested your brother when his party passed through the forest last year. We asked politely then. But he refused, and his party was too large for us to insist. You are very like him, lady. I thought you must be related to old Artinor somehow, though I knew he had no other son. We'll see how much he values you, now.''

"Oh my lamb, you must not grieve . . .'' whispered Nellis. "I took you from your dead mother's arms and raised you to womanhood, and it's like a young goddess you are. What more could I ask life to give to me?'' Nellis' fingers twitched and Shanna took her hand and stroked it. It was thin, so thin, and that more than anything else fed her fear. Through the eighteen years of her life Nellis had been an ample lap and soft breast to comfort her, and sometimes a bulwark against which she could safely vent her rage. What in this world was secure if Nellis could dwindle to such fragility?

"You'll get well!'' she said desperately. "My father will send for us soon. Let me give you some more tea.'' Shanna fumbled with cup and dipper, hardly noticing when hot liquid splashed her hand.

Nellis drank a little and then lay back again. Shanna set down the cup, straightened, and forced a smile for the men watching her from the other side of the clearing. Hwilos, Sandy, and Zan—they were all that was left of the escort that had set out with her. She was responsible for them now.

As she was for Nellis. She looked down at her old nurse and tucked her cloak more securely around her. Nellis had been stunned when the wagon went over; her injuries had seemed slight, compared to those of the wounded men. But there must have been some damage to the body's delicate inner machinery, or perhaps it was the shock of capture. Shanna knew now that it had been criminal to bring an old woman with her on this journey, but she had feared being saddled with some simpering court lady, and she had never thought of Nellis as old . . .

A shadow moved between Shanna and the fire. She looked up, saw Lord Roalt, holding a blanket cobbled together from soft beaver and fox furs. "Will this help?" he said. "It's warm—"

Shanna nodded mutely, torn between anger and gratitude. If it had not been for Roalt, Nellis would not be lying here, but she knew that it was from his own bed that the Prince had taken the furs.

She tried to cover her confusion by carefully arranging the blanket over Nellis' wasted body. When she looked up again she was surprised to see Roalt still beside her, sitting on his haunches with his gaze turned inward as if his thoughts were far away.

Shanna bit her lip at the sudden sense of recognition, and realized that she had often seen her father with just that worried frown. Indeed, the former Lord of Norsith was like her father in many ways—not as Artinor was now, wasted by war and intrigue and anxiety for the son who had never returned from his journey to do fealty to the Emperor in Bindir—but as he had been in her childhood, mighty and resolute and, yes, *kind*. . . .

When Nellis' illness had become apparent, Roalt had sought ways to help her, but there were no farmsteads near the forest to which they could have moved her, and no healers they could call. It was obvious that the old woman could survive neither the long journey back to Sharn, nor, if Roalt had dared it, to Norsith lands.

Angered by her own reactions, Shanna coughed. "Have you heard from your messengers yet, my lord? It's almost two months since you sent them to Sharn. Perhaps they've decided that life in the greenwood's not so fine, now that they've tasted it. What makes you think they are going to return?"

She braced herself for his anger, but Roalt only sighed. "I

suppose I deserve that from you—seizing you was unworthy of a ruler, you would say, and it is true. But with every season my cousin Deneth's grip tightens on my land. The people grow weaker, and the Emperor does not intervene. A sad comedown for a prince to live like a beast in the wilderness, preying on passersby. But what else can I do?''

For a moment an answer trembled on Shanna's lips—he could send her back to Sharn to be his advocate! The scene formed itself in her imagination, and then its sequel, for she knew that having got his daughter safe home, Prince Artinor would never allow her to brave the dangers of the road again. She swallowed. Roalt heaved himself to his feet. The moment passed.

Shanna had been captive for almost three months when Nellis died, and Roalt's messengers to Sharteyn had not returned. The fullness of summer shaded imperceptibly into the first crisp days of fall. Aside from that last obstinate hope that kept Roalt from releasing her, Shanna might almost have been a guest in his camp. His men were impressed by her swordsmanship, and insisted on rounding out her education by teaching her to use the great hunting bow, as well as the kind of weaponless combat that could have saved her from capture.

On a day when the sun shone with almost summer's warmth, Shanna trudged off to the stream to bathe. The Norsith men kept a loose guard on her these days. Beyond warning her not to go too far upstream—and that seemed more from fear that she might run into some danger than that she might run away—they had the courtesy to withdraw and leave her alone.

For a little while she sat on the bank, paddling her feet in the water, getting used to its chill. Then she took a deep breath and slipped in fully, stretching out so that the water, low now at the end of summer, could cover her. It was very clear, but faintly brown and, seen through the water, Shanna's long legs had the warm tint of ancient ivory.

Used to the tiled baths of the palace, at first Shanna had

been afraid of the brown depths of the stream, but she had never found anything more alarming than minnows there, and an occasional crayfish scuttling frantically across the stones. Now she wished only that the water were deeper. Perhaps there were bigger pools nearer the stream's source. Drops of water clung to her body like crystals as she got to her feet and began carefully to make her way upstream.

Shanna had never known the woods to be so peaceful, or so beautiful. She supposed it was because the outlaws rarely came this far, and she had left behind on the bank her clothing that smelled so strongly of sweat and cooking smoke—the betraying odor of mankind. An otter slipped from the stream's edge into the underbrush with hardly a splash; the woods vibrated with small rustles and twitterings—a living stillness very different from the emptiness of the forest around the camp.

Shanna stood for a moment, breathing deeply of the clean air. The tree trunks lined the bank like the columns of a temple. Autumn sunlight glowed through the turning leaves in a hundred shades of gold. The water sang a secret song as it chuckled across the stones, as if it were calling her, and Shanna smiled and went on.

Presently she saw the stream bed blocked by two great boulders, through which the water burst in a miniature waterfall. Her heart lifted; surely such a dam must guard just such a pool as she desired. Eagerly she climbed forward, clambered around the boulders and found herself at the edge of a mirror of water perhaps two dozen feet across. Silver birches surrounded it, like the arches around the sacred pool at the Temple where Shanna had been initiated. With a sigh of delight, she eased her long body all the way in.

Shanna had learned to swim in the cold north sea. What luxury it was to bathe in this water which was so still, yet fresh, as if the pool were fed constantly by some deep upwelling spring. With a few powerful strokes she pulled herself across the pool, and turned on her back to float, gazing up at the gently fluttering golden leaves of the birch trees.

Then the aspiring sun found an opening in the branches, and its radiance shafted downward toward the surface of the pool. Dazzled, Shanna turned over in the water and blinked as from beneath its surface she glimpsed an answering gleam of gold. Curious, she took a deep breath, jack-knifed in the water and dove.

Her reflection rose toward her from the bottom of the pool.

For a moment Shanna found that merely curious, then her startled mind reminded her that one could not have a reflection *underneath* the water, and besides, the hair that swirled around the face that was rising toward hers was pale . . .

Pale, and its bulging eyes were as clear and brown as the waters of the pool as it rose, rose— Shanna's muscles tensed to propel her to the surface, and pallid limbs fastened around her, slick as a trout's belly and *strong*.

Shanna struggled, using every trick Roalt had taught her, but her vision was a trail of sparks through darkness; her pulse roared in her ears. As the strength seeped from her limbs she felt an impossibly limber-fingered hand pass over her breasts and fumble between her thighs. Then the terrible grip released and her body's buoyancy shot her toward the surface.

Shanna gasped, swallowed water and, coughing, stroked toward a rock at the edge of the pool. She lay across the rock, drawing the sweet air into her lungs in hoarse gasps.

"You're not a *man* . . ." said a voice behind her in sweet, aggrieved tones.

Shanna wrenched herself around. The face of her nightmare was floating on the surface of the dark water. Shanna blinked, looked again, and saw the pale glimmer of a body below it.

"It has been so long since they brought me a man to play with, and the last one broke too soon . . ." narrow lips pouted. "But I kept part of him—" The creature rose a little out of the water, and Shanna saw her flexible fingers caressing the scoured curve of a man's skull.

A *nixie* . . . One of Nellis' tales supplied the name. No wonder Roalt's men had feared to go upstream. Shanna wondered if they had ever learned what happened to their missing companion.

"Have you come to pray to me?" the sweet voice went on. "They used to come every springtide. They brought me pretty things . . ."

Shanna's eyes flicked toward the glimmer of gold in the depths of the pool. Forcing trembling fingers to obey her, she worked the golden circlets free from her earlobes and held them out to the nixie.

"Lady, will you accept these as my offering? They are all I have!" As the creature nodded, Shanna tossed the earrings in a glittering arc to splash and disappear.

"My name is Sequilla—" the nixie's laugh was like falling water, but far too many pointed teeth showed when she smiled. She dipped beneath the dark waters in a swirl of pale hair, then surfaced a few feet closer to Shanna.

"Lady Sequilla . . ." Shanna acknowledged, edging backward. She knew better than to make the creature a gift of her own name. "Will you forgive me for swimming here? I did not know the pool belonged to you."

"*Everyone* knows this pool is mine . . ." said the nixie. Then her eyes widened. "But perhaps they have forgotten. They used to come in the springtime, and—"

Shanna sighed as Sequilla repeated her tale. There had been processions, and a priestess, and the music of flutes and drums. They gave her golden ornaments then, and wreaths of flowers, and sometimes men . . . Shanna wondered how long ago that had been. She had never heard of a time when the Forest was not a wilderness.

"But then there was the battle, and after that nobody came . . ."

The nixie's closing complaint recalled Shanna's wandering attention.

"Oh yes," said Sequilla. "Over there—" one sinuous arm indicated a deeper darkness framed by an arch of trees. For a moment she submerged, then bobbed up again. "They are still there, you know. Both of the armies, with all their pretty things."

Drawn despite her will, Shanna got to her feet and moved softly to the edge of the wood. The breeze was freshening, chill on her bare skin. As the branches swayed, for a moment sunlight penetrated the forest canopy, and the humped shadows at which Shanna had been peering showed suddenly the white grin of a skull, the timeless gleam of golden ornaments, and in the midst of them a crown and a skeletal hand that still gripped the wasted spine of a sword.

The nixie gave a sad, bubbling sigh. "They wake sometimes, when new people come, wanting to fight again. So many men . . . but none of them any use to me . . ."

Shanna swallowed sickly and retreated back to the edge of the pool, thinking hard. Two armies of unburied dead, struck down in their hate and fear, would make a powerful haunting. No wonder—no wonder this place had become the *Shadow Wood*! Her skin prickled with something more than cold, and she began to clamber toward the outlet of the pool.

"Don't go—" called the nixie plaintively. "I like you to talk to me."

Shanna shook her head. "I have to leave now. Perhaps I can come again—"

"Come again another day . . ." the nixie half-sang. She swam toward the edge of the pool, and with more haste than grace Shanna scrambled over the rocks that guarded it.

But even as she stumbled downstream, she seemed still to hear the words, "another day" repeated endlessly by the silver voice of the waterfall.

*   *   *

Winter came early, with a bitter wind that searched out every gap in one's clothing, and flurries of wet snow. If Nellis had lived so long this snow would have killed her, thought Shanna, pulling her red cloak more closely around her. Thanks be to the goddess that her journey had been expected to take all winter, and the chests in the wrecked wagon had contained warm clothes. But she had not expected to spend the winter here!

She supposed it must be possible to live through such weather in the wilderness, for Roalt and his men had already done it twice before she came. But this winter the feeling was different. Whether capture or treachery had kept Roalt's messengers from returning, they could not know, but hope was gone. Men's eyes already had a hollow look, and the season was not a month old.

Roalt knows that they have lost their will—thought Shanna as she watched him lay another stick on the little fire. *What is he going to do?* He had been very silent this last week or two, the worry mark between his brows deepening until it looked like a scar. Her fingers twitched with yearning to smooth it away.

Shanna started to her feet to go to him and abruptly realized what she was doing. She sat back in the snow, her fingers curling until they bit into her palm. Her attention went inward, analyzing not Roalt's actions, but her own.

My men gave their word not to try escape, but I did not. . . And it's been weeks since I even asked Roalt to let me go . . . Why am I still here?

She settled on her haunches as deeper levels of awareness surfaced, ignoring the cold.

Roalt has lost. His men stay here because they love him—
—And so do I.

She sat still, with the warm tears rolling down her cheeks to fall unheeded upon the snow, while her memory replayed everything she had ever said to him, all he had said to her.

And after a time another question formed itself in her consciousness.

Why, when hope was lost, hadn't Roalt sent her and the other extra mouths away? Her heart leaped— Was it perhaps because he loved her too?

She jumped to her feet, seeking him, and saw the lookout rushing frantically toward her, almost sliding into the fire as he halted before his lord.

Shanna stilled, her heart pounding. Had she been wrong? Had her father's answer come at last? But the lookout's face held no joy, and Roalt's features were growing grim. Now men were pounding into the clearing from every direction, grabbing for their weapons. Rumors sprang into being to be as instantly denied as they gathered around Prince Roalt and the lookout, listening. Then the Prince nodded at last and turned, holding up one hand for silence.

He got it more quickly than Shana would have thought possible. For a moment the only noises were the crackling of the fire and the occasional "shush" as a branch let go its load of snow.

"We have succeeded in this much, my brothers and comrades-in-arms—" Roalt's deep voice was not loud, but Shanna could hear each word as if he had spoken in her ear. "We have convinced my cousin that we are a danger to him. He is bringing his forces here— A compliment, don't you think, to send an army after two dozen men?"

There was a little wolfish laughter, but Shanna could see them all calculating the options, whether to fight or flee. Big Hwilos gestured to the other two Sharteyn men and the three took up position behind Shanna, who managed a smile for them.

"As for myself"—Roalt's voice hardened—"I will not run again. If in this battle I can destroy my enemy, I will have won at last. If not—well, Deneth will never drag me in triumph through the streets of Ennis Narr!"

Someone began a cheer. Drawn swords flickered pale reflections of snow and sky. "We will stand with you, my lord!" they cried, "Death or victory!"

Shanna swallowed. The battle cry echoed in her ears like the bittersweet lure of a distant horn. Oh yes—was not a swift and glorious ending better than a life of ignominy?

Roalt turned. Shanna began to tremble as his gaze, for once unguarded, focused on her face. But before she could read what she saw in his eyes they changed, and the shield of authority once more hid the nakedness of his soul.

"We will fight then—" he spoke to his men, but his eyes were still on Shanna. "But before that happens, my lady, we must get you clear. I think that even Deneth will honor a flag of truce borne by the daughter of Artinor!"

Shanna glanced at the faces of the men who stood with her, and seeing the disappointment in them, began to laugh. "But my lord, how could I deprive you of a sixth of your army? You wanted an alliance with Sharteyn—you have it now!" She drew her sword with a musical scrape of steel, reversed her grip, and presented its hilt to him.

Now that the decision was made, she felt the exultation. Surely it was a privilege to decide with whom one would die—and to be accepted as a comrade by these men, by *this* man— It was for just such a moment that she had pledged her sword to the goddess Yraine! Curiously, in that moment she regretted the inevitability of Roalt's death more than she did her own.

The Prince frowned; he drew breath to speak—to refuse her offer? But Shanna's own men were nodding, and Roalt's were beginning to cheer again. Then from somewhere not nearly far enough away came the harsh, sequenced notes of a trumpet call. Men's hands gripped their weapons. They stilled, listening.

Then Roalt sighed. "It's the Norsith signal to make camp," he said. "They've had a long march. Likely they'll rest tonight and attack us with the dawn. We will do the same," he went on, "and give them our best in the morning.

Remember, we know the woods as they never will. And Shanna,"—his tone hardened—"I must talk privately with you—"

Shanna sat up, pulling her blankets back around her as the midnight chill penetrated where their protection had been. She had lain down in her clothes—all of them had—but this was the coldest hour, when the icy glow of the moon froze the sky. She heard the regular breathing of the sleeping men around her, an occasional snore, a murmur as someone previewed the coming battle in his dreams.

She was glad they could sleep. She had not been able to manage more than an uneasy doze since she had lain down after an hour's argument with Roalt which neither of them could win. He insisted on trying to protect her, but he must know that he could not keep her from rejoining the battle even if he sent her away. And then both of them would be dead, and it wouldn't matter any more.

Unless—Shanna shivered, not entirely from the cold, for the thought that had kept her from sleeping was surely sufficient to chill one's soul. Terrifying—and quite probably insane. But if Shanna was resigned to death in any case, how could she refuse the risk that might keep Roalt from dying too? If only the past months had given her both the nerve and the woodcraft for the deed she meant to do!

Her seeking gaze found the dark bulk that was Roalt, sleeping on the other side of the fire, and her heart whispered words of farewell she had not allowed her lips to say. At first she had hoped that they could spend this last night together. Why not? Shanna had paid her debt to the Goddess at the Baalteyn Fire a year ago, and he would not have needed to worry about her virginity. But now she was glad. Surely saving Roalt's life was better than sleeping in his arms!

Yawning ostentatiously, Shanna got to her feet and picked her way toward the trees. With luck, the man on guard would think she was going to relieve herself in the trench by the horse-lines. Calur lifted her head as Shanna approached and she laid her hand on the mare's nose to quiet her. But though the horse snorted and sidled at the cold touch of saddle and bridle, she followed Shanna willingly along the moon-dappled path that led to the stream, and stood still for her to mount.

Once, Shanna looked back, and then no more. She must not allow herself to wonder whether Roalt would wake, and finding her gone, believe that she had run away . . . No—better to worry about whether she would recognize the path in the inconstant light of the moon.

After her encounter with the nixie, Shanna had spent some time reconnoitering the borders of the ancient battlefield. The remains of an old road led through it from the edge of the forest to the nixie's pool—probably the long-forgotten processional way. If Shanna succeeded in what she meant to do, that road would lead her out of the forest to Lord Deneth's bivouac fires. . . .

The way seemed very short this time. Shanna guided the mare along the stream, its voice muffled now by the ice that imprisoned it, seeking the pool where the nixie slept beneath a crystal coverlet that glittered in the light of the moon. Stars winked like chips of ice in the moon-paled sky. The gap in the trees that led to the battlefield gaped like an opening door.

"Holy Yraine, sweet Lady of Stars!" Shanna whispered through cold lips, "Strengthen and protect me now!"

Soothing Calur with hands and voice, Shanna guided the mare through that dark doorway into the shadows that had given Shadow Wood its name.

Moonlight filtered through the net of bare branches with a deceptive glow. Was that a moon-silvered shield rim or only the limb of a tree? And there, was it a skull or only a smooth boulder covered with snow? Stepping stiff-legged, the mare minced forward—

—And stopped, trembling, before the bare bulk of a standing stone. Shanna stared at it, noting uneasily that although snow lay thickly elsewhere there was none on the menhir.

Even the ground at its base was clear. And in a moment her adjusting vision showed her other things— Around the stone a ring of mingled fragments of decomposing armor and white bones, and against its base a crumpled skeleton with a skull that seemed to watch her from empty eyes, whose hand still gripped a gold chased sword.

Shanna forced cold-stiffened fingers to close upon the hilt of her own blade. Moonlight shattered and refracted across the face of the menhir as she drew, and struck an answering glitter from the ancient sword at its base.

"Lord of Shadows—" Shanna's voice cracked; she took a hoarse breath and called again. "Lord of Shadows, are you there? I summon you!"

Her voice sounded thin and ghostly in her ears; like departing spirits, white puffs of vapor bore her words away. But soft as her call had been, it was heard. Shanna sensed a stirring around her. Calur pawed unhappily. Shanna felt the powerful muscles beneath her bunch, ready for flight, and shortened her reins.

"Peace, lass, just a moment now . . . I shall want your speed soon!" she whispered, and more softly still, "Blessed Lady of Stars, don't let me be afraid!" But her breathing was ragged. More strictly than she had controlled her mount her reason reined down her fear.

Shadows thickened, dimmed the moonlight. Something quivered at the base of the stone.

"Who is it that breaks our slumbers?" The voice seemed an echo of the earth, a distillation of the air. "The field is ours, through all eternity. Stand, challenger, and face my sword!"

Out of the dark Shanna saw a sharper shadow rising, and was abruptly certain that it would take more than her body's life if it should fall. Her voice rose, shrill, drowning out the gibbering of the terrified soul within.

"I am a herald only, but by the great road an army waits for you. If you would keep your victory, follow me!" And already she was loosing the reins, already her heels dug into the bay mare's sides. Shanna clutched at the dark mane as Calur leaped forward, and the darkness roared like a whirlwind after her.

The mare chose her own way through the chaos of the wood, for all Shanna's will was focused on staying in the saddle, while madness came on behind. And then the trees were thinning, and they burst into a world bleached of color by the moon—white roads, gray fields, and the ghostly, lantern-lit tents of the enemy.

Shanna's drawn sword flared like a silver flame as she careered through the encampment. A startled sentry sent an arrow thrumming past her, but later, remembering eyes whiteringed in terror, she wondered if he had been shooting at her at all. Through the camp she galloped, and out again, but she was a mile into the plain beyond it before she could halt the maddened horse and turn her, flanks heaving and neck white with foam, to look back at what she had done.

She saw shadow like a moving mist staining the moonlight, thinning, congealing, now underlit by torches, then darkening to extinguish them. She was too far away to make out the shapes within that darkness, and she was glad. But she could hear the cries of men driven beyond bravery in their battle with an incorporeal foe.

After a little Shanna urged Calur into a slow walk back and forth across the meadow, lest she should take harm from the cold, but still she watched the storm beside the road, until the moon sank and the dark sky grew pale and the first rays of the rising sun sent the army of shadows in satiated withdrawal back to the Wood to which they had given their name.

When Prince Roalt and his men emerged from behind the ambuscades and defenses no one had tested, to find out what had become of their foe, they saw Shanna, tired almost beyond consciousness but still clinging to the back of the exhausted mare, coming to meet them across the mired fields. She told them that she had heard a strange tumult and gone

out to see what it was. She did not kn
believed her. She did not care.

Where there had been an army the nigh
remained only a few who wandered witless and
who by luck or the grace of the gods had been sp   to hail
as savior the lord they had come to destroy. The others were
dead, slain by fright or their fellows' madness.

Shanna eagerly helped gather wood for their burning, to set
their spirits free, but she said nothing about the cause of their
dying, at first from horror, and later from a kind of shame.
This was not the way she had been taught to face an enemy.
If she had understood what would happen she could never
have summoned the Shadows, even knowing the only
alternative.

And no one questioned her. Prince Roalt was predictably
overwhelmed by the preparations necessary to restore him to
control of Norsith. It was not until he was ready to set out for
Ennis Narr that he found leisure to see Shanna, and by then
she had had time to understand what she must do.

"My Lady!" The Prince rose to greet Shanna as she
entered the pavilion. He was wearing a hauberk of deep blue
leather over steel plates, riveted with gold, that he had found
in his cousin's baggage, and high boots, with a mantle of
heavy indigo wool lined with squirrel fur. Abruptly conscious
of the stains on her own jerkin and her mended breeches,
Shanna pulled the dull scarlet of her cloak around her—not
that the cloak was much better, after having been lived in so
long.

She came to a halt on the Menibbe rug in the middle of the
tent, looking up at Roalt. Clean, dressed as befitted his rank,
the Prince was no longer the bettered woods-wolf she had
known. Their positions had been reversed, thought Shanna
wryly, for surely she was not the pampered princess he had
captured now.

his gray eyes were glowing, his big hands closed on her shoulders. "Lady Shanna," he repeated more softly. "We'll be leaving in the morning. I want you to ride with me—"

"Am I still your prisoner, my lord?" She smiled faintly.

He shook his head, grinning. "For a long time now, I think I have been yours. Come with me as my pledged wife, Shanna—we'll find appropriate clothes for you somewhere. I think your father will consent to the alliance now that I'm back in power!"

His arms encircled her; he tipped up her chin and his firm lips found hers. It was the place where through so many lonely nights she had longed to be, and Shanna allowed herself to relax against him. She understood very well what he was offering—security, luxury, a place of honor—all the things she had been fleeing when she left Sharteyn.

After a few moments she sighed and pulled away. "I must finish my journey to Bindir."

"Oh, sweet Shanna," Roalt shook his head indulgently, "what could you hope to accomplish that an envoy sent by me or your father cannot do?" Something in her expression must have betrayed her then, for he went on, "At least stay with me in Ennis Narr until spring comes . . ."

She stared at him. Would it have been different if he had saved *her?* To protect him, she had stained her soul. There were rumors of her ride in the camp already, and she knew that the shadow of that unearthly battle would always lie between them.

"My oath binds me—" she shrugged apologetically, salving his pride. But it was not the promise she had made to bring her brother home that was setting her on the road again, but another oath, the one she had given to Yraine.

"Well, then, when you return—" His reply did not demand an answer. He kissed her again, this time on the brow, and his arm was across her shoulders as he pushed the doorflap aside.

His gray eyes were glowing, his big hands closed on her shoulders. "Lady Shanna," he repeated more softly. "We'll be leaving in the morning. I want you to ride with me—"

"Am I still your prisoner, my lord?" She smiled faintly.

He shook his head, grinning. "For a long time now, I think I have been yours. Come with me as my pledged wife, Shanna—we'll find appropriate clothes for you somewhere. I think your father will consent to the alliance now that I'm back in power!"

His arms encircled her; he tipped up her chin and his firm lips found hers. It was the place where through so many lonely nights she had longed to be, and Shanna allowed herself to relax against him. She understood very well what he was offering—security, luxury, a place of honor—all the things she had been fleeing when she left Sharteyn.

After a few moments she sighed and pulled away. "I must finish my journey to Bindir."

"Oh, sweet Shanna," Roalt shook his head indulgently, "what could you hope to accomplish that an envoy sent by me or your father cannot do?" Something in her expression must have betrayed her then, for he went on, "At least stay with me in Ennis Narr until spring comes . . ."

She stared at him. Would it have been different if he had saved *her?* To protect him, she had stained her soul. There were rumors of her ride in the camp already, and she knew that the shadow of that unearthly battle would always lie between them.

"My oath binds me—" she shrugged apologetically, salving his pride. But it was not the promise she had made to bring her brother home that was setting her on the road again, but another oath, the one she had given to Yraine.

"Well, then, when you return—" His reply did not demand an answer. He kissed her again, this time on the brow, and his arm was across her shoulders as he pushed the doorflap aside.

out to see what it was. She did not know whether they believed her. She did not care.

Where there had been an army the night before there remained only a few who wandered witless and some others, who by luck or the grace of the gods had been spared, to hail as savior the lord they had come to destroy. The others were dead, slain by fright or their fellows' madness.

Shanna eagerly helped gather wood for their burning, to set their spirits free, but she said nothing about the cause of their dying, at first from horror, and later from a kind of shame. This was not the way she had been taught to face an enemy. If she had understood what would happen she could never have summoned the Shadows, even knowing the only alternative.

And no one questioned her. Prince Roalt was predictably overwhelmed by the preparations necessary to restore him to control of Norsith. It was not until he was ready to set out for Ennis Narr that he found leisure to see Shanna, and by then she had had time to understand what she must do.

"My Lady!" The Prince rose to greet Shanna as she entered the pavilion. He was wearing a hauberk of deep blue leather over steel plates, riveted with gold, that he had found in his cousin's baggage, and high boots, with a mantle of heavy indigo wool lined with squirrel fur. Abruptly conscious of the stains on her own jerkin and her mended breeches, Shanna pulled the dull scarlet of her cloak around her—not that the cloak was much better, after having been lived in so long.

She came to a halt on the Menibbe rug in the middle of the tent, looking up at Roalt. Clean, dressed as befitted his rank, the Prince was no longer the bettered woods-wolf she had known. Their positions had been reversed, thought Shanna wryly, for surely she was not the pampered princess he had captured now.

Her men were waiting for her—big Hwilos, Sandy, and scarred little Zan—already mounted, with the loaded packhorse and Calur. Their eyes widened a little as they saw her with the Commander, but before they could speak she was moving out of Roalt's embrace, taking the bay mare's rein.

"Well, what are you staring at?" she snapped, pulling herself into the saddle. "We've wasted too much time already. Let's go. . . ."

Roalt stood outside his tent, watching her ride away. But his features were in shadow, and when she looked again, she saw him only as a silhouette against the dim masses of the trees. Calur tossed her head, resenting the tight rein, and Shanna turned to let her run free beneath the open sky.

UNICORN'S BLOOD

Bruce D. Arthurs

One of the many temptations which beset an editor—
especially when reading over 400 manuscripts, many of
amateurish quality and multiclichéd plots—is to accept
stories only from writers of proven worth. No editor can
afford to ignore known or "name" writers, and in this
anthology I have printed "repeat" stories by many writers
who were featured in *S&S #1*, feeling that the reader
would greet these writers as old friends; Jennifer Roberson, Diana L. Paxson, Charles Saunders, Phyllis Ann
Karr, etc. But I also feel it obligatory to print the work of
promising newcomers, especially if their stories reach
out and grip me with real excitement. Such a story is
Bruce Arthurs' "Unicorn's Blood."

I must admit that when I first saw the story I groaned.
For some reason or other, unicorns (and dragons) have
become cliché beasts in the last few years, and because
of the legendary purity of unicorns, most of these cliché
stories are filled with such sweetness and light as to tip
an incipient diabetic right over the edge. My tolerance for
cutesy-pie animals is minimal or nonexistent, and I read
the first couple of pages with a rejection slip in hand;
then I got so gripped by the story that I actually forgot it

was by a fan known to me (I am known to be receptive to the work of young writers), and Bruce reminded me that the first three pages of this story had actually been written on my typewriter when he and his wife, Margaret Hildebrand, were staying at my house after a convention. This is not the usual fannish first story. In fact it isn't a first story at all. Bruce appeared once in *Amazing* with a piece of fannish humor, years ago; but this is his first serious piece of fiction.

And serious it is; it's no easy task to make unicorn stories into a serious and gutsy adventure. Which this is. Granted that it's not impossible—another serious and promising newcomer, Robert Cook, in "The Woodcarver's Son" (in my anthology *Greyhaven*) created a bitingly realistic unicorn story. Robert Cook never had a chance to fulfill his early promise; his premature death before the publication of the story prevented that. I like to think that if he had lived, he might have written this, or something like it.

—MZB

The creature stepped out of the darkness beneath the tall trees, into the moonlight shining onto the small clearing beside the bubbling mountain stream. It was the size of a small pony, but with a goatish head and cloven hooves. Its snow-white coat shone silver under the moonlight. From the center of its forehead projected a short horn of twisted bone.

The woman was seated on a large rock beside the stream. Her dress, a simple long-sleeved tunic, was of a fabric as intensely white as the unicorn's coat. Her hair, coppery red, fell in loose waves to the middle of her back. When the unicorn stepped from the darkness, she smiled and raised a beckoning hand toward it.

The unicorn approached, its eyes unfocusing with an irresistible love in the spell of the virgin's presence. It went down on its knees before the red-haired woman and laid its head on her lap, staring up at her adoringly.

The woman stroked the unicorn's throat. The creature made a sigh of pleasure and love, stretching its throat out farther. The woman looked down and smiled.

Then she took the knife from where it had lain under a fold of her dress and cut the creature's throat.

When Kerai rode back into town three days later, she little resembled the woman who had sat beside the mountain stream. The bloodied tunic had been replaced by shirt and pants of dark leather, with high-topped boots of darker leather still. The waves of red hair had been braided and pinned into a knot at the back of her neck. The knife now rode openly in its sheath on her hip, and a shortsword was slung across her back.

The offices of Shar the merchant were in a windowless building whose thick oaken door was guarded by two large, brutal-looking thugs. They stepped aside for Kerai as she dismounted and opened the door with a kick. The guards exchanged nervous glances as she slammed the door shut behind her. Kerai was virgin, and had made clear her intention to stay that way; more than one man had lost blood, and sometimes life, trying to change the status of the deadly red-haired bitch.

Kerai strode past the desks where the clerks and record-keepers worked in pools of light cast by flickering candles, and into the office of Shar himself.

The merchant trader had the body and face of a jolly fat man, with rosy cheeks and a lush white beard, but these were belied by the black, snakelike eyes that mercilessly considered the world from above those cheeks and beard.

There was another man in the office with Shar, Kerai saw as she entered, but dismissed him as no threat. *He* would have been disarmed by the guards out front. She noted only that he was tall, even when sitting in the chair in the corner, that he was thin, and that he was dark of skin; a foreigner. She continued moving without pause toward Shar, opening the pouch on her belt and tossing its contents on the desk.

The blood-stained horn made a curving path as it rolled to a stop in front of the merchant.

"There's your latest horn of unicorn, Shar," she announced. "Just like all the rest. Now give me my money."

The merchant's eyes shifted calmly from the horn to the woman standing before him. "Oddly enough," he said smoothly, "we were just talking about you."

Kerai's eyes darted to the stranger in the corner. He looked back at her with an intent gaze.

"Do take a seat, won't you, Kerai?" the merchant continued, indicating the opposite chair.

Kerai turned her attention back to Shar. "First, my money." She held her left hand out toward him. Her right hand rested casually on the hilt of her knife.

Shar chuckled, then unlocked a drawer in the desk. He counted thirty gold pieces into Kerai's hand, then put the horn into the drawer and relocked it. Kerai put the gold into the pouch where the horn had been.

She sat in the chair, studying the stranger more closely. Shar's business had foreigners traveling through the trader's town fairly frequently, but she couldn't place where this man came from. Dark skin generally indicated someone from Valakar, or the tropical islands even farther south, but the block-printed motifs on the stranger's clothing were designs she'd never seen before. He had a long, thin face, with a sharp aquiline nose and high cheekbones. His eyes looked black in the candlelight, but she thought they might be deep brown in the outside sun. He was serious and unsmiling, but not grim.

"My name is Agrobo," he began, his voice rich in tone. "And I want a unicorn killed."

"A particular unicorn," Shar interjected.

"Why?" Kerai asked after a pause. "Unicorns are rare, but not unfindable. Why one in particular? For all you know, that may have been *its* horn I just brought in."

Agrobo smiled; it was not a pleasant smile, and Kerai suddenly felt that this man might be dangerous after all.

"It's *black*, Kerai!" Shar said. "It's a *black* unicorn!"

That *did* surprise her. She had never heard of any unicorn other than white. "Tell her the rest, Agrobo," the merchant said.

"It is not the same color as your unicorns, and it is not the same type," the dark-skinned man began. "Your unicorns are basically large goats. This isn't. It is a horned horse, a stallion with a jet-black coat and eyes of fire."

"There's only the one?"

"My homeland is Akku, a large volcanic island far west of the southern tip of Valakar. My people settled the island five hundred years ago. Marbakku was there then, and is still there today. No other is known."

Another surprise. Unicorns were, supposedly, long-lived, but Kerai had never heard a claim of more than a hundred years. " 'Marbakku'?" she asked. "Does that mean something?"

"It means 'bad death.' Marbakku dwells in the interior mountains of Akku and is rarely seen. Those who do see him—" Agrobo paused, a distant look on his face—"usually die."

"Can you imagine how much a black horn would be worth, Kerai?" Shar asked with eager greed. "You could charge ten, a hundred times as much for a pinch of powder made from it!"

"What makes you think it would be that much more effective than regular horn powder?"

The trader shrugged. "It would be different. It would be rarer. Who's to know?"

Kerai considered for a moment. "I take it you want me to go to your island and kill this Marbakku."

"Correct," Agrobo replied.

"What do I get out of it?"

"One thousand gold pieces."

Kerai was stunned at the amount. Used carefully, such an amount would make her financially independent. She would never have to do another of Shar's special hunting jobs again, or hire herself out as bodyguard or special courier. She could build the retreat she dreamed of, a place away from the towns and the men that would not let her forget. "It means that much to you?"

"It's not as simple as you might think. The trip there will take three months if we're lucky, four probably, maybe five. When our ship gets there, you'll be on your own. I won't be able to go ashore with you; I have . . . enemies . . . on the island."

"And then another three or four months to bring the horn back to me," Shar said.

"How is payment to be arranged?"

"One hundred gold pieces now. Three hundred when Marbakku is dead. The rest will be held here by Shar and given to you when you bring him the horn."

"It all seems satisfactory," she said after another moment's thought. "One question, though. Why me?"

"Because . . ." The dark-skinned man stopped and glanced at the merchant.

"Because you're a heartless bitch, Kerai," the merchant finished. "The same reason you're the only woman I've ever found willing to kill a unicorn she's attracted. Because you've got a thornbush where your heart should be."

She stared dispassionately at the merchant for a few long

seconds, then turned back to the foreigner. "All right. When do we start, and where's my money?"

"It will take me several days to arrange for the funds. Shall we set our departure for three days from tomorrow morning? A trading caravan is scheduled to leave then."

"All right."

"Can I depend on you to be there?"

"My word is good."

"Very well. In that case," he said, nodding to Kerai and Shar, "I'll go start making arrangements." He lifted himself from the chair and left. He limped badly on one leg, as if the hip would not move properly.

When Agrobo was gone, Kerai turned to Shar. "What's your opinion? Do you think he was telling the truth?"

The merchant shrugged. "Probably. I've only met him once before, in passing a few years ago, but my sources tell me he's known to be reliable and fairly honest."

"What about his saying he couldn't go back to his islands himself?"

"He's in some kind of exile. I don't know the details. I don't know what Akku is like, either. I know it exists, but it's so far off the usual trade routes that that's about all I do know."

She paused. "Would you take the job?"

Shar chuckled again. "It's been a long time since *I've* been a virgin. But yes, I'd take the job if I were you. If nothing else, we've overhunted the unicorns in this part of the world; it took you nearly three weeks to find this last one."

"True. I guess I'd better start preparing for the trip, then." She rose and started for the door.

"Oh, one more thing," the merchant added. "I know you're always on your guard, but you won't have to worry about Agrobo getting any . . . ideas . . . during the trip. My sources tell me he doesn't use women."

*   *   *

The journey from Shar's trade settlement at the crossroads of inland trade routes to the nearest seaport took a month and a half. Shar's sources appeared to have been accurate; in all that time, Agrobo made no advances to Kerai nor, apparently, to any of the women at stops along the way. He kept largely to himself, except when giving directions to the men working with his part of the large caravan, or during the several hours each day he spent teaching Kerai the Akkuan language, a flowing, chanting tongue.

Kerai was not so lucky with other men. A few days out, one of Agrobo's men made a lewd suggestion and tried to put a hand on her. She left him with a long and bloody knife wound across the side of his face, and told him the next time would be across his throat.

A few days after that, some of the first man's friends tried to ambush her. One she disarmed with a slash that left his sword lying in the dirt with his fingers still wrapped around the hilt. The other she cut across the buttocks as he tried to run. Then she went looking for the first man and cut his throat as she had promised.

After that, no one bothered her.

Most of the trip was by ocean, down the coast to the tip of Valakar, then several weeks spent waiting in the port of Valakarsa while Agrobo made arrangements for a ship to take them to Akku. The leather Kerai had habitually worn in Shar's part of the world was unbearably hot in the south, and she reluctantly switched to a loose blouse gathered at the wrists, trousers of lightweight canvas like the sailors wore, and a large-brimmed hat to keep the sun off her head. The knife and sword stayed in their usual places.

She spent most of her time at their inn, the Scarlet Peacock, studying the maps of Akku Agrobo had provided. The island was surprisingly large; even with luck, it might take weeks to find the black unicorn in the mountainous interior.

The stories about her that had traveled down the coast with

Agrobo's trading party kept most unwelcome attentions away from her. There were some hard men, though, determined to see if the stories were true. Kerai finally made arrangements with the innkeeper to use the courtyard in back of the Peacock. Anyone who wished to cross swords with her merely had to pay one gold piece for the privilege; if they won, they would take away ten. She was busy for several days, until it became known that any man who fought her generally went away humiliated. She received one slight wound across an arm from a red-haired giant who had the longest sword she had ever seen. She beat him by sliding under a lunge of his sword and kicking him in the groin. The giant's companions had helped him away.

Kerai was sitting on the veranda that led off the upper rooms of the inn and faced onto the courtyard, studying Agrobo's maps again and stifling a yawn, when Agrobo came in from his latest journey to the docks and sat down on the other side of the table. She felt a twinge of alarm when she saw the glazed, distant look in his eyes.

"Is something wrong?" she asked. "Is it something about getting a ship?"

"Hmm?" He started in his chair, his eyes finally focusing on her. "Ahh . . . yes. We have a ship. An Akkuan vessel that came by Valakarsa several months ago and continued on to trade with the southern islands. I've been expecting it to come back here on its return trip any day, and it arrived this morning. I had a long talk with its captain. . . ." His voice trailed off as his eyes grew distant again, and he stroked his chin thoughtfully.

His next words shocked Kerai with their unexpectedness. "My father is *dead*!" he exclaimed, and he said it with a flash of joy in his eyes and a triumphant smile spreading across his face.

He feels the same as . . . , Kerai thought, then forced the unwelcome memories back into the dark portions of her mind.

Agrobo had risen from the chair in excitement and was pacing between the table and the railing of the veranda. His right hand clenched his bad leg as he limped back and forth.

"This may mean . . . may mean . . ." He stopped in mid stride and shook his head as if to clear it. He turned back to Kerai and spoke to her. "My father disinherited and exiled me. If he is dead, then my younger brother, Pelago, holds the throne. We were more than brothers, we were friends; Pelago will allow me to return to Akku."

A prince. Interesting, Kerai thought. "You said this . . . Pelago? . . . was your younger brother? Does that mean you would have been first in line for the throne if you hadn't been exiled?"

The look of joy dimmed in Agrobo's eyes, and his face turned hard. "Yes," he said. "But for this," his hand clapped against his leg and he lowered himself into a chair, "but for this, *I* would have been the next Akkuan king. A . . . cripple . . . is not allowed to hold the kingship."

"Are you sure," she asked slowly, "that your brother will welcome the former heir to what is now *his* throne?"

"I told you!" he said sharply. "We were friends! We trust one another like . . . like brothers, damn it! Besides—" His voice dropped. "I've accepted my loss. I know I will never be king." He paused, and his eyes glistened. "I just want to go home again."

He pushed himself up and limped to the door of his room. "We'll sail first thing in the morning," he said brusquely. "Be ready."

The door slammed, and Kerai was alone on the veranda again. "I'm always ready," she whispered, and her hand drifted to the time-worn hilt of her knife as she kept the memories at bay.

The voyage across the ocean was plagued by storms, but otherwise uneventful. The strange double-hulled ship rode the rough waves better than Kerai had expected, but not well enough to keep her from being frequently seasick. She vowed to herself that, after she got back to the mainland, she'd never again leave sight of dry land.

Agrobo, after his emotional outburst at the inn, had regained his usual reserve, barely speaking to Kerai. She had asked him, as the ship was taking on its final load of fresh water and foodstuffs, if his plans for her would change if he was no longer an exile. "No," he had answered. "I still want that beast killed."

On the fortieth day out from Valakarsa, the lookout posted above the large square mainsail made the first sighting of Akku. By midafternoon, the verdant cliffs dominated the horizon, and the first of many canoes came out to meet them. The canoes were launched from a beach of sparkling black sand, behind which was a large town. A long dock projected into the water from one end of the beach. Kerai watched as Agrobo gave one of the canoemen a rolled and sealed paper, along with a gold piece, and indicated that it should be taken back to shore. A letter to Pelago, she guessed.

The sun was setting fast, and the ship's captain decided to lower anchor and wait until morning before making the final mile or so to the dock. Kerai wondered why, until one of the crew pointed out the line of choppy water between the ship and the beach, and told her it indicated a sunken reef that would tear out the bottom of the large ship if it wasn't guided through the barrier correctly.

The reef was little obstacle to the light canoes, however, and they continued to go back and forth between the land and the ship all night, guided by torches on the ship's prow. They brought fresh water and food, roasted meat and vegetables, exotic fruits like none Kerai had ever had. Jugs of a potent fruit wine were passed around freely; Kerai took a small sip and decided it would be wiser to pass the jug from then on. News and gossip were passed around between the crew and the regular islanders.

Kerai kept to her tiny cabin, little more than a closet, for most of the night. She felt uncomfortable around the celebrant, and about the attention her fair skin and red hair attracted from the dark islanders.

When morning came, things were quieter, and the decks were littered with sleepers. The captain was up and roaring, nudging the crew awake with a not-too-gentle foot. The last visitors paddled back to the beach, and the sails were hoisted for the last leg of the trip.

As they approached the dock, Kerai got a closer view of the town and its denizens. All the buildings were of wood, she noted; the volcanic stone of the island was apparently too difficult to work, and not strong enough for stone buildings. Many of the buildings had ornate designs and carvings worked into them, and were decorated with bright colors.

A large, ornate litter was being carried through the streets as they tied up at the dock. It was borne by twelve men, six to a side, and was covered with deep carvings and decorated with brilliantly colored bird plumes and sea shells. Other groups of men marched in front and back of the litter, wearing feather headbands and carrying heavy clubs inset with shards of black volcanic obsidian. That made sense to Kerai, too; there was probably no native iron on the island. Weapons like her knife and sword would be invaluable here. The war clubs would leave hideous wounds in a battle, but wouldn't last much more than one fight. She noted that some of the men also wore slings tucked through a belt.

As the litter came closer, the people it passed would drop to one knee and place a hand atop their bowed head. Kerai could see a figure sitting beneath the litter's covered pavilion, but couldn't distinguish it clearly among the shadows. She looked around and saw Agrobo standing next to her, his face tight.

When the litter came to a stop beside the ship, she and Agrobo were the only two people on the ship still standing. "Kneel," Agrobo muttered from the side of his mouth, "or the guards will dash you to pieces and throw your body to the fishes.'' Reluctantly, she knelt, bowing her head as little as she felt safe and keeping her free hand just next to the knife hilt.

There was a long moment of silence. Neither the warriors flanking the litter nor the people bowed before it moved or spoke. The moment stretched, then Agrobo sighed and lowered himself slowly, awkwardly beside Kerai, his bad leg stretched out before him.

Only then did the litter's passenger descend. Kerai could hear his footsteps approaching, then see his sandaled feet as he boarded the ship and approached Agrobo. She felt unsafe with her eyes fixed on the deck, and her fingers itched for the comfort of her knife.

The feet came to a stop before Agrobo, and Kerai heard a voice, similar in richness to Agrobo's but with a deeper tone, speak.

"My brother, Agrobo," the voice said in a near whisper.

Kerai heard Agrobo shift as he lowered his hand and raised his head to the speaker. "Pelago, my brother." He paused. "My king."

Pelago lowered himself into a squat to speak with Agrobo face-to-face. From the corner of her eye, Kerai could see he was shorter and stockier of build than his brother, with a flatter nose and wider lips. *Different mothers*, she speculated. He wore a cloak of brilliantly colored feathers, and around his throat were numerous necklaces threaded with polished steel beads.

"I am sorry," he was saying. "It was necessary to put you through this, however. You had to acknowledge me publicly. You still have many friends who think our father was wrong to exile you."

"And you, Pelago? What do you think?"

"I think as a father he was wrong. As a king . . . I have learned, Agrobo, that kingship sometimes requires hard and painful decisions. You should not regret losing the kingship; it is not a profession for men with kindness in their hearts."

"I no longer regret what I never had, Pelago. I regret the loss of what I *had,* and I have returned to seek my revenge."

Kerai could feel Pelago's eyes shift to her. She had realized that Pelago was apparently unaware she could understand the words being exchanged, and she stayed in place, showing no reaction.

"Your letter said this woman could kill Marbakku for you."

"Yes."

"If this is so, you will have redeemed yourself. Take the woman to the mountains. Bring me the horn of Marbakku, and I will be able to lift your banishment."

"The . . ." Kerai could hear the shock and anguish in Agrobo's voice as he slowly replied. "The horn . . . the horn has been promised to the huntress."

"Ah." There was a long pause. "His head, then. Bring me the rest of his head."

A sigh of relief. "It will be done."

"Agrobo," Pelago said, lowering his voice to a whisper. He placed his hands on Agrobo's shoulders. "Whatever happens, I will see that you spend the rest of your life on Akku."

"If I do not bring you Marbakku's head, brother, it will be because I am dead in trying to take it."

"I know." Pelago stood, then, and returned to his litter. The bearers lifted, the warriors marched, and he was gone.

They set out for the interior that same day. Agrobo was effusive, pointing out the multitudinous plants and fruits that grew on the island, exclaiming over familiar landmarks he had not seen for years. Kerai found it fairly boring, and concentrated on moving along on the narrow, green-bordered trails. The vegetation varied from dense, impassable jungle to areas of sparse, low-growing greenery, apparently differentiated by how recently the area had been formed and how deep the soil had accumulated on top of the volcanic base. Agrobo used a walking staff to ease the strain on his leg as they moved along the steep trails.

"We have many small animals," he was saying, "but Marbukku is the only large one. When I first left Akku and saw my first horses on the continent, I was terrified. People were actually *riding* animals like Marbakku! I was on the mainland for over a year before I rode my first horse."

This was more interesting. "How do your people explain Marbakku's being on the island?" she asked.

"The usual version is that when the Onate created the Small Gods, some were defective or flawed, and were abandoned in the far reaches of the world. Marbakku, supposedly, is the mad incarnation of such a godling. In actuality, the truth is the same as for the goat-unicorns in your land—no one really knows where they came from."

Kerai was not a believer in the gods, large or small, but the talk was disturbing. "Have others tried to hunt Marbakku?"

"Some." He grimaced as a stab of pain went through his leg. "The men, and the non-virgin women, were all killed or . . . maimed. The few virgin women that encountered him had the same experience as is with your unicorns; a spell of mutual love and enchantment. That's why I was so excited when I heard about you."

They spent that night in a travelers' hut, part of a network of stopping places scattered through the rougher areas of the island for the use of hunters and other travelers. Users were responsible for keeping the huts clean and repaired. Agrobo and Kerai rewove some damaged window screens before starting out again the next day.

The trail they followed led across a ridge that lay near a volcanic cone that still fumed and smoked. Occasional breaks in the greenery showed them the layer of cooled lava that spread down the mountainside. Kerai looked at the desolate rock and tried to imagine it red-hot and liquid, boiling out of the mountain. Her mind shuddered.

"Look!" Agrobo said, pointing.

Marbakku galloped across the lava slope, his coat blacker than the rock beneath him. He *was* a horse, but for the long black horn growing from his head; large and heavily muscled, sleek of coat, there was nothing goatish about him. And even from this distance, Kerai saw that his eyes *did* glow, blazing red with an inner fire.

She didn't know if Marbakku was a god, but he was definitely something more than a simple beast.

The beast stopped on a lava swell, tail switching, seeming to look straight in their direction. His head lifted to the sky, and the sound of his scream hit Kerai like a fist; it was a scream of anger and fury, a scream of madness.

Marbakku turned and galloped over the edge of the slope. Kerai turned and saw Agrobo staring at the spot where the black unicorn had been, his face covered with a film of sweat.

"Now we know where he's at," he said at last. "There's a hut on the other side of this ridge. We can work out from there."

"I wish it was me," he said as she finished changing clothes. "I wish *I* could kill him."

"I know." She tucked her knife into the tunic's belt. The tunic was overly warm for here, but she'd worn ones like it on other such hunts, and she felt more comfortable in her mind.

He looked out the door at the clouds gathering in the sky. "There will be a storm soon. The rain isn't cold, but it can be extremely heavy." He turned to look at her. "Be careful."

She realized he wasn't talking about the rain. "I've been out in storms before," she said, and left.

Moving through the dense greenery was the hardest part; moving in a straight line was nearly impossible, and it took her longer to reach the lava slope than she had expected. She searched for some kind of sign, but the rock bore little trace of the unicorn's earlier presence. She climbed toward the ridge Marbakku had disappeared behind.

She stood on the ridge, the wind blowing on her face, and examined the area below her. The lava flow turned into jungle again about a hundred fifty feet downslope. The lava was empty, but she felt something nearby. She felt something in her mind.

She *heard* something on the slope behind her.

She turned, and the world exploded in a ball of red pain. She began to fall, still turning, her hands rising to the blood pouring down her face.

She saw, as she fell, three of Pelago's warriors racing up the slope toward her, one with a sling still in his hand. . . .

She saw, as she twisted down on her knees, Marbakku on the other slope of the ridge, his head raised to give his mad scream. . . .

She saw the bolt of lightning that split the sky and counterpointed Marbakku's scream with its crack and thunder, and she felt the warm rain washing the blood into her eyes as her head hit the ground. . . .

It was a cold rain, but she was safe inside from it. Safe under the covers of her bed, high in the loft at one end of her family's cabin. The rain made only a pleasant humming noise against the thatched roof above her. The fire, almost down to coals, gave a dim illumination to the cabin and a faint smoky smell to the air.

The ladder to the loft creaked. She sat up slightly, still drowsy as a recognizable silhouette came between her and the firelight.

"Daddy?"

"Shh. Shh, Kerai, it's all right." His voice was a whisper, but it was trembling. He lifted the covers and slid in beside her. She woke further, frightened when he slid his arms around her. "Daddy?" she asked again, and now her voice was trembling too.

"Shh. It's all right, Kerai," he whispered. Then he began to touch her.

"Stop." The voice was barely recognizable as her mother's. It was hard and grim, without mercy. Kerai backed into the corner of the loft as her father released her. *"I've seen the way you look at her. How dare you,"* her mother said as she climbed the final rungs of the ladder. *"How dare you."*

Kerai's father wiped his mouth. *"She's old enough,"* he growled.

"She is your own daughter!" The words spat out venomously.

"She is a woman. And I am a man."

"I won't let you." And the knife in her mother's hand glowed dimly red in the faint glow from the fireplace.

Then Kerai was screaming as the two figures suddenly grappled. Something thudded against the floor of the loft, the two figures broke apart, one stumbled and teetered on the edge of the loft, fell and disappeared.

"Mother!" Kerai screamed, crawling to the edge. Her mother's body was motionless on the hard wooden floor below, her neck at an unnatural angle, the eyes wide and unseeing.

Kerai screamed again, and yet again as her father grabbed her and tried to pull her back from the edge. Something was underneath her hand, and her fingers wrapped reflexively around the hilt. She struck out, and the knife's sharp edge cut shallowly into his thigh, then deeply between his legs. Kerai felt a gush of blood over her hand as he screamed and clutched himself.

And then she was running into the dark forest, black and unfeeling, as the cold, clear rain washed her father's blood from the knife in her hand.

Her father was still screaming.

Through a red veil, she saw a club swinging toward her. She lurched back and tripped over a warrior lying on the ground; it was he who was screaming as he tried to hold closed the deep slash across his stomach. The club's swing arced it into the ground, sending shards of broken obsidian flying through the rain. The third warrior was behind her; he swung his own club as she stabbed out with her knife. She cried out in pain as the club drove into her arm; the knife flew out, away from her. The second warrior landed on top of her, growling incoherently as he drove a fist into her face. The other barked a command and pulled him back slightly. They shouted at each other, but Kerai was too near blacking out to understand the words.

They bound her arms and hands with the slings and forced her, staggering, to her feet. The third warrior, evidently the leader, picked up her knife and went to examine the wounded man. He was only moaning now, and blood dripped from his mouth. The leader looked at him for a moment, then drove Kerai's knife into his chest; the wounded man shuddered and was still. The lead warrior removed and wiped the knife, then tucked it into his belt.

The dead man's sling was jammed into Kerai's mouth. Then the two men began moving through the jungle, dragging her with them. She kept stumbling, weak and dizzy from shock and loss of blood. Her arm was numb and swollen, with blood slowly pulsing from the cuts where the club had struck her. The rain that trickled down her face as they moved through the jungle kept her from blacking out again. She kept trying to maneuver the gag out of her mouth as they approached the hut where Agrobo waited.

They slowed as the hut came into view. The lead warrior spoke, and the second clubbed his fist into Kerai's back. She grunted as she hit the ground hard, and it was several seconds before she realized that the gag had been loosened by the fall. The two warriors were sneaking toward the hut as she worked the rest of it out of her mouth.

''Agrobo!'' she screamed. The warriors glanced back at her, cursing, and then Agrobo appeared in the doorway, her sword in his hand.

The warriors froze, then realized they had been seen. The leader straightened and walked out into the open, followed by the second. They stopped about ten feet from Agrobo.

"Your brother said to tell you," the leader said, "that a king sometimes has to make hard and painful decisions." He gripped his war club with one hand and removed Kerai's knife from his belt with the other.

A shudder passed through Agrobo, making the sword point tremble. "He said I could spend the rest of my life on Akku."

"And so you shall." The two warriors spread slightly apart and began to move toward their target.

Kerai had worked herself up onto her knees and was watching. She had never seen Agrobo use a sword, and had no idea how good he might be. Her sword was longer and easier to maneuver than the clubs, but its lighter weight meant it would be difficult to parry any swing of the clubs. And with two against one, and that one a cripple . . . Agrobo might hold them off for a while, but not long.

"Keep your back to the hut!" she shouted. The warriors glanced back, then returned their attention to the swordsman facing them. Kerai leaned against a tree and pushed herself to her feet. Spots danced before her eyes.

The second warrior moved forward and feinted with the club. Agrobo made a slash in his direction, then jumped away as the leader swung his club through the spot he'd been in.

Kerai pushed against the tree with her bound hands, forcing herself into a staggering run. The sound of the rain covered her footsteps. She ran at the leader and sunk her teeth into his ear as she struck him. He screamed, dropping the club, trying to twist her loose as he flailed with the knife.

The second warrior hesitated, uncertain where to turn, and Agrobo slashed at his arm. The club dropped to the dirt, and Agrobo made another slash. The warrior fell on top of his club, dead.

Kerai's teeth came loose from the remaining warrior's ear

and she fell to the ground. The warrior turned and leapt at Agrobo as he finished the second slash. Agrobo tried to recover and turn to meet the new attacker . . . and the knife went into his groin, tearing. He gasped in shock and fell, the sword loosening from his grip.

The warrior stood, panting, for a moment, then turned back toward Kerai. He felt his torn ear, winced, and scowled at her. He lifted the knife in his hand and came toward her.

Kerai had nothing left in her. She could only lay and watch as the man approached.

The scream filled the air, and the warrior's eyes widened in sudden terror as he saw something behind Kerai. Then a black shape flew over Kerai and rammed into the man, flinging him tumbling across the ground. The warrior tried to rise, and the dark hooves pounded into him, pounded into him, again and again and again.

Finally, Marbakku stopped, panting slightly. His bloodied hooves walked toward Kerai and halted before her. His fire-filled eyes stared down at her for a moment, then he nuzzled her gently.

She stirred. She was still alive. She hurt everywhere, but she was alive. She tried to rise, failing. She had to get her hands untied.

She wormed her way, slowly, painfully, toward Agrobo. Agrobo and her sword.

He was still alive. His eyes were vacant and far away, but they focused on her when she spoke his name. "Agrobo," she said. "The sword. Cut my hands free. I'll try to help you." He stared expressionlessly at her. "Agrobo. *Please.*"

His eyes closed, but a hand stirred, and he reached out to the sword beside him, his breath hissing in pain. He couldn't lift the sword, but he turned its edge up for Kerai to saw her bonds against.

When her hands were free, Kerai turned to do what she could for Agrobo. He had let the sword back down, and his eyes were growing dim. She was almost certain he was dying, but she loosened his trousers to see how bad the wound was.

The knife wound was deep and bloody, what she had expected. But the old and twisted scar tissue next to it. . . .

Now she knew what kind of cripple Marbakku had made Agrobo into.

"Kill him," his voice whispered. She looked up, and his eyes were wide as they pleaded with her. "Kill him for me. Ple. . . ." And then he was dead, the rain spattering off his open eyes.

She heard the whinnying of the black unicorn behind her. She turned and saw it standing there, waiting for her to return the love it could not help but feel for her.

Kerai worked herself to her feet, using the sword as a prop. Her knife lay in the grass beside the trampled remains of the warrior leader. She picked it up, careful not to fall down again. Marbakku moved over to her and nuzzled her neck again.

She placed the knife's blade, wet with rain and the warrior's blood, against Marbakku's neck. "You're a beautiful animal," she whispered to him. "But that's all you are, an animal. A stupid animal, just like those one-horned goats. That's all." She increased the pressure against the unicorn's throat.

Clear rainwater squeezed out of the unicorn's coat as she pressed, washing streaks along the blade.

She turned away and lurched over to the hut. "Go away," she muttered, leaning her head against the doorway. "If you're not an animal, you'll go away. If you're stupid enough to come back, I'll kill you. I swear I'll kill you." She lifted her head and stared at the unicorn. *"Go away!"*

The unicorn held her eyes for a long moment, then turned and headed for the trail into the jungle. It turned at the edge of the small clearing and stared again at her. Then it gave its mad scream, turned, and was gone.

Kerai's legs folded under her, and she sat down in the doorway, staring at the carnage before her. The rain had almost stopped, and a beam of sunlight broke through the clouds. There were so many things she had to do: She had to bind her own wounds, and spend a few days recovering. She would have to go back to the seaside village and arrange for passage back to the mainland. She fingered her knife as she thought of the farewell she would give to Pelago. There were so many things to do.

But first she wept.

THE UNSHADOWED LAND

C. J. Cherryh

In general, C.J. Cherryh is associated mostly with hard-tech science fiction—a genre which this particular editor tends to dislike because it tends to neglect people and story values in favor of loving descriptions of the romance of gadgets and the pre-eminence of technology. I hold to the belief that good stories are not about spaceships or technostructures or the societies based on them; good stories are about people and emotions. In fact, Ted Sturgeon once summed up for me what stories are about: good stories, he said, are about passionate emotional relationships.

From Carolyn Cherryh's intriguing *Hunter of Worlds* to her Hugo-winning *Downbelow Station* to the recent Hugo-nominee *Pride of Chanur,* Cherryh manages to keep the focus of her fiction strongly on the people involved.

In general I am content to select only very good stories. This story meets the criterion I use for greatness; it gave the editor goosebumps as I finished it.

—MZB

God turned his left eye to the earth and it shone like silver and burned the land with cold; he looked on the world with his right eye and that eye blazed like gold at melting heat: like the refining of gold it burned. He spread his wings and the wind of them scoured the sands with heat and broke the very stone. He flew, and the shadow of his wings was the sandstorm: so vast were those wings that there was nothing but that shadow in the world. So terrible was the wind of those wings that it mingled earth and sky to the depth and the height and hurled great stones from their seats.

And when God had folded away those wings and looked out again from his white-hot right eye (he watched his brothers and sisters with the other, warily, knowing their ways) —When God looked out on the world it was not the same world; and it was not the same Akhet who walked a crooked line over the sands, for this Akhet was burned, and the sound of the wings of God had entered into her skull, so that she heard them continually in the stillness of the sands, and communed with nothing else, not even memory.

It was the whim of God to turn up old secrets in the sands, in each re-making of the world, curiosities which he had collected and now brought beneath his gaze. Some were mirthful, smiling as they gazed eyelessly upon the eyes of God; some were dried wisps of leather and bone, bizarrely contorted as if they sought in their motionless way to sink into the depths again; others still had an anguished look, as if they protested such violence. Rarest and most amazing, a few gazed upward with profound solemnity, sere flesh almost indistinguishable from bone: they smiled the inward smiles of ancient kings and queens, in their rags or their nakedness. There were beasts also, and stalking carnivores of polished bone, some of twisted horror, others of gaunt, wind-scoured nobleness. There were stones which God had made and his creatures had shaped in imitation of him and his brothers and his sisters. There were the remnants of places which had had great names among such creatures, but God himself gave

them no names and they had none now, like Akhet, who had
forgotten that she was Akhet, or what direction she moved.

She walked among these treasures. Sometimes it was one
way and sometimes it was another: she forgot. But she found
fellowship with these memories of God, and laughed with
them, for she saw that the skin of her flesh became like their
flesh, seamed with fine lines; and she fancied that her face
was the face of the kings and queens she found, sere-lipped
and hollow-cheeked and terrible as God.

She laughed; and was alone with that laughter in her skull,
which rang in sudden silence, for the roar of the wings,
which had never yet ceased in her ears, did cease. She stood
in the white-hot sight of God, in the light of his right eye that
left no shadows on the land, in his terrible light that left no
color but its own, and shone round the rocks so that they cast
no shadow. There was no dark place in all the land. The eye
of God looked into Akhet's heart, and the light of his eye
shone all round it as it did the stones, and it was one color
with the stones and the land, as all things were. The silence
became that color and that taste, which was like the smell of
molten copper in the nostrils; and that silence drank up her
laughter and gave it back again.

Aaaa-ha, ah-ha, ah-ha, ah-ket, akhet, akhet, akhet, Akhet.

Her voice had become the voice of God, and that voice
called her name, so that she turned and came, trusting as a
child.

"Akhet!" she cried now and again, seeking herself. Or she
was God, seeking Akhet. God's voice forever called her
name, in a voice multiplied and strange.

"Akhet, Akhet, Akhet!"

She had thirsted; she had water and had forgotten this,
when the wings had left her deaf. Now it made a small
welcome sound as she walked, like the river-song. (Indeed
she trod on the stones of another of God's forgotten secrets,
the very mummy of a river, which was sere as the forgotten
dead. The stones of its bed clicked beneath her feet, and the

shreds of her sandals caught and made her stumble.) She carried other things she had forgotten. They burdened her, but she did not let them go, having recalled that they were Akhet and Akhet was these things. She drained the stagnant heat of the waterskin and let it fall empty at her side. She laughed and God laughed, redoubled her laughter, and slowly closed his eye.

It was the moment of shadow, of half-real things.

She saw cliffs. And those cliffs were red as blood. And they echoed with the voice of God—*Akhet, Akhet, het, het*—

"Aiii," she cried in this blindness, when the eye of God had left her, and in the shadow-world she suspected God's mirth, and delusion.

Aiii, ii, ii! the cliffs gave back. She walked, and the delusion of a river became moisture under her feet, and the pain and the moisture grew—it was a river of blood in the dying of the light; and the cliffs were stained with it; and the shadows multiplied and moved.

"God!" she cried. (And *God—god—god—*, the stones.)

A jackal came to meet her, beside the riverbed. This was God's brother, and she was uneasy, for the brothers of God were his enemies, and this one was sly. He knew how to steal a soul away in his jaws, and take it down among his shadows before his brother saw. He laughed, and she walked on the blood, sure that she knew the river now, that it was the Dark River she had found; and the jackal-god would wish to lead her if he could.

She bent and gathered up a stone.

"Go away!" she cried. (*Go away-way-way*, the cliffs gave back.) She hurled it, and the god jumped aside, then trotted off a few paces and stood in recovered solemnity, his great ears pricked up, with which he hears his brother's thoughts and every counsel in the world. He smiled, and his jackal's teeth were sharp.

She threw another stone, and it became a spear in mid-flight; it became a spear in her mind, and flew with the noise of voices and the sound of waters. She wept when she had cast it, and stood still and shocked, in a place of rocks, in the blindness of God.

A stone turned and clicked. Another moved. She spun about to see, and the stones betrayed her, and she crashed down to her knees, blinking at this stranger the shadows made, this pale shape on whose breast a pectoral glittered in the wan last light: and on whose wrists the sheen of night-wrapped gold. Gold lapped her waist and spilled like flood on her thighs, and the linen of her robe was night-bound white; and the smell of her was like the smell of myrrh and smoke.

"Goddess," said Akhet, in the blindness of God, when he searched the worlds for his brothers and sisters, their doings. But one of the gods was surely here; and another was there, the jackal in the shadows; and Akhet forgot the stone on which her hand had fallen. Her knees quaked under her, for the goddess walked the trail of her blood and her face was the hollow-cheeked face of the queens of the dust. Her eyes were the pits of their eyes; and her mouth held the sere, fixed pleasure of their mouths, which hold secrets and do not share.

"What is your name?" that mouth asked.

"Akhet," said Akhet.

"And again: what name?"

"Akhet."

"Again: what name?"

It was a spell, Akhet was sure, and her bowels went to water and the wounds of her feet stung. She stank of sweat and trembled, and remembered the stone in her hand, so that her hand began to shake. She wished to throw that stone. But her own name froze in her mouth and stopped in her throat and barred her breath, or her soul would have come out into the night that moment, into the goddess' hands.

"It is not your name," the goddess said, and it was not. She was robbed and desolate and shivered in the cold. She had no hope then, that God would look and drive her Death away. God would open his silver eye but she would have no more name than the other secrets of this plain, and she would be no more than that to him.

"Mine is Neit," the goddess said.

It was a Death. There were many. This was hers; and she became calm then, and put her stone neatly back among the other stones. She remembered she carried things. One was an empty waterskin. One was a sheathed sword. One was a quiver of arrows, but she had lost the bow. She gathered these things into her lap, against her knees, and held to them as hers.

But the goddess sat down before her, her fine linen and her gold glimmering in God's blindness. Her smell was sweet attar and lotus amid the myrrh. "Why have you come here?" the goddess asked.

She tried to recall. She hunted this memory through her wits and it turned and leapt on her, black and sudden, so that she shook and hugged the remnants of herself.

"I came to die," she said; and a portion of herself came back to her, so that she winced and rocked with the grief of it, clutching at the sword. Red blood ran on sand and swirled in river currents, scarlet thread in brown. Cities burned. Tombs stood desolate. "Where have I come?" She blinked and lifted her eyes and gazed about the cliffs. There was no river, only a dry bed of stones between dead banks. "Goddess, where have I come?"

"Where you are. Lift up the sword. Lift up the sword, child."

She blinked, clenched the hilt to draw it closer. It was her defense. This alone she had. But the hilt slid from the sheath and the blade was broken.

—had broken, in her hand. *The children wailed, wailed in the fire and smoke; the chariots swept down on the morning gates*—

She shook and trembled. The quiver spilled arrows of spoiled fletchings and dulled points. The sheath fell empty at

her knees. She cast the blade after it and bowed her head and
wept.

"What happened, daughter?" The voice came gently from
those sere, awful jaws. "What became of the children?"

"O Neit, the chariots, the bitter swords—"

"Iron," the goddess named them. "The swords are iron."
And the word went through her bones.

"No," she cried, and pressed her hands against her eyes.
"O goddess, my children—"

"You fought."

"They killed my children!"

"They burned your cities."

"My cities. . . ."

She shuddered and wiped her eyes. There were bracelets
on her wrists. They were an archer's bracelets. Her right hand
had an archer's calluses. And some of herself came back. Her
back went straighter. She stared at her death with her chin
lifted and her heart beat stronger. "Can we not be done with
what you have to do?"

"What is your name?"

A pain struck her heart, bleak and terrible.

—*the jaws of crocodiles, the dead devoured, the mummies
of kings hurled into the waters with the lately dead, stripped
of all their gold*—

"I lost," she said to the goddess. "I lost. Is there more
name than that?"

"Bronze swords," the goddess said, "are no match for
iron. Weak metal breaks."

"We had no iron."

"They gave your children to the crocodiles."

"*We fought!*"

(—*fought, fought,* the echoes said.)

"You fought. You fled. This is the unshadowed land. God
burns it with his left eye and his right scours its secrets to the
surface. Here is the resting place."

"*This?* This is paradise?"

"For the failed, the lost, those who forget their names. Those who give them up."

"I gave nothing up!"

"Would you do battle here?"

"For what? My soul?"

"Your name."

She drew a breath that ached with myrrh and lotus. With the smell of eternity. She let it go and laughed a weak, tearful laugh. Something broke then, like a scar tearing in her heart; but torn, it let the breath gust from her and come in again greater than before. She thought of her dead and her cities, of the thunder of the chariots like the wings of God. She rose to her feet with the sword hilt in her hand, and its pitiful small blade. The goddess rose, and the wind stirred her robes with the scent of dried leaves and sunbaked death.

"And if I lose, O Neit?"

"Do you ask?"

She drew another breath, freer than the last. She shook her head and the weight of braided locks swung about her face. "No." She went to fighting stance. "No need."

The goddess stretched out her hand. The sword grew cold as the left eye of God himself and shattered in her hand.

She hurled the hilt, and the goddess flung up her hands to ward it off; in that instant she rushed forward and flung her arms about her death.

It was utter, bitter cold. And Neit whispered in her ear: "You have won, daughter. I will tell your name. Let me go."

"Do you swear?"

"By the left eye I swear." And Neit became like smoke, flowing backward from her grasp, so that she stumbled to her knees. "Dear sister."

"My name!"

"It is Sekhmet."

—*temples ravaged, gold spilled, images of the lion-eyed*

tumbled and stripped of ornament, her name erased and scarred—

"No," she cried. "I never was!"

"Sekhmet, my sister. They have burned your cities, slaughtered your babes, and your priestesses—can you forget? Can you forget your land?"

—*priestesses dying in the courtyards, the young men before the walls*—

"Do you not hear them?"

It was a murmuring, like the river, like the wail of babes and the keening of the doomed.

—*A few struggled in the dark, in the shadow, a few still struck and ran*—

"I have no sword!"

Goddess! Sekhmet! Lion-headed, lion-hearted, help us or we die—

"One can always forget again," said Neit. "One can lie down and sleep in this place of forgotten gods."

"A curse on you!" Sekhmet cried, and picked up the bladeless hilt.

"With that?" Neit mocked her. "You left your shield. Your bow is broken. You have no sword."

"Iron," Sekhmet said. She drew a great breath, and hurled the hilt through Neit's insubstance. There came a sweet taint of corruption in the air. And blood. She walked upon it. Her feet slipped upon the stones.

"Where are you going?" Anubis asked, jackal-headed. He stood in shadows close to the path. His ears pricked up. His voice came strangely from narrow jaws. "What are you hunting, Sekhmet?"

She turned her face on him and he stepped back. "Follow in my steps," she said; and her voice had changed. Her step had grown softer and catlike sure.

"What do you seek?" asked Neit, behind her, her voice grown faint and far. "What do you seek?"

"Worshippers. And swords."

Then there was no voice. She leapt from rock to rock.

The wind stirred, for God spread his wings. He turned his left eye to the world, and the silver cold of it spilled down the cliffs and onto the stones and round their edges until there was no shadow anywhere. There was only cold, cold to crack the marrow and break the rocks.

A lion stalked the unshadowed plain, headed riverward, though that river was long distant. At some distance a jackal followed in the distracted way of his kind, seeking this and seeking that, but never losing the track, not quite. The great terror was loose again; war stalked on lion's feet, seeking lost young, lost prey, and her steps had the smell of blood. He always followed her, did the jackal god.

SHIMENEGE'S MASK

Charles R. Saunders

The first of the "theme" stories for this year is by
Charles R. Saunders, who is rapidly achieving a reputation for masterly fantasy with an African background. His
two novels, *Imaro,* and *The Quest for Cush,* have created a mighty hero in an ancient African background.
Last year, in *Sword and Sorceress I,* his "Gimmile's
Songs" introduced us to Dossouye, the woman warrior of
the Abomey—who were, Charles assured us, historical
figures and might have been the originals of the Amazon
myths. This story, "Shimenege's Mask," introduces the
first of our Chosen Maidens. Furthermore, Charles says
of this story: "Not long ago I realized that I haven't made
any use at all of one of the most significant aspects of
African culture—masks. I have more than a few books
on African masks, but for some reason the stories and
novels I've written simply haven't had any scenes or
cultures in which masks play an important part. The
Masai, after whom Imaro's people are modeled, don't
make masks. So, with this Dossouye story, I decided to
try a story in which masks are a primary focus. The
masks described in the story are real; the plot is out of
my head. I decided to try writing my own folk tale. Deep

down inside, the story may also reflect how I feel about missionaries."

I found this story perhaps even more subtle and fascinating than the first of the Dossouye stories.

—MZB

Her name was Shiminege, and she was crying in the sunlight. She had made certain she would be alone before allowing the tears to come. She was sitting on a log in a clearing in the bush beyond the yamfields of her people, the Yaoule. Although there were leopards in the bush, Shiminege did not fear them. The thing she feared presaged a fate beside which the fangs and claws of a leopard faded to insignificance.

Shiminege was a short, squat girl who had only recently seen her fourteenth rain pass. Her charcoal-colored skin stretched tightly across a round, broad-featured face. Already her hips had widened and her breasts were full. Her only garment was a leather apron knotted about her hips.

Like all Yaoule women, she wore thick coils of blue beads that extended in twin loops from her temples to the nape of her neck. The leather band to which the loops were attached cut deep into the skin of her forehead. A copper plug protruded beneath her lower lip.

In her lap, Shiminege held a mask that stared impassively at her as her tears spattered its surface like rain. Its wooden face had acquired a smooth patina from years of handling by Yaoule women. Like Shiminege's, the face of the mask was round. Its eyes were thin, rectangular slits surrounded by carved semicircles that represented cheekbones and brows. The mouth was a straight, expressionless line with only a hint of lips. Although the mask was large enough to cover her face, Shiminege did not put it on.

"*Mwana Pwo*," Shiminege said softly. "Why did you choose *me?*"

The mask did not reply. It gazed up at her in sublime indifference, as if it knew that the answer to Shiminege's question already lay behind her eyes.

It was then that Shiminege heard a rustle in the bush behind her. Leaping to her feet, she held the mask at arm's length before her. Through an emerald veil of leaves, she could see the approach of a large, dark shape.

A leopard? she wondered. It did not matter. *Mwana Pwo* would protect her this day, and the next.

A head pushed through the foliage. Shiminege screamed and nearly dropped the mask. For the head did not belong to a leopard. A huge buffalo shouldered the bush aside and stepped into the clearing. In the first moments of her shock at its appearance, the Yaoule girl saw only the sweeping, scythelike horns of the beast and the muscles that bunched and relaxed beneath its smooth, dark hide. Then she realized that the buffalo bore bridle and saddle; that a rider was mounted on its back.

Shiminege's knees grew weak and fear blurred her vision. She thought she knew all the demons that haunted the other-world of Yaoule belief, but she had never before heard of one who sat astride the one beast even the leopard feared. Still clutching the mask of *Mwana Pwo,* Shiminege sank to the ground, blackness blotting out the sun.

A moment later, Shiminege awakened in the clasp of strong arms. Her eyelids fluttered open, and she saw a narrow female face peering down at her.

Then she remembered the buffalo—and its rider. With a squeal of fright, Shiminege squirmed out of the strange woman's embrace. Her bead-loops bumped against her head, and her back collided painfully with the log that had been her seat. *Mwana Pwo* still rested securely in her hands, and she interposed the mask like a shield between herself and the stranger.

Shiminege's eyes involuntarily catalogued details of the woman's appearance. The stranger's face was narrow; her body tall and thin. Her skin was dark as any Yaoule's, but its shade tended more to indigo than charcoal. Her torso was encased in light leather armor, and a helmet of the same material protected her skull. A long slim sword was belted at her side.

The clothing confounded Shiminege. Among the Yaoule, men and women alike went nearly naked except during times of ritual.

The stranger gazed steadily at Shiminege, her face as unreadable as *Mwana Pwo's*. Almost of their own volition, words pushed past Shiminege's lips: "Who are you? Where do you come from? Why are you here?"

Tilting her head to one side, the stranger appeared to weigh the words of the Yaoule girl. Then she spoke, her voice surprisingly soft, her accent subtly reshaping the tones of Yaoule speech.

"I might ask the same questions of you, child. But this is your country. My name is Dossouye."

"Where do you come from?" Shiminege asked again.

"Nowhere."

"Where are you going?"

"Anywhere."

Shiminege stared at Dossouye. The evasive answers, the strange accent and clothing . . . Shiminege was not yet beyond the thought that she might be confronting a demon.

Then she remembered the buffalo, and her eyes grew wide with fear, and she hid her face behind *Mwana Pwo*.

"The buffalo," she stammered. "Where is it?"

Dossouye's hand gestured behind her. The buffalo stood quietly. Only its tufted tail moved, flicking at insects buzzing in the humid air.

"Gbo will not harm you. And he is not a buffalo. He is a war-bull, not some untrained wild animal."

The distinction was lost on Shiminege. But the Yaoule girl carefully laid *Mwana Pwo* in her lap and repeated an earlier question: "Why are you here?"

"To learn why you cry alone."

Shiminege blinked. Dossouye's last reply was as cryptic as any of the others she had given the girl. Yet the stranger's eyes held hers like dark lodestones, and she found herself speaking, giving voice to thoughts she would never have dared to reveal to another Yaoule. . . .

In the rains when the grandmother of Shiminege's grand-mother was a child, the demon Umenya Kwi came to the country of the Yaoule. So fearsome was Umenya Kwi's countenance; so overwhelming his strength that the warriors of Yaoule were unable to resist him. The chieftain, the spirit-women, and the elders had gathered in haste to learn what it was Umenya Kwi required of them.

When the demon made his demands known, the elders shuddered in helpless abhorrence. At each rain, during the time that marked the transition from the dry season to the wet, the Yaoule were to produce a girl of early marriage age to be the bride of Umenya Kwi. As well, the Yaoule were accorded the option of sending a champion to fight against Umenya Kwi for possession of the bride. If the champion bested the demon, Umenya Kwi would depart forever from the country of the Yaoule. If the demon won . . . the Yaoule would mourn the loss of two of their young people that rain rather than one. In all the rains since the coming of Umenya Kwi, none of the youths who ventured forth to battle the demon had survived.

Only once did the Yaoule dare to defy Umenya Kwi and refuse to proffer a bride. That rain, Umenya Kwi carried off five Yaoule women and killed half a score of warriors who sought to rescue them. The Yaoule themselves slew the chieftain who had counseled resistance.

As the rains passed, the spirit-women devised a Ritual of Choosing that distracted the thoughts of the Yaoule from the anger and hopelessness and madness that threatened to corrode them from within. For the spirit-women's mandate included the quieting of the souls of the living as well as the dead.

Masks were carved by the eldest of the spirit-women— masks sufficient in number to fit over the faces of every woman in Yaoule country. All the masks save one were *Bachi:* smooth-faced, devoid of features other than semicircular slits for eyes. The one mask unlike the others was *Mwana Pwo:* the One who Chooses.

Every rain, the spirit-women would assemble the masks in a long row, one mask for each girl of marriage age. The masks were hidden beneath the huge leaves of the plant called elephant's ear. In a ceremony presided over by the spirit-women, each girl would uncover a mask. The one who uncovered *Mwana Pwo* was Chosen.

This rain, *Mwana Pwo* had chosen Shiminege. With the rising of the next day's sun, she would be given to Umenya Kwi.

"Will a champion fight for you tomorrow?" Dossouye asked when Shiminege finished her tale.

"Yes," Shiminege replied. "His name is Bosedi. Before *Mwana Pwo* chose me, Bosedi did. Now, he wants to fight Umenya Kwi even though he knows he cannot win. I tried to convince him not to do it, but he says without me, he'd rather be dead."

Dossouye fell silent. Watching her, Shiminege wondered what thoughts passed behind the ebony brow of the warrior-woman. Had she known those thoughts, she would not have understood them.

For Dossouye had wandered long and far from her native

kingdom of Abomey, away to the west. There, she had learned the battle skills that made her an *ahosi*, a soldier in the army of the Leopard King. There, she had first learned that beliefs inculcated through generations of lifetimes were sometimes false, sometimes lies. . . .

The Abomeans believed that two of their three souls were embodied in umbilical cords buried beneath palm trees. If the tree were destroyed, the souls would die. And if the souls died, the body would soon follow. On her last day in Abomey, Dossouye had seen the tree that guarded her souls lying on the ground, cut down by an enemy. Her tree was dead; her souls were dead. Yet she was still alive. The belief was a lie. Or was her continued existence the lie? Dossouye did not know.

Since her departure from Abomey—where she was a living contradiction—Dossouye had roamed aimlessly among the tribes of the vast wilderness that separated the kingdoms of the west and the east coasts of Nyumbani. During those wanderings, she had encountered more instances of false belief, of lies that were believed to be true. She had seen; she had judged; but she had done nothing. The delusions of others were of no concern to her.

Now, as she looked at Shimenege, as she felt the girl's terror and confusion flow through the air like wind from a cold horizon, Dossouye became aware of a resolve forming within her like steel emerging from iron.

For she had guessed who Umenya Kwi was. And if she had not saved others from their delusions, she would save this girl. . . .

"Your Bosedi will challenge Umenya Kwi tomorrow?" Dossouye asked.

"Yes."

"Tell me where."

Shimenege told her of the clearing the spirit-women had prepared for the combat and the ceremony that would follow.

"And where is Umenya Kwi to be found when he is not stealing women from your people?"

"In the Grove of Weeping Trees. When the wind blows, you can hear the crying of the brides of Umenya Kwi. Soon, my voice will join theirs."

"No it won't!" Dossouye shouted. Shiminege flinched; this was the first outward display of emotion she had seen from the warrior-woman.

"Now, tell me where to find this Grove of Weeping Trees," Dossouye instructed. Her voice was calmer, but still commanding.

Shiminege provided directions to the grove. Then she said, "Are you going to— No, you *can't!* You have never seen Umenya Kwi! He'll—"

Dossouye took two long strides, gripped Shiminege by the arms, and lifted her to her feet. Shiminege trembled; the warrior-woman's hands were like claws of iron.

"Listen to me, child," Dossouye said. "You will tell no one in your village that you saw me today. You will undergo tomorrow's ceremony as you have been taught to do. And you must make me two promises. First: Whatever happens during the ceremony, do not let anyone know who I am. Second: After the ceremony, if Umenya Kwi does not take you, meet me here before the sun begins to set. Do you promise me these things?"

Shiminege looked deeply into Dossouye's eyes. They were large eyes, dark eyes; pieces of a starless sky embedded in a midnight face. And at that moment, Shiminege believed Dossouye could slay Umenya Kwi and save her life and Bosedi's.

Believing that, she said, "I promise."

Dossouye held her gaze a moment longer. Then she released her grasp. Shiminege would have rubbed at the circles of pain where Dossouye's hands had been, but she still held *Mwana Pwo*.

"Go back to your village now, child."

With that, Dossouye turned and mounted Gbo. Moments later, warrior and war-bull disappeared in the bush, leaving hardly a sound to mark their passing. Shiminege turned the mask over in her hands and said: "Did you send her, *Mwana Pwo?*"

Mwana Pwo did not reply.

The sun was about to touch the western horizon. Crimson rays lit the leaves of the trees that surrounded the lair of Umenya Kwi. The slim branches of the trees bent downward, as though weighted with a heavy burden of sorrow. In the scarlet sunset, the trees appeared to be weeping drops of blood.

Umenya Kwi smiled in satisfaction as he laid his demonic mask and his raffia-layered costume alongside his weapons. Even without such guise, the appearance of Umenya Kwi was daunting. His body was tall and gaunt, but beneath his earth-colored skin swelled ropy thews that promised a strength that was more than human. His hairless skull sloped to a peak, and his ears were pointed like those of a jackal. His jaw protruded in a beastlike muzzle. Within that jaw, a carnivore's teeth gleamed as Umenya Kwi smiled.

Only the eyes of Umenya Kwi betrayed his human origin. They were crafty, calculating eyes. Behind them was a mind that had long ago decided that costumes would serve him better than would his true appearance. Only his brides ever saw him as he truly was, and none of them lived long enough to tell anyone what she saw. . . .

Tomorrow, another, mused Umenya Kwi. His eyes scanned the darkening grove. The limbs of the Weeping Trees were festooned with loops of blue beads—all that remained of his previous brides. Each bride sacrificed her life so Umenya Kwi could continue a lifespan that had already lasted several generations.

Umenya Kwi was the last of his kind, but he experienced none of the desolation such solitude might be expected to bring. Others like him had perished in the cities of the kingdoms of the west; they had been fools. For all their preternatural strength and vitality, Umenya Kwi's kind were still vulnerable to physical assault, though they were exceedingly difficult to kill. Armed and armored soldiers were deadly foes; wilderness tribesmen were not. Umenya Kwi had foreseen the fate of his kind in the cities. He had fled; the others had died. He did not regret their absence.

A sound in the grove reached Umenya Kwi's ears. He tensed, then whirled, his eyes piercing the gathering gloom. His blood raced with excitement. Could one of the Yaoule have mustered sufficient courage to challenge him in his lair before the ceremony? Many rains had passed since the last such attempt. . . .

Then the intruder stepped out of the shadows, and Umenya Kwi saw that it was not a Yaoule. And his eyes grew wide with recognition at the sight of an *ahosi*, a woman soldier from Abomey.

Dossouye stood calmly, sword bared, both hands gripping its hilt. When she spoke, her voice carried above the sigh of the wind through the leaves.

"I was right," she said. "There is one of your kind left. My ancestors did not complete their task—*sichi*."

"Yet you remember," Umenya Kwi murmured. "You remember our name, and you remember what we do."

"You sold yourself to the Mashataan—the Demon Gods—to become what you are. You infested our cities and villages like rats, stealing lives to prolong your own. We destroyed you; yet here you are, battening like a spider upon those too weak to oppose you."

"Did your people send you to slay me, *ahosi*? If so, where are the others?"

Dossouye said nothing.

Umenya Kwi bared his fangs in an unpleasant grin.

"You are alone, then? Foolish woman! Do your legends not tell you how many of your kind it took to bring down one of mine? I am a *sichi*, yes! I am worth ten of you! Pray to your ancestors, *ahosi*, for your armor will adorn these trees before this night ends!''

The *sichi* bent down and caught up a barbed spear lying next to his costume. He rose quickly, in case Dossouye attempted to attack him while he was momentarily distracted. Dossouye stood still, sword upraised, knees bent to spring into action.

Umenya Kwi's grin became a snarl of bloodlust.

''You will be easier than the Yaoule 'champions,' *ahosi*,'' he taunted.

''I am not alone,'' Dossouye said.

A loud crash through the trees behind him brought the *sichi* whirling about. And as he saw what approached him, Umenya Kwi's face betrayed an emotion he had not felt for more than one hundred rains: fear.

The sun washed the circular clearing in a hard, metallic light. Scores of dancers swayed and sprang to the beat of unseen drums. All the dancers were women: only one man would participate in the ceremony of challenge to Umenya Kwi. The men who played the drums were hidden in the surrounding bush.

Shiminege danced. She was surrounded by the girls who had not been chosen by *Mwana Pwo*. The blank-faced *Bachi* masks hid their faces. Otherwise, they were naked save for brief skin aprons. The *Bachi* girls danced to the slow, steady throb of bass-voices drums.

Shiminege wore the mask of *Mwana Pwo*, and she was clad in a length of dark blue cloth that covered her from shoulder to knee. Her movements were linked to a different rhythm: a sharp, staccato beat that spurred her to frenetic gyrations that cut across those of the *Bachi* girls, yet interwove in a pattern of deep kinetic complexity.

It had been difficult for Shiminege to remain silent the previous night. She had ached with the need to tell her mother, her sisters, the spirit-women, and Bosedi about the woman who rode a buffalo and challenged a demon. But she knew intuitively that Dossouye's secret must be kept until she accomplished what she could against Umenya Kwi. Thus, Shiminege had guarded her tongue and behaved no differently than did the many other girls *Mwana Pwo* had chosen.

Now, Shiminege wore the mask of *Mwana Pwo*, and she *became Mwana Pwo*, and she saw through *Mwana Pwo's* eyes and she felt with *Mwana Pwo's* body as she moved through the intricate steps of her dance.

Abruptly, a new element was added to the drumming—a note of anticipation, expectation. It was then that Bosedi appeared in the clearing.

Shiminege's lover wore no mask other than the stoic expression he affected to conceal his deadly fear. He was a stocky, well-built youth armed with an iron-tipped spear and an oval shield fashioned from oxhide. His charcoal skin was slashed with geometric designs rendered in stark white pigment. By those signs, Bosedi's ancestors would recognize him as a man who had died bravely. . . .

Bosedi did not dance. He was awaiting Umenya Kwi.

Umenya Kwi came.

For a moment, Shiminege was no longer *Mwana Pwo*. For a moment, she wanted to cease her dance and cry out her bitter disappointment. Dossouye had not defeated Umenya Kwi. The demon stood in the clearing as always. The yellow raffia costume he wore concealed his true dimensions, for the body was covered with layered streamers and the arms and legs were encased in fringed sleeves.

And the mask. . . .

It was a white helmet incised with black linear patterns; loops and scallops and whorls that covered its entire face, creating a visage of abstract terror. From the top of the mask cloth cylinders of orange and black projected like the bent legs of a gigantic spider. From its bottom hung a cascade of brown, mossy material that resembled an overgrown beard.

Umenya Kwi was wise. The costume and mask were indeed far more fearsome than was his natural appearance.

In his hands, the demon carried a barbed spear. He disdained the use of a shield. Although he could easily have defeated an armed man barehanded, Umenya Kwi was proud of his skill with weapons and chose to maintain it.

The drumming and dancing stopped, leaving silence to fill a soundless void. Umenya Kwi moved forward. Bosedi raised his spear and crouched behind his shield. In the last instant before she again became *Mwana Pwo*, Shiminege dared to hope that Dossouye would come charging out of the bush on her war-bull to save Bosedi. . . .

The battle for Shiminege began. Umenya Kwi awaited Bosedi's attack. The Yaoule's body was bent nearly double behind his shield. His leg muscles quivered as he attempted to contain his fear. Umenya Kwi waited. Time crawled.

Finally, in an effort to end the agony of fear that gripped him, Bosedi emitted a shrill cry and rushed toward Umenya Kwi. His spear-thrust was clumsily executed; the demon parried it effortlessly. Umenya Kwi's return thrust glanced from Bosedi's shield. Bosedi stumbled backward, shield raised high. Umenya Kwi jabbed his spearpoint into the Yaoule's shield, forcing the frightened youth to retreat until bush foliage scraped against his back.

The onlookers lowered their eyes in resignation. Umenya Kwi was toying with their champion, as he had with so many others. The outcome of the challenge was as predictable as the coming of the wet season. . . .

In desperation, Bosedi swung his spear like a club. The flat of its blade connected against the raffia costume. And Umenya Kwi staggered away from Bosedi.

Bosedi stared open-mouthed at the demon. Was Umenya Kwi mocking him? Umenya Kwi shook his head, and the spider-legs of his mask moved as though they were alive. But the demon made no move toward his challenger.

Again Bosedi lunged forward, stabbing his spear toward

the middle of the raffia. Umenya Kwi dodged the thrust. Again, the demon's counter-thrust was deflected by Bosedi's shield. A second thrust sailed well past the youth's head.

Bosedi was beginning to remember the fighting skills he had mastered only a few rains before. His fear was fading. Feinting with his spear, he slammed his shield against the demon's body. The impact sounded like a stone falling into grass.

Umenya Kwi fell. Bosedi jabbed his spear toward the raffia, but Umenya Kwi rolled away from the point and rose to his feet. Emboldened, Bosedi drove his point toward the demon's throat. Umenya Kwi raised his shaft in time to block the thrust, but the force of it knocked him down again.

Bosedi's spearpoint slashed through a raffia fringe as Umenya Kwi rolled away. The youth's fear was vanishing swifter than morning dew as he charged the fallen demon. Umenya Kwi barely made it to his feet before an aroused Bosedi was upon him.

The Yaoule's spear flickered like lightning in his hand as he stabbed again and again at Umenya Kwi. Although the demon parried most of Bosedi's thrusts, he could not get his point past the youth's shield. Teeth bared in triumph, Bosedi drove Umenya Kwi from one end of the clearing to the other.

Finally, with a desperate surge of strength, the demon shoved Bosedi off-balance. Struggling to maintain his footing, Bosedi raised his shield to ward off a renewed attack. Umenya Kwi lifted his barbed spear—and plunged it into the ground between himself and Bosedi.

Then Umenya Kwi turned and fled into the bush, raffia rustling as he vanished from sight.

Bosedi stood motionless, transfixed by utter disbelief. Shiminege, the *Bachi*-dancers, and the spirit-women remained still as leaves on a windless day. Umenya Kwi had been defeated, and there was no aspect of the ceremony that provided for that possibility.

Even as her mind alternated uncontrollably between being

herself and being *Mwana Pwo*, Shiminege remembered her promise to Dossouye:

If Umenya Kwi does not take you, meet me before the sun begins to set. . . .

And Shiminege knew she would keep her promise.

It was close to sunset when Shiminege returned to the clearing in which she had first met Dossouye. The events that had occurred after the flight of Umenya Kwi swam giddily in her mind, like fish in a whirlpool.

Bosedi was a hero. He had led a band of newly courageous warriors to the Grove of Weeping Trees to dispatch Umenya Kwi. But they had not found him there. There was blood on the trunks of the trees, and the earth was torn, as though a ferocious struggle had taken place there.

They found ragged strips of leather scattered about the grove. The leather told them nothing. They found blue bead-loops hanging like lifeless fruit from the trees. The beads told them much. The warriors collected the bead-loops and carried them back to the village.

Shiminege had become a totemic figure. It was through her that *Mwana Pwo* had breathed strength into the limbs and courage into the heart of Bosedi. The girls who had not been chosen by Mwana Pwo looked at Shiminege in envy; the spirit-women regarded her with undisguised awe. Thus, she had not found it difficult to convince the other Yaoule that her role as the vessel of *Mwana Pwo* had exhausted her to the point that she would not be able to participate in the feasting and dancing that would celebrate the end of Umenya Kwi. Bosedi had been more difficult to convince than the others, but she had managed.

Leaving the mask of *Mwana Pwo* in her dwelling, Shiminege had slipped unnoticed from the village. Now she was standing in the clearing, staring at Dossouye.

As before, Dossouye sat astride the war-bull. Her posture was slumped, as though she were fighting a losing battle against weariness. Most of her leather armor was gone; her lean body was scored with recent wounds. The hide of the war-bull was also marked with scarlet lines.

Shiminege's eyes were captured by what she saw hanging from the front of Dossouye's saddle: the costume and mask of Umenya Kwi.

Dossouye straightened, then held out her hand.

"Climb up behind me," she said. "I have something to show you, and there isn't much time."

Wordlessly, Shiminege did as she was told. So shaken were the foundations of everything in which she believed that she refused to acknowledge the connection between Dossouye and the limp mass of raffia that hung across the saddle.

Gbo galloped toward a desolate place far from the lair of Umenya Kwi. The two women did not talk. Shiminege fixed her gaze on the shift and play of muscle across Dossouye's back. Beneath her, the war-bull's haunches rose and fell at a steady pace.

Dossouye stopped at a small ravine. She dismounted, then helped Shiminege down. Taking the Yaoule girl by the hand, Dossouye led her to the lip of the ravine. Shiminege looked down, choked in revulsion, and looked away. Dossouye forced her to look again at the trampled, hacked thing that lay at the bottom of the ravine.

"That is Umenya Kwi," Dossouye said.

"H-How?" was the only word Shiminege could say.

And Dossouye told her what Umenya Kwi was, and how he had deceived the Yaoule, and why the Yaoule need never fear retaliation from others of the *sichi*.

"But how did you kill Umenya Kwi?" Shiminege asked incredulously. "His strength—"

"Was more than enough to have slain me had I faced him alone. But Gbo was with me, and the *sichi* had forgotten it was the war-bulls that finally helped us to drive his kind out of Abomey."

"And you wore his costume and took his place in the challenge. But why? Bosedi could have killed you!"

For the first time, Shiminege saw a smile on Dossouye's face.

"No," Dossouye said. "He is not good enough. I made him look better than he is."

Dossouye was staring intently at Shiminege. In the girl's face, she saw all the indications of the collapse of a lifetime of beliefs and assumptions. It was like watching the erosion of soil in the wet season. Dossouye's face had appeared much the same when she saw the tree that guarded her souls lying dead on the ground. . . .

Dossouye's hands closed on Shiminege's arms. Her eyes stared deep into Shiminege's soul as she spoke: "You must make me another promise. Again, you must never let your people know you saw me. And you must never tell them what you saw here. Allow them to think Umenya Kwi fled in cowardice, in shame. When the next rain comes, and Umenya Kwi does not come again, your people will be free. Do I have your promise?"

Shiminege nodded. Dossouye pulled Umenya Kwi's mask and costume from the saddle and tossed them into the ravine to lie with the corpse of their owner. Then she mounted Gbo and raised Shiminege up behind her. And they rode back to the small clearing to which Shiminege had come to weep the day before.

As Shiminege slid from Gbo's back, the sun was beginning its descent into darkness. Dossouye's last words to her were, "You will keep your promise."

"Yes," Shiminege said.

Lifting her hand in a farewell salute, the warrior-woman touched her heels to Gbo's flanks. A moment later they were gone, hidden by a green mask of bush foliage.

Shiminege stared at the spot where she had last seen Dossouye and Gbo. Then she turned toward the village and the yam-fields. Her mind stirred with new thoughts, new emotions. . . .

*   *   *

At a river not far from Yaoule country, Dossouye watered Gbo and reflected upon what she had done. She knew it had been essential that she replace Umenya Kwi during the challenge. If the *sichi* had simply failed to appear, there was the possibility that a Yaoule filled with dark ambition would seek to take his place. Dossouye had seen that happen many times before. She knew only public disgrace would eradicate both demon and ambition.

If only she keeps her promise, Dossouye thought as she splashed water over her wounds. She was confident Shiminege would not betray her trust, despite all the inner dislocation the Yaoule girl must be experiencing.

"She kept her first promise; she will keep the second," Dossouye said aloud. "By the time anyone stumbles across that ravine, the scavengers will have scattered all that is left of Umenya Kwi."

Shaking herself dry, Dossouye mounted Gbo. In the darkening sky over Yaoule country, she saw a faint glow of flame.

A celebration, she thought. And Dossouye guided Gbo northward, satisfied in her shattering of a false belief that had held a people in thrall.

She never knew Shiminege failed to keep her promise. She never knew what she had awakened in the soul of the Yaoule girl. She never knew that Shiminege had decided she was now the vessel of Dossouye, not Mwana Pwo. She never knew how Shiminege burst upon the Yaoule village like a meteor from the sky, shouting the truth of Umenya Kwi's deception and downfall. She never knew that Shiminege had taken the mask of Mwana Pwo and hurled it into a cooking-fire. She never knew that the horrified Yaoule, led by Bosedi and the spirit-women, had seized Shiminege, bound her, and thrown her into the same fire.

She never knew. . . .

THE BLACK TOWER

Stephen Burns

One of the best ways to make a sale to a fantasy market is to invent an intensely interesting character; and one of the best ways to make a second sale is to write a story about the same character and sell it to the same editor.

In this volume of *S&S*, I chose a second of Phyllis Ann Karr's *Frostflower and Thorn* stories; a second story about Shanna from Diana L. Paxon; and a second story about the African warrior Dossouye from Charles Saunders. And in this tradition, when Stephen Burns sent me a story about his young woman thief Clea, who outshadowed the protagonist of his first story in *S&S #1*, "Taking Heart" (which, judging by the mail I received, was liked better than any other story except Emma Bull's "Rending Dark") I felt I had received an offer I couldn't refuse.

Not that Steve Burns relies on a piggyback sale; a postscript to his letter offering me this story told me he had just made a sale to the highly prestigious *Analog*. I'm sure he deserved it, but hope he doesn't abandon sword-and-sorcery fiction for high technology

—MZB

Even at seventeen years of age Clea would laugh if someone spoke of luck. But if she had believed in luck, then she would have been forced to admit that it had gone bad of late.

She trudged grimly across unending sand under a blazing, pitiless sun, her footsteps filling in behind her as the restless, comfortless wind stirred the sand as if bent on wiping out every trace of her. The nearest human enclave was still many days distant, and her chances of reaching it were poor as she had no food and her water was gone. She had only the clothes on her back, no money, and only a small belt-knife to call a weapon. She still mourned her friend and recent mentor, old Ad'Rhow, dead since two nights past, killed by his own carelessness.

The hood of Clea's cloak was pulled low, covering her midnight hair and giving her wide-set black eyes some shade as she searched the horizon continually. If there was any succor to be found in that acrid, unforgiving place, she did not intend to miss it.

She labored up the side of a steep dune, struggling against the sliding, treacherous sand. The view from the dune's crest gave no cause for hope, and she half-slid and half-ran down the other side. Once in the trough between the dune she had descended and the one before her, she followed it in hopes of finding damp sand.

She had not long been on that path when something broke over the dune-crest to her right and leapt to the ground before her, landing in a spray of sand. That leap alone should have been beyond any mortal attacker.

Clea threw herself backwards and landed in a fighting crouch, already pulling her knife free of its sheath. She had to crane her neck to take in the full height of the thing confronting her for it was well over twice as tall as she.

It was no man, but a creature or demon-thing. Inky black it was, black as the eternal night in the deepest of poor old Ad'Rhow's now-collapsed caves. But it was not a dull black, like soot; instead it had a glazed and shiny look to it, as if the thing had been carved from the purest obsidian. It was roughly manlike in form, but freakishly tall. Its limbs were long and spindly, with barbed, armored joints and legs that bent backwards. The thing's head was similar to a locust's, its eyes faceted jet globes at the sides of its gleaming, plated head.

Clea stared at the thing, poised to attack but withholding. The knife she held looked small and ineffectual when measured against the creature. The demon-thing's thin limbs had no look of weakness about them, and each was edged along its length, those edges looking sharper than the blade Clea held. Sharp enough to cleave through bone like soft cheese.

The huge black devil-thing moved its clawed, three-fingered hands, Instantly there was a knife in each hand. Black, both blade and hilt alike, they seemed to appear out of the hot desert air.

Clea's crouch tightened as she readied herself to dodge or leap. The nightmarish thing confronting her stared at her blindly, not even making the small motions that would prove it drew breath. After a moment its barbed mouth opened, and it spoke in a voice like plates of rough brass rubbing and clashing together.

"Drop your knife. While you hold it you will think of nothing other than how to hurt this one. You can not hurt this one, and this one will not hurt you if you obey."

Clea shivered and gritted her teeth, for the thing's voice hurt the way iron scraping stone can. But her black eyes never left the thing and she gripped her small blade more firmly. "No. I will not be tricked."

The creature said nothing. Without warning, it acted. Faster than any human hand and arm could move, it sent the two knives hissing toward Clea. She reacted instinctively, and flung her knife in return.

A heartbeat later Clea stood perfectly still, holding her breath. The demon-thing had plucked her knife out of the air as if it had been a slow, lazy fly. The two knives the thing had thrown had not touched her. One hung in the air a hand's-breadth away from her throat, neither falling nor coming closer. The other was poised in the air a finger-joint away from her belly as if waiting to be told to drive home by its master.

The creature cocked its locust-like head. "There is a word. Trust." It stabbed Clea's knife at its own eye, striking the faceted, fragile-looking globe harder than any human hand could. The blade shattered, raining bronze slivers around the thing's feet. The hilt was idly crushed to powder in its hand.

Regarding Clea steadily, the thing gestured. One of the strange black knives flew back to its hand like a trained bird. It reversed the knife, dispassionately began to push the blade into its own chest. Tar-dark fluid welled around the rent in its glassy hide. Its brassy voice unchanged by pain, it spoke again.

"Only one kind of weapon can harm this one." The knife at Clea's throat backed off, turned, slid hilt-first into her hand. She looked down at it in wonder, thrilling at the throb of power it sent up her arm.

The creature flung its knife into the sand between them and, plucking another from the air, buried it next to its mate. "Will you trust this one?" it asked, folding its legs and sinking to the sand. "This one would have your counsel and help if you would give it."

Clea looked at the knife in her hand, then at the creature. She sat down across from it. "What help could such as you need?"

The creature's posture changed, becoming less rigid. Obviously relieved at Clea's answer, it told her.

"This one is no demon," the creature said, "Though it may look to be one. But this one is not of earthly life either, being a made thing and not born, formed from the power and

malice of its maker and master, Okkatal. This one was brought
into the world to be the instrument of that terrible malice.

"Okkatal was once the High Priest of Nomana, a city near
the Eastrise Mountains. His hunger for power and domination
knew no bounds, and led him into dark searchings and darker
undertakings. Through his schemings and, served by magic,
cruelty and murder, he sought to usurp the rightful rulers of
that place. His power grew as the darkness at the sun's
setting, and with that power he wielded terror like a whip.

"But the brave folk of Nomana and the few rightful Lords
he had not yet murdered or subverted were able to cast him
out before his hold was complete. They could not kill him,
for his sorcerous might was great and any hand raised against
him burst into flame. But at a terrible cost they struggled free
of his growing dominion, driving him from Nomana and
closing the city against him.

"Okkatal's power was diminished by this turn, and his
wrath burned hotter than a forge-fire. He wandered for a
time, seeking new lore and tending his resentment until it was
a pyre inside him. All of his old power returned to him in
time and redoubled under the force of his unending malice.
He came to these wastes and raised up a tower of black glass,
a tower built by necromancy and maintained by ill will. Into
that tower he went to begin his real work.

"For more than a score of years Okkatal has labored
toward his dark dream of vengeance on the city that cast him
out. Many works were begun toward this end, and this one
was to be his greatest."

The strange black creature shifted restlessly, almost shyly.
It made a small metallic *clack-clack-clacking* that might have
been laughter, then went on: "No earthly soldiers would
serve Okkatal's purpose, for they could be killed and they
could betray. He wanted a servant as terrible as his will, and
strove to create an awesome, invulnerable creature whose
aspect was terror and whose form was killing made flesh. It

was to be an intelligent thing, capable of craft, planning and reasoned intention.

"This one he made, and named *Ruin*." The creature said the name again, as if it gave some unhappy pleasure. "Ruin. But Okkatal, old and mad with poisonous intent and best-forgot learnings, made better than he knew. This one could flatten a city like a storm, if it wished, or cut down a thousand soldiers like wheat falls to the scythe. But this one would not. Could not. This one learned of something called pain as Okkatal's will blew against it like a wind-driven fire, yet this one knew it must bear that agony and refuse its master's commands."

"You knew right and wrong," Clea said. "Men have some small sense of it, too."

"This one is no man." The creature's voice was a mere rattle. "This one was unsuitable to its master's purposes, and his anger turned day into night. He could not unmake or harm this one, though his trying could have cracked a mountain open like an egg. *Fail*, he named this one then, and cast it out, setting a Forbidding that this one could not enter the tower again.

"Lesser creatures, called *garsk*, he creates now, ones bereft of thought or will, and forged of malice entire. Okkatal increases their number with each passing day, and soon they will be turned toward the purpose for which this one was made."

Fail huddled in on itself, bowing its head. It stared at Clea with one glittering ebony eye, and though no emotion colored its voice, its confusion showed as plainly as its shadow on the sand.

"This one was cast out, just as Okkatal was from Nomana. This one is like Okkatal in that it too desires to return to the place it was cast from. Fail would reenter the forbidden tower to kill its maker and end his plans if it could. Is this one as evil as Okkatal for its wishes are the same as his?

"You are human-born, not a poor made thing. Answer this one's despair."

Clea smiled at Fail. She went and sat beside it, returning its knife. "You must tell me everything about Okkatal and his tower if we are to bring it down, my friend," she said.

The sheet of black glass shimmered, then cleared and an image appeared. Okkatal watched a small, cloaked and hooded figure ride toward his tower on the back of the creature he had named Fail. He frowned, trying to understand how that was possible.

The strange pair halted. The one riding Fail threw back the hood, revealing a young woman with short black hair and wide-set dark eyes. Still seated on her steed, and seeming to stare straight at Okkatal, she put her hands on her hips and shouted, "Hail the tower! Would Okkatal keep an old woman waiting in this damned sun all day?"

Okkatal's frown deepened. Old woman? He sent four of his *garsk* soldiers out with a silent command. Moments later he watched the four mantis-like creatures surround the intruder. The young woman looked them over coldly. "Shoddy work," she said, shaking her head. She dismounted, then headed toward the tower, tossing an order to *stay* over her shoulder at Fail as if it were a dog. Fail huddled face-down on the sand like a whipped cur.

This was a riddle which demanded an answer. Okkatal ordered the four *garsk* to escort the woman to his chamber. He ordered the mirror carried away and waited to meet this peculiar visitor.

Clea was taken directly to Okkatal, escorted by the four silent *garsk*. These creatures were smaller than Fail, and although the same glossy black, they were more mantis-like in construction, with undersized antlike heads. In the claws that served them for hands, each carried an all-black spear with a leaf-shaped blade.

Okkatal was ensconced on a throne of gold in a chamber of black glass so faceted that the few small lights burning were multiplied to a thousand dazzling flickerings. A phalanx of *garsk* lined either side of the path to Okkatal's throne in a spear-bristling double line of menace.

Clea marched straight up to the front of Okkatal's raised dais and glared up at him. "You are a fool, young man!"

Okkatal was old, very old. His skin was yellow and tautly stretched over his bones, marked by snaking courses of blue veins. His eyes were the color of pus and seemed to rest unmoving in his head. All his hair was as gone as his youth, and he had a slow-moving reptilian look about him, as if his mouth were full of poison.

"Not so young as you," he said at last in a dry papery whisper. "And as you dare come into my lair and bait me, not such a fool either."

Clea met his viper-eyed gaze squarely. "They say it takes one to know one, child, but such is not the case with fools. I see you sitting there on your fool's throne, making ants while the scorpion stings you again and again. That is your folly, and I would leave you to it but that it touches me as well."

Okkatal frowned, wondering what that strange comment meant. He would know soon, whether she wished to tell him or not, but first he wanted some answer to the riddle of her mastery of Fail.

"You came here riding one of my failures as if it were a broken-spirited horse. How is that so?"

Clea laughed. "Ah, that creature was a better work than these toys with which you now surround yourself. It is worth a thousand of these ants." She gestured at the four *garsk* guarding her still and the others ranked inside the crystal chamber.

"To master such as the thing I rode in on was no great task. Had you a hundred years more to study the matter, you might be able to bend it to your will as well."

She spat on the floor and grinned at Okkatal. "We reach

the reason for my visit. You die, child, and little time remains to you—far less than a year. You shorten your own span of years, though you are too much the fool to know it. Well, I have lived thrice your span and plan to live it thrice again. But tell me, would you like to live a little longer? Long enough to enjoy your triumph over Nomana?''

Okkatal stared at the woman before him, tempted to let his creatures use her for sport and be rid of her. His eyes told him that she was not that long past being a child, and he suffered no one speaking to him in such a fashion.

Yet she had ridden to his tower on a creature he knew capable of laying waste to an entire city, a creature which had resisted his every attempt at mastery. That bespoke either power or learning in plenty. If this witch's claims of great age were true, then she might hold the solution to a predicament that rankled and rubbed his nerves raw, in that by the time he was ready to grind Nomana to dust under his heel he would be that much closer to the death whose rank breath he felt cold on his neck.

Could this one have learned the secret of passing through the ages untouched by time? The thought of having a hundred years to extract payment from Nomana thrilled him as his dreams of vengeance had ceased to do of late.

''Is that what you have come to offer?'' he said at last. It took a great effort to keep hope from showing on his face or in his voice.

''I offer nothing. I come to set a matter aright, and you have but to choose between aiding me and living long after, or opposing me and dying this very day. But can a fool choose wisely?''

''Do not taunt me!'' Okkatal's bruise-colored eyes blazed, and he gripped the arms of his throne tightly with his thin, skeletal hands. The *garsk* surrounding Clea moved closer, raising their spears higher. ''Speak the reason you intrude straight out, or I will have these creatures you dare call *ants* pull you to crumbs for my sport and theirs!''

Clea sighed. "I will tell you, but not from your threat—I wish you to know the extent of your folly. In the making of the creature you named Fail, and in the making and controlling of these lesser creatures you used a *zenghen-s'tu*, a great black jewel which you drew from the Dark Realm. Is that not so?"

Okkatal was surprised that the young woman before him could know of such lore. It had taken him years of study to learn of the *zenghen-s'tu*, the Stone of Hatred, and years again to master the arts needed to procure it. Only in the past year had that come about, and half that time had been spent trying to master it enough to produce Fail. That she could know such gave credence to her claims of great age.

"Yes, that is so."

Clea grimaced. "Of course it is so! And you employ the jewel just as it came to you, uncut and unshaped."

Surprised again, Okkatal merely nodded.

"Fool!" Clea cried, stamping her foot. "That is like using a sword whose hilt is as sharp as its blade! You work your work, all the time withering and turning old as your tool cuts your hand and drains the life from you! Weeks of travel distant is my home, yet even there I felt its hunger lick against me! If you wish to die, that is your affair. But I plan to live long and lose not a day more to your folly.

"So I come to do one of two things; to either destroy you and your bungling, or to teach you to form the thing aright. I care little how you choose, and offer the second choice only because you and I are of one kind." She crossed her arms and said no more.

Okkatal dismissed her threats as idle boast. He knew his power, and feared no other mortal. But if it were true that a simple reshaping of the great black jewel would give him renewed life and a greater power over the worms of Nomana—!

Okkatal gestured, his skull-like face wearing a feral grin. The four *garsk* warriors closed in on Clea, two seizing her arms in their claws. "I have decided. You will show me how to reshape the gem. Then, if you beg sweetly, I may let you live.''

Clea showed no fear. "Oh child, I will help you," she said. "But as to after . . ." She spread her hands and shrugged.

Okkatal was picked up to be carried, throne and all, by a dozen of his insectile minions. Another dozen surrounded Clea. She followed behind as he was carried out, walking inside a circle of spears as if she were alone in an open meadow.

After the procession left the throne room of Okkatal, it made its way up a broad stair that narrowed as it climbed, emerging into a high-ceilinged chamber one level up from the ground.

This room was huge and round, its outer walls formed by the walls of the tower itself, and through those walls filtered an ashy-hued, gloomy light. All but the center of the chamber was empty space, and there stood a rough-hewn stone pedestal on a raised obsidian dais. The *zenghen-s'tu* rested on that gray stone pedestal.

It hurt the eyes to look upon the great black jewel. It reflected back no light, and looked less like something brought into this world than a wound in the world that allowed some darker place to show through. The whole room thrummed with its power, yet for all that power the chamber was cold, bitter cold.

Clea's steps faltered as she was led into the gem's presence, and the look of insolent confidence she wore slipped from her face for a few dangerous moments. Had Okkatal turned and seen her just then she would have been undone, for he would have seen that she was no lore-wise old woman hardened to powers such as the *zenghen-s'tu's*, but a brave and arrogant young woman facing a venomous power that would daunt the staunchest of mortals.

But Okkatal had eyes only for his gem. He was borne toward his pride and his power, his papered-skull face twisting into something like a look of love as he gazed avidly at the beating heart of his dreams of power and revenge. His breath came from his seamed mouth in a gray plume in the chamber's cold and his little-but-bone hands trembled in eagerness to reshape the gem into a tool better suited to serve his purposes.

One of Clea's hands found the other. She dug her fingers into the back of her hand, harder, harder, her knuckles whitening and blood welling around her nails. Her eyes slitted for just a moment, then her hands relaxed.

She clapped them together, and threw back her head and laughed aloud just as Okkatal's *garsk* bearers were lowering his throne to the dais on which the pedestal rested. The renegade priest's eyes left the sight of his beloved jewel and sought Clea. She strode toward him, as if more eager to begin than he was.

"I wonder that you are still alive!" she cried. "You wrought greatly when you brought this from the Dark Realm, and it is no wonder that I felt it even in my far-off place!"

She grinned at Okkatal approvingly. "You must be sternly made to yet live while so close to such tremendous unshaped power for so long. You are not the blind dabbler I thought you! I apologize, young man, and that is indeed a rare thing for me!"

Okkatal breathed a sigh of relief that his rude intruder had passed the final test and not fallen into utter dismay before the vast raw power of the *zenghen-s'tu*. The yellow mask of his face showed that relief and no small hope.

"It is indeed a beautiful thing," he said simply. "It is also the fruit of a score of years' labor. Can a simple reshaping truly make it burn away the price of that labor?"

"Yes it can. Would you begin?"

Okkatal's eyes smoldered with eagerness and his withered mouth worked hungrily. "I would."

"Then you have but to do this," Clea said. "Remember when you were young and strong, when your limbs served you well and your blood ran thick and hot, when the life in you was a blaze and not a banked and failing fire. Fix that in your mind, banishing all else. When you see that earlier self well and truly, seize the stone and drive that image into it. With your mind mould it to look as you did then, and so shall you reshape and return to that happier state. If your will is sufficient for this, and your strength, then you will be able to wade through the ages as if time was but a shallow stream with no power to pull you down or carry you away."

"Such a simple secret," Okkatal breathed.

"Simplicity lies at the heart of all great power."

Okkatal did not reply. Already he was beginning to follow her instructions that he might forge the *zenghen-s'tu* into a remembrance, and thus a renewal. He gave a moment's passing thought to having his creatures kill the witch then and there, but decided against it. She might know other useful things.

Putting all else aside, Okkatal remembered, casting his mind back across the years, recollecting what had been worn away by the years. He remembered, and when he was ready, reached out with shaking, skeletal hands and grasped the *zenghen-s'tu*.

Red fire erupted from the jewel at that contact, fire that coursed up his arms and enveloped his body in an instant. Cloaked in twisting crimson flame, he stiffened and was pulled erect so that he stood facing the jewel as if swearing allegiance to it.

Sudden heat, candent and dire, rolled off the jewel in waves, forcing Clea back. Okkatal's throne of gold began to slump and run, too close to the raging power of the *zenghen-s'tu*.

The jewel began to pulse and seethe like a living thing under Okkatal's hands, taking on a rounded shape, then the crudely formed aspect of a human head. His mouth stretched in a soundless howl, he bent every iron-forged sliver of his will against the stone's monumental resistance.

It was then that a thunderous concussion shivered the tower and there came the far-off clash of breaking glass. In the clamor that followed, Clea turned toward the stair and began to put more distance between herself and Okkatal, who was oblivious to all but his efforts to master the *zenghen-s'tu*. His will was prevailing; already the potent black stone wore the shape of a vaguely sketched face and it appeared that a hand of years had fallen away from him.

But the struggle took everything he had. That part of his mind which had maintained the Forbidding against a single creature he had formed and then cast out as insufficient had been bent to his present trial. He had no choice; the *zenghen-s'tu* gave him no leeway for reserving himself. Had he tried to hold back, he would have been consumed like a dry leaf in a bonfire.

At the moment the Forbidding had faltered, Fail had acted, hammering his way through the adamantine walls of the tower as if they were but thin plaster. Aided by surprise, it had gained the stairs before full opposition could be mustered against it.

Fail gained the top of the stairs, beset by a swarm of *garsk*, in time to meet another swarm of the vicious black creatures head-on. It glanced once at Clea, then its eyes found its maker, Okkatal. It threw back its locust-like head and loosed a cry like tearing brass and bells being crushed between great stones, then began to fight its way toward its maker.

Nothing in this world ever moved or fought as Fail did then. It flung off the *garsk* which had thrown themselves upon it during its moment's pause, and felled a score more in the space of a heart-beat. A dozen *garsk* thrust at Fail at once with their spears, and a dozen spears—and the arms gripping them—fell to the ground from a single knife stroke. One *garsk* was launched at Fail from behind. He turned and struck it with one three-fingered fist. It burst like a hammer-struck melon. One of Fail's hands moved ceaselessly, the uncanny all-black knives flying and striking like ebon lightning, then returning to be thrown again faster than the eye could follow. A space cleared around Fail as any *garsk* coming within reach was dashed to bits by Fail's fist or feet. Slowly the taller creature forced its way through its lesser brethren and deeper into the chamber.

Clea was no less busy. The *garsk* had no orders to destroy her; they had surrounded her at Fail's appearance. But two of the mantis-like creatures had stepped inside the circle of spears to restrain her, and she had responded by snatching the spear of one from its claws, spitting it, then its accomplice. The circle had closed tighter around her, and she whirled the spear to keep them back.

"Hurry!" she shouted. "Okkatal changes!" She feinted as another *garsk* stepped into the circle, then drove the spear's blade into its throat.

Okkatal's years were peeling away like the layers of an onion, and the red-pulsing gem was a furnace that burned so brightly that the bones of his hands and arms could be seen through his flesh as if it were glass. The golden throne was a red-gleaming puddle on the floor and already a rough, leering face could be seen in the jewel.

Fail waded toward its creator through a seething black surf of *garsk* and their broken bodies flew like spray. More of the things streamed into the chamber and flung their weight and mindless malice into the writhing mass that sought to bring Fail down. The great creature was losing tar-black blood from a dozen wounds by then, for the spears of the *garsk* were lesser versions of its knives and capable of piercing its vitreous carapace. Beset by numberless *garsk*, some spears got past its guard.

Clea would have fought her way toward Fail but her own foes came too fast. A spear nicked her ribs, and she ripped it from her attacker's claws and drove the hilt into its eyes. The unrelenting press of spears and claws ground closer to her, surrounding her like a storm.

Fail was all but buried in scrabbling, stabbing *garsk*, and it seemed that for every one tossed off two more took its place. Heaving itself forward in the midst of that boiling madness of *garsk*, Fail gained the dais. With an effort that would have been beyond any other thing on this earth, Fail struggled its arms free and brought its misshapen hands down on the *zenghen-s'tu*.

There was a detonation that bowled everything but the jewel, Okkatal, and his first creation over like bottles on an upended table. As Fail touched the jewel the crimson fire went white, running up its arms and turning its body into a torch of pure and colorless incandescence.

The tower groaned and shivered, the *garsk* lay unmoving. Clea watched from behind a pile of their bodies with slitted eyes as the white fire loosed by Fail burned the renewed youth from Okkatal in the space of a heartbeat.

But Okkatal's will was strong. He clenched his teeth and met the assault. Slowly a red stain began to color the white, and Fail, who had been reshaping into something white and more human, began to lose ground to its creator.

More red bloodied the white and Fail's locust-like head swiveled from side to side in agony. A scream like smashing brass and breaking glass was torn from it, and the black of its body took on a fiery tinge, like heated iron.

"I . . . made . . . you. . . ." Okkatal hissed. "Grovel! *Fail!*"

Fail shuddered as if struck. Its barbed shoulders hunched, and it fixed Okkatal with one glittering, faceted eye. "This . . . one . . . I—" Fail's voice grew stronger, and it stood straighter, daunted no more. "*I . . . will . . . not!*" With a convulsive effort Fail squeezed the gem with all the might Okkatal had been able to bestow on its form.

There was only a slivered moment for Okkatal to scream before the *zenghen-s'tu* left the world. It was as if lightning had struck the pedestal a thousand times at once.

The world went white, then black, then silent.

*   *   *

Clea forced herself to her feet, coming out from behind the pile of dead *garsk*. Blood stained the side of her robe redly, the rest of it was smeared with tarry *garsk*-blood. She shook her head to clear it, brushed her midnight hair from her eyes, then limped toward the dais.

Okkatal's poisonous dreams of vengeance were ended. He had been blasted flesh from bone, his soul gone to whatever dark pit awaited it. Greasy smoke arose as those remaining bones smoldered sullenly.

Clea turned away and sought Fail. She found the creature, and first thought it dead. But after a moment Fail's head swiveled weakly and it turned one black eye toward her.

"I am. . . .content," Fail said, and though its voice still sounded of clashing metal, a quiet pride and peace shone in it. "I thank you."

Clea said nothing, her face solemn and the beginnings of a tear collecting in one dark eye.

"I am near over," Fail said, turning toward her weakly. Black blood began to trickle from its mouth. "Would you be tricked one more time?"

Clea was given no time to answer that strange question. Fail's hand moved suddenly. One of the all-black knives appeared, then left its hand faster than an eye blink. A second and third knife appeared and were thrown, one after another.

Clea reacted instinctively, trying to slap the blades away. The first slammed into the palm of her right hand, drove through it. She cried out and the second knife pierced her hand next to the first. The third struck her left hand, the point of the knife coming out of the back of that hand. She fell to her knees, turning shocked, unbelieving eyes on Fail.

"Pull the knife out," Fail said weakly. Clea stared at the creature as if seeing it truly for the first time. *Monster*, her eyes said, *Betrayer*.

"Pull the knives," it said again. Dazedly, gritting her teeth against the agony of her hands, Clea managed to catch the hilt of one of the knives between her hooked fingers and pull the blade from her flesh. It came free, leaving no wound. She clumsily pulled the other blade spiked into her right hand, and it came free to leave no mark either. She grasped the last knife in a whole hand and withdrew it. Her whole arm thrilled at the feel of the hilt in her hand. No wounds, no pain, and she knew she could cut through stone like water with that knife. She stood full of wonder.

"A last trick, and payment." Fail said. "Throw one."

Clea flung one of the uncanny black knives at a *garsk* body on the far side of the chamber. Unerringly it found its mark, going in up to the hilt.

"Call it," Fail whispered, like beads rolling on a brass tray.

Clea stared at the distant knife. It pulled free, then flashed back to her hand. She moved her hand, and it was gone, yet she knew that if she wanted it, or the other two, they would be there. She turned toward Fail to thank him.

The great black creature was dead.

Clea knelt next to Fail's body for a moment, and this time there were tears in her eyes, running down her cheeks. She moved her hand, and instantly one of Fail's knives was there. She brought the blade to her brow in salute, then stood and began to limp toward the stair.

Clea found a skin of water, and one of wine. She filled a sack with food Okkatal would never need, then walked out into the evening through the gaping hole Fail had made in the tower of black glass.

She walked away without looking back. She did not see the tower crumble and fade, covering the sand with drifting black dust.

THE LADY AND THE TIGER

Jennifer Roberson

Last year, in *Blood of Sorcery,* it was my pleasure to introduce Jennifer Roberson as a brand-new writer. Since then she has had a novel, *Shapechangers,* published, and is fast becoming known. New writers don't stay that way very long, certainly not if they have any talent.

In addition to talent for telling a story, Jennifer has a talent which may be even more rare. She runs a writers' workshop, and this year, one of her assignments to the writers in Phoenix was to write and submit a story for *Sword and Sorceress;* several stories made their way from Jennifer's workshop to my post office box, and the results gave the lie to the much-repeated axiom that nine-tenths or more of workshop stories are worthless or talentless; from her workshop I bought two stories, and found two others worth keeping for a second look, even though in the end I did not buy them. Both Michael Stackpole's "The Five Wards" and Bruce D. Arthurs' "Unicorn's Blood" came from this Phoenix group; so that Jennifer has contributed more than perhaps any other single writer to *Sword and Sorceress:* her own fine story and the encouragement of two more fine writers.

For the benefit of the feminists in the audience, there

155

was a point at which I figuratively threw this story across the room in exasperation, shouting "Hell! She's blown it! Why did she do that?" But I found the story so fascinating that I *had* to go on reading and finish it, even though I was convinced that I could not in conscience offer this story to the female half of my readership. And, as you will see, Jennifer magnificently redeemed my trust.

—MZB

"Tiger," the girl said, "you aren't paying any attention."

Oh yes I was. Just not to *her*. Not anymore. I slid her an absent sideways glance and smiled without any real enthusiasm. "More aqivi?"

She tipped her wooden mug to show me hers was mostly full. Much of what sloshed in the cup was probably water; cantina girls learn real quick how to water their aqivi so they stay sober while the patrons get drunk enough to spend all the coin in their pouches.

I sighed. She was growing suddenly tiresome. Especially when I saw the lower lip creep out to jut forward in a childish pout that did not become her young-old face. But I couldn't really blame her. Competition had just walked in the front door.

Competition was a tall, lean, fair-skinned, blue-eyed Northern blonde gorgeous enough to make my eyes water. My mouth was already salivating. Hurriedly I swallowed, got better control of my innards and managed some semblance of dignity. It wasn't much—I don't have much to start with—but it was enough to stiffen my spine and make me watch in narrow-eyed appreciation.

She moved with a liquid grace. Her hair was loose and hung past her shoulders, rippling as she glanced around the cantina. She wore a white silk burnous that only enhanced her fairness even as it hid her charms, but somehow I had no doubt that what lay beneath the fabric was the finest I had ever seen.

Every other male in the cantina knew it as well as I did. Conversation stopped dead as she entered, then started up again and eddied abstractedly, circling and bobbing and going nowhere because no one was listening to what anyone was saying. Everyone was watching the girl.

She knew it. She shook back her hair and lifted her chin a little. Those glacially blue eyes slid over every man in the place. I wondered if she found us all lacking to some degree, for her expression didn't change one bit. She merely looked at the purveyor of local spirits a long moment, seemed to discern some form of acquiescence in his face and nodded once. He smiled weakly, dazzled as a baby, and shrugged.

The girl planted her sandaled feet, arms hanging loose at her sides. She didn't have to raise her voice over the din of the cantina because everyone stopped talking at once.

"You men," she said in an accented voice, "I have business with you." Briefly amusement flickered in her eyes. "A different sort than you are used to from a woman, perhaps, but business all the same." Her eyes were judgmental; her mouth pursed a little in contemplation of her audience. A faint line appeared between her pale brows. "I have need of money. But I wish to get it fairly, without selling my body."

One of the men hooted. "What else have you to offer, my girl? A smile? Those are free in this place."

Her eyes fastened on him at once. She did not smile, as if unwilling to barter away something she could very well sell. A smile from that mouth would be worth the gold.

"Afterward," she said, "the smile may cost you nothing. But you will have earned it, then."

The jokester hooted again. He made an obscene witticism

that elicited a titter from several men, but most said nothing. Like me, they watched her.

Her mouth tightened. "You are betting men, are you not? Willing to wager a few coins in a worthwhile game? Well, I have such a game to offer." Her eyes swept the room's denizens again. "Most of you wear swords. Some of you may even be adequate with the blade. I challenge one of you, or two—or even three—to a sword-dance."

My brows shot up. A woman challenging men to a sword-dance? Unusual. As a matter of fact, unheard of. Here in the South only men carry swords; women are veiled and guarded and treated softly. None of them would consider touching a dainty finger to a sword hilt, let alone lifting one against a man. Yet this beautiful Northern girl had challenged the entire cantina to a sword-dance.

That rankled. For one thing, a woman has no business meddling about with a man's concerns.

For another, the sword-dance is nothing to take lightly. It requires skill, strength, endurance, intelligence . . . well, to be perfectly frank it isn't the sort of thing just anyone can do. Those who do it are generally professionals, men who make their living hiring out their swords. Like me.

I scowled at her. She didn't see it; I was in a far corner tucked into a niche with a small knife- and sword-hacked table in front of me. Somehow I had managed to slide most of my impressive length underneath the table so that I sat on the end of my spine, and what little of me showed was not arranged to draw her attention. Especially with the sulky black-haired cantina girl seated hard against my right side.

For a long moment no one, absolutely no one, said a word. She stood there in white silk with her slender hands showing at the ends of her loose sleeves and her sandaled feet at the hem of the burnous. The hood hung from her shoulders, mostly obscured by the gleaming curtain of her hair. And those blue, blue eyes bored a hole into every single face in the cantina.

"Well?" she asked. "Have I come upon a nest of albino eunuchs?"

I winced. I didn't particularly want to see all that beauty ruined by an angry male. If she kept up with the insults she might find herself in a real sword-dance, and there was no doubt she would lose.

Mutters made the rounds of the room. I saw some smiles and raised brows, but no one seemed to take her seriously. I marked the tension in her body even beneath the enveloping silk; anger was in her eyes. The chin thrust upward again.

Before she could resort to insults again I spoke up. "Show us your weapon, bascha." The Southron word was a compliment, but I didn't know if she knew it. "We might take you more seriously if we knew you had more than just a well-honed tongue with which to fight."

The pale brows lanced down, wrinkling the skin between her eyes. It was a half-glare, half-scowl she cast in my direction, but she followed my suggestion. Sort of. Before I could push myself into an upright position—the better to appreciate the results of my suggestion—she'd stripped the burnous from her body and stood before us all in a sleeveless brown leather tunic that hit her mid-thigh. Blue stitching edged the borders—some form of runic glyphs—but I didn't pay much attention to them. I was too busy checking out the scenery.

She had legs a mile long. I'm tall, topping most men by a head and a half, but I was willing to bet the crown of her head came up to my shoulder. Her arms were long as well, slender and fair, and taut with subtle muscles that slid beneath the flesh. Criss-crossing her chest—equally admirable—was a supple leather harness, and over her left shoulder peeked the hilt of a sword.

She tapped the hilt with her right hand. "Now," she said, "who will join me in a circle?"

She wasn't joking. She really did want a sword-dance. Sword *fights* are common enough in the South, but the

ritualistic— and dangerous—sword-dances are not. Her words
rang false in my ears.

"You said you needed money," one man called out. "What
are you wagering, then, if you have none?"

She didn't miss a beat. "My smile," she said. "And a
little of my time."

I wet my drying lips and swallowed heavily.

"What do *we* put up?" another man shouted. "Our good
looks?"

She didn't smile. She waited for the laughter to die down.
"Your gold," she said coolly. "It will cost you a gold
piece—or its equivalent—to step into the circle with me."

That silenced a lot of them. This cantina isn't the best—it
isn't the worst, either, but it comes closer to that than the
best—and most of the patrons don't have gold to wager. Not
even gold to drink on. But a lot of us, looking at her, reached
into our pouches and fingered the weight of our coins.

Eventually, of course, someone found the required amount.
Amid much joking and loud raillery he got up from his table,
executed a clumsy bow and tapped the sword hanging at his
waist. Already I discounted him; a man who carries a sword
at his waist is always an amateur. Professionals go in harness.

Automatically my hand went up to my own. It snugged
against my chest beneath the green burnous I wore; Singlestroke
reared his heavy hilt above my left shoulder through the slit
in the seam of the burnous. Of course sitting slumped the way
I was, the blade was hardly in the best position for a quick
unsheathing, but then I had no plans to show Singlestroke's
edge to the patrons. Or the blonde.

She draped her white burnous over the nearest table, then
flicked her fingers in a come-hither gesture. I saw the light in
her eyes and realized she relished what she did. And yet she
was cool. I saw no hint of anger or pride or the sort of
emotion that could get a sword-dancer into trouble; more
often than not the man who loses his head in the circle will be

carried out of it. Frowning, I scratched at the claw scars on the right side of my face and waited.

Almost at once the cantina floor was cleared. Tables and stools and benches were dragged out of the way; the patrons stood in groups wagering among themselves, ringing down coin against the tables and tossing bets to others. I did not doubt that most of the bets were going against the girl. Maybe all of them.

She waited. Her arms still hung at her sides. I saw her shake her hands a few times, loosening her limber wrists; her feet were spread slightly, one a little in front of the other. She did not stand high on the balls of her feet; not yet. I thought it might come to that when the sword-dance began.

But it was not a dance. It was a travesty. No sooner had she whipped the sword from its sheath across her back than she had torn the man's weapon from his hands. It clanged against the wooden floor with the dull thud of poor tempering; there was the hint of a smile in her eyes but she did not look at the sword as it lay before them both.

The man's hands clenched three times. His face was red with embarrassment and shame. I saw the idea pass through his eyes to call foul or some such thing, so he could pick up the sword and go again, but he didn't do it. I think he understood what she was about, for all he did was toss down the gold coin so it rang at her feet.

Not a muscle twitched in her face. Instead she remained silent, watching as he bent and retrieved the sword. Then, with only the ghost of a smile, she flicked some hair behind her back. "Who is next?"

She did not pick up the coin. It emphasized her contempt for her first opponent better than I could have done with a single word. All eyes strayed to the gold glinting against the wine-soaked wood, then went back to her. If she didn't pick it up, no one else would either. The loser, churlish and childish, had hurt himself more than her.

The next man fared little better. Oh, he kept his hands wrapped around the hilt of his sword a little longer, but in the end she twisted it out of his grasp with a subtle maneuver and stepped back as he bellowed his surprise. But he, at least, was a better loser; he handed her his gold and then retrieved his sword with a bow in her direction.

She said nothing. Words from her would underline his failure and she owed him better than that. Already the collective masculine pride in the place was smarting; comments from the victor would worsen matters. She knew that much of us, at least; I wondered how she had learned it.

I saw the odd wiggle of her fingers. Come hither, it said. For a moment I considered doing just that, then decided against it. It would serve no good at all to destroy the reputation she was building. She stood no chance against me. And I was enjoying her dance; I had no wish to end it so soon.

A third man stepped into the center of the cantina, crossing over the imaginary line into the circle. In sand the circle is drawn; a sword-dancer stepping outside the boundary loses at once. But inside a cantina, with no circle upon the floor, the dance is changed. A subtle change, but evident. Every man there knew exactly where the boundary lay. So did she.

I saw her eyes narrow. For a brief moment there was a flicker of consideration in them, though her face remained calm. Then I saw the harness criss-crossed over his chest and back and realized he was a sword-dancer. I didn't know him—the South is big and even I can't know them all—but it was obvious he was a professional. There were no unnecessary twitches and shiftings and fidgetings from him. He stood quietly before her, waiting politely, and I saw the beginnings of a smile on her face.

"Have you seen enough?" she asked.

"Enough to know better than to discount you."

"For that, my thanks."

He smiled. "Save your thanks for when I have allowed you to leave the circle alive."

It wasn't bluster. He meant it. He was a professional and would behave as one. In the circle it's hard to do otherwise.

It wasn't a true sword-dance. For one, they began with swords in their hands. In close quarters it's common enough—there is no room for a true dance—but it does change the parameters. It means, usually, the thing can be ended with the first thrust, because the circle is too small for the customary variations. I wondered how he would end it. I wondered if he would leave her alive.

Anyone else would. She had wagered herself to the winner. But to a sword-dancer the dance is a serious matter. In such a challenge as this generally the dance is friendly enough, an exhibition of skill more than anything else, but occasionally you'll find it to the death. He was within his rights to kill her. She had claimed herself a sword-dancer—heresy enough, in view of her sex—and her death in the circle was well within the rules.

Still, I doubted he'd kill her. He was all male and she magnificently female. It would be more of a courtship rite.

The swords swung up. Clashed. Rang as they twisted apart and meshed again. He was taller and stronger than the girl, but she was quicker. I saw it almost at once. Before she had held back, winning quickly because she saw no need to tease and bait the others. Now she danced. Now she twisted that supple body, blonde hair flying, and danced.

He led, she followed. Changed. She dominated, then faded, feinting, ducking a swipe of the blade that would have chopped a ragged hole in her shining blonde hair. She followed that with a trick of her own, pricking one of his bared ribs with the tip of her sword and then sliding away as he blinked at her in surprise. She could have had him then. But she leaped away, circling warily, as if she could not believe it herself.

I swore. She moved well and handled the sword with more skill than I could have imagined in a woman, but she was sloppy. Unprofessional. She had let her man go free. Had it been *me,* I'd have chopped him down instantly.

"Fool," I muttered. "Even boys know better. . . ."

A moment later the sword-dancer had drawn a crimson line across one flashing thigh. I saw the frown in her face and the shock in her eyes. I thought then the thing would end; I had seen apprentices lose all their skill and aggression the moment blood flowed, even so much as a prick. No doubt the scratch stung, but it was hardly the thing to concern a professional.

But she wasn't one. She was a woman, and suddenly everyone remembered it. Including the man she faced.

He stepped back at once. He did not lower his guard but neither did he follow up his advantage. He stood pat, waiting for her shock to pass, and in that moment she had him.

Her blade flicked out and caught him once on each forearm, then across his knuckles, and as he swore at her she slid the tip beneath one of his thumbnails. Blood fell and so did his sword.

The thumb went into his mouth. Then out of it. He wore an incredulous expression that warred with the pain in his eyes. Then he swore again and stared at his bleeding thumb, at a loss for what to do about it.

My own thumb ached in response. But my pride didn't. He deserved to lose. No man should ever discount his opponent in the circle, not even a woman.

And *I* didn't intend to.

I felt it almost at once. Faces turned in my direction. Whispers started up. I heard the mutters, though none were clear—just bits of "Sandtiger" and "sword-dancer." Slowly I straightened up on my bench and rested one shoulder blade against the wall. I waited. And eventually, of course, someone came over to see if I was interested.

I was. But I waited until the price was right. Then, lazily, I uncoiled my long legs and rose, letting them all see my

height and the considerable width of my shoulders. And
Singlestroke, hiding coyly beneath my burnous.

"I'm a fair man," I told them all. "I don't want to cheat
anybody. You know that; you know *me*. But there is something at risk here." I waited a beat, then grinned my lazy
grin. "My reputation."

It brought the expected laughter. Relief sped around the
room and suddenly the patrons were boisterous again, rowdy
and happy, positive I would uphold the pride of the male sex
against this woman. Even if she *had* bested three men—and
one of them a professional—none of them had been the
Sandtiger. None of them had been that legendary sword-dancer.

She stood in the center of the invisible circle, clutching the
coins in her hand. Her other held her sword. I saw the color
standing high in her face and the anger in her eyes; all to the
good. This was a grudge-match no matter how you looked at
it.

"You deserve something for your trouble," I told her.
"What do you say to a ninety–ten split? Ten to you if you
lose." I thought saying "if" showed some sensitivity on my
part; I could have said "when."

"Winner take all." It was clipped off, strangulated by her
Northern accent.

I grinned at her. "That means all of you *and* the money
. . . when I win." This time I couldn't bypass the truth.

She turned around, marched to the bar and slapped down
the coins. Two gold pieces. The first coin still glinted against
the floor. When she spun back around the color was brighter
in her face. *"Winner take all."*

"Fine with me." I glanced around at the intrigued audience.
"What about a purse? Put up some coin for your enjoyment.
Let's have something worth dancing for."

It had the desired effect. Someone passed around the pouch
and by the time it had made a circuit of the room it was
nearly full. Not all of it was gold, of course, but it was still a

substantial amount. They would all make something on their side bets, and the girl or I would take home the spoils.

I grinned at her. "Last chance for a decent split."

"You heard my offer." Her face was perfectly blank.

I sighed. "Still, I refuse to hold an unfair advantage over you. Unless, of course, you *know* who I am."

"An overlarge, somewhat drunken man," she said distinctly. "What more?"

I scowled at her. "I am not drunk."

She eyed me consideringly. "That, the circle will discern. . . . Very well, who are you?"

"My name," I said, "is the Sandtiger."

I saw it go home. She was a Northerner and therefore a stranger, but she'd been South long enough to hear of me. Most people have. My reputation gets around.

"Sword-dancer." She said it softly, rolling it over on her tongue. "Are you truly the Sandtiger?"

Idly I stroked the claw marks on the side of my face. "Call me Tiger for short."

She took a deep breath that did wonderful things to her frontal anatomy. But when she let the air out again I knew her decision was made. "We have an agreement."

"You're sure?"

Her eyes swept the waiting faces. "I have no desire to dash the hopes of all these men who wish to see me skewered by the greatest sword-dancer of them all." An ironic smile was in her eyes. "Dance with me, Tiger."

"Outside," I said. "Let's make this a proper dance."

She tilted her head a little, then nodded. And we took it outside.

The Southron sun is very hot. It bakes the sand until you want to scream with it, but you don't. You haven't got the saliva for it. You learn to live with it. Or you die with it.

This time of year the heat is not so bad. Just hot enough to make a sword hilt warm in your hands and your feet flinch away from the heat that bakes through your sandals. Almost at once I shed my burnous and faced her in my brief leather dhoti. Then I stripped out of my harness and dropped it on top of the pile of silk, once I'd drawn Singlestroke, and I waited while two men drew the circle.

The grip fit my hand in a perfect intercourse of hard flesh and beaded metal. Early in my apprenticeship I had experimented with wrapping leather around the grip to cushion my palms, but I had learned I was better without it. My hands were so thickly callused I hardly felt the grip and the heat was only a faint underscore to the brightness of the gold. Sunlight ran down the blade like light against a mirror. I smiled.

We paced to the center of the circle. I put Singlestroke in the precise center and measured her blade with my eye as she set her sword down. It was a big blade for a woman, but it was no match for Singlestroke. Not many swords are.

"Luck, bascha," I said.

"I make my own." She turned her back on me and marched to the edge of the circle. I saw her mouth move and realized she had begun her song.

She had not used it inside. Perhaps she had thought her opponents unworthy of the honor, for honor it was. Even the sword-dancer she had bested had not elicited a song from her. I frowned at her, trying to sort out her motivations, and then I shrugged and scuffed through the sand to my own portion of the circle. The two blades, side by side, glowed in the sunlight.

I felt the familiar tautening of my muscles and the knot of tension forming in my belly. Almost instantly it loosened, dispelling the familiar sensation of anticipation. I was cool and calm, untouched by the heat or the moment; I waited, and so did she.

I heard her song. It was sung very softly, privately, and yet it carried to my side of the circle. She meant me to hear it. I couldn't understand it—it was sung in her Northern dialect—but I understood its fundamental meaning. It wasn't a deathsong but a lifesong, a salute to her opponent, a commendation of the skill yet to be displayed and a celebration of the dance. Whatever else she was, she was professional after all.

I smiled. "Winner take all—" And we were running.

I am big but I am quick. I reached Singlestroke first. I snatched the sword out of the sand, letting the hot grains slide away as I settled my hands, and made the first move. But she caught me by surprise.

I knew she had less energy than I; she had spent some of it in three previous dances. But she threw herself down into the sand, rolling, grasping and coming up in a single fluid movement. From underneath her blade slashed upward, grating against Singlestroke as I brought my sword down. I saw the sinews tighten in her forearms clear to her shoulders; she held the posture long enough to break my momentum, then twisted and danced away. I was caught flat-footed in the sand, untouched but definitely lacking her finesse.

I scowled across the circle at her. The dance would take longer than I thought.

She didn't laugh. She circled and watched, coolly professional with no more come-hither effects. She balanced on the balls of her feet, always moving; her shining hair was shoved behind her ears and hung past her breasts as she bent forward in a subtle crouch. She had stopped singing, but she didn't need to anymore. The purpose had been served.

Our blades met again, shrieking in contrapuntal song. I nicked her forearm twice, then felt a stinging across two knuckles. That she had slipped past me at all, even for that much, was miracle in itself.

I was barely aware of the audience. A hum of voices surrounded us, forming a second circle. I heard shouts and comments and laughter, and the clink of coin as more bets were laid.

The girl smiled. "Dance with me, Tiger."

We danced. The sand flew and the swords flashed and the sweat ran down our flesh. I blinked stinging salt out of my eyes and felt the dry pain lodged in my throat. Again and again Singlestroke flashed out to parry or strike down her blade; again and again she came back with her own counter-moves. Where I was tall and strong, she was supple and quick; where my reach was longer, hers was more subtle; where my skill was more obvious, hers was unexpected. And it was all to her advantage.

Finally, having grown tired of the inequities of such a dance, I decided to end it. She was good. She was much better than I expected. But she was the woman and I the man.

And the Sandtiger never loses.

I grinned at her, though it was a rictus of exertion. "Good dance," I said. "But tonight I desire a different sort of battle. . . ."

"In bed?" she scoffed. "First you have to win."

And I did. Of course. I leaned on her a little, let Singlestroke taste a little more of her pale flesh, and knocked the sword from her hands. I stepped on it before she could lunge to grab it up. "Enough," I said charitably. "The dance is won."

Cheers and applause broke out. Backs were slapped, coin was exchanged and drinks were offered by the management. But I didn't go in at once. I watched as she faced me, filmed with sweat, empty-handed and proud, and saw her force a smile.

"You are indeed the Sandtiger."

I tapped the string of curving black claws hanging around my neck. "Did you doubt these?"

"No. Nor those marks on your face." She sighed and pushed an arm across her forehead, shoving damp hair away from her eyes. "But I hoped I might win."

"The first time I lose will be the last," I told her. "Did you want to kill me so badly?"

"I *have* killed," she said defensively.

"That isn't what I asked."

She grimaced. "No. I didn't want to kill you. I just wanted to beat you."

"Because I'm a man. . . ."

The pale brows lanced down. She stared at me in genuine puzzlement. "No . . . because I wanted to *win.*"

I bent and picked up her sword. The audience, for the most part, was heading for the cantina, but a few well-wishers remained behind. As I handed back her sword I smiled my sandtiger's smile. "We'll dance again, bascha . . . tonight in bed. This time maybe I'll let you win."

"*Let* me!" she flared. Anger leaped into her eyes. "What I do, *I do!* No one *lets me!*"

The well-wishers laughed. It shut her up immediately, as if she had no desire to be thought a poor loser, or worse: a frustrated woman. But I saw the scarlet flags high in her cheeks as she turned to walk into the cantina.

I put out a hand and caught her shoulder. "For what it's worth, you danced well."

"For a woman?"

"For anyone." My fingers squeezed lightly as I saw the interested onlookers. "Come inside and I'll buy you a drink."

"With my gold?" She smiled crookedly. "Well, I did lose it. Fairly. And I always pay my debts." I felt her sidelong appraisal. "Maybe it won't be so bad."

I smiled. "I'm the Sandtiger, remember?"

She laughed. "So you are."

We retired inside the cantina and spent the rest of the afternoon swilling aqivi.

She drinks as well as she dances.

In the soft, small hours when even the rats were quiet, I felt the warmth of her breath against my ear. I opened one eye, then both. "What is it?"

"How much?" she asked. "How much was in the pouch?"

I grinned. "You mean, how much did you lose?"

"That is only one way of putting it."

I shifted over onto my back and thrust an arm beneath the pillow. The other arm slid down to cradle her head against my shoulder. The smooth, lean length of her was warm against my body. "Enough to last us a month, at least. If we are not terribly vulgar about spending our wealth."

"I am never vulgar."

"I thought you might be this afternoon, when I nicked you on the arm."

She harrumphed. "You would have deserved it, cutting me that way. Why did you do it?"

"You were careless. You'd already let that sword-dancer draw blood. I just wanted to wake you up."

"Was it worth it to see me bleed?"

I set my mouth against the mass of her hair. "I wanted to slit him open from guts to gullet, Del. But you took care of him for me."

She sighed. "Tiger . . . we can't do this forever."

"No. They'll catch onto it soon enough, and we'll have to come up with another scam."

She was silent a moment. The room was dark and I could hardly see her, but her hair was a dim glow against the shadows. Then she sighed. "I did not become a sword-dancer to trick stupid men out of their coin."

"Neither did I, Del. But for now, until we find an employer, it's all we've got."

"I know that." She moved closer. "I think I'm just tired of having to lose."

I grinned. "*You* know these Southron males would never bet as much coin if they thought a woman might win. That isn't part of the game."

Silence was her eloquent protest.

I rolled onto my side and leaned over her. "Besides," I said drily, "you and I both know you can cut the legs out from under me in the circle. I wouldn't stand a chance if you *really* decided to dance."

She smiled. And then she laughed. Just once, but it was enough.

What else can you say to the truth?

FIREWEB

Deborah Wheeler

Although the heroine of this story seems to have
committed herself to the sword—in the end her
commitment is to life, not death, and healing, not
war.

Deborah Wheeler's first sale was to the first of
these anthologies; her story "Imperatrix" betrayed the
author's interest in martial arts and animals. Deborah
Wheeler is a black belt in, I believe, kung fu (if I am
mistaken I know Deborah will forgive me; to me one
martial art is indistinguishable from the next, and the
only physical art in which I have any skill is ballet)
but the other skill which Deborah shares with the heroine
of her story, healing, is also a serious preoccupation;
Deborah is actually a licensed chiropractor and like
many who study that discipline, has a healer's skill in
her hands to which the muscles and backs of the whole
community can attest.

She has a young daughter, Sarah, and also a cat.
(Doesn't everybody?)

—MZB

The selith came down hard, three-pronged hooves battering the dusty road. He bounced stiff-legged, recovered, and then arched his neck for another wrenching buck. The modified scales along his crest struck Orlly across the face, and she lost her temper.

"Of all the stupid, hell-stinking conniptions to pull! Get your head up where it belongs, or I swear I'll make you wish you'd never seen the ground!" Screaming at the top of her lungs, Orlly hauled on the reins, using all her strength to jerk the selith's head around. Rebellious, the animal bared his teeth and dipped his head in unmistakable threat.

"Don't even think of it!" she shouted, booting the selith's tender nose with an aggressive foot. He squealed in pain and staggered, giving her the chance to pin his bony head to one shoulder.

Orlly's arms ached with strain as the selith halted, sides heaving in great trembling gulps of air. She loosened her grip on the near rein, allowing the animal to stretch his head skyward in a gesture of surrender. Then she directed her gaze to the cause of the crisis. A young woman her own age stood not two paces beyond the selith's bucking orbit, waiting quietly in her leather and knotted silk armor.

Orlly's anger surged another time. "You stupid blockhead! Don't you know any better than to run right up to a selith? Now I'll have to settle him again, and he was just barely fit to rent as it was. That's two days' hire you've cost me, plus whatever business I've lost after that little show. If you can get your worthless legs to carry you, take yourself from my sight before I get really angry."

The young swordswoman's mouth twisted a little, but she kept her hands quietly at rest, well away from the hilt of her sword. "Let me make it up to you. You seem competent enough, and I want to hire a guide and mounts. I'll pay you for the two days' rest as well as a trip across the Pass."

"Done!" cried Orlly. She kicked her feet free from the carved wood stirrups and jumped down.

"Where exactly are you bound? I'll need to know how many are in your party, any beasts you may already have, and your level of conditioning—"

"I suggest we begin with names. I'm Valeria Langua dy Ostrander," the swordswoman said with a friendly smile.

Orlly ducked her head, resenting not for the first time her single, ordinary name. "Orlly" was honorable enough, being the name of her maternal grandmother, until her death the headwoman of the tiny farming village where Orlly had spent her childhood. She might have claimed the village as part of her name, had she left it by choice. Her face hardened reflexively, but she made an effort to keep her tongue civil. "Call me Orlly. Everyone does."

"That's sensible. Mine's such a mouthful, I shortened it to Val. Can you imagine someone trying to get in all those syllables in the middle of a swordfight?" She laughed lightly.

Orlly stared at her. *With a name like that, dripping of gentility and old family honor, she jokes about chopping it.* "Where are we off to?"

"Kasimire, through Breakheart Pass."

"I *know* where it is," Orlly snapped.

Val's pale violet eyes flicked across Orlly's face, but her friendly tone did not change. "There's me and two guards, we'll have our own kits and clothing . . . and an elthim." Orlly drew a quick, astonished breath, but the swordswoman went on conversationally, taking her arm and steering her toward the nearest ale-house. "She's old, in her fourth cycle; her speed may be our limiting factor. I don't know how fast laden selithi can travel, but it's vital we not overtire her."

Orlly gulped as Val urged her to sit down and called for ale. She had never seen an elthim, but in her childhood village they had been legendary, the tattered fragments of a once powerful, magical race.

Val took two tankards, paid for them, and shoved one in front of Orlly. "How soon can we start?"

Orlly sipped her ale, a rare luxury for one who lived with

nothing but her wits and her selithi. "Depends on how quickly 'we' can make peace with 'our' mounts."

Val laughed, throwing back her head in uninhibited gusto. "And I thought you were only pretending to be angry at me to ask a higher price! You mean that display of riding wasn't an advertisement for my benefit?"

Orlly shrugged. With ordinary handling, he would not be fit to hire, but she could use her special gentling techniques and then ride him herself. "He could carry me. I wouldn't trust him with a stranger. But I have only the three selithi for four riders. I'll have to buy another."

Val handed her a small, promisingly heavy purse. "Buy what you need. You can give me a reckoning tomorrow when we set out."

"What's to keep me from taking this and never showing up?"

Val downed the last of her drink and stood, her body moving in strong, graceful gestures. "You'd miss the rest of where that comes from. I'll see you at dawn at the northern gates." She sauntered out of the inn, leaving Orlly to enjoy the rest of her ale in puzzlement.

Orlly pulled tight the last strap on the new selith's hackamore in the dawning light. Val's generous purse had bought a strong young female, plus extra blankets and good food; she had even managed to justify the purchase of a new double-lined riding cape. The other selithi, Sa, So, and Sy, stood quietly, heads together. So, the fractious male Val had startled into rebellion, kept one ear swiveled hopefully in Orlly's direction. She had spent hours the night before, stroking him, finally smoothing his restive spirits into contentment.

Orlly saw the elthim first, tall and silvered in the strengthening light, arms and torso concealed beneath a flowing, intricately embroidered robe. Her four clawed paws moved with deliberate, almost delicate grace, her beautiful but inhuman face sculpted into permanent lines of serenity. Val trotted at her side, talking animatedly, while two men guards brought up the rear. Orlly stepped away from Sey, the new selith, and assumed a characteristic posture, hands on hips with elbows thrust out aggressively.

Val touched the elthim's side, reaching up with an ease of familiarity and affection. "Elth'ua'lth, this is Orlly, who will be our guide. Orlly, this is H'ma Elth'ua'lth, and Taggart, and Dev." Taggart blurred in Orlly's sight as young and dark; Dev was middle-aged and looked competent in a grim sort of way. She took in their faces from the corners of her vision as she stared at the stately elthim.

The beautiful, mobile mouth opened. "You are welcome to my presence, my child," spoke a melodious, three-toned voice. "Am I to yours?"

"Y-yes," stammered Orlly, furious at her own awkwardness. The elthim, with her serenity and kind words, reminded her too much of the healer Ama, who had sheltered and taught her.

Orlly said, "Each selith bears food for five days; that's twice as long as the trip usually takes. We can night-over at the travelers' shelters, so we can sleep out of the wind. Let's get going."

Orlly had managed to recover her emotional balance by the time she had the three humans mounted and had swung herself on So's back. She could feel the results of her work in the steadiness of his gait as he stepped out at the head of the line. Next came Taggart on the gentle Sa, then the elthim, striding along with her curious gliding pace. After her came Val on grizzled Sy and the veteran Dev on Sey.

They rode easily through the wildflower-dotted foothills, the well-marked trail gradually thinning to a ribbon of itself. Orlly left the head of the train to let So stretch his legs and to check on the others. Taggart would have saddlesores before the end of the day, but he had the sense to leave Sa's head alone, and the selith bobbed along contentedly, happy to be out of the stench and bustle of the town.

The elthim paced steadily along the steepening trails. She had shed her intricate cloak and packed it in the bags strapped to her slanting back. Orlly had heard legends that once elthim lived side by side with humankind, scarce even then, but each one using her magical powers to secure the safety and peacefulness of her territory. *If only her village had had a resident elthim,* she thought in a burst of private grief; but their ways had faded long before her birth.

Orlly touched So into action beside Val's Sy. "We'll stop for midday meal soon. There's a flat place not too far ahead, although no water."

Val's face looked taut and set as she glanced around her, scanning the sculpted peaks. "Don't the selithi need to drink?"

"Not now. There's a spring farther up, and they'll drink a day's worth there. After that, we'll go more slowly, but we should reach the shelter by dark."

Orlly squinted up toward Breakheart Pass. From this angle, she could not see even the beginnings of the cleft through the tall Killian Mountains. She need not fear bandits with three armed fighters in her party, even if the elthim did not exude a mystical aura of protection. As yet, she was not in territory familiar enough to remind her. . . .

She blinked back tears, unable to tell if their source was anguish or outrage. The rest of the journey would be a constant battle to forget that on the far side of the crest of the pass lay a narrow, almost invisible thread of a trail, and at its very end, nestled in a valley of hidden green, her heart's unattainable desire. And she could never go back.

On the grassy flat, she jumped from So's back and began unpacking food. "Leave the reins tied around their necks so they can browse," she told the others. "They'll stay close, and the green feed will do them good."

The three warriors sat in a little circle around the elthim, who seated herself gracefully with her clawed feet drawn up under her body. The men relaxed, chatting as they broke open their packets, but Val squashed together some waybread and cheese, and ate while she paced the green borders of the flat.

Orlly was too awed by the elthim to feel very comfortable in her presence and had no wish to socialize with the soldiers. The selithi welcomed her to their midst, rubbing their bony heads against her thighs.

So came alert first, ears cupped toward the upward trail. Sey, the new female, whickered as her head spun around. Orlly reached a hand to calm her, but as soon as she touched the animal, she knew something was wrong.

The next sound was Val's hoarse shout, and then the calm flat erupted in black fighting bodies. Dark-sheathed riders galloped down the trail, mounted on heavy lowland solethi. The omnivorous cousins of the selithi bared ivory fangs and screamed angry, mindless cries as their riders spurred them on.

Val had drawn her sword, running to encounter the first rider before he could reach the rising elthim. In a lightning arc, she slashed through the reins. The overweighted soleth staggered, fighting for balance. Val glided to one side, avoiding the dark beast's massive shoulder, and dispatched its rider with a sharp upward stab. His whip dropped from his hands; the soleth scrambled over his body as he fell.

Taggart and Dev had each taken a defensive position around the elthim. The three remaining riders reined their mounts into a savage circle. Orlly shrank against So's quivering flank, her childhood nightmares vivid before her eyes.

It took her a moment to realize that she was cut off from the protection of the guards, an easy target. One of the dark riders shouted and wheeled his muscular soleth in her direction, brandishing his whip. Orlly looked up to see the rider's masked face for a terrible instant before the whip lashed around Sa's off hind leg.

Sa cried out in fear and pain as the rider jerked on the whip handle, wedging it against the high pommel of his saddle. Orlly heard a sickening snap, and Sa fell heavily to the ground, her cries escalating to pure agony. The pungent smell of the selith's blood stained the air as it seeped from her fractured leg.

Fury, molten and blinding, surged through Orlly, drowning all fear. *They were not after her, they were attacking the selithi! What kind of monster would stoop to unprovoked attack on the inoffensive animals?*

Orlly heard Val's piercing shout, then a thud, and the rider slowly crumbled from his prancing soleth, whip slipping to the grass from lifeless fingers. The hilt of a long throwing knife protruded from his back. The two remaining riders wheeled their mounts and fled, followed by the riderless solethi.

In the sudden stillness, Sa's anguished cries shot through Orlly's heart like a charring blast. She did not see Val and the others stooping over the fallen riders as she knelt at Sa's side. The raiders had bought their own deaths; her animals, innocent of all malice, were another matter.

Sa lay on her side, the splintered ends of her leg bones protruding from the mangled flesh. Her cries had subsided to a croon of mindless agony, her eyes glazing as if already dead. Orlly drew a sobbing breath and felt the sting of tears as she reached out a hand to soothe the suffering animal.

She took Sa's angular head in both hands, and brought her around to stare directly into her eyes. "Peace, peace, my beauty, my love," she whispered. "It will all be over soon."

Sa's eyes darkened, clearing, and she grew quieter. Orlly felt her own throbbing grief calm under the certainty of what she must do. She slipped her knife from its sheath in her boot and pierced the selith's carotid artery. Sa quivered but did not struggle. Orlly held her as the blood flowed downslope to pool beneath a large rock. Finally Sa gave a relaxed sigh and closed her midnight-colored eyes.

Orlly laid Sa's head down as So's anxious whicker reached

her. She went to him and led the three remaining selithi away from the pool of blood. Val looked up from where she knelt beside Taggart. The cloth of his sword arm shone red as the young swordswoman slit the fabric and gently drew the strips back from the wound. Orlly felt her throat convulse as she met Val's eyes. She could not speak.

Elth'ua'lth said, "They will not come again."

"No," Val agreed. "He'll send worse. We've no time to spare now." She finished tying the makeshift bandage around Taggart's arm. "We'll have to leave them as they lie." She nodded toward the two inert bodies.

"They were human, however misled. Should we leave their bodies, the temples of their spirits, to the scavengers?" asked the elthim, her face still reflecting unearthly calm.

"They were Bakkar's henchmen, sent to delay or destroy us!" Val cried. "If we stay to bury them decently, we give him time to summon what we cannot face. We might as well turn around and go back now."

The elthim moved to her side, resting one small, graceful hand on the swordswoman's shoulder. "In our pursuit of the greater good, we must not lose sight of the particular." She raised her head toward the cascading peaks. "Yet I think your words carry wisdom, my child. Since secrecy will no longer serve us, speed must."

Val helped Taggart to his feet, and stepped toward Orlly. "We've got to move on fast. I'm sorry about your selith, but on the whole we came off lightly. It's too bad we couldn't have caught one of their beasts to use instead."

"You knew about the attack," Orlly whispered. "You knew there was that kind of danger, and you led me right into it without telling me. How dare you risk my selithi like that?"

Val's face clouded as she took Sy's reins and led him to Taggart, helping the injured man to mount. "No, I didn't know, not precisely. Besides, that's part of the dangers of the trail, isn't it? Surely even you must have realized that an armed guard must be armed *against* something." She strode over to Sa's body and, with a grim, set face, began dividing the food parcels and tying them on the three remaining selithi.

Orlly turned her face to the elthim. "With your magic you could have stopped the attack—you could have saved Sa." She added, with wrenching bitterness, "Aren't we good enough for you to care about?"

"All life is sacred, daughter of the mountain. The loss of your beast diminishes me as much as you. What would you have had me do?"

"Blast them into nothingness, shrivel them in their saddles before they could draw their whips, I don't know. All the tales tell of your marvels. You're supposed to be so powerful, so magical, so wise. You tell me what's to be done."

"Oh, my dear." The elthim laid one shapely hand on Orlly's shoulder, looking down with eyes soft and gray. "There have been such stories told of us, and you have unwisely put your trust in them. The powers I have are not the sort which could blast an assassin from his saddle, even if it were lawful to do so. I am not magical, at least not in the sense you mean."

"Then you could not have protected Sa . . ."

"I might have eased her passage, but you yourself had the love to do it better. Your parting gift to her was closer to magic than you know. It was of the spirit, of the heart, which is where true enchantment dwells."

Orlly moved away from the light touch. Despite all the stories she had heard of their legendary abilities, the elthim had been powerless to act. Just as the people of her village had been powerless against the army which had marched across it, slaughtering mindlessly.

She thought for a moment of gathering her remaining selithi and heading back down the mountain trail to safety. The elthim, Val, and the others could fend for themselves. Their future was none of her concern; they could bring her nothing but sorrow. Yet honor stopped her; she was pledged to their care from the moment she had touched Val's purse at the inn. Her best course would be to get them all through the Pass as soon as possible.

The elthim still fixed her with that deep gaze, moonlight dancing behind her silvery eyes. Orlly muttered, "What's the use of magic then?" Before the elthim could reply, she turned back to Val. "I agreed to guide you, not fight off brigands. If I am to risk my selithi, as well as my neck, to earn my fee, I'm entitled to know what to expect. And why."

Val touched her shoulder gently. "This attack means we've been found out, and we have no time to spare. Come, I'll walk beside you. Fall in behind us, Taggart," she called, "and then Elth'ua'lth. Dev, guard our rear."

"Right." He reined Sey into line behind them.

"I should have warned you earlier," Val admitted, "but I had hoped my fears were groundless. It's my business, not yours, to plan Elth'ua'lth's defense."

"Who would want to attack an elthim? Even if they aren't magical?"

"They are, but not in the sense you meant, not in being able to instantly vanquish a human enemy. Long ago, my people used to listen to their wisdom. Elth'ua'lth's line-of-descent was pledged to the service of Kasimire generations ago, when it was still a village. The elthim arbitrated, judged, ensured peace with neighboring settlements. Then the world changed, the towns grew, and the elthim faded into their far retreats over the years. Men learned to fight."

"That's nothing new," Orlly commented grimly.

Val went on, her voice still even and measured, her breath in easy rhythm with her stride. "There's a dispute now over the rightful heir to the Kasimirsh crown. The usual tangle of collateral branches and power bids; it's such a mess I don't think it's even possible to tell whose claim is legitimate. But once Konray and Vistiane decide to fight it out, the whole country will fall into civil war. That must not happen," she said fiercely, balling her hands into hard fists.

"You're not much of a peace-keeping force," Orlly said tartly.

"I bring Elth'ua'lth in response to the Regent's summons. If Konray and Vistiane agree to her arbitration, as I pray they will, countless lives will be saved. If one agrees, the other will be forced to, if only to appear devoted to the welfare of Kasimire. They both know that no matter who wins a war, the country will be devastated, and an easy prey for greedy neighbors."

"If yours is such a fine cause, what are you worried about? Who would want to sabotage such a noble mission?"

"Bakkar, Duc dy Lanola, and rumored to be a black magician. He tried to marry Vistiane a few years back, but she knew he was only after power in Kasimire, and laughed in his face. Now he can just wait until she and Konray thrash it out, and then destroy their exhausted armies. To do that he's got to make sure Elth'ua'lth never reaches Kasimire."

Orlly felt a sudden fury spark within her. Her village had been only one of many tiny obstacles in the way of an army bent on some such cause, caring only for its own purposes. She thrust the memory from her. "Since you came from Kasimire, you crossed the Killians yourself to find your precious elthim. Why did you need a guide at all? You could have bought your own selithi, or walked on your bare hands for all I care, without dragging me into your troubles."

Val's face clouded and she moved her right hand toward the hilt of her sword, but she drew in her breath and answered evenly, "I never intended you to fight our battles. That's what Taggart, Dev, and I are for. You're being paid well for your work, and I did need a guide. I didn't come over the Killians, I went around through Norroway and the Salten Lakes. I had to follow the retreat path of Elth'ua'lth's line-of-descent before I could find her."

Orlly lowered her eyes to the steepening path before her. It was hard to stay angry at one who admitted so casually to a legendary search. She bit her lip at the unfairness of her feelings and forced herself to say, "I can see why assassins are of no importance to you after the Norroway cannibals and sea-dragons."

Val laughed. "The people of Norroway may be strange to us, but they're not man-eaters, and I only saw one sea-dragon from very far off. It was small and quite shy, more frightened of us than we of it. Have you never traveled, and found that the tales which frightened you as a child were but fantasies to beguile the credulous?"

"I was told stories, the same as any other youngster," Orlly retorted. "Who knows if there are true monsters in the world? I only know that some of them wear a human form."

"Yes, there are those to whom laws exist only to be broken. I think there will always be a need for a good sword in a steady hand to keep the peace."

"What could you possibly care for peace? You who march to war as to a pleasure faire! You who brandish your sword and throw knives into men's backs as if they were so much target practice! You—"

"But I'm not like Bakkar's raiders. I'm trying to *stop* a war! I serve the cause of peace."

"Do you think Sa gave a fig for your cause? She was only an innocent beast, and yet she lies dead now because of your cause, dead like all the little villages trampled in the name of a *cause*. No animal would have done that—only humans!"

"Poor child, what could have happened to leave you so bitter? Have you never known human kindness then? Never mind," seeing Orlly's face tighten, "I don't wish to pry into your secrets. The forces of chance have hardened us in different ways, but we are not so very different, you and I."

Orlly stared down at her with stark, flat eyes. "No," she said, "we are nothing alike." She touched So with her heels and felt his startled leap, loping ahead to scout the next stretch of trail.

* * *

Orlly signaled So to a halt where the trail whispered into a shadow along the barren heights. The high peaks seemed nearer now, drawing closer to her beneath their everlasting snow. She shook her feet free from the stirrups and slid to the ground.

"Damn her to hellsleet," she muttered, leaving So to browse for the few sprigs of hardy herbs between the rocks. "They can all go chop each other to bits! If only Sa hadn't been their first victim . . ." *If only she didn't have to remember.* The destruction of the village, viewed from afar by a frightened herd-child cowering amid her father's selithi was one thing, dimmed with time and distance. But the fresher, more piercing loss could not be pushed aside so easily. She had thought she had found her home, only to have it wrenched from her.

. . . She had stood at the gate, trying to stem the hot, angry tears. The mountains had curved around her gently, protectively, even in farewell.

"My dear child," Ama the healer had said.

She had turned to see the familiar lined face, the eyes wells of dark light, bright with compassion. The old woman's lips had moved across her face like a whisper. "You cannot stay."

"I have no place to go."

"You have everywhere to go. To stay is to learn healing, to touch the core of life with your soul and let that energy flow through you. But your heart is filled to the brim with anger. How can there be room for anything else? How can your gift escape your hatred?"

"I can't help what I feel. I had nothing left when you took me in, now this is my whole life. Besides, I'm good with animals. You said I had the touch for it."

"That I have never denied. You can heal a selith or a squirelle, but your heart is closed to your own kind. I cannot teach you."

"Tell me how to change. I'll do anything to stay." She

had kept her eyes fixed on the far peaks, glistening pure in the sun, afraid to look back lest her control snap and she fall to her knees in pleading tears. After a long silence she had realized she was alone . . .

They rode on through the rest of the day, stopping at the spring to let the selithi drink and to unpack warmer clothing. Orlly bundled herself in her new double-lined riding cape. The elthim donned her intricately embroidered cloak, and Val and the men covered their armor with warm, fitted jackets which permitted free movement. Val and Dev took turns walking to let the injured Taggart ride.

They reached the travelers' shelter well after dark. The ambush and forced slower pace had taken their toll of time, so that when they stumbled into the stone building, they were all chilled.

The shelter was divided into two large rooms, one strewn with the remnants of hay. Orlly helped Taggart to dismount and led the animals to the stable sheds. "Go on," she told Val, "get a fire going and warm up. I'll see to the selithi and join you later."

"Dev can do that. You're just as tired and in need of hot food as any of us."

"I'm fine," Orlly protested, forcing her cold-numbed fingers to manipulate the buckles of So's girth.

"Nonsense, the selithi carried all of us. You shouldn't have to care for them alone."

Orlly lowered So's saddle and turned to push the other woman aside. "I don't need your help," she said sharply.

Val looked at her, surprise and sudden understanding in her widening eyes. "No, I can see you don't." She turned on her heel to join the others.

Orlly, stung by the bleak tone of Val's voice, unsaddled the selithi and rubbed them down. Her back and shoulders ached with the effort of stroking their long, powerful muscles as they began to bubble their pleasure. They thrust their muzzles at her, fodder trailing from their flat, heavy jaws, pleading for more, filling her with secret joy. Even the newcomer, Sey, rubbed against her arm. She smiled and murmured in the young female's ear, then went to attend to the demands of her own body.

Whoever had built the fire had made a competent, compact blaze, a cookpot hanging from the hook embedded in the rock fireplace. Dev, his fingers wrapped in a cloth, lifted the lid to stir the contents. "Done. Are you hungry, lass?" He looked up at her, his grizzled features reddened by the light of the flames.

Without waiting for her reply, he took up one of the light trail dishes, filled it with jerky-laced porridge, and handed it to her. Orlly took it and sat by herself in a corner, cupping her fingers around the warmth. She watched Val tending Taggart's wound, talking with the elthim, and her heart pulsed unevenly within her. She longed for the familiar comfort of the selithi. The young guard winced as Val snapped tight the ends of the bandage. Reluctantly, Orlly put down her meal and went over to him.

"No, not like that," she said curtly, telling herself that her only motive was that she despised incompetence.

"Look," Orlly said, smoothing and easing the fabric with her fingertips, "it's no good if you cut off the circulation and let gangrene set in." The knots beneath her touch felt wrong, so she unwrapped the whole bandage, peering at the deep slash. Even in the faltering light of the fire, she could see the edges of the long, deep wound gape and dark blood seep out. She pursed her lips.

"That bleeding will continue draining his strength until I close the gap." She held Taggart's elbow and moved his arm backward and forward, watching the skin strain on the slash. She shook her head. "No, there's no position that doesn't open it further," she said, gently swabbing the blood. "I'll have to stitch it closed."

"With what?" Val asked, clearly fighting to keep the sharpness in her voice under control.

"I've a sewing kit with silk thread. We'll have to boil it, but I've sutured selithi wounds with silk and it works fine."

Orlly went back to her corner while Val sterilized the short metal needles and lengths of silk thread. She had not worked at healing a fellow human since her time of refuge and study with Ama. She did not want to remember what once had been hers and was now no longer. Yet here it was, thrusting itself back into her life like a corpse that would not stay decently buried.

She laid out her materials and bathed the wound with boiled water. Val held a torch close by at her shoulder.

"That feels good," Taggart told her. With his tousled dark hair and his face shadowed in the uneven red light, he looked very young. "Will it hurt much?"

Orlly smiled. "You needn't be afraid. Close your eyes, feel my touch here," between his eyes, fingertip like a tiny sun of warmth and life, "here," at the base of his throat, "here," on the inside of his elbow on the injured side, "here . . ."

She found her voice settling smoothly into the cadence and inflection she used with the selithi. The lines of pain and tension in his face softened. Stroking the skin above the wound gently, she began to hum and watch his response, a deepening of the breath. She picked up the threaded needle, turning so that her hand would cast no shadow across the wound, and thrust the point through the gaping flap of skin. The boy did not flinch, but continued breathing softly and evenly.

Quickly she sutured the slash, matching the wound edges as closely as she could in the uncertain light. Her hum rolled on, wending its own way through her movements. After she tied the last knot, she bathed the wound again and bandaged it lightly. "Let him sleep," she told Val. "He needs rest more than anything else, as do we all."

While the swordswoman tucked blankets around the young guard and made ready her own bed, Orlly washed and dried her needles and repacked her supplies. Without looking up, she knew that the elthim watched her through serene, alien eyes. She grabbed her bedroll and rose to carry it into the other room, preferring the comfort of her selithi.

The elthim stood before her, faintly luminous despite the near darkness. The fire had descended into ash and embers. "You have a rare gift, child."

Orlly shrugged. "A lot of good it does me," she muttered. *Not enough to save gentle Sa, only to sew up some young idiot so he can go out and get slashed up all over again.* "I did little enough, just patch up a cut so we can move on tomorrow."

"You know that you did far more than 'patch up a cut.' Why do you hide behind old anger?"

Orlly gasped, snapped that it was none of her business, that her gift for healing was no one's business except Ama's, who had thrust her out like a cull from the herd. The pain of that parting still wrung her heart. The elthim stood firm, quiet in her steady radiance. Orlly swallowed her words and pushed by her, breaking into a run to reach the selithi.

She awoke cold and stiff, with old Sy nuzzling her anxiously. Orlly forced her lids open to see his dark eyes, almost black with age. She stroked his chin and pulled herself upright. Something was clearly bothering him. She pulled her cape around her shoulders and stumbled over to the makeshift chamber pot.

In the other room, Elth'ua'lth stood at the door, holding it open a crack and staring into the swirling whiteness outside. Val, looking pale and tired, knelt by the fireplace, fumbling with her flintstone and tinder.

Orlly went to the door and peered outside, shuddering as a sudden blast of icy air met her cheeks. She could see only a few feet through the howling snow. "Blizzard," she commented, shivering. "Well, we can't travel in that. I don't understand it, there's never snowfall this low at this season."

"Yonder is no ordinary weather," the elthim said. "Valeria, come here and see this."

Val put another stick of kindling on the growing fire and stood up, wiping her hands on the front of her trousers. "I've never seen a storm like that."

"It is a fimbul-winter," Elth'ua'lth told her, "a storm of magic sent to bind us here." She turned to the young swordswoman and shut the door firmly. "I cannot guess what might be sent to take us while we bide the storm, but we must not be here when it arrives. Let us eat and dress as warmly as we can, for we must force our way through it or suffer worse."

"You're crazy!" Orlly exclaimed. "Even if my selithi could travel through that, we can't! I can't see three paces in front of my nose in that snow. We'd tumble down a mountain, or lose our way, or get drifted in before midday and freeze to death. Our only chance is to wait it out here."

"That is just what whoever sent the storm wishes us to do. I must confess I am not overeager to plunge into it myself," the elthim said gently. "I know very well it may mean my death. But to stay here in the tempting comfort of the shelter will be the end for all of us, even your beasts. Will you take my sworn word? Or would you have me describe the horrors that might come while we are pinned down here?"

The silvery eyes blazed with light, the musical voice raw with truth. Orlly felt it resonate in her bones, felt the stir of the same tremulous certainty as when Ama had spoken. She nodded and said grudgingly, "If we must, we must. I'll do my best to get us all through. But I still think that going out in that blizzard is daft."

They filled their bellies with hot porridge and fruit-meal, then used their bedrolls to fashion extra cloaks for themselves and blankets for the selithi. Orlly insisted that Val ride behind her on So.

"You'll only waste your strength fighting drifts," she argued. "So's the only one strong enough to carry double, and I can't watch you and the trail at the same time. I want to know you're safe, not sliding into some crevasse."

So snorted as he stepped out into the thick swirls of white. His skin shuddered as the first flakes touched him, and he extended the spiny crest of his neck in alarm. Orlly sent him in the general direction of the trail, relying more on memory than vision. He sniffed the fallen snow and pawed at it, prancing.

"Elth'ua'lth once said that animals can smell evil magic," Val commented.

Orlly nodded, for once content not to argue.

So swiveled his ears at the sound of her voice, moving slowly and carefully. The other selithi bunched closely around the elthim, as if trying to protect her from the wind with their solid bodies.

They inched forward with agonizing slowness. At each step the selith took, Orlly's heart pounded with fear that he would overstep the edge of the trail and carry her and Val to their deaths, or else plunge into a drift-filled hole and snap a leg. She was not sure she could survive another death such as Sa's; the cliff might be easier.

She found it better to close her eyes; she could barely see past an arm's length anyway, and any attempt at guidance would only undermine So's confidence in himself. She could feel him moving slowly but powerfully beneath her, the solid bulk of Val behind her. She imagined she could touch the selith's life-force like a steady, glowing sphere floating through thick honey. Behind her soared another, of a different hue: Sy bearing the injured Taggart. Then floated a shimmering silver disc spangled with jeweled facets of heart-searing beauty that must represent the elthim. Finally came the fiery orb of young Sey. Her inner vision shifted as she focussed on the balls of brilliant living light, Dev and Taggart and Val behind her. They drifted together in a gossamer web of golden and platinum strands.

So's whicker brought her up short from her dreamy vision. The trail stretched before her, visible even in the clearing snowstorm. He perked his ears happily and surged forward.

"I don't understand. We haven't been traveling that long. How could it just disappear?" Orlly asked in amazement.

"Longer than you know, child," came the elthim's sweet voice. "Whoever taught you, did well."

They began to climb in earnest now, leaving the last flakes of enchanted snow. Val offered to dismount, but Orlly, seeing her pale tired face, insisted that she ride, and walked at So's head herself.

They stopped for a midday meal in the partial shelter of a bleak stone face, a stark contrast to yesterday's nooning. Orlly nibbled at her meal as she checked the selithi, inspecting their feet and girths.

"Orlly, will you look at Taggart's arm?" Val asked. "It seems better to me, but I'm no healer." She had unwrapped the outer bandages to reveal the sutured cut, healing with only a trace of redness.

"What makes you think I'm one?"

Val opened her mouth in surprise, but did not reply.

Orlly gentled her voice. "What about the elthim? She's slogged it along with the selithi through worse than I'd care to walk through."

"I've been trying not to think about it," the swordswoman said in a small, uncertain voice. "She knows more about what we have to face than I do. If she says we dare not rest, I can't gainsay her."

"Let's be off, then. The hardest part of the Pass is still ahead. We must make it over before dark. It's too dangerous to travel without daylight, and there's no shelter on this side."

The selithi plodded on while Orlly and Dev took turns riding or scrambling over the rocks on foot. There were no more magical snowstorms or bands of assassins, only the barren loneliness of the heights. Orlly had often felt peace in the clean swept stillnesses above the tree-line, where the wind was the only other voice she heard. Now she sensed only emptiness, lifelessness, and the soaring fatigue that had given Breakheart Pass its name.

They passed the crest of the pass just as the sun began to dip toward the jagged horizon. With luck they would reach the next shelter at tree-line before total darkness.

Making excellent time downhill, they were within sight of the plain rock structure of the shelter as a full moon rose, flooding the last stretch of trail with light. Orlly suppressed a cry of relief.

"Hold!" came from the elthim, her voice now rough and uneven. Orlly whipped her head around to see her halt on unsteady, exhausted feet, her small hands raised in a warding gesture. "Gather behind me, all of you! Quickly!" Her voice deepened into imperative, undeniable tones.

Orlly found her legs obeying the elthim's command. Val slid her sword free and jumped from So's back, and Dev did the same, moving to her side. Instinctively Orlly reached one hand to touch So. *I'll die before I'll let them have another of mine*, she promised, thinking she meant only the selithi.

"Look!" Taggart, still astride Sy, pointed.

In the pool of moonlight before the shelter, the ghost of an orange ember flickered and then ignited to a ragged ball of flame, throwing out arms of coarse, condensing light. Val stepped forward, sword held at ready. She was trembling visibly.

"No, get back," Elth'ua'lth commanded. "Your blade is useless here, you would only throw your life away to feed that thing."

Val obeyed reluctantly. "What do we face, then?"

"Were-dragon. Stay here, all of you. You can do nothing.

If I fail . . .'' Her voice faltered for the first time. ''Die gladly if you must, do not give it your fears.''

She stepped forward as the violent orange mass elongated, its jagged projections spreading into writhing wings, a distorted body, a fang-armed head. Blackness leered from its eyes; Orlly could smell its dank breath from where she stood.

The elthim held fast, her four claw-footed legs spread slightly, glimmering as the moonlight touched her own radiance. The dragon-shape slithered hissing through the air and reared before the elthim, dwarfing her.

Elth'ua'lth spoke, her voice carrying calm in the night air, and the orange monster spun away as if struck, shrieking vile curses in its own unintelligible language. It touched the edge of the shelter in an explosion of stench and sparks. The stone began to smolder where contact had been made.

''I don't understand,'' Orlly whispered to Val. ''She said she had no magic to fight the assassins. How can she now do this?''

''No magic to slay any living creature,'' the young swordswoman answered. ''The were-dragon is not alive.''

''But deadly?'' She did not need to see the expression of tightly controlled fear on Val's face to know the answer.

Orlly turned and buried her face against So's muscled neck. The dragon's shrieking tumult degenerated into hoarse glottal bellows, drowning out Elth'ua'lth's light sweet voice.

Orlly could feel the elthim pulse of light falter, exhaustion gnawing at her sharp focus. The strands of evanescent light linking her to the silver disc began to dim. Behind her closed eyes, she saw the were-dragon looming like a black pit, its obscene maw reaching for the elthim's shining sphere. Orlly lashed out in fury and denial, surprised to see a flash of white flame speed toward the dark. The black mass halted, its edges rippling and curling inward. The sparkling globe grew brighter, recovering.

Orlly opened her eyes to see a filmy shape coalesce above the standing elthim. It stretched upwards, reflecting the pure clean light of the full moon, then solidified into a pair of extended wings radiating rainbow glory, a noble head, and outstretched arms holding two slender daggers.

The dragon-thing coiled in on itself, its empty eyes rolling in distress. It shook its tail and rattled its misshapen wings; then Orlly saw the blocky muscles of its haunch tense for a leap. It sprang into the air before she could even gasp in alarm, its coarse whistle deafening to her ears.

With lightning speed the moon-silver form rose to meet it, tipping the daggers inward, great wings fanning the air. Orlly caught a scent of sea-tang masking the dragon's stench for only an instant before the dagger points met its eyes. Then she fell to the rocky ground at Val's side, clutching her ears in a vain attempt to mask out the horrendous din of the wounded were-creature. Even through the agony which filled her skull, she felt So brush against her, trembling, felt Val's strong body contract as she fought for control . . . felt the elthim stagger under the massive weight of the magic which fueled the dragon.

She looked up, eyes watering in rebellion. Elth'ua'lth had fallen to her knees before the were-dragon, now a shapeless, writhing mass no larger than a newborn selith. It seemed to be struggling to reassert its form, vague gestures of wing or snout or tail emerging from the central lump, only to melt back at a gesture from the elthim. Elth'ua'lth had fought it to a standstill, but how long could she continue? How much strength did the were-dragon have left?

The racket had died down, all noise evaporated except for the soft whimpers of the selithi and whispered commands of the weakening elthim. Orlly could hear her own heartbeat rampaging through her skull.

Val, kneeling at her side, raised her head with a sob. Orlly saw her face convulse in despair as she reached for her sword.

"You fool, you can't go out there!" She grabbed the sleeve of Val's sword arm and pointed to the still-smouldering rock of the shelter where the were-dragon had touched it. "That thing'll only burn your sword, and then you. Idiot!"

"I don't care," Val sobbed, her voice filled with anguish. "I've got to do something. Bakkar may be burnt out if the dragon is, but if Elth'ua'lth dies, there will be war anyway. Whatever you may think of me, I can't let that happen. I can't let all those people die. Don't you understand? Don't you care about *anything*?"

Orlly met her pale violet eyes with a steady gaze. "Yes. But if you go out there, you won't be able to stop it, and you'll only waste your own life for nothing."

Val slid her sword back into its sheath, her shoulders shuddering with her silent weeping. Without thinking, Orlly flung an arm around her, closing her eyes in shared grief. *I can't let that happen . . . I can't let all those people die.*

She watched the jeweled orb dim, sinking perceptibly into the darkness. A memory leapt to her vision—the complex network of interconnecting strands she had seen during their struggle through the fimbul-storm. Now she could sense only a few dying threads, and she tried to imagine what they had looked like.

To her surprise, the threads pulsed brighter with a beat of life before subsiding. She reached out with her memories again, willing herself to see a growing web of iridescent fibers. More appeared, tenuous at first, then firming under her repeated mental insistence that they *did exist*. Rainbow hues, deepening to healer's green, spread outward from her focus, sliding along the glistening strand to reach the silvery disc. To one side she noticed a concentration of weaker colors, dancing like tiny stars from a triad of suns—the selithi were joining her. She caught at their unfocussed atoms of light, imagining them woven into a steady flow, and then saw what she had evoked.

Emboldened now, she reached into her memory for the luminous globes which were Val and the two men, spun their light into a veil of living color, and tossed it like a fishing net along the webwork to Elth'ua'lth's strengthening gem.

The elthim's sphere regained its silvery radiance, set in a fireweb of light. Before her the darkness receded, curling in on itself, shrank to a pinpoint, and vanished.

Exultation shot through Orlly as she opened her eyes. Val huddled in the shelter of her arm, no longer sobbing. In the clearing before the shelter, Elth'ua'lth still knelt before a blackened circle. Orlly pushed Val away and scrambled to her feet to run to the elthim.

She reached her just as Elth'ua'lth fell slowly to the bare earth, moving as if time itself were thickened. Orlly reached out to touch her side, now flat gray instead of her usual luminous silver. Beneath her fingers, the elthim's ribs moved tremulously, drawing in a shallow breath.

"No!" cried Val, racing to Orlly's side and flinging her arms around the elthim's narrow shoulders. "She can't be dead!"

"She isn't," Orlly said quietly. "She's still breathing."

"She isn't wounded, I don't see any blood," Val babbled, her words spilling over each other, barely coherent.

"I don't think it's that sort of wound." Orlly trembled as sudden fatigue seized her. She sank down, reaching out with both hands to keep from falling. "I don't know what's wrong with her." She steadied herself, closing her eyes once more for an inner vision. Nothing met her eyes but flat darkness and hot tears.

"Hellsleet," she whimpered, too exhausted to curse with imagination. "The first time I cared, and I couldn't do a damned thing. I couldn't save her."

"I wouldn't say that," said a stern, familiar voice.

With a wrenching effort, Orlly lifted her head. Ama stood on a little knoll above the shelter, her intricately carved staff in hand. She shook one gnarled finger at Orlly.

"You couldn't make that much psychic racket without my knowing. Come, child, wipe your tears. There's nothing wrong with you that a good night's sleep won't cure. I've waited years for you to be ready to continue your studies."

"But the elthim," Orlly gasped. "If she dies, there's war."

"And that makes a difference to you?" The healer raised one grizzled eyebrow.

"Damned clear it does. Do you think I want to be responsible for other little villages getting flattened as mine did?" she stormed. Then her words dried up. How could she describe the web of life linking her to the heart-searing glory that was the elthim's spirit? To her selithi, giving love in return, and to her comrades? Warmth instead of perennial ice filled her heart.

Ama smiled, her seamed face crinkling into a dance of kindly light. She turned to the fallen elthim and touched her lightly on the forehead. "Nothing but a little backshock from your over-enthusiasm. She'll recover in a few moments."

Val cried aloud in inarticulate joy as the elthim's eyelids twitched and opened. She reached out a small hand to the young swordswoman and got gracefully to her feet.

Elth'ua'lth looked down at her, and Orlly felt herself bathed in the silvery radiance behind her gray eyes. The elthim took her hand and kissed her gently on the brow. The touch seared her with cool, crystalline light, reaching to her very heart. Beyond the elthim, she could see Val's tear-streaked, jubilant face.

"Say good-bye to your friends, child. It's time to go home," said the healer. "They don't need you any longer. Let them use the other two selithi; that boy can't walk down the mountain on his own legs, but So will answer only to you and ought to come back with us."

To Elth'ua'lth she said, "The trail is broad and clear; you'll not need a guide now. Good fortune attend you."

Val flung her arms around a startled Orlly. "I don't know how you did it, but I thank you with all my heart. I promise, I'll care for your selithi as well as you would. When you've finished your training, come to Kasimire to get them and visit me."

"Where?" blurted Orlly, uncomprehending.

"To the Regent's palace; he's my father." She brushed her tears with the back of one sleeve, set her hand on sword hilt in a characteristic gesture, and marched towards the shelter. "Come on, a good night's rest and then we've got a war to stop."

Orlly turned to the healer beside her. "I don't understand. I'm going back with you?" Hope and new understanding dawned within her, washing away the bitter taste of old grief.

"Oh yes," said Ama. "You were much too clumsy with the life web. As you're a healer, you must be more skillful. I've a great deal to teach you now."

COLD BLOWS THE WIND

Charles de Lint

In every anthology there is a story that comes in late, and I know that, without knowing it, I have been holding a place for this story because the anthology would be incomplete without it. This year, that story was Charles de Lint's. One of the reviews of *Sword and Sorceress I* complained that the anthology was heavily weighted in favor of swordswomen against sorceresses; this story is almost—but not quite—an old-fashioned ghost story, but it somehow manages to be strong and positive. In general I do not like ghost stories in a sword-and-sorcery collection; but every editor knows that every rule goes out the window when you find a story good enough to make you forget your own guidelines.

I honestly think this one is.

—MZB

THE UNQUIET GRAVE (Folk ballad)

Cold blows the wind o'er my true love
And a few small drops of rain,
I never had but one true love,
And he in the grave is lain.

My lips they are as cold as clay,
My breath is earthy and strong,
If you should kiss my cold white lips
Your life would not be long.

Don't go by night, they said. But she did. Don't stray
from the road, they said. But she did. Don't follow
the fire; don't listen to its music. But she did. They
meant well, she knew, but they didn't understand. She sought
the blue-gold fire and the fey music of Jacky Lantern's
elusive kin. It was all she had left.

It was the night they camped by Tiercaern, where the heather-
backed Carawyn Hills flow down to the sea, that Angharad's
people met the witches. There were two of them—an old
winter of a man, with salt-white hair and skin as brown and
wrinkled as a tinker's hands, and a boy Angharad's age,
fifteen summers if he was a day, lean and whip-thin with
hair as black as a sloe. They both had the flicker of blue-gold
in the depths of their eyes—eyes that were old and young in
both of them, of all ages and of none. The tinkers had
brought their canvas-topped wagons around in a circle and
were preparing their supper when the pair approached the
edge of camp. They hailed the tinkers through a sudden
chorus of camp dogs and Angharad's father, Herend'n, went
out to meet them, for he was the leader of the company.

"Is there iron on you?" Herend'n called, by which he
meant, were they carrying weapons. The old man shook his
head and lifted his staff. It was of white wood, that staff, cut
from a rowan. Witches' wood.

"Not unless you count this," he said. "My name is

Woodfrost and this is Garrow, my grandson. We are travelers—like yourselves.''

Angharad, peering at the strangers from behind her father's back, saw the blue-gold light in their eyes and shook her head. They weren't like her people. They weren't like any tinkers *she* knew. Her father regarded the strangers steadily for a long heartbeat, then stepped aside and ushered them into the wagon circle.

''Be welcome,'' he said. When they were by his fire, he offered them the guest-cup with his own hands. Woodfrost took the tea and sipped. Seeing them up close, Angharad wondered why the housey-folk feared witches so. This pair was as bedraggled as a couple of cats caught out in a storm and, for all their witch-eyes, seemed no more frightening to her than might beggars in a market square. They were skinny and poor, with ragged travel-stained cloaks and unkempt hair. But then the old man's gaze touched hers and suddenly Angharad *was* afraid.

There was a distance in those witch-eyes like a night sky, rich with stars, or like a hawk floating high on the wind, watching, waiting to drop on its prey. They read something in her, pierced the scurry of her thoughts and the motley mix of what she was to find something lacking. She couldn't look away, was trapped like a riddle on a raven's tongue, until he finally dropped his gaze. Shivering, Angharad moved closer to her father.

''I thank you for your kindness,'' Woodfrost said as he handed the guest-cup back to Herend'n. ''The road can be hard for folk such as we—especially when there is no home waiting for us at road's end.'' Again his gaze touched Angharad. ''Is this your daughter?'' he added.

Herend'n nodded proudly and gave the old man her name. He was a widower and with the death of Angharad's mother many years ago much of his joy in life had died. But he still had Angharad and if he loved anything in this world, it was his colt-thin daughter with her brown eyes that were so big and the bird's nest tangle of her red hair.

"She has the *sight*," Woodfrost said.

"I know," Herend'n replied. "Her mother had it too— Ballan rest her soul."

Bewildered, Angharad looked from her father to the stranger. This was the first *she*'d heard of it.

"But, da'," she said, pulling at his sleeve. He turned at the tug to look at her. Something passed across his features the way the grass in a field trembles like a wave when the wind touches it. It was there one moment, gone the next. A sadness. A touch of pride. A momentary fear. "But, da'," she repeated.

"Don't be afraid," he said. "It's but a gift—like Kinny's skill with a fiddle, or the way Sheera can set a snare and talk to her ferrets."

"I'm not a witch!"

"It isn't such a terrible thing," Woodfrost said gently.

Angharad refused to meet his gaze. Instead, she looked at the boy. He smiled back shyly. Quickly Angharad looked away.

"I'm not," she said again, but now she wasn't so sure. She wasn't exactly sure what the *sight* was, but she could remember a time when she'd *seen* more in the world than those around her did. But she'd been so young then and it all went away when she grew up. Or she had made it go away. . . .

Angharad smiled as she left the road, remembering. The forest closed in around her, dark and rich with scent and sound. The wind spoke in the uppermost branches with a murmur that almost, but not quite, buried the vague sound of a fey and distant harping that came to her from deeper in the wood. Her witch-sight pierced the gloom, searching for the first trace of a will-o'-the-wisp's lantern, bobbing in among the trees.

*   *   *

As though the coming of the witches was a catalyst, Angharad
found that she *could see* what was hidden from others. There
was movement and sound abroad in the world that went
unseen and unheard by both tinkers and the housey-folk who
lived in the towns or worked the farms, and to *see* it, to *hear*
it, was not such a terrible thing.

Woodfrost and Garrow traveled with the company that
whole summer long and will she, nill she, Angharad learned
to use her gift. She retained her fear of Woodfrost—because
there was always that shadow, that darkness, that secrecy in
his eyes—but she made friends with Garrow. He was still shy
with the other tinkers, but he opened up to her. His secrets,
when they unfolded, were far distant from the sort she supposed his grandsire's to be. Garrow taught her the language
of the trees and the beasts, from the murmur of a drowsy old
oak to the quick chatter of squirrel and finch and the sly
tongue of the fox. Magpies became her confidants, and badgers,
and the wind. But at the same time she found herself becoming tongue-tied around Garrow and, if he paid particular
attention to her, or caught one of her long dreamy glances, a
flush would rise from the nape of her neck and her heart
began to beat quick and fast like a captured wren's.

The smile grew bittersweet as Angharad moved deeper into
the forest. It was on a night like this, between the last days of
Hafarl, the Summerlord's rule and the first cold days of autumn,
on a night when the housey-folk left their farms and towns to
build great bonfires on the hilltops and would sing and dance
to music that made the priests of the One God Dath frown,
that she and Garrow made a mystery of their own. They made
love with a gentle fierceness and, afterwards, lay dreamy and
content in each other's arms while the stars completed their
nightly wheel and spin above them. The tears that touched
Angharad's cheeks as she continued through the trees,
remembering, were not the same as those that night. *That*

night she'd been so full of emotion and magic that there was no other release for what she felt swelling inside her. Now she was only . . . remembering. . . .

The tinker company wintered in Mullyn that year, on a farm that belonged to Green George Snell who once traveled the roads with Angharad's people. There they prepared for the next year's traveling. Wagons were repaired, as were harnesses and riggings. Goods were made to be sold at the market towns and the horses were readied for the fairs. When the first breath of spring was in the air, the company took to the road once more. Angharad and Garrow still rode in Herend'n's wagon, though they had jumped the broom at midwinter. Newly married, they were still too poor to afford their own wagon.

The road took them up into Umbria and Kellmidden that summer where the company looked to meet with the caravans of other travelers and to grow rich—or at least as rich as any tinker could get, which was not a great deal by the standards of the housey-folk. They looked forward to a summer of traveling on the road, of gossiping, trading and renewing old acquaintances. Instead, they found the plague waiting for them.

The memory of that first devastated town was still too fresh in Angharad's mind. It cut deep into her heart. She stumbled in the forest, foot caught in a root, and leaned against the fat bole of a tree. The bark was rough against her skin and snagged at her hair as she moved her head slowly away from it. As though echoing her pain, the fey and distant harping faltered and grew still. She lifted her head, afraid of the sudden silence. Then faint, faint, the music started up once more and she went on, trying to keep the memories buried, but they rose, constant as air bubbles in a sulfur spring, the pain spreading through as pervasively as those noxious fumes.

*   *   *

The corpse had lain in the town square, black and swollen. Surprised, the tinkers' shocked gazes found more—in alleyways, in doorways—sprawled bodies, black from the plague. Too late, Herend'n realized their plight. The town had been silent, empty, but there had been no hint, no rumor of this. Too late, he turned the wagons. Too late.

Two nights later the first of the company took sick. In retrospect, Herend'n realized that one of the dogs must have spread the sickness. Angharad and the witches *saw* the plague spreading under the skin of Marenda's son Fearnol and Herend'n turned the wagons into their circle and they set up camp. Too late. By nightfall, half the company was stricken. In two weeks' time, for all the medicines that Angharad and the witches and the rootwives of the tinkers gathered and prepared and fed to the sick, the greater part of the company was dead. Nine wagons were in that circle and sixty-two tinkers had traveled in them. On the morning that the last of the dead were buried, only one wagon left the camp and only three of the company rode in it. They were thin and gaunt as half-starved ravens. Jend'n the Tall. Sheera's daughter, Benraida. And Crowen the Kettle-maker. There was a fourth survivor—Angharad. But she remained behind with her dead. Her father. Her husband. Her kin. Her friends.

She lived in her father's wagon and tended their graves the whole summer long. She cursed the *sight* that had made her *see* the black sickness speed and swell inside the bodies of the stricken, killing them cell by cell while she stood helplessly by. Garrow . . . her father. . . . She cursed what gods she knew of, from Ballan the Lord of Broom and Heather to Dath, the cold One God, and even Hafarl's daughter who had always seemed the most real to her. Gentle Tarasen, who kept safe the beasts of the wood and the birds of the air. Even she had failed Angharad in her time of need.

She stayed there until the summer drew to an end and then she remembered a tale once heard around the fires of a tinker camp, of marshes and Jacky Lantern's kin and how the dead could be called back in such a place if one's need were great enough, if one had the gift. . . . She took to the road the next morning with a small pack of provisions slung over one shoulder and Woodfrost's white staff in her hand. She went through a land empty and deserted, through villages and towns where the dead lay unburied. Past farms that were silent and as forsaken as broken dreams. She traveled through the wild north highlands of Umbria and when she crossed Kellmidden's borders it was to come to a land that the plague had never grasped in its diseased claws and she still did not understand why she had been spared when so many had died.

Hafarl's grip was loosing on the land as the autumn grew crisp across the dales and hills of Kellmidden's lowlands and the constellations that wheeled above her by night were those of Lithun, the Winter Lord. She stopped to sup in a last inn, ignoring the warnings of the well-meaning housey-folk that stayed warm by the fire when she went out into the night once more. She went empty-handed now, her provision bag depleted and the rowan staff no longer needed for she knew she was approaching the end of her journey. As she had eaten her supper in the inn, she'd *heard* the sweet fey music . . . calling to her, whispering, drawing her on, unattainable as fool's fire, but calling to her all the same. When she left the road and entered the dark forests, Garrow's features swam in her mind's eye, a familiar smile playing on his lips, keyed to the fey unearthly music that came to her from the depths of the forest, and she knew her journey was done.

Now the land sloped steadily downward in the direction of her travels. The forest of pine, birch and fir, gave way to gnarly cedar and stands of willow. Underfoot, the ground softened and her passage was marked by the soft sucking noise of her feet lifting from the marshy mud. A sliver of a horned moon was lowering in the west. Last quarter. A moon of omens. The muck rose to her ankles and the long days of her journeying and sorrow finally took their toll. Weary beyond belief, she collapsed on a small hillock that rose out of the marsh. The fey harping was no louder than it had ever been, but somehow it seemed closer now.

On arms trembling from fatigue, she lifted her upper body from the ground and rolled over to see the makers of that music all around. They were tall ghostly beings, thin as reeds and glowing with their own pale inner light. Their hair hung thin and feather soft about their long and narrow faces. The men carried lanterns filled with flickering light; the women played harps that were as slender as willow boughs with strings like spun moonlight. Their eyes gleamed blue-gold in the darkness.

"Strayed," the harping sang to her, a ghostly refrain. "Too far . . . too far. . . ."

She looked among their ranks for another slender form—a familiar form, with black hair and no harping skill—but saw only the ghostly harpers and lantern-bearers.

"Garrow?" she called, searching their faces.

The harping fluttered like a chorus of bird calls, grew still. Angharad's heartbeat stilled with it. She held her breath as one of the pale glowing shapes moved forward.

"You!" she hissed, her breath coming out in a sharp stream as she recognized the man's features. Her pulse drummed suddenly, loud in her ears.

Woodfrost nodded wearily. "You are still so stubborn," he said.

She glared at him. "What have you done with Garrow?" she demanded. "I didn't come for you, old man."

"As a child you could *see*," Woodfrost said as though he hadn't heard her, "but you saw soon enough that others couldn't and, rather than be different, you ignored the gift until you became as blind as they were. Ignored it so that, in time, all memory of it was gone."

"It was a curse not a gift. How can you call it a gift when it allows you to *see* those you love die, while you must stand helplessly by?"

"So many years you wasted," Woodfrost continued, still ignoring her. "So stubborn. And then we came to your camp, my grandson and I. Still you protested, until Garrow drew the veil from your eyes and taught you your gift once more—taught you what you had once known, but chose to forget. Was your gift so evil?"

Angharad wanted to stand but her body was too tired to obey her. She managed to sit up and hug her knees. "Garrow was alive then," she said.

Woodfrost nodded. "And then he died. Death is a tragedy—no mistake of that, Angharad—but only for the living. We who have died go on to . . . other things; as the living must go on with the responsibility of being alive. But not you. Oh, no. You are too stubborn for that. If those you love are dead, then you will go about as one dead yourself. It is a fair thing to revere those who have passed on—but only within reason, Angharad. Graves may be tended and memories called up, but the business of living must go on."

"I could call him back . . . in this place, I could call him back," Angharad said in a small voice.

"Only if I let you."

Anger flickered in Angharad's witchy eyes. "You have no right to come between us."

"Angharad," Woodfrost said softly. "Do you truly believe that I would stand between you and my grandson if he were alive? When you joined your futures together, there was none happier than I. But we no longer speak of you and Garrow; we speak now of the living and the dead, and yes, I must come between you then."

"Why is it so evil? We *loved* each other."

"It is not so much evil. . . . Let us leave the talk of evil and sins to the priests of Dath. Say rather that it is wrong, Angharad. You have a duty and responsibility while you live that does not include calling forth the shades of the dead. Death will come for you soon enough, for even the lives of witches are not so long as men would believe, and then you will be with Garrow in the land of shadows. Will you make a land of shadows in the world of the living?''

''Without him there is nothing.''

''There is everything.''

''If you weren't already dead,'' Angharad said dully, ''I would kill you.''

''Why? Because I speak the truth? You are a woman of the traveling people—not some village-bound housey-folk who looks to her husband for every approval.''

''It's not that. It's. . . .'' Her voice trailed off. She stared past him to where the will-o'-the-wisps stood pale and tall, silent harps held in glowing hands, witchy lanterns gleaming eerily. ''I could live ten years without him,'' she said softly, her gaze returning to the old man's. ''I could live forever without him, so long as I knew that he was still in the world. That all he was was not gone from it. That somewhere his voice was still heard, his face seen, his kindness known. Not dead. Not lying in a grave with the cold earth on him and the worms feeding on his body. If I could know that he was still . . . happy.''

''Angharad, he can be content—which is as close as the dead can come to what the living call 'happiness.' When he knows that you will go on with your life, that you will take up the reins of your witch's duties once more—then he will be at peace.''

''Oh, gods!'' Angharad cried. ''What duty? I have no duty, only loss.''

Woodfrost stepped toward her and lifted her to her feet. His touch was cold and eerie on her skin and she shrank back from him, but he did not let her go.

''While you live,'' he said, ''you have a duty to life. And Hafarl's gift—the gift of the Summerblood that gives you your *sight*—you have a duty to that as well. The fey wonders of the world only exist while there are those with the *sight* to *see* them, Angharad, otherwise they fade away.''

''I see only a world made grey with grief.''

"I have known grief as well," Woodfrost said. "I lost my wife. My daughter. Her husband. I, too, have lost loved ones, but that did not keep me from my duties to life and the gift. I travelled the roads and sought blind folk such as you were and did my best to make them *see* once more. Not for myself. But that the world might not lose its wonder. Its magic."

"But. . . ."

The old man stepped back from her. In his gaze she saw once more that weighing look that had come into his eyes on that first night she'd met him.

"If not for yourself," he said, "then do it for the others who are still blind to their gift. Is your grief so great that they must suffer for it as well?"

Angharad shrank back, more frightened by quiet sympathy in his eyes than if he'd been angry with her. "I . . . I'm just one person. . . ."

"So are all who live . . . and so are all who have the gift. The music of the Middle Kingdom is only a whisper now, Angharad. When it is forgotten, not even an echo of that music will remain. If you would leave such a world for those who are yet to be born, then call your husband back from the land of shadows and live together in some half-life—neither living nor dead—both of you.

"The choice is yours, Angharad."

She bowed her head, tears spilling down her cheeks. I'm not as strong as you, she wanted to tell him, but when she lifted her anguished gaze he was no longer there. She saw only the wraith-shapes of Jacky Lantern's kin, watching her. In their faces there were no answers, no judgements. Their blue-gold eyes returned her gaze without reply.

"Garrow," she said softly, all her love caught up in that one word, that one name. There was a motion in the air where Woodfrost had stood, a sense of some gate opening between this world and the next. Through her teary gaze she saw a familiar face taking shape, the hazy outline of a body underneath it. "Garrow," she said again, and the image grew firmer, more real. For a long strained moment she watched him forming there, drawing substance from the marsh, breaching the gulf between the land of shadows and the hillock where she stood, then she bowed her head once more.

"Good-bye," she said.

The grief swelled anew in her. He was lost now, lost forever, while she must go on. She could feel his presence vanish without the need to watch. Her throat was thick with emotion, her eyes blinded by tears. Then there was a touch on her cheek, like lips of wind brushing against the skin, here one moment like a feather, then gone. In the midst of her grief a strange warmth arose in her and she thought she heard a voice, distant, distant, whisper briefly, *I will wait for you, my love,* and then she was alone in the marsh with only the ghostly will-o'-the-wisps for company.

Through a sheen of tears, she watched one of the harpers approach her, the woman's pale shape more gossamer than ever. She laid her harp on Angharad's knee. Like Woodfrost's hands, it had substance and weight, surprising her. It was a small plain instrument—like a child's harp. She touched the smooth wood of its curving neck.

"I . . . I'm a witch," she said in a low soft voice, the bitterness in it directed only at herself. "I can't make music—I never could." But her fingers were drawn to the strings and she found they knew a melody, if she did not. It was a slow sad air that drew the sorrow from her and made of it a haunting music that eased the pain inside her. A faery gift, she thought. Was it supposed to make her grief more bearable?

"It must have a name," the wraith said, her voice eerie and echoing like the breath of a wind on a far hill.

A name? Angharad thought. She watched her fingers draw the music from the instrument's strings and wondered that wood and metal could make such a sound. A name? Her sadness was in the harp's music, loosened from the tight knots inside her and set free on the air.

"I will call it Garrow," she said, looking up. The ghostly company was gone, but she no longer felt alone.

The tinker company was camped by a stream with good pasture nearby when the red-haired young woman with her old eyes came to their wagons, a small harp slung from her shoulder. She called out to the tinkers in their own secret tongue and they welcomed her readily with a guest cup and a place by the fire. Sitting in the flickering firelight, she looked from face to face and smiled as her gaze rested on a lanky girl named Zia who was thirteen summers if she was a day. Zia blushed and looked away, but inside her she felt something stir that had been buried a year ago when she learned the ways of a woman and set aside her favorite doll with its cloth face and broom and heather body. The red-haired woman smiled again and began to play her harp.

SWORD OF THE MOTHER

Dana Kramer-Rolls

Most of the women who take part in the medievalist
Society for Creative Anachronism are content to behave
like medieval women and limit their participation to
embroidery, singing and dancing, writing poetry, and bak-
ing pies and confections for banquets. Although Dana,
known in the Society as Maythen of Elfhaven, does all
these things superbly well, from the beginning she chose
to join the small minority of women who went into the
fighting and fought in many tournaments against men
twice her size. She acquitted herself well, and was the
third woman to be knighted in the West Kingdom. She
chose to enter the lists in serious competition for the
crown—and to the dismay of many men (and women) in
the Society, actually won the tournament, overcoming
men in the fighting events and men *and* women in the
nonfighting ones. There was consternation in the ranks—
could a woman be Prince in her own right? This appeared to be a place where the best man for the job was
definitely a woman; she had won fairly by her skills.

Dana, mother of three children, looks very much like
her own heroine, a sturdy woman, graceful and strongly
muscled. She has cut back on her tourney fighting in

favor of aikido; in fact, she wrote this story while recovering from a broken collarbone suffered in aikido practice.

This is her first professional sale, though she is working on a novel.

—MZB

Kaarin held the lump of ore in her hands. She hefted it, eyed it, turned it. Then she closed her eyes and *felt* it. It was good. It was the best she had ever seen. She hobbled on her game leg to her workbench, paused to examine the ore again, and thumped it down. She retrieved her staff and limped back a step or two, never taking her eyes from the darkish uneven lump. Never had a smith been elected a Master so young, never had so great a burden been laid at a Master's forge. She was in her mid-thirties, her hair, long and black as a maiden's, was tied sensibly and firmly behind her and tucked in her leather tunic. A twist of rag held back stray wisps, and the sweat of her trade. She wore brown leather trews and heavy boots clad in plates of her own invention. Only one heel touched the ground.

"Damned priests," she muttered, "Don't trust 'em." She hobbled around her shop, poking and prodding with the tip of her crutch at the piles of ore and sharp caltrops formed by castoff detritus of finished projects. "Damn, where is it?" She talked to herself when her sons weren't here to teach and help and get underfoot.

This sword was her gift. Not the priests'. "It is the finest piece of ore," she mused. Uncertainty made her stop her rummaging. "Maybe I'll destroy its quality. Maybe they've enspelled it." She watched the charcoal dust she had kicked up settle out of the low shaft of winter light from the door.

"No," she said aloud. Her eye lit on a fist-sized pitted lump on a wooden shelf. "There you are, my skychild."

It was very heavy, very dark. It seemed to throb in her hand. "You fell from heaven for this. Your time is come."

The commission and the ore had been delivered last week, but the moon was on the wane. No time to start things. She had taken the time to plan this. A new Great Sword for Tremain, a personal weapon for the Queen who would be consecrated in some seventy sunturns. Kaarin began to form the face of Sheira in her mind as she looked at the two lumps before her. Her face tensed with an old agony. She mastered it, as she had mastered pain and despair and steel. The two lumps now sat side by side on the bench. "Like Sheira and me," Kaarin mused. "One fine and blessed by the priests; one heavy and pitted and starfallen. Together at last." She grinned and then laughed a deep hearty laugh. "I will forge the finest and purest weapon ever made. I face the challenge, as I faced war. Without fear, with love of battle." She raised her knotted arms. "Mother, hear me. I swear this." She fell toward the bench, but steadied herself and added softly, "Mother, help me." She hobbled to the courtyard and bellowed, "Vlat, Erkin, Samish, muster forward! We have work to do."

The two lumps had fused in the melting. The fire was so hot they had feared the furnace would crack. She had fired it with a mixture of charcoal and the burning stone she had traded for years before. Stone like charcoal, but hard and slick. She would need to husband every piece. The heat it put out, oh, Goddess, the heat!

The night the ingot cooled she had sat at table with her husband and three boys—the two of her body and the sworn prentice. "Valder, I want you to make the scabbard. But I ask you a favor. Let me pick the subject of the decoration."

Her husband sat in silence awhile. "It would be an honor.

It would give me my Master's cap. But would it be mine if you designed it?"

"I can't pick out images in grains of gold, Valder. I was her bodyguard, her lover. I owe her. I will forge her sword. Will you not make its sheath? We cannot leave this to some court toad who gained his goldsmith's cap by bending over for some priest."

Valder chuckled. "Let me think awhile."

She had become tense; she always did when a major work began, but this time she was distant and quiet. He sighed. There probably wouldn't be a shared bed until Hearth Mother's Night.

The next day Kaarin and her older son and her prentice cracked out the ingot. It had a luster, even rough.

"Heat the forge. And I want your little brother here. There will never be a sword like this again. You will *learn* more from this than the whole Guild could teach. You hear me?"

And they began. She heated the ingot and hammered, heated and cooled and chiseled scores and cut it into lumps. As the boys took turns aided by the older prentice and even the old farm hand who lived with them, the metal was drawn and twisted into long plaits.

"Hold the tongs tightly, Vlat. Pull, pull. See how to twist it, Erk? When we beat it into a pattern and pound it, it will weld into one piece, strong but flexible. Samish, is it red enough? See the difference in the color now? It's the glow within the redness that tells you it's ready. Pull, Vlat, it releases the pain in metal. Like stretching after a sleep."

The ingot was no more. Now a rough sword emerged with the crisscross of the pattern welding still visible.

"You boys run off awhile. I need some quiet."

"Mother, would you like some bread and beer?"

"Not now, Samish." She tousled her younger child's hair and smiled, but she was already years away. She went back to her anvil and began to pound the hammer song. Tap klink, tap klink, tap klink.

It was the worst battle of the war, of her life, of anybody's life. Not the clean swift moves of the practice yard. She had seen farmgirls kill hens with more finesse than she had hacked this man to death. His neck was half severed, his arm lacerated, his guts showing. Oh, sweet gods, he moved. She swung again, this time taking off the head. She slipped on the mud and gore and fell on his bloody wet corpse. She was so tired the tears trickled down her face. "Oh, Mother, Mother, let me just get up, up. One step, another, Mother." The stench of death made her want to scream, but she was too tired. Then she saw her liege lady, her beloved. Tall and slender, still standing and swinging against a foeman. "How I love her. For her, for House Tremain!" She lurched forward and scrabbled up to her liege lady.

"Sheira, it's me, I'm on you, love. At your left. I've a shield. Watch your right. He's going to thrust. Hang on." By now two others had joined the foe and they stood two to three outnumbered. They were good and fresh. Then Kaarin felt a blur behind them from the right. "Sheira." She leapt as the shriek carried across the field above the noise of battle. The searing pain. "Mother, save her." When she awoke, she was in a field hospital. "I don't think we can save your leg." "The hell, *you will*. Is Sheira alive, My Lady? Tell me." She pushed herself up and grabbed the healer priestess by the tunic.

It took three old veterans to subdue her. "She is unharmed. She is unharmed." A tall woman in the banded headdress and plaque of a High Healer came. There was murmuring. "You are in the guard of Sheiralith, Royal Lady of Tremain, Guardsman Kaarin?"

"Yes."

"Bodyguard of our Royal Lady?"

"Yes."

"You saved her life with your body and your prayer." She poked and prodded at Kaarin's body wounds and then lifted the dressing from her mutilated leg and studied it. She looked directly into Kaarin's eyes. "I will save your leg." But she had never again walked with both feet on the ground. And a crippled soldier is no use to a Royal Lady. Kaarin's uncle had taken her in and taught her to make the tools of war. No other had ever learned so fast or achieved mastery so young. But all she could feel was the shame and guilt of her failure to stay at her lady's side.

The hammer sang. Tap klink, tap klink. Her tears sputtered as they vaporized on the hot steel. "My tears are your temper, child of my art. I give you all the love and loyalty I could not give before. I commit to the forge-fire my shame and guilt. But to you, my child, to you I forge in you my fealty and protection for her whom you will serve. Guard her from death and treachery."

The next day brought a late winter blizzard and for three days the work ceased. Kaarin was glad for the rest at first, but soon rest turned to restlessness. Finally, a cold clear morning dawned.

"It is time to teach you tempering." Heated and quenched in the Mother's own sea water (she had ordered it brought by mule for this day), then heated and peened with precise firm taps and cooled slowly by the winter's breath. Fire, earth, water, and air all commingled time and again to gain the best of strength and yielding, of edge and spring. And all blessed in the charcoal-firerock heat. Kaarin explained to her boys each stage, giving them a knowledge to take to their own children in time, a knowledge beyond anything known before. Kaarin's eyes glowed as she taught, with passion.

"Look, see how you draw the steel from the brine while it is still warm enough that the water steams dry slowly. When it cools slowly, as it does here or in the wind, it is softer but it is not brittle." And later: "See how to place the steel in the charcoal and firerock. This will cause it to harden. It will cut rock." Finally, satisfied and exhausted, she looked at the young faces around her. How she loved them all. But how she had loved her Lady. "Go and have Greta set out dinner. I'll be in soon."

She sat looking at the sword, fingering it, tang to tip. "How I love you, my Sheira." The years slipped away. Her fingers now could feel Sheira's firm, gentle body. How awkward was their first time together. Five years the senior, Kaarin was only a guardsman. "You love me only for my body," she had teased.

"Let me commission you."

"No, please, no. I can take nothing, Lady."

"*Lady*? Here? Now?"

"Beloved, you are second to the throne. Please don't shame me."

But she had been commissioned nonetheless, after Sheira had taken a young Count from Court to her bed. Tears hit the cold, rough blade. "No, I'll not put jealousy or anger into you. Only love and loyalty. I loved your body and your soul and you were young." Kaarin got up to go in to eat.

As she reached for her staff, she turned suddenly to the door of the shop. The view took her breath away. The rolling hills were blanketed with snow, golden in the light, pale blue in the shadow. And the trees, the trees. Etched black against the snow and each branch and twig encased in crystal beauty. "Mother!" Kaarin leaned on her staff. "You gave me the best. Thank you, my mother."

They had a dinner of soup and bread, and Greta produced some sausages she had husbanded against the late winter, as Kaarin had misered each chunk of firestone. Greta bustled through the kitchen, round and red-faced. Her children grown and breeding in the surrounding countryside, she had adopted the elderly farmhand who had come to cut wood for a crust and stayed to be part of this family. Greta embroidered with a Master's skill, but, alas, embroidery was not a guild craft. Samish was soon asleep on the floor with his favorite dog.

"Vlat, how about a game of nine-pegmen?"

"Sure, Valder."

"Dad, can I go see Hera? I'll be back before dark," Erk pleaded.

"No, boy."

"But it's only two miles to her dad's farm."

"Wind's blowing up. May storm. Better wait a day or two."

Erk looked so sad Kaarin laughed. "Never any died of love," she sang from the old songs. Soon they were all singing and laughing and telling old stories. But the restlessness returned to Kaarin. She'd been putting off testing the metal.

Finally she took a lamp and went back to the shop. "Damn. The metal seems so good. Only one way to tell." She limped to the grinding wheel. She had built it to drive with a treadle and pulleys so she could drive it with one foot. Now many had abandoned the heavy flywheel in favor of her innovation. When it was up to speed she placed a burr on the tang against the stone wheel. It sparked, short tracks, thousands of them. The starstone in the metal struck stars from the sword like all the stars in the sky. Here was the proof. Never had she seen or heard of steel hard enough to spark tracks like this.

"It sparks, hoorah!" she shouted. "It's as hard as . . . hard as . . . hard as me own black heart!" she sang as she rose from the grinder and danced, wobbling, around the shop. With joy and abandon she swung the blade by the tang. It sang, even gripped by the tang, it sang. It slipped from her hand and sailed into the cold coals and stuck, vibrating. "All right, all right, tomorrow, child." She laughed and cried and wiped tears from her eyes and the ash from the unpolished blade. She tenderly wrapped it in a sheepskin and laid it on the bench. "Goodnight, my child."

The next days were polishing and polishing and polishing. And on the tang Kaarin carved "Made by Master Kaarin for Queen Sheiralith" and the date. "You must *never* dwell on any ill wish when you work a weapon," she instructed her charges, but the endless polishing was tedious to her, not like the alchemical pleasure of forging and metalcraft and she kept herself steady by watching the snow and imparting its smooth brightness into the blade. But she was glad when it was done. She and her husband collaborated on the finely carved quillons, grip and pommel, she doing the coarse work and he carving and beating in the gold designs. Finally, she bound the hand grip in leather strips and it was done. Her last act, alone, was to put her lips to the sword and whisper its own true name.

Next day at dinner she braved the subject of the scabbard again. "I must have an answer. The priests will be back by Hearth Mother."

He rose from the table and wiped his hands on a cloth. He went to the bed-closet they shared and reached under and pulled out a long bundle and brought it to the table. "My work, my subject." He unwrapped it, and there lay a wooden scabbard, covered with beaten gold, with the scene of an ancient battle formed of grains of gold. In the center of this history of Tremain was a panel showing a victorious queen, cradling in her arms a wounded guardswoman. "Is that what you had in mind?"

"Yes, oh, yes! You know, Valder, it's all been worth it. If it had not been thus, we would not have had all this. It's your masterwork." The glow between them sent the boys and servants off to an early bed.

The royal messengers rode in the day of Hearth Mother Eve, the beginning of the thaw, the honor of the Queen of the Gods, who was Warrior, Hearth and Forge.

Kaarin waited in the court with her whole clan. There had not been time to tidy or dress as for a festival. They were as they were.

A tall woman dismounted, dressed in brightly embroidered red wool and fur-lined riding coat, fine-dyed blue leather gloves and fur cap. She would be a beautiful queen.

Kaarin's heart skipped and her stomach hurt. Sheiralith. "My liege!"

"Did you think I would send servants to you?" She reached

out her arms to the older woman. "It's my turn to take the lead." They crushed each other in an embrace. Grown apart on separate paths, they still loved. But now we are sisters, Kaarin thought.

"Let me see it."

Kaarin held the sword in its scabbard out to her, then drew back.

"This is my work and Master Valder's work." (He had received his cap at a Guild meeting just the fairday past.) "And the work of every prentice and worker on this farmholding. But mostly it is the work of the Hearth Mother. I would give it to you in Her presence."

Kaarin heard the words coming from her with gentle authority. Part of her mind was asking the other part, *Who are you and what are you saying?* The other part of her mind said, *Be still, my child.*

They went together to the household circle, just out of sight of the house. Some of the priests and priestesses had made a move to come, but Kaarin shot them a look that froze them into a circle of their own, shuffling and gossiping among themselves.

As they crunched through the snow past the thawing trees which dripped their crystal tears to reveal the pastel buds beneath, they entered the circle at the East and stood facing each other at the center, before the altar, Kaarin's back to the North.

She held out the sheathed sword for Sheira's inspection. Sheira reached out her fine long fingers and traced the scene in the middle and looked Kaarin in the eye. "I have missed you. Truly. Your honesty. Your solidness. But it's not the same since my older sister died. There will be no more front-line campaigns even for me."

"I know." Kaarin's solid body clad in its sweat-stained and spark-scorched leather seemed more at home here than Sheira's finery.

Kaarin drew the blade and placed the scabbard on the altar. She took a cloth from her belt and draped her hand to protect the blade from human touch. Then she lifted and displayed the shining blade across her outstretched hands. Sheira's eyes were riveted on the blade. "It's beautiful. No. There are no words."

"They will touch the blade when the oath is taken."

"It can't be helped. There is a fine smith at court. I'll take care of it. What have you named it?"

"Sword of the Mother."

It hummed in the crisp air.

"I will remember."

They stood together thus for a moment, their eyes locked. Slowly, Sheira slipped off her gloves and placed them in her belt, placing her hands over the sword. Kaarin found herself channeling the words again, words she had heard but once as a child at court, but words she did not know she knew.

"Swear here, before the Great Mother, to be the Sovereign of Tremain. In body and in spirit, in life and in death, be thou Highest Priestess of all, be thou Liegewoman of your Oath-kin, Mother-Protector of the Land and its Children, Master of all Masters of the Guilds. . . ."

"I here swear before the Great Mother and upon my body and spirit that I am the Sovereign of Tremain. . . ." The Oath reverberated in the circle and to all the land. The trees and deer heard it, the mountains heard it, the sky heard it. The Gods heard it. Soon the priests and people of Tremain would hear it. But that would be for the priests and the people. It was already done.

The Queen took the sword and made to sheath it.

"Wait." Kaarin mopped off the finger marks. They both giggled. It was their secret. Theirs shared with all the land of Tremain. Sheira stood taller.

"If they can't see it I'll know what fools my ministers are. Come, my friend." She put her arms around Kaarin's waist. "You'll be at my coronation, won't you?"

Kaarin hesitated. All those people. Perhaps some she knew.

The Queen watched her and then said gently, "I need to honor you, for this." She shook the sword in her hand. Kaarin's face clouded, but the Queen went on. "No more commissions. I promise. But hear me. Your tools are in your shop below. You create this," she rattled the sword again, "from lumps of rock. My tools are ceremony and ritual. I lead a Great Meeting Dance of every living person and beast in Tremain. My task is to spark each woman and man, young and old, into steady warriors or holders who cherish their plot of land or craftsmen who do this." She shook the sword again. "Come, let us show those lumps how the dance is done. Please. I need, yes I *need*, a friend I can trust there. Besides—" with half a smile, she added, "there will be those almond-paste cakes you love at the feast."

Kaarin looked at her, as she spoke, with intense wonder. An icicle broke away from the altar table and crashed and shattered. Kaarin's last fear melted like the melting winter ice. Yes, here was liegewoman, priestess, guildmaster, all the attributes of the Oath. She would deserve the sword, and the crown. Sheira prompted again. "Will you come?"

"Almond crescents?" Kaarin grinned. "Why didn't you say so before? I wouldn't miss it for the world!"

They bowed and left the circle.

"Let's see how it swings." Sheira whipped the sword out. It sang in the air. "The balance is perfect." She struck at a branch and it sheared off, and fell.

"My turn," and Kaarin took the blade and made passes in the air then sighted a likely target and with years of black-smithing skill easily lopped off the offending branch. They galloped like girls, whooping and slashing. Finally breathless they slowed and stopped.

Sheira wiped the blade, inspected it once more with pride and wonder, and sheathed it. "We must go back now, Mastersmith." She took Kaarin by the hand. They walked down the hill, mustering all the decorum they could. By the time they reached the waiting group in the courtyard, Sheira had forgotten Kaarin's limp. So had Kaarin.

HUNGER

Russ Garrison

This, the second of the "Chosen Maiden" theme stories,
is about as far as one can get from the high seriousness
and exotic setting of Charles Saunders's "Mask."

Russ Garrison is a psychiatric nurse on the midnight
shift . . . "a fertile atmosphere," he says, "to work on
macabre twist endings and interesting characters." This
is his first sale; and I've observed that writers who make
their debut with a humorous story frequently go far.

—MZB

The manacles were lined with leather and not uncomfortable and her wrists were wrapped with rags to
cushion their chafe. Delois didn't fight their tight grasp;
she'd done her struggling when they'd tried to put them on
her. Ruefully she grinned down at the ruins of Myrda's
wedding dress. How Myrda had howled when her husband
had taken it to dress the ogre's offering!

Upward, past the shattered top of her column and through the branches overhead, she squinted at the darkening sky. Nightfall came early deep in the forest but she knew it must be near sundown. The chain rattled behind her as she idly banged the cuffs against the cracked marble column. She soon stopped—the clatter was too harsh and loud in the stillness. For it was still. The birds and the animals seemed to be holding their breath and even the dripping from the rainwet leaves had ceased.

She shook her head to chase the morbid fancies and leaned back against the marble. With a gasp she pulled away to the ends of her chain. The damp stone had chilled her skin through the thin, ripped dress and sent shivers down her bare arms. She sneezed and with a sigh slid down onto the cracked stone floor of the temple. Sitting with her legs outstretched, she shook the dark, damp hair out of her eyes and stared unseeing into the forest as the light gave way to dark.

"An ogre's been sighted on the road into the village," Elron had said as he practically dragged her off the street. "Come inside the inn where it's safe."

Reluctantly Delois joined Elron's parents and their customers inside the inn's strong walls. Ironically those very walls had led to her present predicament.

"Bring me virgin or I destroy!" the ogre roared. "Next dark. Old stones in forest. I destroy!"

Too late she'd seen Elron's father looking at her thoughtfully and then there'd been no place to run or swing her staff. Safe, ha!

The undergrowth crackled suddenly. Branches snapped, leaves rustled and deadwood exploded as something big forced its way through. Her time had come. She pushed herself to her feet (no easy task with one's hands locked to the ends of a length of chain around a pillar). Fortunately, if one could speak of fortune at a time like this, she still had her heavy, sturdy shoes. At least she would get in a couple of good kicks before the ogre killed her.

The crackling drew closer and was accompanied by an odd moaning sound. She fretted and sawed the chain from side to side. If only she had her staff, then she'd see if his head or his privates were unbreakable.

Blinded by the dark, she thought she saw a deeper patch of shadow moving off to her left. Her eyes and ears strained for those few additional seconds of warning. The moaning was replaced by a muffled wheezing. Wet branches snapped under heavy feet in the clearing. Quietly drawing back her foot, her mouth filled with saliva for one last act of defiance. She was, under the circumstances, pleased not to be dry-mouthed.

"Delois? Delois, are you there?"

"Elron?" she asked incredulously. "Elron, what in Morath's name are you doing here?"

The shuffling continued, followed by a thud as something soft collided with something hard and immovable. He suppressed a curse. "Delois, keep talking so I can find you. It's so dark."

"Of course it's dark; it's night. Didn't you bring a torch?"

"Certainly, but I didn't want the ogre to see the light."

"Ogre or not, you can't rescue me if you can't see me. That is why you're here, isn't it?" She began to have her doubts about the whole affair.

"Oh yes, rescue you, kill the ogre or, failing in that, die gloriously," came his cheerful voice.

"Oh, Morath," she groaned. Too many sagas. "Light the torch and get me out of these cursed chains."

Flint clicked against steel with an occasional spray of sparks. He cursed in a monotonous undertone and blew out the sparks before they could catch. Clumsy as usual, she thought glumly, or clumsy as Elron, as the village brats said.

She swallowed, resisting the urge to grind her teeth or blister him with a curse. "Please hurry. It's already dark and the ogre was supposed to claim the offering at sundown."

The clicking stopped. "Claim the virgin, you mean," he snickered. "What if there were not a *virgin* waiting for him?"

She didn't like that line of thought. Maybe she would need her shoes after all. "Elron, wherever did you get the brave idea of rescuing me?" she cooed. "My hero, I'm so grateful."

There was a pause and the clicking resumed. "Well, actually it was Dakra—you know, the King's Recruiter—who suggested it. We were just talking about what a damned shame it was that the village decided to offer you as a sacrifice instead of standing up to the ogre. Well, one thing led to another, and Dakra said I looked like a likely lad," his voice puffed with pride, "and that maybe the two of us could rescue you."

The torch flared up and revealed a short, pasty-faced and spotted youth with a cheerful, gap-toothed grin. Really, she thought, he looked more like one of his mother's dumplings than an ogre-slayer. She considered him critically even though she had known him most of her life. Almost her age, he was the child of his mother's dotage and never allowed to play rough games with the other boys or chase the girls. His pudgy hands twisted the torch nervously as he waved it around and peered with light-blinded eyes into the forest. She shook her head minutely.

Apparently satisfied that nothing lurked within torchlight, he turned back to her. "Hullo," he said with his cheerful grin. "Myrda's dress never looked so good on her." Then he stared at the long diagonal rip over her left breast. He licked his lips slowly and the torch drooped. "I never realized your skin was so fair."

"Elron, where's Dakra?" she said desperately. "You said she was coming with you. Where is she?"

Elron shook himself and smiled again. "I think she got lost. For a King's Officer she sure is a lousy forester. Why, I lost her not ten minutes into the forest."

"Uh, yeah. Come on, help me out of these chains. Why are you standing there? Elron!"

The torch fell so that it hung slackly from his fist and the flames licked at the damp debris covering the temple floor. His mouth dropped open and she swore that his wide eyes grew even rounder.

"Elron, talk to me. What's the matter?"

"Dakra, Dakra's got the key to the manacles. She was supposed to steal it from the smith and follow me here. Then we were going to set you free and run away before the village knew what happened."

He ducked his head and shuffled his big feet. Uh-oh, that was a bad sign. Either he was lying or he didn't want to tell her something.

She kept her tone neutral. "And then what?"

He was almost whispering now. "Then she said she would help us get away, far away from the forest." His voice stumbled and died. "Then, you know, the two of us . . ."

She didn't know for sure, but she could guess. Ever since she'd grown breasts, Elron and the village boys, aye, and most of the men, too, had tried to corner her alone. Too many times to count she'd had to defend herself with her staff or take to her heels. Elron, at least, was sweet—sweet but exasperating. He'd follow her around like a puppy, bringing bundles of flowers and sweets stolen from his mother's kitchen. He was staring up at her again with those sad puppy eyes.

Slowly and calmly she spoke to him as if to a small child. "Elron, we must get out of here quickly. Come on, come over here. If I stand on your shoulders I might be able to lift the chain over the top of the column."

With a look of relief Elron nodded and grinned, eager now that someone was giving him directions again. He wedged the torch into a pile of rubble and came over to stand docilely in front of her. Once again he stared at the torn bodice.

"Elron!" He jerked his head up with a guilty expression. "Bend over and make a stirrup with your hands. A little lower, about knee-high, that's right. Now, I'm stepping into your hands and big, strong Elron is going to lift me up until I can step onto his shoulders. Ready? Now!''

Elron panted heavily at the exertion but dutifully spread his legs, bent over and lifted. She rose slowly, her shoulders and hips bumping along the cold marble. Her foot was about level with Elron's waist when she was suddenly pinned against the column by his heavy body.

''Oh Delois, you're so light and soft. I've longed to hold you in my arms like this.'' His words were muffled, spoken as they were into her dress and right thigh.

Delois drew back her fist and pushed her other hand back to give her the slack she needed to box his ear. Then she heard another sound, the sound of his sobbing.

''You're so beautiful, so wonderful, and I love you so much.'' His voice was hoarse and near breaking and, incredibly, she could feel the moisture of his tears through her dress.

Hesitantly she uncurled her fingers and stretched them slowly toward his head. Touching his soft, curly hair, she snatched her fingers back as if burned, then determinedly stroked his head and murmured soft words of noncommittal reassurance.

She whispered his name. ''Elron? Now's not the time to talk of such things. La-later, after we've escaped, I'll owe my brave, noble, fearless rescuer—my affection, my respect and my gratitude. But right now we have work to do. Come, big, strong Elron, and lift me higher so that I can stand on your broad shoulders. We're almost there; I think I can see the top.''

Slowly, raising his tear-drenched face from her skirts, he smiled gratefully up at her. Snuffling, snorting, and wiping his cheeks and nose on his shoulders, he grunted once more and lifted her smoothly upward. As she stepped onto his shoulders, he swayed and stumbled slightly.

''I can see it! Just a little more, a little higher . . .''

There came a roar to blot out her thoughts and an odor of

rotting meat and stagnant swamp to choke her. From Elron there was a sound somewhere between a groan and a grunt and then she was falling, scraping along the column as Elron jumped away.

Skinned and bruised, her ankle twisted under her and stabbing pains lanced up her leg. Her teeth slammed shut on her lower lip and she tasted salty blood. Her multitude of pains distracted for a moment and then she was staring around wildly for the source of the roar and the stench. Elron had grabbed the torch and was waving it around, turning around so rapidly to look behind him that he stumbled over his own feet.

Somewhere in the darkness the ogre roared again, but this time the roar had words, crude words filled with grunts, gobbles and growls. "I smell virgin. Give me virgin. I hunger! So cruel."

It was a voice, she thought wildly, to sour the milk in the cow and send dogs howling in terror. Gathering her feet beneath her, she swallowed, choked, and was annoyed to find her mouth dry. She cleared her throat experimentally before testing her voice. The unseen beast continued his shuffling advance, snorting and slobbering.

"Elron, I want you to run now. Go on, hurry. It's better this way."

Unfortunately, her voice, strained and quavering a bit, seemed to rouse him from the torch-holding statue he'd frozen into at the beast's words. Shaking himself, he threw down the torch into a pool of rainwater and yanked out his belt knife, a pitiful length better suited to table use than to fighting. He brandished it wildly at the darkness.

"Virgin, pretty virgin, I see. Come, pretty virgin. I hunger!" If the inhuman voice could be said to have human emotions, then the ogre sounded joyful—and ravenous.

"Good-bye, Delois. I wish, just once, that I had kissed you."

The torch extinguished abruptly with a sizzle and the last

thing she saw was his screaming charge down the temple steps toward a monstrously large shadow.

"Elron, no! Don't be a fool. Your dying will be for nothing. Come back! At least take the torch."

There was another roar, an enveloping explosion of sound, then the shriek of a mouse caught by a cat and, finally, the shrill clatter of metal on stone. The roaring dropped to a rumbling like distant thunder and Elron sobbed fearfully. Delois mourned the brave but foolhardy boy and longed to be able to blot out his final, horrible moments. However, the sobbing and rumbling grew fainter as if growing distance separated them. Even the air smelled cleaner.

Forgetting her own predicament, she called out. "Elron?"

There was a blast of a roar and she shut up abruptly. Heart pounding, she tried to sort out the puzzling events of the last few minutes.

"Careful. I doubt it, but she might just come back."

She whirled with a clanking of chains, searching for the cool, amused voice. "Who's there?"

A torch burst into flame, revealing a round, smooth face dominated by a great blade of a nose and capped by a cowl of mail. A deep, mocking bow swept a long, dark cape away from a thick, mail-clad body and a worn sword. "Dakra, the King's Recruiter, at your service. If you'll hold still, I'll see about having those manacles off. Unless, that is, you fancy heavy jewelry?" She moved closer and bent over the manacles with a crude key.

What did she know about Dakra? Nothing. Last night she had been just a rather broad, indolent figure among the other travelers cowering inside the dark inn. At least Dakra, to her credit, took no part in her capture.

The last manacle fell off with a clank and Delois kicked it away. "What about Elron? Why didn't you help him?"

"That foolish boy?" She laughed. "I had absolutely no interest in him. 'Twas you I meant to save. You are much more—attractive—to me. By the way, do you recall what you promised Elron? Something about your affection, your respect and your gratitude?''

Delois ducked her head and scowled. ''Aye, and I pay my debts, but I can't leave without trying to save Elron from that monster.''

''Oh, he's quite safe as far as being killed or eaten goes. Despite their terrible reputations ogres as a rule aren't maneaters or killers. However, if you insist on chasing after him, I can't guarantee your safety.''

''But if the ogre didn't take him to kill him or eat him, why did he?''

''*She*. It was an ogress, not an ogre. I took the liberty of looking at the monster through a crack in the shutter and noted certain, ah, characteristics that to a woman of the world such as myself signaled that it was the female of the species.''

Delois recovered quickly. ''So it was a female and not a male. What difference does that make to Elron?''

''Obviously you don't understand the ways of the world and ogresses. The ogrish race is a solitary and dwindling one. I fancy the poor thing hasn't seen a male of her species for some time. Also, her command of humanspeech is poor. She was clear about one thing, though. She wanted a tender virgin. She got one, too.''

''You mean . . . Elron?''

''Yes, I think it should clear up his spots nicely. But don't worry: ogresses are a fickle lot and he'll come limping home in a few days. However, if you or anyone chases after them, she's liable to kill him and the rescuers. When they're in love, they're extremely jealous.''

Delois, filled with horrified understanding, was torn by a mad desire to laugh, the kind of laughter where you're too embarrassed to do anything else. ''Poor Elron,'' she gasped. Then she steeled herself. ''But what about you? What reward do you claim for my rescue?''

Dakra leered. ''Your body and four years of your life.''

She staggered and tasted bile. "You.— So be it. I'll be your slave and I'll share your bed but nothing more."

"Oh well, one can't have everything. But it's not for me." She reached into her pouch and brought out a piece of parchment. "Just make your mark here, and I'll keep the King's silver—thank you—for my troubles."

"What?"

"Mark your enlistment papers, dear. You're just in time for the King's dragon offensive. It's not slavery; it's an adventure."

ON FIRST LOOKING INTO BRADLEY'S GUIDELINES
OR
STORIES I DON'T WANT TO READ EITHER

Elizabeth Thompson

As mentioned in the preface, I sent out a set of guidelines for contributors to this anthology. As well as reminding the writers about standards for professional submission, I listed about twelve cliché stories of which I had read far too many. I added, however, that I would break any or all of these rules if the writer could avoid the "Oh, not *that* one again" reaction on my part.

One of the no-nos I emphasized was "No poetry," but this turned out to be so amusing that I wanted to share it with the readers.

—MZB

There's a story with which I am bored,
of a scanty-clad girl with her lord:

the girl, who's a zero,
stands around while the hero
chops the evil ones down with his sword.

I think that I've read this one, too:
there's a sexy cute sorceress who
has flashing white thighs
and also a wise
old male wizard who knows what to do.

Haven't I read these before?
There's gratuitous rape, lots of gore,
an evil old hag,
and Conan in drag,
and the Goddess Herself; and there's more.

There's a princess who's off on a quest
with her unicorn into the west.
She's sweet and demure
and unspeakably pure,
and the hero—but you know the rest.

There's a female chauvinist pig
with a sidekick who's hulking and big.
He's clumsy and dumb
and he's under the thumb
of Beowulf wearing a wig.

There's a strong-minded woman who must
find a hero in whom she can trust.
The key to the plot
is that freedom is not
as rewarding as true love (or lust).

There's a commune that's idealistical,
and a lesbian priestess sadistical,

by the woman who can
ruin his Magic in ways shamanistical.
and a challenge to Man

There's also romantical rot:
a simpleton stuck in a plot
whose only solution
is the great institution
of Romance—and that's all it's got.

There's verse epic, pretentious and rough;
and as if that weren't enough,
there's crude sophomorical
fake prehistorical
phantasmagorical Stuff.

There are man-hating women in leather;
there's polemical feminist blether
dressed up as a story
of how Woman's glory
is to do without Man altogether.

I want to read tales that are new
and exciting or thoughtful—a few
could be light-hearted fun—
and every damn one
had better be well written, too.

THE CHOSEN MAIDEN

Raul Reyes

When I was a young girl just beginning to read science
fiction and fantasy in the adventure pulps, the magazine
covers invariably featured the form of a scantily clad
maiden, being lustfully—or hungrily—surveyed by some
form of bug-eyed monster.

Because of this lightly draped virgin, my parents disap-
proved of my reading this sort of thing. In vain I reas-
sured them that the stories were invariably as pure as
Elsie Dinsmore; their answer was always "Then why do
they put those covers on them?" I had no answer then,
and I have no answer now, except that perhaps, in those
days, the reading of fantasy fiction was considered
unmanly, and a "sexy dame" on the cover meant that a
man could be seen reading it without fear of derision,
since he was engaged in reading "manly stuff" filled with
sex and blood-lust.

In the decades that have elapsed since I was a young
girl, the pulp magazines have vanished, and the paper-
backs which replaced them have admitted that their audience is at least half female; they no longer seek to lure
readers with a false promise of pornographic delights.
Nor has the lustful bug-eyed monster returned. But even

then, I knew better; I knew enough biology to know that if the bug-eyed monster had any interest in the maiden, it would be to regard her as dinner, rather than as a love object.

This third of our "Chosen Maiden" stories addresses directly the question of why a dragon, or other maiden-eating monster, should be assumed to care about the morals of his sacrificed victims. Raul Reyes is a young writer from Berkeley, previously a member of the police department; this is his first professional sale.

—MZB

"**B**ut I don't want to be a virgin!" Stephanie cried. "I hate it, I hate it!"

"Hush that," her mother scolded. "What do you think you are? And what will the neighbors think, if they overhear you?"

"I don't care," Stephanie cried again. "I don't like it. Anika is already three months' pregnant, and due to marry her lover next feast day. And Tomira has laid with half the boys in the village, and maybe almost as many of the girls, and here I am, never touched in all my days. Why should I be punished for virtue? And I've been told I'm pretty!"

"Pretty what?" Lauranne asked wickedly. Her younger sister was chubby, and with a wise attitude to match. She licked at a spoon half covered with sweet syrup. "I think," she drawled slyly, "that you're just afraid of going to the dragon next feast day."

"And what if I am?" Stephanie asked in answer. "Would you want to end in some dragon's gullet as a sacrifice?"

"Don't talk like that," her mother admonished her. "How

do you know that it will be you? The lottery has over thirty
names in it this year. It's not too likely that you'll be chosen.
We've a good crop of virgins this year." Stephanie didn't
answer. She sulked, spooning her soup to her lips and scowling into the bowl. She knew she stood a better than equal
chance of being chosen. Everyone knew the lottery was
rigged sometimes, as it had been three seasons past when
Jaimy had been the betting favorite among all. This year
Stephanie would be the one with her name on more than half
the ballots, and for the same reason. Like Jaimy she had
resisted the advances of Ottar, Chief Priest of the temple.
Ottar, who differed from the rest of the village temple priests
only by being more porcine and vile than the rest. Better the
dragon's gullet!

"Well," Lauranne continued in a voice as sticky sweet as
the syrup she was licking, "if it really worries you, there's
always something you can do about it." She smirked wickedly
at her older sister, then yelped as her mother's fist rocked her
head sideways.

"Such language!" their mother snorted. "What's this younger generation coming to? Don't listen to her wicked talk,"
she went on to Stephanie. "Being a virtuous maiden is a very
good thing to be. Pay no attention to any that says otherwise.
When you find a husband you'll find that all that wickedness
is not so good as all the talk has it," she finished primly.

"You seem to enjoy it!" Stephanie retorted, then yelped in
her turn as her mother's hand slapped her.

"So you've been listening at keyholes again!" she yelled.
"For that you go to sleep with no supper." Stephanie looked
up at her, eyes blazing, then rose in a huff and stormed off to
her room.

Alone in her bed, staring up at the darkness, she pondered
the ways of fate. Already in her sixteenth year, with a lithe
and firm young body and a rather pretty face, she could count
no lover in a village where the annual sacrifice of a virgin
made being a maiden a rather dubious blessing. As virgins

went, she was already an old maid! But she hadn't really been pretty until her face cleared up in the last year. And as luck would have it, it had been Ottar who had first noticed her. She glared into the dark, made up her mind with a grimness beyond her years. She was not going to slide down a dragon's gullet.

The next day dawned fair and bright. Clear blue sky and crisp early autumn air made a good combination. She dressed carefully, modestly enough so that her mother would not say anything, but with her blouse with the front buttons that she could leave opened just enough so that the upper swell of her firm young breasts could be seen. With luck, she would not be dragon fodder by the end of the day. She already had her quarry chosen. Neil, who had glossy black hair, clear blue eyes, and a strong young form from working his father's fields. He would do, she thought. He would do quite well.

"Stephanie," the young boy said, shaken. "What are you saying? Do you think you are a common girl of the village, to be taken carelessly? I have too much respect for you to treat you as anything but a virtuous maiden." His name was Eric, it was near the end of the day, and Stephanie was getting rather impatient.

"But not too much respect to save me from a fate worse than your clumsy lovemaking?" she flared. Her face was flushed, she stamped her foot, her eyes tearing. Neil had been indifferent to her charms, his interest being taken up with his new companion, a rather handsome young man from a neighboring farm with hair like cornsilk and eyes almost as blue as his own. Eric had been her second choice. She hadn't counted on an attack of chivalry.

"Stephanie," he said, trying to be understanding. "You are distraught. You know that with more than thirty maidens this year, you stand little chance of being chosen for the honor." It was amazing, he thought, how blue the sky could be. Even seen through one eye, it was a crisp clear autumn blue that took his breath away. His other eye was already swelling from Stephanie's roundhouse punch and he was flat on his back very much aware that a stone was making a deep impression on his left kidney.

"He was so dense," Stephanie was saying. She was sitting with her friend Lisette, a young pretty girl of fifteen already safely past her maidenhood. "I did everything but tie him down and he starts talking as if I were a maiden of some lord, being saved for a diplomatic marriage."

"He's not so dense," the younger girl replied. "The virgin sacrifice doesn't have to be a girl you know. It has been a young boy some years. And the whole village knows that you turned Ottar down." Stephanie looked up, shocked. Lisette nodded sagely. "The smaller the village, the greater the gossip," she quoted. "The boys know that if they thwart Ottar's petty vengeance, they may be the ones to dive off the board this next feast day. And since they have no way to prove they are no longer virgin, they dare not give offense to him. You can't blame them for being scared stiff."

"They're not!" Stephanie cried. "That's the problem!" She blew noisily into her hanky. "It's not fair," she said. "I won't even have a choice."

"Life isn't fair," Lisette quoted again. "That's what our good King Cartoris said." She looked up at the sound of dinner bells ringing all over the village. "Time to eat," she said. "See you tomorrow." She was gone in a moment, leaving Stephanie to trudge home disconsolate.

"I hear you had poor luck today." Lauranne smirked while their mother's back was turned. Their father had finished his meal and gone to talk with the other men of the village, as was his custom. Aside from their mother only old Uncle Willis in the corner kept them company. Stephanie frowned, said little. "It looks as if you will have to dive off the board this year after all," she went on. The smirk vanished as their mother returned with their sweet pudding for dessert. Stephanie only picked at her portion. That brought a frown to her mother's usually placid face.

"Are you still worried about being chosen?" she asked, stroking Stephanie's shining tresses. "Don't be. And even if you are chosen, it's an honor. You don't want the dragon to leave his den in the volcano and ravage the countryside?" she asked. "We all have to take our chances and someone has to prevent that calamity. Think of your great aunt Gwennis, who made a beautiful swan dive when she was chosen, or Tarrin's daughter twelve years back, who did a triple gainer off the board." She looked off into the distance. "No," she said, "they don't make virgins like that anymore."

"Neither do I," cackled old Uncle Willis from the corner. "Neither do I."

"Hush," their mother admonished, rapping him smartly across the head with a heavy wooden spoon. "Is that any way to speak to maidens? You should be ashamed of yourself."

Stephanie finished her dinner, the seed of an idea in her head. Old Uncle Willis wasn't the only dirty old man in the village. There was Old Sam, the sailor, reputed to have been a pirate in his youth, and certainly no one the priests could accuse of virginity. He as one-eyed, vulgar, uncouth and unwashed, but certainly a better choice than a dragon.

It was another clear autumn day when Stephanie set out on her quest once more. A few strolls past old Sam's hut in the course of her errands were enough to catch his attention, and by the end of the day he was sitting on a stool in front of his hut, his leering eye following her every move.

"Ah, my pretty," he drawled evilly as she walked by with a jug of water balanced on her head. "Stately and under full sail ye are, ye are. Like a sloop cutting the waters of the Southern seas ye are." She smiled at him, standing with her hip saucily at an angle.

"You'll turn my head," she said, "with talk like that."

"Ah," he replied, "ye turn my head, like a compass needle in a storm, ye do, ye do." She set the jug on the ground near him, stood looking down at the old pirate with a saucy grin on her face.

"Oh," she said. "You're an evil old man, who can easily lead a maiden astray."

"Aye," he cackled. "Aye, and then follow a straight course after too." She smiled at him some more, ignoring the stench of rum on his breath. It was certainly better than a dragon's sulfur!

"He may have been a pirate in his young days," Stephanie complained to Lisette later, "with a girl in every port. But there hasn't been any wind in his sails since before I was born!" She blew into her hanky, which had certainly been put to much use lately. Lisette gave her a fresh one.

"Everyone has bad days," she commented. "Maybe tomorrow will be better." Stephanie blew noisily into her fresh hanky.

"No," she cried. "I'm dragon doomed for sure!"

Dinner that evening was quiet. Even her mother seemed to have caught the mood of despair. She cooked a berry pie that Stephanie normally loved. Lauranne got her share, and Stephanie's too, when Stephanie showed little interest.

"We all have our destiny," their mother said, as the dishes were being cleared. "Safeguarding the valley from the dragon's depredations is a good fate."

"Is that all I am to you?" Stephanie cried suddenly. "Dragon vittles?" She threw her towel down and ran to her room, locking the door and throwing herself on her bed to sob her tears out. Wisely her mother did not follow.

Late that night, alone in her darkened room, Stephanie considered her options. There were other boys, she reasoned, outside the village and beyond the priest's grasp. One of them would have to do.

There had been an abundance of clear autumn days lately, and the next day was no exception. Stephanie clasped on her cloak against the chill of the morning and took her basket in hand, announcing she was going to get some berries. Once outside she took the road out of town heading for the copse outside of the village on the side of the towering volcano where the dragon dwelled. The woodchopper was reputed to have a comely young son. He might do very nicely.

Before too long Stephanie had to admit that she had managed to get lost. The copse was really a small forest, and she had never been that far out of the village. She looked around. All the trees looked the same. She let out her breath slowly. Think, she told herself. Now what? She narrowed her eyes, looked at a pile of rocks partway up the hill, dominated by a massive out-cropping of dull brown stone. That might make a good observation point. She set out for it.

At the edge of the rock field she stopped to catch her breath, gazing about at the brown grass and stony ground around her. Pretty dismal, for sure, she thought. Up ahead was the big rock she was aiming for. She picked up her basket to resume her march when her heart suddenly stopped. The big rock had moved.

For a long time she stood as still as the stones all around her. Then she slowly began to retrace her path. With the same perseverance it had displayed so far, bad luck dogged her steps; now she cracked a twig. With all the menace of a rising thundercloud the dragon raised its head, peering down at her from a lordly height.

"Hello," she said. "How are you?"

"Fine," the dragon replied. "And you?"

"Fine," she replied, rather glad she had managed not to stammer. She looked around, they were all alone. "Nice day, isn't it?" she went on. Not very original dialogue, but then, what do you say to a dragon? He seemed aware of the lack of common topics and merely nodded, then resumed probing about the rocky ground.

"Excuse me," she went on. The dragon looked back at her. "Uh, what are you doing?" she asked.

"Looking for my supper," he replied. With an ease that was menacing he turned over a rock the size of a peasant's hut to expose a warren of mountain marmots, each half the size of a sheep and fat from the lush summer. Like flickering lightning his forked tongue shot out, once, twice, and thrice, each time making a fat marmot into a dainty dragon snack. Stephanie had to admit it was fast, which did give her some relief. At least she did not have to worry about pain, if and when it came to be her turn.

"Is that what you eat?" she asked, curious at the spectacle. He nodded, gazing down at her in a somewhat avuncular manner. Really, she thought, he wasn't a bad sort, for a dragon.

"Among other things," he said.

"Like virgins?" she asked, gathering her courage. He peered down at her.

"When and if they're offered," he replied. "But they're not my choice."

"They aren't?" she asked, surprised.

"Hiss and hoot, no," he snorted. "Skinny young things, hardly with any meat on their bones at all."

"But the priests say you want virgins," she said. He snorted in disgust at that.

"Now why would I care about a young woman's personal life?" he asked. "I have enough troubles with my own. Not that I have a personal life," he went on. "All my friends and all the female dragons are far to the South, in warmer lands. And I'm stuck in this miserable place, where a decent meal is hard to come by, and all they feed me is skinny virgins. Now if you don't mind." He turned from her, turned over another rock, and ate some more marmots. She watched the feeding dragon, and an idea began to form in her head.

"Uh, Mr. Dragon," she said. "Can we talk?" He looked back down at her for a long while, then sat back on his haunches and bade her begin.

They were blessed with another clear day the next feast day. True to her expectations her name had been drawn in the lottery, and all the other maidens had expressed relief by congratulating Stephanie on her selection for the honor. Now, dressed all in white and gold, she led the procession up the slopes of the volcano, borne on a palanquin carried by the young men of the village. Temple priests in gold and red robes swung incense burners and chanted hymns, led by Ottar, his waddling bulk obscene in his robes. Soon enough they came to the edge of the volcano, where the diving board awaited them. Far below they could hear the sound of the dragon ascending the inner walls of the crater.

Ottar led the prayers and chants. "We call upon you, oh majestic slitheriness," he intoned, "to accept our humble offering in the spirit with which we offer it." More incense was burned, more chants chanted. The sound of scales on rock became clearer. Under her exterior calm Stephanie's heart pounded. What if the dragon had lied? With studied composure she allowed Ottar to help her from the palanquin seat. But instead of going alone by herself to the edge of the wall and then out on the board she indicated that he was to lead her to the board himself. With a shrug he led her out, followed by the twelve chanting priests. The sound of scales rasping on stone drifted up from the fuming crater. Ottar and the others stayed at the edge while she stepped out on the board alone, heart pounding. She looked down into the swirling smoke and dust. A darker shadow became clearer, formed into a distinct image. It was the dragon.

"Mr. Dragon," she called down. "It's me. I'm here."

"I know," he grumbled in reply. Suddenly he was on the edge of the crater, forearms propped on the edge, looking over the crowd with interest. His gaze settled on Ottar and his band. His tongue licked out, the twin tips like snakes weaving before a charmer's flute.

"Mighty dragon," Ottar intoned, "accept our offering."

"Thank you," the dragon replied, his voice rolling like thunder. He continued looking them over. "Uh, we hope you like the virgin," Ottar went on, less sure of himself. What could be wrong with the beast?

"And why should I?" the dragon asked mildly. Ottar looked bewildered.

"Well," he asked. "What would you like?" The dragon smiled down.

"Something fat," he said.

"Fat?" Ottar squeaked.

"Fat," the dragon confirmed. With a speed like a striking heron spearing a fish, his tongue shot out, the twin ends grasping Ottar's bulk between them. In a moment Ottar was in the air, and barely had a moment to scream before he was gone and the tongue had shot out once again, snaring the next priest in line. He too vanished, and then the next and the next. By then the remaining temple denizens had taken to their heels, but years of soft living and accumulated bulk exacted a toll, and the tongue caught up with them all, bringing them in to join their erstwhile leader, Ottar.

With a satisfied burp the dragon looked at the fleeing villagers and gazed sideways at Stephanie. "A very good meal," he said. "Thank you very much." His tongue reached out, more slowly this time, but still too quick to evade, and plucked her from the board, lifted her in the air, and set her down on solid ground. With a last wink he slid back down into the murk.

It was a very happy homecoming meal her family gave her when she returned that evening. The villagers were still getting used to the idea that they didn't have to sacrifice young virgins anymore, although some of the portlier citizens were looking a bit concerned about their future. Her mother had baked her favorite berry pie, and for once her sister didn't try to take her portion.

"Maybe we can lure some priests from the village down the road," Lisette was saying, "to supply next year's offering."

"Maybe," Stephanie replied around a mouthful of berry pie. "We'll have to think about it." They were interrupted by a shout from outside. Setting down forks they all rushed out to find the villagers looking up. As soon as their eyes became used to the dusk they saw what the shouting was about. The dragon was leaving the crater, giant wings beating the air, sending thunderclaps rolling away in all directions. He circled the village, dipping his wings in salute, then veered away to the South and was soon lost in the night sky.

"He's gone," Lauranne said unnecessarily. Everyone nodded in agreement, then suddenly began chattering in relief.

"He's gone!" they all shouted. "He's gone!" Grins broke out, laughter was heard. In a moment the whole village was cavorting like a bunch of fools. Lisette and Stephanie hugged each other. Lisette was surprised to see tears in her friend's eyes.

"Don't tell me you miss him!" she exclaimed. Stephanie shrugged.

"He wasn't so bad, for a dragon," she replied.

"Well," Lisette said gruffly. "He's gone, and now maybe we can set about to find you a lover!"

"Tomorrow," Stephanie replied. "It's been a long day."

RED PEARLS

Richard Corwin

From a new writer, a story of a sorceress and her revenge; colorful and fantastic.

Richard Corwin is a graduate student, a photographer/artist, currently working at early childhood education; this story is definitely not for the kiddies.

—MZB

"For the five people who told me that I should write it anyway."

It began with the beating of the drums. Beating slowly, sonorously, rhythmically, hypnotically in the night's still air. Weatherbeaten hands held weatherbeaten mallets. Thick as a man's wrist, worn smooth from beating skins of stretched horsehide. Sounding out a slow heartbeat that moved the dancers of the circle through their smooth synchronous movements. Bare feet stamped lightly to the timing of the graceful rhythm, as the dancers traced out a carefully drawn starlike pattern in the sand. The snapping flurry of long silk sleeves circumscribed wavelike arcs, tossing shadows over white-painted faces that flickered red in the fire's glow.

The drum beat doubled and re-doubled. Punctuated by additional sharper-pitched taras, dancers whirled, kicking up red dust. Swirling and eddying about the circle, the white-robed Kojiro-Dahaka brought those beyond the circle to clapping in syncopated time to the drums. The spell became hypnotic. Winding. Binding. Blinding. The smoke-dust congealed into a pillar within the circle. Bending, swirling, and twisting it came to take a form of blood-dust. And the transfiguration began.

The chants condensed into wailing as the spell tightened, until the dust turned a carnelian in an explosion of light and heat, leaving a single form standing in the clearing haze. The figure of Ranghi stood cocooned in silken spiderwebs, save a single feminine hand extending outstretched in a frozen gesture of expectation. The drumming died down until only one pair of hands formed the music's beat. The Kojiro stepped within the circle of dancers bearing a pair of leather gloves dyed the color of blood, embroidered with silver threads and red pearls. Stepping before the cocoon, he placed the gloves into the open hand. Ruby fingernails closed slowly, stiffly around them.

A soft, distant sigh was heard from inside the cocoon before it disintegrated into a thousand floating wisps of filament. And slowly the form within was revealed. Encased in crimson-burnished armor adorned with rubies, red pearls, and silver filigree that traced aggravated curves; smooth blood-red surfaces with shapes sometimes resembling dragons, sometimes lions. The carved ruby helmet fitted the head snugly, and bore the sculpted crest of a curling dragon that clutched a slim silver moon in its claws. A queue of roseate hair flowed from an opening in the helmet and spilled down past her shoulders.

Her eyes were gold, and her skin was silver. Coral-colored lips moved. "It is the Spring, yes?"

"Yes, Houri-Ranghi," the Dahaka chieftan replied.

Ranghi had been the leader of her tribe for three hundred and fifty years. She remembered times long ago when the Dahaka had numbered into the hundreds. Now there were only twenty-seven. A war had begun in the time of her father, between themselves and the Asana. It had escalated into a feud of extinction, in which she had been their last surviving sorceress. In the Winter cold of the previous year she engaged in her death battle with Ameshet, the last wizard of the Asana, in the slag wastes near the Black River. They fought for three days, taking the forms of ogres, half-beasts, and demons, using any weapon they could conjure. Ameshet was stronger though. He took on an aspect more powerful than any Ranghi could become. Through luck, he trapped her and rent her body into five pieces, until he found her heart. Then he tore it from her; and made ritual to strengthen himself by eating it: it became an extra heart to pump for him.

Ranghi died slowly: it took nine days. After Ameshet left her to die, she began to weave a final spell to enable her to return to the earth to gain her revenge upon Ameshet. Before she died, Ranghi summoned Gabbath, the Kojiro-Dahaka to her and bade him to bury her body in the slag wastes, because the shoulders of the earth were strong there. She instructed him to return to her in the dark moon of spring-tide, and to call her back with tribal drumming. She then gave Gabbath her gloves and told him to restore them to her when she took her form in a body of dust. "They will return some of my power to me," she told him.

"Through the drumming I have been restored," she told her people. "It is through your drums that I may be sustained where sorcery cannot avail. Drum for a hundred years if need be, but do not fail. I am the only hope the Dahaka have to defeat Ameshet. I am weak. The coin of my sorcery is not strong without a body of flesh. My body is of dust, so you must be my strength. Your hands must be the line that holds me to this earth. I will not fail you. I promise to return to you as I have promised to return to you before."

As she spoke, the dust in the air coalesced around her, forming into a pair of beautiful golden wings. Weightlessly, she rose from the ground and began to fly northward to where her final battle lay. Behind her the drums chorused into complex rhythms, slowly becoming faint, far-away sounds in the distant night.

Moving through the belly of the desert's night winds, she came to the place where alabaster towers rose above white sands. Landing in pergolaed gardens of polished basalt pillars covered with vines bearing blue flowers, she approached a door of carved ivory. Two silent, muscular sentinels stood before it, hands hanging loosely about crystal-hafted spears with snakestone tips. With a gesture only, the solemn ones became crystal too, their hands merged forever with their weapons. She smiled lightly as she passed them, approaching the door. Gracefully disintegrating into dust again, she began seeping through the cracks around the single slab of ivory, passing easily through an invisible barrier that barred weapons both magical and otherwise. She entered an octagonal room of white walls, punctuated by carved screens that were trimmed with blue and green embroidered curtains. She glided on the breeze over a carpet bearing a maze-like design trimmed in runes. The intent of the carpet was to destroy or slow attackers of mortal flesh—but not those of dust.

In the center of the room was a tall dais of lapis, mounted by a fan-shaped chair of exquisitely carved emerald. On the chair, amid frozen reliefs of dancing gryphons and eagles, he sat: Blue and green armor of silk and steel trimmed in gold fittings, onyx hair pulled into a topknot, his white powdered skin caressed jade eyes. Ameshet. Kneeling before him on a cloth pillow was a white-garbed and also white-powdered man, leaning forward and speaking in quiet tones.

Circling the dais, she sprinkled motes into his eyes, blurring his vision with a curtain of tears as she reformed before him. She stood with hair that mingled with the train of her flame-colored robes. "Oh how you should cry, Ameshet," she said condescendingly.

The white-garbed one produced a jeweled knife and flew to his feet. Her smile turned to ice. Taking her attacker by his upraised arm, she threw him across the room like a discarded toy. Crackling tongues of blue fire licked him as he flew above the carpet's designs, enveloping him as he crashed into the wall, his body shattering into a thousand exploding smoldering fragments.

Ameshet cleared his half-blinded eyes, and drew himself up from the chair. "Is it Ranghi returned from her grave, or may you a phantom be?"

"No phantom," she replied.

"Then you may be slain again . . ." his voice trailed off into a hiss as he moved to a whitewashed wall to remove an opal sword from a gem-encrusted scabbard, ". . . and you *will* be slain again."

Dancing across runes that would not be triggered by dust, Ranghi moved to the opposite wall to a silver blade which she took into her two slender hands. She turned to face Ameshet. He had grown a full head taller. His shoulders had become wider, his teeth longer. He bore down upon her like a tidal wave. Crashing in armor, he rolled his sword arm in circular movements until the blade looked like iridescent flotsam amid the white foam of his hands. With a shrill scream she parried, engaging his blade for a moment, then shifting her fulcrum, sent his wave onward to eddy beyond her. She turned to face him. He had grown to nearly twice again his previous height, his head barely clearing the ceiling, his teeth had become snarling tusks. In his hands which had become ragged claws, the sword seemed scarcely a poiniard. She moved catlike backward, her long hair becoming rippling fur, her muscles becoming thinned and feline. She slashed at him with her sword, shattering his blade with the impact. Roaring, she leapt sword-first at his white gnashing face.

And then it was no longer there. She fell with a wounded howl into a pile of oversized armor.

"Over here, Beast," he called mockingly from the opposite wall. Brandishing a long lance with a double-edged blade at its tip, he asked, "As I do not know why you have returned, would you tell me before I undo you?"

"To watch you suffering," the reply.

Padding toward him, she began to whirl the blade over her head. He began his counterattack by feinting to her left, then swinging upward into her flurry, illuminating them both in a shower of yellow sparks as he disarmed her. He then arced the lance tip at her neck, beheading her almost soundlessly. Ranghi's head laughed a distant, hollow laugh as it rolled across the floor. The headless body stooped to find its lost member, searching furtively for what it could not seem to find. Ameshet's laugh joined with hers as he impaled the head with the lance and drew it into his left hand. Taking the still feline face by the hair, he examined it carefully but quickly. Ranghi's open eyes glared at him with a pale fury.

Ameshet smiled. "It seems that disembodiment has not killed you. Still, I suspect that your body will be quite useless without your eyes to guide it," he remarked. "Nor do I think that your head will survive overlong without your body."

Ranghi's head replied, "I think you overestimate yourself."

From the corner of his right eye, he saw a blur that became darkness as it raked across his eye, leaving behind a stream of blood that fell like tears. Half-blinded, Ameshet swung the lance at the body, but failed to more than beat it back as he retreated for the nearest open door. Sliding through the egress, he closed and bolted the bronze door behind him, and flew down the hall to a lacquered door. Expecting only a small lead to be gained from the obstacle now between himself and the body, Ameshet rested the lance and the severed head on the floor near him and then turned to face the opponent that would soon come. Taking a ring from his finger, he began to weave a hasty spell. As the bronze door began to buckle inward, Ameshet unleased a tumultuous ball of fire that sped down the hall and exploded like thunder as the leonine-human form broke into the hallway. Stooping to retrieve his charges, Ameshet's smoke-stung eyes saw what they had not expected. The beast was padding toward him through the ash-thick smoke.

A swell of fear rolled through him. He clutched the head with nervous fingers and sped through the door behind him, not bothering to close it. Down the next corridor, Ameshet pivoted into a small square room with three doors, lined with shelves bearing various equipment. He hastily scanned the room for usable weapons. From a table he took a small brown vial and three rings for his fingers, onyx, emerald, and sapphire respectively. Then his hand dove into a jar of herbs, retrieving them to put on his now useless eye. Finding a pouch of three-hundred rings, he tucked Ranghi's head therein, and bound the purse to his hip. As the headless body appeared at the doorway with a throatless snarl, Ameshet took a vial of brown potion and cast it upon the blue tile between them. A tongue of great brown earth sprang up between them, arched over Ranghi's body, and enveloped it in a tight ball.

Ameshet breathed a sigh and leaned heavily upon the nearby wall for a moment. He mopped the coagulation of ash, sweat, and white powder from his brow, retrieved the lance, and approached the spherical prison. In the blinking of an eye, a catlike forepaw sped from the ball dislocating Ameshet's shoulder with a crack. The dust-creature reformed itself utilizing the earth that had been intended to imprison it. Ameshet stared for a moment, then fled through the door at his left.

At the end of this next hallway, he threw open a door and

was greeted with a chorus of startled whinnying. He threw a bridle over the nose of a stallion and mounted it without saddling. Nudging the ribs, he steered the mount around the stall and through the open archway that led into the open night. Lance in his right hand, severed head at his left hip, he rode West.

A hundred yards from the stable he heard the sound of screaming horses behind him. There was no need to look back. He knew. He spurred the horse on faster.

Far away, the drums continued . . .

Taking the reins in his teeth, Ameshet thrust the lance into his belt. He then bit harder into the reins as he snapped his dislocated shoulder back into place. As his scream hissed through the leather, a chuckle rose from the pouch at his side.

Ameshet looked back after a few minutes and saw that Ranghi's body had lost all of its human attributes, becoming now entirely leonine . . . save that it was lacking a head. He rode on faster, gradually forming a lead between himself and the paws running silently behind him. As the night hours wore on, his lead slowly grew. In the gentle still heat of the hour before dawn, Ameshet looked behind him again. The beast was still following him, but it had become only an unwelcome stain at the edge of his night vision. With his good eye he gauged it to be about one league behind him. He directed his horse toward a distant waterhole in the desert with the intent of resting briefly, while alternately hoping that the sun's rays would dissolve his pursuer into a dreamlike specter.

But it did not.

At the sun's rise, the shadow still followed behind. Ameshet approached the waterhole and let the horse replenish itself. He pulled the pouch from his side and drew the head from it. Ranghi's eyes rolled open into an amused gaze. "Even dead you are still a strong sorceress. Tell me how you have done this?" he asked her.

"Let us call it a last enchantment, Ameshet. When you

killed me, I swore one day of vengeance for each piece of my body that you scattered.'' She grinned, pleased with her achievement.

''This means that you will hunt me for six days, does it not?''

''If you last that long . . .'' Her voice trailed off.

''But I have your head. Without it I see that your body can only flounder and falter after it, occasionally doing random injury to me,'' he replied.

''Yet it flounders after you,'' she snapped, ''And you have failed to show sufficient strength to stop it thus far. The greater sorcerer has managed only to flee in terror from it.''

''I am strong enough to stop it. I have my means,'' he snarled as he callously stuffed the head back into the pouch.

He considered for a moment ways that he might stop her. Necromancy would hardly work on one already dead. Considering her strength, and the previous encounter, open battle might prove fruitless. He had hardly brought any useful implements for strong sorcery, due to the speed of his flight. He had three rings, however. They would prove useful. Still, it seemed to him that he had won a small advantage already by gaining her head and riding just ahead of Ranghi's body. This advantage could be parlayed into victory if he stayed ahead of his opponent and kept her in sight, avoiding surprises, outrunning the spell. His horse would sustain him for a while, that would buy him enough time to think out the best ways of dispersing the resources that he had.

Behind him, Ameshet noticed that Ranghi was now about a third of a league from him. He then crushed the first of his rings into powder, and began to weave a spell. He clapped his hands and stamped his foot. The earth swelled between them, creating a high mountain of sand where there had been none before. He walked to his horse, remounted it, and resumed his near-random flight.

Far away, the drums continued . . .

Near nightfall, he galloped into another waterhole, this

time with a two-league lead. The horse was dying; he had
exhausted it. He estimated that it would last only another few
hours. They rested a short time while he clapped his hands
twice and stamped his feet twice, causing another mountain
to rise. Astride the stallion again, he jabbed his heels into its
now unresponsive flesh. His mount reared and a wet cough
gurgled from its throat. It staggered a few feet and collapsed.
Ameshet cursed softly at the inopportunity of the moment of
his charger's demise. He turned toward the mountain and
summoned a windstorm to slow the cat-beast even more.
Then, regarding the horse, he crushed the second ring into a
powder and sprinkled its green crystals over the body. He
wove a complex spell whereby the corpse would continue to
carry him by drawing power from its own decaying flesh.
The strength of his mount would carry him even in death. He
pulled the pouch from his belt and drew out the head. Shouting over his wind, he said, "See Ranghi! I will defeat you
again! I will continue onward, and you will expire before you
can retrieve your head!"

Ranghi's eyes opened, and her coral lips grew into a smile.
"That is what I have always admired in you, Ameshet. You
are so easily manipulated." Punctuating her statement with a
laugh neither evil nor complacent, her head melted away into
dust upon the wind. At the top of the hill, Ranghi's feline
body appeared with a roar of satisfaction. From where he
stood, he could just make out the shape of a lioness' head
placed where it should be between the shoulders. He watched
as the shoulders sprouted eagle's wings and tested them in the
wind. With a second roar, of challenge now, Ranghi stretched
her wings in the midday sun and began to swoop at him.

He mounted the reanimated stallion and charged away from
the gryphon behind him, the windstorm following directly at
his back. The windstorm remained behind him, blowing inter-
minably at Ranghi. Nonetheless, she flew over a half league
behind him, undaunted, tacking the wind. As the moon waned

on the end of Ameshet's first day of flight, his security and bravado began to turn into fear and terror.

Far away, the drums continued . . .

Dawn of the second day came. Ameshet's charger had begun to show signs of noticeable decay. The fur, epidermis and flesh had been consumed, leaving the superficial muscles plainly visible. Its eyes seemed white pearls. By the evening the muscles, too, were lost. Ameshet's attention was divided between maintaining the spell that continued the horse's progress, and reassessing his situation. Now the prospects did not look so good. There was not enough time for him to weave a spell of teleportation, neither was there enough time to make a strong spell to stop Ranghi. Now there seemed only time to run, to hope that an idea to stop her might come.

Early in the third day, he came to an oasis and briefly checked his flight to get water to refresh himself. He had not eaten or slept for three days, and had not drunk in two. Approaching the water, he stopped to look briefly at his reflection. His brightly embroidered silks were the dun-gray of the desert's dust. The white powder on his face had long since sloughed off with his sweat, and had been replaced with a thick caking of dried mud. His good eye was flecked with clouds and punctuated by angry red lightning. The other eye was as yet nearly swollen shut. His hair was matted with coagulated dirt and sweat. The desert had transformed him.

As he knelt to wash away the grime, he saw in the reflection the gryphon-form of Ranghi dropping on him from high above. He was at once consumed with panic. He lurched aside as the descending claws rent the previously dislocated shoulder. The lance he had held tumbled into the once-welcomed waters. A frustrated roar swooped upward ahead of him, and then banked into a turn to attack again. Ameshet instinctively jerked his arm in a rising gesture, and a hail of stones erupted from the lake, hurtling toward Ranghi. The missiles beat at her body with such great speed that they stunned her momentarily, causing her to alter her course to avoid further projectiles. She looped around the oasis, altering her shape as she went: above her waist she returned to human form in all its naked beauty, but below the waist, lion's paws became talons of brass tipped with ruby claws, and eagle's wings became a cacophony of brass feathers. By the time she had circled the oasis, Ameshet was riding away, leaving a thin ribbon of dust behind him. The windstorm had ceased; he could no longer maintain it. She shrieked a gleefully bellicose shriek. Her plan was proceeding well. She beat her wings on the suddenly still desert air, and followed after him.

The moon rose on the end of the third day to see a ragged man riding a mount of decaying bones. Behind him, in a flurry like the ringing of bells in a storm, a woman-bird of brass and rubies zigzagged after him like an obscenely gilded bat.

Far away, the drums continued . . .

At dawn of the fourth day, the gaunt mount crumbled into dust. Ameshet lifted himself from the ground to which he had been thrown and looked behind him. She still followed. He knew he had to continue. Despite his riding sores, his distended and torn shoulder, his swollen eye, his bruises, abrasions, starvation and exposure, he had to continue. He somehow summoned sufficient strength to transform himself into a black wolf, but the grime of the desert made his fur appear dun. He would run on his own strength now. Mustering his courage he issued a long howl of challenge. It was echoed by a scream like a torturing of the damned. "I have been there," it seemed to say. "And soon, you shall be there too." Ameshet turned to face the low dunes before him and began to run on onyx-clawed paws.

The sores of the dawn of the fifth day were great, but Ameshet continued despite them. Loping over the terrain that he had encountered the day before, he was allowed at least the occasional patch of shade. As he neared the lands of the setting sun, the heat became more intense, taxing him greatly.

He needed water and rest, things that Ranghi seemed not to need. Heedless of the heat, Ranghi soared high in the sky, seeming sometimes to be a brazen crow, sometimes to be merely a glimmer in the sun. Occasionally, her uluating howls would form shapes in the air to swoop at him and claw harmlessly at his ears. Advantages seemed to be all hers now . . . but if he could continue another day he knew he would defeat her . . .

Far away, the drums continued . . .

The sixth day came. There had been no waterholes for three days. Ameshet's thirst was becoming a thing of near-delirium. The dunes and the shade that they had provided were gone now, leaving only open desert to run in. Only the dream of the scattered corpse lay behind him now. He girded himself for the final sprint as dusk approached, hoping to gain a sizable lead. He needed time to crush the final ring, to call the final spirit to defend him. As the night would dissolve, he would dissolve her with the fury of a final storm. Slowly he began to gather speed, moving ahead as the hours passed into night. As the moon neared its apex, signaling the end of the sixth day, Ameshet stopped and turned to face the approaching Ranghi.

He returned his form into that of a man clothed in armor of green tortoise shell and jade. He pulled the final ring from his finger, it was lapis strewn with rivers of gold. He crushed the stone into blue powder in his palm and blew the powder into the night breeze. The powder formed a cloud that rose into the sky, ballooning and mushrooming until it stretched across the horizons, obscuring the moon into blackness. Ranghi closed the distance of a quarter-league. He could see that she was human again, armored in her rubies, flying on crisp white wings. He waved his hands, causing the wind to whip around him in a towering vortex. Ranghi became caught in the strength of the winds, and was slowly blown away from her target. The force of winds made it difficult for the dust that was her to remain together. He smiled. Only a few minutes and the sixth day would be done, she would return to the darkness where she belonged. He clenched his swollen fists and rain began to pour from the clouds, turning the growing tornado into a hurricane. She seemed to be confounded in flight. He was certain that she would be grounded soon. The time was almost nigh. "All I need do is wait." The rain began to hit the ground. It was the music of victory to Ameshet's ears.

It was also the sound of victory to Ranghi. For the falling of the rain on the earth made a sound: the sound of drumming. The sound of ten thousand drums. The strength that summoned and sustained her. It had never been a question of six days, it had been a question of drumming. Here were more drums than her tribe could give her. Ameshet had unwittingly exploded her spell. Feeding hungrily on the power, she began to expand herself. Her wings grew longer and surer in the wind. Stronger now, she beat her wings faster, caught the winds, and banked into them. She dove into a long, rapid arc that catapulted her into the eye of the hurricane, landing before Ameshet in a flurry of feathers. She raised herself up to thirty feet. He, in turn, grew to the same, sprouting ram's horns, scorpion's claws and leathery wings. The storm was spent. He was not strong enough to maintain it. As his claws slipped into a fierce grip around Ranghi's throat, he said, "Your sixth day is almost gone. The spell you laid is about to be undone."

"The dead are not bound to the laws of the living. I lied."

His arms slackened their grip momentarily. A moment, no more. But in that space of time Ranghi's arms slashed upward, breaking his hold. Her upraised fists pummeled down upon his head, smashing it aside with a cracking like a felled oak. Injured and exhausted, Ameshet fell to the ground, nearly helpless. Her hands rained down upon him again, turning the lower half of his face into bleeding flesh and fragmented bone. She had removed his opportunity to utter a final curse. "You were so unwise to rely upon your strength, Ameshet.

Did you think that you would always be strong?'' His only reply was a look of helpless terror. ''You will unfortunately be unable to learn from your mistake, as I did. There is something, though, that I need of you before I reduce you to the dust that I have been—your heart. As you took mine, I will take yours to beat strongly for me. It will make me a part of this world again.'' She smiled.

She gestured with her hand, and his ribcage split open soundlessly. His heart wrenched itself out and raised itself up into her hand. It was then pushed gently through her armor, turning dust into firm flesh as it passed. Between her breasts, a drum began beating. The true Power returned to her again. She drew her first breath into her new lungs and exhaled. The desert air tasted sweet.

No longer a phantom, she waved her hands above Ameshet's body and his flesh slowly was desiccated into dry dust. As it began to dissolve, a final scream rasped from his ruined throat. When only porcelain white bone remained of Ameshet, Ranghi knelt beside him to inspect her handiwork. She plucked one red pearl from each of her gloves and placed them in the sockets that were once his eyes. When the Asana found the corpse, they would know its slayer. She would return to her people now. Soon they would eradicate the last of the Asana. She lifted her wings to the sky, raising a small cloud of blue-green dust as she headed toward her home.

THE WOUND IN THE MOON

Vera Nazarian

One of the greatest pleasures in an editor's life is the discovery of new talent. In the first volume of *S&S*, I published "first stories" by Charles Saunders, Charles de Lint, and Jennifer Roberson, all of whom have had, between their two appearances here, first novels published: Charles Saunders' *Imaro* which exploits an African background to the Dossouye stories; De Lint's excellent *Riddle of the Wren*, a low-keyed fantasy of great beauty and charm; and Jennifer Roberson's *Shapechangers*. Each of these has a second novel (in Saunders' case a third) ready for print.

Vera Nazarian is the youngest contributor to this anthology. In January of this year, she sent me a story for the anthology, saying that she had been told by other editors that it was too long, but she hoped I was more flexible. Since the story exceeded by about ten thousand words the "maximum" length I had set in my guidelines, I would normally have returned it with a noncommittal "does not meet wordage requirements," but since the author was a schoolgirl of seventeen, I read the story and found it excellent; however, I was compelled to tell her that there was no market for a story of this length (almost 20,000 words) though it would have been just right for a "lead novel" in the old pulps. I suggested she try something shorter; and she did.

This is a good story by any standards. Vera Nazarian is now about to enter college, and is eighteen years old; and this colorful piece reminds me of the early work of Tanith Lee. Finding something like this is why editors cheerfully wade through slush piles; now and then one discovers a new writer of astonishing talent. In this volume there are a number of "first stories" but few by writers so young.

—MZB

A s the late afternoon sky stood lavender upon gold in the great city, the thief was imprisoned for the highest crime there was. The stranger had raised her eyes and gazed at the Al-Eralir, lord of Aerhad-el-Rass, as he rode by in a procession, surrounded by obeisant slaves, haughty, beautiful, and cold as death.

The great multitude all around had sunk to the earth in worship, the faces of men and women hidden, the eyes shut tightly, so as not to risk a sacrilegious glimpse of the Al-Eralir, demon lord. But she, an outsider, had stared in curiosity first at the graceful magnificent stallions which walked, bejeweled, and barely under control of the crimson warrior guards of the Al-Eralir.

And then her gaze had slid higher, from the mirror-bright trappings of the great black beast in the center of the procession to a mounted figure of stonelike bearing. She was stricken by the sight of empty amber eyes in a perfect face. After he had passed by the blood-clad warriors of his guard brutally captured and manacled her, not giving her an instant to react.

Under more normal circumstances the thief *could* react, swiftly and ferally. She could, when provoked to physical violence, move lithe as water to strike and leave no trace. Only this time she had looked and tarried much too long, as if something in the air of this huge city dulled her wits. When they took her, she did not even desire to resist.

From the start, she had never admitted that she was a thief. It must have been the agility in her eyes and the brightness, that made them all assume, and she went along, passive and uncomplaining. They were intense gray-blue, those eyes of hers, and peculiar in their own way. Peculiar, maybe, because neither the jailer nor the guards had previously seen such eyes in a commoner, and even less, a thief.

The jailer also noticed her oddly fine looks, as he searched her for valuables. She had then, to facilitate his efforts, surrendered two rings, a neck chain of precious metal, and the ready information on the nature of her occupation. All this to end the further probing of his lecherous fingers. The jewelry took its permanent place in the jailer's collection, but he only guffawed when she told him she was a warrior. And the thief was moved on for further inspection by the jailer's next superior.

One of the crimson guards believed he saw a glimmer of a dagger in her boot. But that came as a second thought, after the definite stirring of desire at the sight of a slim leg and calf encased in masculine trousers. Her body was limber and well-formed.

The dagger was confiscated. And then they had wheedled a name out of her, Lyren, by force of threats. That had been one thing she was loath to part with. However, threats were threats, and for one who was dead in Law already, cooperation meant an easy or not-so-easy way to end.

Knowing what was good for her, Lyren did not resist when they stripped her and gave her a penitent's rags to wear, Thus she was to appear before the demon lord himself whose lips were to utter her punishment.

"When you are summoned, bitch, dirt beneath His feet, you shall fall flat on your face. Then you shall crawl to His Seat, never lifting eyes from the floor," she was told, and a guard dealt her, as a reminder, a lash of the whip. It fell across her cheek, cutting a thin crimson welt that burned like hot coals. She never flinched.

Afterward they threw her into a cell, dark with rotting night. And when true night came to lie over the city, she slept, knowing what was to come.

They said that Aerhad-el-Raas, pearl of cities, stood the first in the way of the rising sun, before all of the lands of men, in the East of all the easts. It was the hallowed Seat of the expansive unconquerable Empire which from the city took its name.

In all of the Empire of Aerhad there was no other such city, no other such exquisite luxury, and no other such decadence. Contrasts prevailed throughout—beggars and lepers lined the squalid bazaars with their fly-covered bodies, and man-filled rags huddled in filthy alleyways and under the bridges crossing Urthad, the River of Smells; in the rich quarter the streets were paved with gold, sparkling crystal fountains ran with wine, and from the palaces and gardens of the nobles came exquisite music and softly muted laughter of courtesans.

Over all this ruled Sahtiel, the beautiful demon lord, whose mother was said to be none other than the moon herself. The previous Al-Eralir, his mortal father, built Aerhad-el-Raas, city of cities, and his son added the Empire.

Sahtiel surrounded himself with beauty in the truest sense. Godlike in appearance himself, with golden hair running like honey to his shoulders, skin of pale ripe olives, features reminiscent of a statue from a holy shrine of Cxeris, and amber eyes of the mountain cats, Sahtiel attained twenty-three summers, conquered the East in another three, so that rivers of blood irrigated the lands, and then decided he had no more desire to see ugliness in any form.

In the luxurious rooms of the Palace of the Al-Eralirs musk and incense were burned day and night, and the sweet scent carried out into the gardens to eclipse the fragrance of the roses with its sensual delicacy. Beautiful youths served the Al-Eralir, for he was known to take only male lovers. His crimson guard was composed of the finest warriors who served their stern master with fanatical loyalty, for his charm had conquered their souls. It was told among the people however, that the present Al-Eralir, having demon blood in him, held strange orgiastic and occult feasts, where terrible perversions were practiced.

Sahtiel had decreed that no commoner was ever to lift eyes outright at him, and no woman approach him without crawling upon the ground, so as not to defile him with their baseness. He also gave orders never to have the sick or the ugly within his sight. All this was on pain of death, for the Al-Eralir had no mercy. And the punishments he dealt out were such that instant death could only have been a blessing. . . . .

It was before the demon lord that Lyren, thief, and stranger, was to be brought forth.

In the morning Lyren awoke in her cell, and the understanding of the way things really stood smote her. The day before had been like a daze, in which she only remembered two cold amber eyes, lovelier than any human ones she had seen, and terrible. But now her practicality had set in.

Utter fool! What in Aldiz's name made me dawdle like that? He resembles someone—she did not finish the thought, the implications of which were too unclear to pursue. Instead she forced herself to ponder on the purpose of her presence here in this accursed city of the corrupt.

Somewhere in Aerhad-el-Raas was Haderi, alive, she knew, for the carnelian stone in her earlobe remained warm and pulsing with his heart. Her blood-sworn promise to him still stood, and so did the half-conscious love which had managed to insinuate into her relationship with him since the last summer of their travel companionship. Haderi, unlike her, was not a renegade *sehjir* warrior, but a thief, one of the most sophisticated and highest-placed in the Guild. He had taught her all the tricks and the grace, which now helped her to pass easily for one of the Guildmembers.

Lyren remembered the strange skirmish in a small town tavern, which involved her and Haderi with a group of men from the city. Haderi killed one with a throw of a knife, and she bowled over two others. They had left the place swiftly, but not before she had seen a bit of oddly rich clothing show from under the folds of the cloak of one of the fallen men. Like a cold wave came the suspicion that these were disguised noblemen. Indeed, the land ran with rumors that nobles from Aerhad-el-Raas often came and went in the semblance of commoners, for perverse entertainment. And if it were so in this case, then the two of them were in great danger.

Her suspicion came true, for the next morning Haderi left her on some private business and did not come back. Never quite sure of his intents, Lyren waited a week. And then she knew that a venture to the city was now inevitable.

She had once promised herself not to approach Aerhad-el-Raas closer than an arrow's flight. It was as if some inner sense stood as a warning against the lure of that decadent trap. Only now the moment of truth was at hand. The business contract which had first bound them was now only second place. Lyren had to rescue the man she had been hired to protect, for his own sake.

Curiosity killed the moth, ran a common saying among the people. Only Lyren would never quite see the truth of it, not even when she was entering the city where there were so many perilous things to be curious about. What harm would it do, she had thought as she stood with the multitude before the procession, to glance one time at the Al-Eralir? How in the world could she be noticed among the crowd, and even then, why couldn't she swiftly escape? Lyren was not aware, however, that the crimson warriors knew which sorts to watch more carefully than others. She, as a stranger, had not prostrated herself quite as correctly as necessary, or soon enough. She had hesitated. And that drew their attention.

Lyren thought about death, as footsteps echoed down the prison corridor, and her cell door fell open. Two guards entered, roughly lifted her from the cold stone slabs of the floor, and removed her outside.

Before being brought into the demon lord's presence, Lyren was made more presentable by two slaves who brushed out her short, higher than shoulder-length dark hair, and gave her water to wash the grime off her face and hands. The rags remained, for the sake of humiliation, but the Al-Eralir was to see no dust or disarray.

The great arched doors opened before her, and she was pushed from behind to fall forward on her stomach into a great dimly lit chamber.

For several instants she was too surprised to do anything, only lay feeling the cool mosaic of the exquisite floor tiles against her cheek. A harsh whisper sounded from somewhere nearby: "Crawl!" it hissed. She opened her eyes and saw, at the level of the floor, the feet of the guards which lined the two walls.

By Aldiz, what a fool I must be making of myself, she thought, as she began to slither along the floor. She had a long way to go.

"O, Exalted One," a voice from someplace spoke out, "this *nothing* huddled before you on the ground, penitent and groveling, has committed the ultimate crime of seeing your Visage. Pronounce, if you will, the manner of its death."

Lyren liked this not at all. *Neither Am I* "*huddled*," she thought, *nor* "*penitent*"—*for I do believe I'd do this again, given the chance, only with greater caution. And even less am I "groveling." Aldiz knows, I don't govel. This bastard assumes too much.* And abruptly, unexpectant to herself, she gave an audible snort of contempt.

Rarely had it been that such a simple thing as that could have so great a meaning or such a peculiar effect upon a room full of people. Almost, echoes were heard from that one sound, so silent became the great chamber.

And then something prompted Lyren to repeat the great crime, the terrible crime that had gotten her here. She looked up.

The young man with long golden hair, half-reclined on the great filigreed throne, observed her blandly from underneath the lazy slits of his bored eyes shadowed by a fringe of long sable lashes. *Eyes too beautiful even for a maiden*, Lyren thought.

At his feet sat a dark-haired youth with the coal-black eyes of a doe, dark-skinned, and delicate-boned. He was watching with a sleepy look the proceedings, his head languidly leaned to the knee of the Al-Eralir. Sahtiel's elegant hand was absently toying with the strands of the boy's silky hair.

Lyren's raised eyes met the look of the empty golden ones. And then suddenly, there came a spark of interest in those yellow melted amber eyes.

Sahtiel carelessly glanced at the ragged beggar at his feet. *It* was human, of indefinite sex. The Chancellor had promised it was to be the last one for the day, not to be put off because of the magnitude of its crime.

Chancellor Razd proceeded to describe in his usual groveling voice the crime. It was another one of those who had "looked."

Sahtiel listened in silence, listlessly, absent-mindedly stroking Jieri's hair. Jieri. This night they had not slept much, for the Al-Eralir had experienced a resurge of passion toward the youth, which was beginning to wane since last week. Now

Sahtiel wanted to lean down and breath in the scent of Jieri's sweet silken locks, but held himself back for the sake of maintaining the formal atmosphere of the audience chamber.

Razd finished his speech. The human on the ground suddenly squirmed, making a very definite snort of derision. And then it raised its head of dark unclean hair. In a young face two uncharacteristically piercing gray-blue eyes met his. Sahtiel involuntarily felt a reminiscence of *something* wash over him. His interest was quickened.

"Gods of Aerhad!" exclaimed Razd, "The wench dares to look at you once again, O Glorious One! Order her maimed limb by limb, her breasts cut off, her womb filled with molten lead. . . ."

The woman on the floor slightly turned her head in Razd's direction, and her remarkably clear eyes filled with cold anger.

"I'll maim you, hairless devil, monkey, son of—" she hissed, no longer caring of the consequences.

Razd's mouth fell open.

And then Sahtiel laughed.

Every crimson guard watched in silence as the Al-Eralir laughed, his voice cold as crystal, inhuman, echoing in the great chamber.

The woman watched too. Only there was no awe on her face. She seemed quite annoyed.

"When you're finished, great Al-Eralir," she said in a strangely calm voice, "Do proceed to condemn me for your idiotic crime. Aldiz help me if I listen to any more of this without reverting to violence. I wonder, can demon-kin withstand strangling?"

"What is your name?" said Sahtiel, and she saw his amber eyes were now alive and burning.

"My name is mine. To give or to keep. Why is that boy looking at me like that?"

Jieri was staring in near shock at this pile of common rags, which suddenly began to speak back to his lord.

Her insolence was so new that Sahtiel involuntarily straightened in his seat. "Rise," he said quietly, "Come here."

"Now *such* orders I like. The floor was getting cold."

She stood before him, wrapped in nondescript concealing rags, but he saw that she was tall and slender. And again, those eyes of hers were indeed remarkable. Sahtiel had not previously seen such brazen clear-eyed insolence in a woman.

Her head leaned slightly to the side. "Well, what now?"

"Yes, what now?" he said, "I will not have you killed yet. Who are you?"

"I am Lyren."

"You give me your name, when before you refused."

"I am deliberately provoking you." She bared her teeth in an angry grin.

Sahtiel glanced around the chamber. "Leave us, all of you." His gaze included Jieri.

"Illustrious One—" began Razd.

The amber eyes burned.

When the chamber was empty, the Al-Eralir turned to Lyren. "I do not know your motives, but you intrigue me."

"I intrigue many people—is it permitted to sit down?"

"Sit, here, by me. Tell me things."

"By Aldiz, you're not as blood-thirsty and cruel as I thought. I expected to be torn and maimed—immediately." Lyren sat down in a light crouch before the throne, her clear eyes trained on his. Despite her unsightly appearance, there was grace in her movements.

"I hope, O Al-Eralir, that you don't mind my stink. People brought forth from prison customarily give off an odor. Have you considered cleaning the place, ever?"

"Your words are too clever," he mused, "You must be a thief."

"Hm, we were speaking about odors—"

A smile passed his fine lips, sensuous and pale. "Nevertheless, I shall call you thief." He watched her closely, in silence, studying, it seemed, everything about her.

"Interesting?" Lyren asked. She was feeling discomfited by this.

"So, thief," he said. "So, you hint with utmost subtlety that you desire a bath. And a change of clothes. Should I allow you that, I wonder? Or maybe it might be more interesting to have you beheaded?"

"Not at all. From what I've heard, you've overused the method already. Besides, that wouldn't *look* nice at all. And I know you don't like things that don't look nice."

"*You* don't look nice." The golden shadowed eyes watched her, unblinking.

"Ah, but again, *that* can be remedied—"

"I wonder." The mockery was very subtle from underneath the indefinite expression of the refined face, but once again she knew, by the slight curving of his lips, that the verbal game they were playing pleased him.

"If you, O great Al-Eralir, don't try me, you'll never find out."

"Well then, you have stirred my curiosity." Sahtiel said, and summoned slaves to the chamber.

Lyren was indeed curious to look at, later that day, after she had bathed and donned an elegant masculine outfit. Her once listless hair now fell in dark soft curves around a pale fine-featured face with its evocatively clear intense eyes. The dark expensive material of her well-fitting caftan and trousers emphasized her willowy stature, almost too tall for a woman. As she walked to Sahtiel's quarters, those who saw her pass often mistook her for a young handsome nobleman going on the demon lord's business.

Sahtiel had invited her to dine with him that night, a particular honor. Lyren hoped that his interest toward her would not wane before it could be beneficial for her and her search for Haderi.

As Lyren approached the lord's quarters, unchallenged (she was given permission to walk around freely), she thought wary thoughts. People had said strange things about the present Al-Eralir. He was not human, they said. He had no compassion. And many doubted if he had a soul. His refinement was so acute that it had turned into perversion. He took beautiful youths from the finest families of the Empire for his lovers, putting to death those who displeased him.

And they said that he did other worse things.

Lyren paused before the guarded doors of the private quarters, frowning at the two crimson guards (who probably would've loved to frown back—the Al-Eralir's short-lived favorites were envied and disliked, often for good reasons). The doors were opened for her, and she entered into a luxuriously furnished room, once more, dimly lit, as it was characteristic of Sahtiel.

Rich exotic carpets hung on the walls and covered the floor, while mosaic tiles decorated the ornate ceiling. Lyren however, immediately turned her attention to the great arsenal of weapons hanging on one of the carpeted walls. She turned around and, seeing no one in the room, quickly advanced to examine the objects closer.

Among the barbed pikes, spears, battleaxes, swords, *Ahri* knives, daggers, throw darts and discs, she saw one sword that took her fancy. Lyren had made it a habit, since in the employ of Haderi and the Thieves Guild, never to carry weapons more conspicuous than a dagger. Now, lacking even her one small throw-knife confiscated by the jailer, she remembered with involuntary envy her own longsword which she had had to turn in to the Guild for "safe keeping" before beginning her work with them. This sword before her, slim and of a simplistic workmanship, brought memories of times both good and bad. And Lyren, on a newly learned Guild habit, did not hesitate to take it down from the wall.

She slid the blade out of the long scabbard, weighed it in her hands, then tried the feel of the handle with both hands separately (she was ambidextrous). Then came the practice swings which she felt compelled to try. Lyren was deeply engrossed in a very pleasant practice bout with a ghostly opponent, when a voice sounded from behind.

"The elegance of your movement fits the weapon. The sword is yours."

Lyren had thought, since the beginning, that his voice was oddly memorable, and now, once more, the clear quality of the sound jerked her out of her concentration.

Like crystal breaking . . . beautiful, she thought, as she turned around, somewhat embarrassed by her display.

Sahtiel, his golden hair a stream of pale liquid honey in the semi-twilight, had come in through a small hidden door, and was watching her for several moments now. He wore a long white robe with a wide ornate belt over ankle-length trousers, and his perfectly proportioned body was arrow-straight. Despite the fine-boned semblance of diminutive delicacy, Lyren realized that he was taller than she.

She was unable to hold the words back: "Is it true what they say, that you are the son of Ilenvis, the moon?"

His dark arches of brows moved slightly upward. "And what *do* they say, thief—or should I say, warrior?"

Lyren lowered the sword and approached him. "They say, O Al-Eralir, that you take blood—human blood—and you drink it from a silver vessel when the moon is full. And then, your mother descends from the sky, leaving the sphere unattended. She comes to you, out of love, to tell you the truths of this world and others. And you kneel to her—" She paused. "And then there are other things, darker ones, that you do, that I don't comprehend. . . ."

Sahtiel looked at her, silent, his expression indefinite. At this proximity she was better able to examine the details of the face, and sensed a welling of apprehension. The peculiar charismatic quality about him was beginning to have its effect on her.

"Must I tell you everything, my thief?" he spoke then, and drew his face down to hers, so that their eyes were inches apart. And then his hand touched her left earlobe. His fingers brushed against the carnelian stone, warm and living.

"What is that?"

She blinked, coming out of a reverie. "Nothing. An earring."

"No. It is more, I can feel it. It is some kind of a living transfer link. With whom?"

She was surprised, then wary. "Whatever do you mean?"

The amber eyes glowed. "Do not attempt to withhold anything from me. You *know* what I mean. With whom?!"

"What does it matter? With a friend."

"Why?"

"By Aldiz, what is it to you?" she exclaimed, now angry. And then she felt a wave of fear at the sight of an even greater anger, cold, and strange, in the golden eyes.

Lyren lowered her gaze. "I am looking for a man," she said, "A man of the Thieves Guild. I am his hired bodyguard. This—" she pointed to her ear, "is to establish permanent contact. I know he is here in the city."

"Is that all?" The eyes were still cold.

"Yes! What else could there be?"

"You said, 'a friend.' "

"I lied. My employer."

"No, you lie now."

"Demons be damned, why do you insist this? What do you care?"

"His name is Haderi-e-Relavis. I know him . . . well."

"You—how did you—"

Sahtiel watched her intensely.

"How did you see what I was thinking?" Lyren said.

"Didn't you know? I had glanced into your soul. My Mother gave me the gift together with Her blood."

"I suppose she had also given you the right to freely assume power over everyone?" said Lyren, angered by the diffident arrogance.

"I do not assume. I *have* the power."

"Hah!" Lyren snorted and turned away from him. There was a pause.

She paced the room. "Well, then, find him. Find Haderi for me, if you truly can."

She did not see as Sahtiel smiled. "I have already found him," he said.

Lyren froze.

And then she felt a chill sweep down her spine as a hand came to lie against her left shoulder, from behind.

"You shall have Haderi tomorrow," he spoke softly, close to her ear, "In exchange for—for this . . ."

Surprise came too late, as she felt the languid yet hard pressure of warm lips against her throat. As his other hand slid around her waist in a tightening embrace, she managed to breathe:

"And how do I know the—truth of what you say? . . ."

"You have my word," answered Sahtiel, Al-Eralir, as for the first time in his life he felt passion toward a woman turn him to fire.

The nightingale stopped singing some while ago, replaced by the morning birds, when Sahtiel opened his eyes. In the tentative rose glow of dawn coming through the great arched balcony windows, Lyren lay asleep, the slender body naked under the light silk covers of the great bed. He drew closer to watch the face in repose, washed by the last blue shadows of the fleeing night. She was not just fine-featured, but truly beautiful, he saw now. The aristocratic lines of the face reminded him of something, only what, he could not recall. Under the dark brows, her long lashes lay against the pallid skin of her cheek, and the dark soft waves of her hair flowed in disorder against the pillow. Her pale full lips were parted slightly. So pale. . . .

She was so very fine and dark and pale. . . . His mind blurred for an instant, and he thought he saw, in the strong angle of her chin, in the heavy line of her brows, a youth. It was as if a man were lying beside him, not a maiden.

This was how he had first seen her, with her defiance, her manner of nonchalant ease, and her quick, witty answers. The way she dressed also aided the illusion, in particular the night before when she was practicing with the sword. Sahtiel was infatuated with her, with the illusion, until the two were intertwined into one complex object of desire. And when he discovered the body of the woman, the novelty only kindled the desire further, so that all night he burned, his passion greater than that ever experienced before.

Sahtiel watched her and thought of what he had done. From the first he had known, despite all her words, that she loved Haderi, and the memory came to him of the raven-haired thief who had once stolen his heart and his soul with a glance. Haderi had had the same, almost the same effect on him as Lyren. Haderi was quick, clever, brilliant, and his dark handsome elegance was noticeable everywhere from a distance.

And Haderi, although the mesmerizing golden beauty of the demon lord had touched him, did not submit to his advances. He was not usually a lover of men. And women, as Lyren knew, also held little interest for him whose life was quicksilver and ambition.

Sahtiel hated him then, after the handsome dark thief had rejected him. That had happened years ago, when the Al-Eralir breathed with the passion of conquest of the East. Somehow Haderi had escaped his wrath, maybe because Sahtiel had not tried very hard to apprehend him.

But now, once more, Haderi was within reach. It was a strange discovery for Sahtiel to make that the thief was even now imprisoned in the dungeons of the city for a reckless act of murder of some nobleman.

Sahtiel thought only briefly before doing what he did, thought very briefly how he had once loved Haderi, and then, how Lyren loved Haderi, and how he now wanted Lyren.

And then, still loving Haderi, and newly loving Lyren, he summoned a guard in the middle of the night, when she slept in his arms, and told him to throttle with a silken cord a dark handsome man in the thirty-seventh prison cell on the right, the one with a tiny window facing east, and the rising sun. . . .

Lyren woke up from the cold. It was a cold that slithered its way from her left ear to the rest of her body, insinuated unnaturally into her blood, so that it seemed to slow in her veins. The carnelian stone burned with cold.

Her eyes flew open and she sat up in the great bed. Next to her Sahtiel lay back on the pillows, his eyelashes shadowing the amber eyes, watching her lazily and indifferently.

She stared at him, at the indifference, and suddenly a great surging tidal wave of emotion came welling in her, a wave of anger.

"He is dead," she said, softly, and her clear eyes shone bright.

He spoke nothing but at that moment something slowly forced the corners of his lips upward. A tiny cynical smile.

Lyren remembered that tiny smile. It was a catalyst. She turned on him then, turned on the Al-Eralir of Aerhad-el-Raas.

"He is dead!" she cried, "You betrayed me!"

"I did not betray you."

"What?! You dare say this now, when you gave me your word—"

"My word is still yours. You shall have Haderi as I promised."

She stared at him, suddenly cold in anger and understanding.

"Yes," he said, "You see now. You did not specify *how* you wanted him. I give him *dead*."

"But why?"

He reached out with a hand to brush his fingers against her cheek. She did not draw back, but flinched. There was a tiny trace of a scar there, a whip scar. It had healed incredibly fast, overnight.

He ran his fingers along the scar. "Because you are beautiful," he said. "And Haderi was—beautiful too. There shouldn't be such beauty together, as yours and his. Dark with dark. No. . . ."

"You are mad . . ." Lyren said softly.

"No," he continued. "Dark should be with gold. I am gold. . . ."

"By Aldiz and all the gods, may you be damned, but you're mad!"

And Sahtiel laughed. It was a crystal clear cold laugh. "No. I am not mad. I am omnipotent. Which in itself is a sort of madness to those others who cannot know what I know or have. . . ."

"And what is it that you know and have?" said Lyren as she stared closer into his eyes.

They were golden and cold with emptiness. And he did not answer.

Suddenly Lyren sprang from the bed, throwing back the covers, and stood naked before him. "So, you think that you know and have things greater than the rest of us ordinary mortals?"

And then, she ran to the open balcony, past where the gauze lavender curtains fluttered in the morning breeze.

Before he could react with surprise, she was on the balcony, looking down, high above the city, her lovely willowy body tinted lilac and gold by the rising sun.

The breeze was strong where she stood, and dark specks of birds circled the towers and turrets of the palaces nearby, blue-gray against the lightening sky. Aerhad-el-Raas, drowning in the pale milk-fine mists of morning, spread all around her, immense, boundless, teeming with confusion of lowly life. Lyren, her hair flying in the wind, looked around her, then raised both hands to the sky, and cried, sending great echoes resounding against the walls of stone and the emptiness of the great abyss:

"Hear me, O Aerhad-el-Raas, city of the mad and the

meek! I, Lyren, challenge Sahtiel Al-Eralir to a duel! Let the Al-Eralir fight a woman, if he has any courage in him! Let him fight me with sword, a duel of honor! You, O corrupt rotting city, hear me well! Hear me well and bear witness to my words! Witness now this Formal Challenge!''

The echoes rang and dwindled into living silence. She lowered her hands and breathed in the pure air. The deed was done.

At the doors of the balcony Sahtiel stood, naked as she, his countenance full of surprise, anger, and odd sorrow.

"What have you done?" he whispered. "What have you done, O fool? Now I'll have to kill you . . ."

She barely turned her head at his voice, and her eyes were calm and intense and clear, as she answered: "No, demon lord. Now is the time that I wound the moon. She has forgotten, I think, what mortal pain life contains. Through her son She shall remember."

At midday all the city came to watch the duel of Sahtiel Al-Eralir of Aerhad-el-Raas, and the woman *sehjir* warrior. By law, a Formal Challenge could never be ignored or refused, by beggar or lord, or the one to abstain from the duel would have been forever termed coward and less than a man. A Formal Duel was usually to the death, but this was never specified by law. The winner determined the final terms.

At the Field of Combat, just outside the city, space was cleared, and a wide square platform erected, for all to see. All around, thousands milled, seethed, expectant.

The two opponents were given only armor and longswords, according to the rules of combat. Sahtiel, slender, elegant, clad in silver, stood before Lyren, easily swinging a longsword. The helmet with its white plumes hid his face under its visor. Lyren faced him, equally armed with a sword. She wore black.

"Foolish thief," spoke Sahtiel, "I did not want you to die."

And as the Duel was called to begin, Lyren answered, cold and impassive, swinging her sword up for a strike: "Fight me now, demon lord. Fight while you can."

They came together, two birds of prey, to tear each other's hearts. Lyren was swift, but Sahtiel was fire. Their swords flashed white in the sun, as they met and separated, leaving searing lines of light in the empty space. The crowds were silent, watching.

Never had Lyren met such a skillful and strong opponent. And she remembered in snatches how people had spoken of the Al-Eralir's prowess. In the time of Conquest, he had ridden in front of his armies, merciless destroyer, brilliant swordsman. He sliced human flesh like a reaper in a field of wheat, yet he was never wounded.

"The moon must indeed love Her son!" Lyren cried, breathing hard, in a tiny free moment.

Laughter was his only answer, as he increased his attack, pressing forward, and forcing Lyren several steps back.

"However," she gasped, "she does not love you enough. It is said—it is said that the sun also loves His children . . ."

"Save your strength, my thief," came the clear cold voice, as he dealt her a blow that nearly shattered her sword.

"The sun," cried Lyren, "The sun loves His children! The sun, Arev, loves His daughters. And He loves His one daughter so much that He has given her a gift . . ."

Sahtiel advanced on her, step by step, lightly, tirelessly.

"It is a great rare gift," she continued, "A gift of feeling mortal pain, of being tired and then resting, of ignorance and then experience, of indifference then love. It is a gift of living, of being mortal. Here, look at this scar on my cheek—I bleed and can be wounded! For I, Lyren-e-Arev, daughter of the sun, have this gift from my Father . . . And the moon— the moon, Ilenvis, had forgotten. She had forgotten to love Her son enough to give him true life."

Sahtiel seemed to falter for an instant, and his sword left a crooked arc in its wake, before striking hers.

"You, O Al-Eralir, have never been alive truly. You have never loved. Haderi you destroyed, as you now attempt to destroy me, because we are both alive, more alive than you'd ever be, and you, having nothing, had unknowingly wanted that life for yourself. I fight you now not for revenge—there can be no revenge for an act of one who is not alive, not humanly alive. I fight to give you mortal pain, so that you would feel, so that the moon would know what She has done. . . . This city—its darkness is the work of Her hands, Her misdeed. I free you and it. . . . Let the wrong be righted!"

Suddenly, swift as light, Lyren swung with the sword, the same longsword that he had given her in his half-love, half-life. He was somehow, for a single instant, petrified, his reaction too slow. Her sword cleaved his in half, and continued its fall to slash through the light silver armor of his right shoulder, and then his flesh.

Blood, red human blood sprang forth in a fountain. It ran and stained the silver, like a great rose flower opening its petals. The wound was not fatal, yet deep.

Slowly, without a sound, he sank to his knees. The handle of the broken sword fell out of his limp hand.

Lyren stood above him, not triumphant, not sorry. "It is a hard way. To learn life," she said softly, almost kindly.

The silence was universal, profound, all around. Laying down her sword, she reached out with her hands to remove the silver helmet from his head. The golden hair spilled out in a stream of radiance to lie about his shoulders. His face was of marble pallor, and the eyes lowered to the ground. The cruelty was absent from the countenance, together with strength.

"If what you say is true . . ." he whispered, then was silent.

"Look, O people of Aerhad-el-Raas!" Lyren cried. "Look upon His face! Look freely, for you are now free!"

Like great rumbling thunder the voices swelled, all around.

Lyren turned back to Sahtiel. "I shall not kill you," she said, "I almost loved you once, lord. You, like Haderi. But I

can't now. Now that I know what you could have been . . . I
pity you . . .''

Suddenly she took hold of his hair, gathered it behind him,
and taking her sword in the other hand, cried out once more:

''Behold, O Aerhad-el-Raas, free city! Let this make him a
man!''

The swordblade came down, shearing off the great golden
mass. She held it up for all to see.

And Sahtiel, Al-Eralir, wept, for together with the cropped
hair was gone his pride.

The sky stood lavender upon gold over Aerhad-el-Raas, as a
rider left the city on a great black steed. Immediately behind,
a train carried in state the body of a handsome dark man with
the marks of strangulation on his throat. The rider, Lyren,
warrior, stranger, and someone else, never looked back to see
the young demon lord watching her from the highest tower in
the city. His wounded shoulder was bandaged, his hair short-
cropped, and his face pale with sorrow and mortal pain.

That night, people said, there was seen a blood-red wound-
blemish on the face of the pale full moon.